PRAISE FOR ELMER KELTON

"Kelton's exquisite style develops the themes of a love of liberty and a suspicion of authority that taps deep into Texas's heritage." —James L. Haley, *Passionate Nation: The Epic History of Texas*

"San Angelo novelist Elmer Kelton knows intimately the work and ways of the West. That's why real cowboys love his writing." —*Southern Living*

"One thing is certain: As long as there are writers as skillful as Elmer Kelton, Western literature will never die." —*True West* magazine

"Elmer Kelton writes of West Texas with unerring authority." —*Fort Worth Star-Telegram*

"Kelton, like fine wine, just keeps getting better and better." —*Tulsa World*

Forge Novels by Elmer Kelton

After the Bugles
Barbed Wire
Bitter Trail
Bowie's Mine
Buffalo Wagons
Captain's Rangers
Cloudy in the West
Dark Thicket
The Day the Cowboys Quit
Donovan
Eyes of the Hawk
Hanging Judge
Hot Iron
Joe Pepper
Llano River
Long Way to Texas
Many a River
Massacre at Goliad
Pecos Crossing
The Pumpkin Rollers
Sandhills Boy
Shadow of a Star
Shotgun
Stand Proud
Texas Rifles
The Time It Never Rained

Hewey Calloway Novels
The Smiling Country
The Good Old Boys
Six Bits a Day

Sons of Texas
Sons of Texas
The Raiders: Sons of Texas
The Rebels: Sons of Texas

Texas Rangers
The Buckskin Line
Badger Boy
The Way of the Coyote
Ranger's Trail
Texas Vendetta
Jericho's Road
Hard Trail to Follow
Other Men's Horses
Texas Standoff

Brush Country
(comprising Barbed Wire and Llano
River)

Lone Star Rising
(comprising The Buckskin Line,
Badger Boy, and The Way of the
Coyote)

Long Way to Texas
(comprising Joe Pepper, Long Way to
Texas, and Eyes of the Hawk)

Ranger's Law
(comprising Ranger's Trail, Texas
Vendetta, and Jericho's Road)

Texas Showdown
(comprising Pecos Crossing and
Shotgun)

Texas Sunrise
(comprising Massacre at Goliad and
After the Bugles)

TEXAS SHOWDOWN

Two Texas Novels

ELMER KELTON

A Tom Doherty Associates Book

New York

TEXAS SHOWDOWN: TWO TEXAS NOVELS

This is an omnibus edition comprising the novels *Pecos Crossing,* copyright © 1963 by The Estate of Elmer Kelton, and *Shotgun,* copyright © 1969 by Coronet Communications, Inc.

Pecos Crossing was originally published in 1963 by Ballantine Books as *Horsehead Crossing. Shotgun* was originally published in 1969 by Paperback Library as *Shotgun Settlement* by Alex Hawk, a pseudonym of Elmer Kelton.

A Forge Book
Published by Tom Doherty Associates, LLC
175 Fifth Avenue
New York, NY 10010

www.tor-forge.com

Forge® is a registered trademark of Tom Doherty Associates, LLC.

The Library of Congress has cataloged the hardcover edition as follows:

Kelton, Elmer.
    Texas showdown : two Texas novels / Elmer Kelton.—1st ed.
        p. cm.
Contents: Pecos crossing—Shotgun.
"A Tom Doherty Associates book."
ISBN 978-0-765-31152-8
    1. Texas, West—Fiction. I. Title.

PS3561.E975 P43 2007
813'.54—dc22

                                                2006050989

ISBN 978-0-7653-1020-0 (trade paperback)

First Edition: March 2007
First Trade Paperback Edition: December 2012

Printed in the United States of America

0 9 8 7 6 5 4 3 2 1

CONTENTS

PECOS CROSSING

I

In the 1890s a mile was a distance that a man could respect. From Sonora, Texas, up to San Angelo, and from there west to the Pecos River was a long, rough, dangerous trail, especially when a man paused every so often and turned in the saddle to look back with worried eyes for someone who might be following. . . .

A lot of Texas maps didn't even show Sonora, for scarcely more than a decade had passed since it first began as a trading post on the San Antonio-El Paso Road. Much of it was fresh and new, the unpainted lumber not yet blistered and darkened in the sun. But to Johnny Fristo and Speck Quitman, riding in after spending the winter in a cow camp far down on the Devil's River, it wouldn't have mattered if Sonora had been a hundred years old. It was there, and so were they. A long winter had bowed out to spring, and this was going to be payday.

Speck was as eager as a new-weaned pup loosed on a fresh scent. "She's a peach of a town, ain't she, Johnny? Didn't seem this pretty when we left here last fall."

Johnny Fristo made a more sober appraisal of the scattered frame buildings and Mexican adobes huddled in open sunshine between the rough limestone hills along the river's dry fork. "No town looks like much when you're ridin' out of it with your pockets emptied."

For that matter, they weren't bringing much back. All these cowboys owned, they carried on their horses. Tied behind the high cantle of each saddle was a yellow Fish Brand slicker, a wool blanket and a warbag, bulging with their "thirty years' gatherings." The latter was a misnomer because neither had lived thirty years yet. Johnny was twenty-two and admitted it. Speck was the same and claimed twenty-five.

They had had a run of luck last fall, both good and bad. They had worked all summer with a wagon crew gathering cattle from the rocky hills and the liveoak thickets of the broad Edwards Plateau. After fall branding, the boss paid them off. They drifted into Sonora hoping to find something else. They hadn't found work, but the chuckleheaded Speck had found a man who was willing to teach him about poker. The lessons came high. By the time Johnny Fristo found out Speck had lost all their money, the "teacher" had vanished, bound for San Angelo and points north. The cowboys would have spent the winter swamping out saloons and sleeping on a porch if a hawk-faced cow trader named Larramore hadn't shown up. Larramore was looking for somebody to work cheap and take care of a steer herd he planned to winter down on the river. He was paying pasturage to Old Man Hoskins, who had more grass than he was using. Johnny and Speck spent the winter in a picket shack that was really half dugout, pitifully short of coffee and tobacco but a healthy distance from all temptation.

A few days ago a worried-looking Larramore had ridden into camp with a couple of extra men to gather the steers. He lamented that the cattle market had gone as sour as last week's milk, but he had finally managed to find a buyer.

"You fellers stay and patch up for Old Man Hoskins," Larramore said as he drove the cattle away. "I'll meet you in Sonora Friday and pay you off."

Luckily for Johnny and Speck, the good-natured old rancher had come by the camp. "Forget about patchin' up," he had said. "You punchers have coyoted out here all winter. Go git yourselves a taste of civilization. And drink one for *me*."

Now Speck licked dry lips and glanced toward the first saloon. "Larramore'll be real surprised. Reckon he's got the money for them cattle yet?"

Johnny nodded. "I expect so. Shouldn't make him any difference whether he pays us today or pays us Friday. Comes to the same figure anyhow."

They were a contrasting pair, not much alike except in age. Folks usually took a liking to the swivel-jawed Speck. He talked all the time, though sometimes he got so carried away that his talk quit making sense. Speck was short and bandy-legged, with a round face and freckles. His hair was rusty, his eyes a laughing blue. He could ride any bronc they led out to him and could rope anything that would run. Some folks said Speck had probably been sitting on a fence telling a windy when the Lord was passing out brains. At any rate, he hadn't quite gotten his share. If occasionally some rancher flared up and fired Speck for the tomfool stunts he pulled, he was likely to hire him back in a day or two. He was a good cowboy. A man could put up with a little flightiness.

Another reason ranchmen tolerated Speck's shenanigans was because they had to take Speck if they wanted Johnny Fristo. When you hired one, you hired both. When you fired Speck, Johnny went too.

Johnny didn't often have much to say. With Speck around, he didn't get much chance to talk anyway, and he had long since quit trying. Johnny was taller, thinner of build. He didn't share Speck's flashy ways, but he was always around to help pull his partner out of a jackpot. Johnny would be out doing his job with a quiet competence while Speck was still talking about it.

He could ride along with his gaze on the horizon, his mind a hundred miles away, nod agreement to everything Speck said and not actually hear a word of it.

They had spent their boyhoods in the Concho River country up around the army post and cow town of San Angelo, sixty-five miles north of Sonora. Johnny's father raised cattle on a small ranch back from the North Concho. Speck had been brought up in San Angelo by an aunt till he was about fourteen. Then he had landed a job as a horse jingler out on Spring Creek. Once or twice a year Speck worked up courage to make a duty call to his aunt. He would get away as quickly as he could.

"She's a sweet old lady," Johnny had heard him say with a certain reverence. "But she's mean as hell."

Today they came into Sonora by way of the Del Rio road. Eastward, halfway up a hill, stood the new Sutton County courthouse. Horses lazed at hitching racks and posts along the sloping, dusty street. Sweating freighters grunted at the weight as they unloaded store goods from a heavy wagon that had hauled them down from the railroad in San Angelo. A pair of smaller wagons, one tied behind the other, groaned under a load of early-shorn wool.

Speck eyed the first saloon but rode on by it. "Heard a feller say once to always pass up the first one. Shows you got willpower."

Johnny grinned. He knew this saloon had been the site of that cardsharp's *school.* "Speck, if it's all of a whatness to you, I'd rather clean up first."

Speck reined in at the square frame front of the second saloon, stepped down and wrapped his reins through a ring in the hitching post. "You wash the outside and I'll wash the inside."

They had a little money—not much. Larramore had advanced them a few dollars last fall. He owed them for a winter's work, so they would have plenty when they found him. Johnny had counted his money several times before leaving the cow camp, and now he counted it again. Main thing he wanted to begin with was a change of clothes. Those he wore had spent a hard winter, washed periodically in the river, beaten with a rock and slept on to press some of the wrinkles out.

After a while, with new-bought clothes bundled under his arm, he walked into a barbershop which advertised a bathtub. The barber was busy shaving a customer. "Have a seat, cowboy."

Johnny picked up a copy of the weekly *San Angelo Standard,* looking hopefully for items about people he knew. He didn't find his father's name in it, but he hadn't expected to. Baker Fristo was just a little rancher, and he didn't get to town much. Johnny read the trespass and cattle brand notices and shook his head in doubt over ads for patent medicines supposed to cure everything from adenoids to hemorrhoids.

Finishing the paper, he began wondering idly about the man reclining in the barber chair. He couldn't tell much except that the customer was very tall, had a new black suit and wore a pair of high-laced shoes on feet that probably were more used to boots. A new broad-brimmed black hat and a suit coat hung on a rack by the front door.

Rancher, probably. Or a cattle buyer.

The barber was as talkative as Speck Quitman. "Folks say

you've bought a ranch up on the Colorado River, Milam."
The man named Milam couldn't answer. The barber was
scraping whiskers from his jaw. "Yes, sir," the barber went on,
"I was up in that Colorado City country once. Sand country, it
is, and good for cows. Man don't go stumblin' around over
rocks all the time."

The customer had a firm, deep voice. "Any country is
good, Jess, when you own a piece of it yourself."

The barber wiped soap off of his blade. "Used to think
that way myself, till I lost my little place in the big panic.
Found out it's easier to scrape chins than to try and scrape a
livin' off a piece of hard-scrabble land. But, then, I reckon you
wouldn't buy anything but a good place, Milam. Bet you and
Miss Cora are goin' to be real happy."

"We will," the man said. "She'll be mighty pleased with
the place, the way I've got it fixed up for her."

"When you takin' her?"

"We're leavin' tomorrow mornin', takin' the Sonora Mail
to San Angelo."

The barber finished. As the customer stood up, Johnny saw
that the tall man was around forty—maybe a little more. The
outdoors had weathered him badly. His hair showed streaks of
gray, but his moustache was still coal black. Crowtracks were
etched at the corners of keen gray eyes that looked as if they
had seen aplenty of hardship. For a moment those eyes lighted
on Johnny. They were not unfriendly, but they looked as if
they could read whatever was in a man's mind. Johnny nodded, wondering what it was about this stranger that made him
feel suddenly uncomfortable.

"Howdy," said the man Milam, and that was all. He put on
his hat and coat, paid the barber and left.

The barber turned to Johnny. "Shave? Haircut?"

"Both. And then a long, slow bath." Seating himself, Johnny jerked his chin toward the door. "Who was that?"

"Him? Why, friend, I thought everybody knew Milam Haggard."

"Name sounds kind of familiar."

"He was a Texas Ranger down on the Rio Grande. Married Miss Cora Hays here, and she talked him into takin' off the star. He's been off up the country, buyin' them a place to live."

Johnny stared out the open door. He vaguely remembered now. "This Haggard, he's got a name for bein' a bulldog in a fight, hasn't he?"

The barber shook his head knowingly. "A man couldn't have a better friend than Milam Haggard. Or a worse enemy. There's no end to what he'll do for a man he thinks is in the right. He's been known to ride fifty miles in the rain to fetch medicine to a sick Mexican kid. But break the law and you got trouble. He hates an outlaw. He sticks to a trail, Milam does. I don't suppose he ever let a man get away, once he ever got the scent. I recollect one time he trailed a pair of horse thieves plumb down into Mexico. I seen him come back leadin' their horses. Their gunbelts was looped around the saddlehorns, and the saddles was empty. Milam never did talk about them hunts. But he didn't have to."

With bold snips of the sharp scissors the barber took off Johnny's winter growth of hair. "Miss Cora, she made him turn in his badge and put up his guns. She was afraid someday somebody would be a-bringin' *his* saddle in empty."

Johnny took a slow soak in the barber's tub, lazily enjoying the luxury of castile soap. Out in a cow camp, a man was lucky to have plain old lye soap that took off the hide along with the dirt. Finished, he tucked the bundle of dirty clothes under his arm, mounted his horse and walked him to the saloon. Speck's horse was still hitched out in front, head down, one hind foot turned up in rest. Johnny shook his head. Likely as not Speck would forget that animal and leave him standing out here all day. Johnny untied the horse and led him to a wagonyard with his own. Might as well turn the horses loose in the stableman's corral and give them some feed; they weren't going anywhere today.

Unsaddling, he asked the stableman, "All right if we bed down over here tonight, me and my partner? We won't bother nothin'."

Hotels were for ranchers, drummers and the like. Cowboys generally slept in the wagonyard or down on the riverbank.

"Help yourself. Just don't be doin' no smokin' around that hay. I'd hate to sell you a burned-down barn." Critically, the stableman looked Johnny over. "You couldn't pay for it no-way."

Walking back, Johnny told himself it was fortunate Speck didn't have enough money on him to get into a poker game. Put Speck to work in the country and he was usually worth his wages. But turn him loose in town and he was likely to kick over the traces, bedazzled by the flash of cards and the slosh of whisky. It was like he hadn't grown up, and maybe never would.

Johnny had let Speck have three dollars this morning. He figured that wasn't enough to get him drunk or into a poker game. Entering the saloon, he found out how wrong he was. Speck pushed away from a gaming table and threw his hands up in a gesture of defeat. "That cleans me." He spotted

Johnny. "Hey, partner, come here and give me enough for a fresh start. I'm just about to clean these fellers' plow."

Johnny covered his impatience with a grin he didn't mean. "Looks to me like it's *your* plow that shines."

"Aw, Johnny . . ." But Speck could see Johnny meant to be firm. He didn't beg. He leaned on Johnny, looking instinctively to his partner to help him keep his nose clean.

One of the gamblers called to the bartender, "Lige, give them cowboys a drink. I'm payin' for it with their own money."

Speck and Johnny leaned work-flattened bellies against the short granite-topped bar. Speck lifted his glass and said, "Here's to Larramore and his speedy arrival."

Johnny almost choked. He knew he had tasted worse whisky, but he couldn't remember just when. Speck had a fondness for the stuff; Johnny could take it or leave it alone. This kind was better left alone.

A man appeared in the saloon's open door. He started to walk in, then stopped abruptly, seeing Johnny and Speck. Quickly he backed out and walked off up the street.

Johnny straightened. "Speck, that was Larramore."

Speck hadn't noticed. "Maybe he didn't see us."

"He saw us. He backed out like somebody had shot at him. I don't like the smell of it."

Speck frowned. "You don't think he would . . ." He broke off, doubt in his eyes. "You know, he just might."

Johnny nodded grimly. "Let's go find out."

Larramore was walking briskly away. Johnny called, but the cow trader appeared not to hear. Johnny and Speck broke into a long trot and caught up with him in front of a general store.

"Mister Larramore," Johnny said, coming up behind him, "just a minute."

Larramore turned and looked surprised. "By George, it's Speck and Johnny. Wasn't expectin' you-all till Friday."

Johnny said, "Old Man Hoskins told us to come on in. So we're here, Mister Larramore, and we sure do need our money."

Larramore's face was blank. He was watching someone walking up the street. "Money? What money?"

Johnny's voice hardened. "We put in six months of work for you, Larramore." He wasn't using the *mister* now. "You promised us twenty dollars a month. Now we want to get paid."

Johnny was hardly aware of footsteps on the plank walk behind him, or of a man with a badge who passed them and started into the general store. But Larramore had seen him, and he raised his voice.

"I've already paid you. I paid both of you at the ranch. What do you mean now, tryin' to browbeat me into payin' you again?"

The man in the doorway stopped and turned, his attention caught.

Speck Quitman's face boiled full of rage. He grabbed both fists full of Larramore's shirt. "You're a liar! All you ever gave us was a few dollars advance last fall. Now, damn you, pay up!"

Watching the sheriff, Larramore stood his ground. "Get your hands off of me, you halfwit! I won't stand for bein' robbed!"

The insult to Speck made Johnny clench his fists. "*You're* the one who's a thief, Larramore."

The sheriff had heard enough. He stepped up and placed a

big hand firmly over Speck's fist, his eyes stern. "Turn him loose, cowboy."

Speck turned angrily upon the intruder, but his mouth shut as he saw the badge.

A cow trader has to be quick on his feet or he doesn't survive. Larramore was quick. "Sheriff, it's a good thing you came by. These boys are tryin' to pull a fast shuffle on me."

The sheriff's grim eyes flashed from one man to the other. "All right, everybody simmer down a little. Tell me what the trouble is."

Larramore spoke quickly, heading off Speck and Johnny. "I hired these two last fall to watch over some cattle I was winterin' down on the Devil's River. The other day I picked up the cattle and paid these men. Now they're tryin' to claim they've still got wages comin'. It's not my fault if they've drunk it up or lost it playin' poker."

Johnny said, "He's a liar, sheriff."

The sheriff frowned. He leaned close and sniffed suspiciously. "You-all *have* been drinkin'. I can smell it."

Johnny said, "Just one is all I've had. It was bought for me. We're not lyin' to you, sheriff. *He* is."

The sheriff studied Speck. "Seems to me I remember you boys. You was in town last fall." His eyes lighted. "Sure, you lost your wad down yonder tryin' to beat one of them Angelo gamblers. You was dead broke."

Larramore cut in, "That's right, sheriff. I gave them a job. Do a man a favor and he'll spit on you every time."

Johnny protested, "He *hasn't* paid us."

The sheriff looked at Johnny's new clothes. "If you haven't been paid, where did those duds come from?"

Johnny could tell the sheriff was almost convinced now,

and not in their favor. He started to tell about the advance Larramore had given them last fall, but he realized it would sound hollow. How many cowboys could keep anything all winter out of a fall advance?

Johnny had a sudden thought. "Old Man Hoskins knows. Why don't you ask him?"

A shade of doubt appeared in the sheriff's eyes. "Ely Hoskins? Sure, his word is as good as his bond. But it's a long ways out there."

"If you're interested in the truth, you'll go ask him."

Larramore said, "They're just stallin', sheriff. They're caught in a lie. They belong in jail."

Speck Quitman exploded. His fist came up and caught Larramore full in the face. Larramore staggered backward against the clapboard wall of the general store. For a second Johnny thought the trader was going to fall through the front window. Speck roared forward to follow up his punch, but the sheriff reached out and grabbed him by the collar. With a sudden thrust of his mighty arm, the lawman threw Speck off balance and sent him sprawling backward into the dust of the street.

"That done it!" the sheriff thundered. "I was halfway inclined to go along with you boys, but now I'm goin' to let you sweat awhile in the jailhouse."

Larramore swayed, one hand behind him to brace him away from the wall, the other lifted to his face. His nose was bleeding.

Johnny urged, "Sheriff, Speck's hotheaded, and what he did wasn't smart. But it don't change the fact that Larramore's lyin'. Give us a chance. Go talk to Old Man Hoskins."

The sheriff scowled down at Speck Quitman, who was

shakily pushing himself up out of the dust. The lawman pondered. Something about Larramore seemed to make him uncertain. "I don't know what I'm wastin' my time for, but I'll do it. I'll send a man out to talk to old Ely. Till then, you boys are goin' to enjoy Sutton County's hospitality. Behind bars!" He glanced at Larramore. "I'm expectin' you to stay in town till I get the straight of this."

Larramore nodded, holding his handkerchief to his face. "Sure, sheriff, anything you say." He avoided looking at the cowboys.

The sheriff took hold of Johnny's and Speck's arms. "Come on." They walked up the street, the sheriff holding them tightly. The few people who were outdoors paused to look. It was evident the two were under arrest.

A tall man and a woman stepped out of a store and almost directly into their path. The man caught the woman's arm and moved her gently aside. Johnny recognized Milam Haggard. The handsome young woman would be the wife the barber had been telling about. Her eyes touched Johnny's, and he thought he saw sympathy there.

But he found no sympathy in Milam Haggard. The longtime Ranger stared with stern gray eyes. Any friendliness he might have shown in the barbershop was gone now. It wouldn't matter to Haggard what the trouble was about. He could tell the cowboys were in custody. That was enough for him to pass his judgment.

The sheriff took his hand from Johnny's arm long enough to tip his hat. "Howdy, Cora . . . Milam."

The three walked by. Johnny glanced back, for no particular reason. Milam Haggard was still watching him.

II

A bugle sounded. Johnny Fristo awoke to the rattle of trace chains and the clatter of horses' hoofs. The Sonora Mail was leaving for San Angelo.

Johnny opened his eyes and glanced up at the barred window. Sunrise. He arose stiffly from the hard cot and stretched his back to try to work the ache out of it. The air was cool and fresh. Johnny's movement aroused Speck Quitman, who peered dourly at him a moment, then swung his sock feet down to the floor and started probing around sleepy-eyed, trying to find his boots.

A limping man entered the jail's front door, carrying a covered platter. "You boys up?" the pleasant old jailer asked needlessly. "Brought you-all some breakfast."

He unlocked the cell door and dragged in a small table. He did it carelessly, as if not even considering that the two prisoners could easily jump him and get away. He had brought a big mess of scrambled eggs with pieces of fried beef alongside, and some biscuits. "Hope you fellers don't mind eatin' off of the platter. Too far to pack extra dishes."

Leaving the cell door wide open, he went to the stove and picked up the coffee pot. "Now, don't you boys go gettin' the wrong idea; we don't treat all our prisoners this good. But I figure you-all been out in a cow camp all winter and ain't had no eggs. Besides, like I was tellin' the sheriff, it's probably that Larramore who ought to be in here 'stead of you two."

Johnny and Speck went after the eggs like a pair of starved

wolves. The talkative jailer sipped the scalding black coffee, his lips immune to the burn. "I used to cowboy, too, till I got stove up. I looked you two over and decided you was all right. Besides, I heard about some cow deals Larramore was mixed up in. He's no deacon in the church."

Johnny asked, "Hear anything yet from Old Man Hoskins?"

"Nope. Thought he might be in the crowd that was down while ago to see Milam and Cora Haggard off on the Sonora Mail. But he wasn't." He smiled, remembering. "My, she sure did look handsome. Folks was afraid she would wait around and be an old maid, but I guess she was just waitin' for the right man. And she got him." He paused. "You know about Milam Haggard?"

Johnny nodded. "Some."

"*Mucho hombre,* that Milam. Sure did hate to see him turn in his badge. But I expect most of the devilment is over anyway. Country's turned respectable. Milam has outlived his time as a lawman. We don't need his kind of lawin' anymore. This is the '90s now, and we're about as modern as we can ever get."

Eventually the sheriff came, his face creasing as he saw the open cell door. "Ad," he spoke sharply to the jailer, "this is a jailhouse, not a *hotel*. One of these days somebody's goin' to walk right out over you."

Standing up, the jailer said defensively, "I wouldn't do it for just anybody, but these boys are all right. Like I was tellin' you last night . . ."

The sheriff nodded, his rueful gaze passing from Johnny to Speck and back again. "I remember what you told me, and it turns out you were right. Boys, you can go."

Johnny smiled. "So you heard from Old Man Hoskins?"

The sheriff was chagrined. "Didn't have to. I just found out Larramore sneaked off to the edge of town while ago and caught the stage hack for San Angelo. If he'd been on the square, he'd have stayed here like I told him."

Johnny swore. "Damn him! He's tryin' to get off and keep from payin' us what we got comin'."

The sheriff shook his head. "He'll pay. If you boys will get saddled up and put them ponies through their paces, you can get to Angelo ahead of the hack. Go see the sheriff there. I'll write you a letter to give him. He'll see that Larramore pays what he owes you or he'll shove him way back in jail and forget where the key is at."

Speck and Johnny waited impatiently while the lawman scribbled a note. The officer said, "I'd go myself, only I just got word of some trouble down in the south end of the county that's liable to lead to a shootin' if I don't stop it."

Speck said with bitterness, "How am I goin' to explain to my Aunt Pru about me spendin' the night in jail? And all for nothin'."

The old jailer grinned. "Well, look at the bright side: you had supper, breakfast and a bed, and it didn't cost you a cent."

"Some bed," gritted Speck. "I've slept on rocks that was softer."

The jailer grinned again. "We don't advertise for repeat business."

Johnny folded the letter the sheriff had given him and stuck it in his pocket. "One thing sure, *we* don't intend to come back."

The sheriff followed them down to the wagonyard and watched while they saddled their horses. "Stop in at Pete

Smith's ranch halfway to Angelo and tell him I said lend you a pair of fresh horses. And one more thing: don't try to do nothin' on your own. Just go around that hack and get to Angelo ahead of it. Let the Tom Green County sheriff take care of Larramore his own way. That's his job. You-all leave Larramore alone."

Anger edged Johnny's voice. "He owes us more than wages now, sheriff. He owes us for a night in jail."

The sheriff repeated, "Don't you-all do anything, do you hear me?"

Johnny and Speck heard, but they made no reply. They rode out of the wagonyard gate, touched spurs to their horses and moved into an easy lope on the mail and freight road that led north toward San Angelo.

Twisting along at the foot of the hills, the trail made a slow climb toward the top of the divide which separated the sprawling watershed of the Devil's River from that of the three Conchos. From where the cowboys rode, rainwater would drain generally southward, first to countless draws and creeks, then to the Devil's River and finally by a tortuous, canyon-cutting route to the Rio Grande.

Spring had come with color and hope to this high, rocky limestone country known as the Edwards Plateau. Winter rains had preserved the holdover moisture stored last fall, and now fresh grass rose tender and green amid the tall brown leavings of last year's bluestem growth. Cattle already were slicking off, shedding their coarse winter hair. Frisky calves were fat and shiny.

Johnny and Speck came upon a band of sheep, scattered to

graze on an open flat where the grass was shorter and more to their liking. Fat young lambs lifted their heads to watch the riders passing. Many of them scampered away bleating. A Mexican herder stood up at the cowboys' approach and nodded a silent greeting, his eyes narrowed in distrust. Too often the *gringo* did not come in peace.

Johnny asked, "How long since the mail hack passed this way?"

The herder just stared at him, as if he did not understand. Speck broke in to repeat the question in a halting, broken Spanish. The herder did not smile at Speck's mistakes. But neither did he give a clear answer. "*¿Quién sabe?* A while. I have no watch, *señor.*"

Speck seemed disposed to try again, this time in anger, but Johnny said, "Let it go, Speck. That's all the answer we'll get. We're makin' some gain, and we'll catch up."

They moved on, putting the horses into an easy lope and holding them in it as long as they dared. Every so often Johnny would pull down to a trot. Usually he would have to call to Speck, who didn't stop until he saw that Johnny was going to, with or without him.

"Speck, we can't make it if we ride these horses down."

They would trot along a mile or so, then Speck would impatiently spur into a lope again. Johnny noticed Speck wasn't doing any talking. That in itself was a bad sign. The rusty-haired cowboy's jaw took a hard, angry set, and his eyes were narrowed.

Speck was talking inside, to himself. Johnny knew the signs. When Speck was like this the inner heat would crackle and build until there had to be an explosion of some kind.

There was no other outlet. That was a side of Speck Quitman most people didn't know about, for it didn't often show. Most regarded him as a scatter-brained cowboy with a lot of bark and no bite. But Johnny had seen him bite a few times. He didn't like it.

They came out atop the divide in a wind-rippled sea of short green grass. Speck reined up and stood in his stirrups, peering out through a scattering of liveoak trees which were shedding their old leaves and putting on a new set.

"Johnny, I think I see the hack up yonder, ahead of us."

Johnny squinted. It took him a minute, but finally he saw it too. Speck turned in his saddle and untied his warbag. He dug around in it, then pulled out a six-shooter, wrapped in oilskin. It was old and tarnished, and on one side a knife-whittled piece of mesquite wood had replaced the original black rubber grip. Relic though it was, Speck prized it above anything else he owned. He had bought it from a broke cowpuncher when he was only fifteen, and he had carried it around with him ever since. He had given it the loving care a man might give a horse. He had never used it in anger, though sometimes Johnny Fristo got a cold, ominous feeling that Speck hoped someday he could. Speck began to punch cartridges into it.

Tightly Johnny said, "Speck, you got no use for that thing. The sheriff told us to go to the law in Angelo, not to try handlin' Larramore ourselves."

"It wasn't the sheriff he cheated. It wasn't the sheriff that had to spend the night in the Sonora jail like some drunk sheepherder."

"Speck, you better put that thing back into your warbag before you do somethin' you'll wish you hadn't. What if you was to accidentally shoot him? A dead man don't pay no wages." He thought at first Speck might be listening to him. But Speck shoved the loaded pistol into his waistband.

"I'm not fixin' to shoot him. But I sure do intend to scare him to death."

Speck's spurs tinkled as he touched them to his horse and surged forward. Johnny held back a moment, trying to figure some way to reason with him. Then he hurried to catch up. "Speck, listen to me. The sheriff made sense. This is the kind of thing they got sheriffs *for*."

"A man ought to stomp his own snakes. And Larramore is a snake."

"We can make a little *vuelta* around them and get to Angelo first. Larramore won't have any idea we're around. We can spring the sheriff on him as a surprise."

But Speck was hot as a wolf, and he was riding, not listening. The thought of that pistol made a cold chill run down Johnny's back. Somehow it always had. He would as soon touch a rattlesnake.

Still, he knew the only way he could stop Speck now would be with a club. All Johnny could do was stay close and try to keep things from getting too badly out of hand. They were partners, right or wrong, smart or otherwise. Several times before, Johnny had come close to riding off in disgust and leaving Speck. But always in the end he would shrug and stay with him.

He stayed with him now.

Ahead of them the trail took a bend around a big motte of liveoak trees to avoid a wheel-breaking gully. Speck cut across, Johnny close behind him. They loped around the heavy motte and came back into the trail ahead of the stage hack. Speck slid

his horse to a stop. He raised the pistol to signal the driver to
halt.

It would have been hard to gauge which showed strongest
in the driver's face—anger or alarm. A robbery on the Sonora
Mail was unheard of! "What do you two peckerwoods want?"
he demanded. "We got nothin' on board here that's worth
stealin'."

Speck Quitman replied in a tense voice that didn't sound
at all like his. "Don't fret yourself, mister. We didn't stop you
to steal anything."

"Then put that cannon away before you scare the lady!"

Johnny pulled his horse up beside Speck's. "For God's
sake, Speck, put that damned old smoke-belcher down. We're
fixin' to get ourselves in a mess of trouble."

Under the rolled-up side canvas he could see the frightened face of Cora Haggard, her hands tightly clutching Milam
Haggard's arm. Haggard stared at the cowboys, his gray eyes
challenging and unafraid. But he was helpless, for he wore no
gun. In the seat behind the Haggards, the trader Larramore was
trying to crouch down out of sight.

The hack driver had a heavy brown moustache and a loud,
harsh voice. "If you didn't come to steal nothin', put that gun
back where it belongs. Somebody might get hurt. Besides,
you're stoppin' the U.S. mail. That could get you sent to the
pen."

Johnny decided it was time for him to do the talking. Speck
wasn't getting them anywhere but in trouble. "Mister, we don't
mean to hurt anybody, and we're sure not fixin' to tamper with
the mail. But you got a passenger who left Sonora owin' us
money, and we want it."

"Cowboy," said the driver, "your private feuds ain't any

concern of the Sonora Mail. The man is a passenger. You take up your complaints with the law."

Speck Quitman waved the pistol. "We brought our own law. Larramore, you get yourself down from there, and be right spry about it!"

Larramore stood up partway, his head touching the canvas. "They're lyin'. They come to rob me!"

Milam Haggard spoke in a rock-steady voice: "You heard what the driver said, boys. I don't know anything about the merit of your claim on this man, but I do know that the way you're doin' this constitutes robbery in the eyes of the law. I suggest you stand back and let this hack go on."

"Mister Haggard," Johnny said, "there's already *been* a robbery, and it was us that got robbed."

Haggard studied him a moment with eyes so stern that Johnny couldn't hold his gaze against them. "I remember you. The Sonora sheriff had you in tow yesterday. That doesn't make your argument sound very good to me."

Johnny reached for his shirt pocket. "I've got a letter here . . ."

Impatience jabbed its spurs into Speck Quitman. "Forget the letter. We're takin' Larramore off this stage and gettin' our money!"

Angrily Haggard said, "There's a woman in this hack. You put that gun away!"

Haggard's severe voice got through to Speck where Johnny's pleading hadn't. Speck was a little afraid of the man. He lowered the barrel, but he rode around closer to Larramore. "How about it, Larramore? You gettin' down, or do I have to shoot you in the leg or somethin'?"

Face white, Larramore began climbing out. "All right, I'm comin'." Stepping to the ground, he turned to plead with Haggard and the driver. "Are you goin' to let them get away with this?"

The driver said, "Mister, I got no gun. Neither has Milam."

Johnny held his breath. Now he began to feel the thing was going to go over all right. Maybe there wasn't going to be any more trouble. He rode around to the off side of the hack, where Larramore stood. He dismounted a couple of paces from the cow trader. Speck's anger gave way to anticipation, and he stepped down from the saddle.

"All right, Larramore, a hundred dollars apiece."

Larramore replied shakily, "I got the money in my bag." He turned and lifted a canvas grip out of the hack. Speck shoved the pistol into his waistband and eagerly stepped closer to look as Larramore opened the bag. The trader reached inside. "There now, I've got it."

He brought his hand out with a short-barreled Colt revolver.

Johnny didn't hesitate. He jumped at the trader. Larramore squeezed the trigger. The hammer fell on the empty shell he kept in the cylinder for safety, the empty shell he had forgotten in his anxiety. But the next cartridge would be a live one. Johnny grabbed the man's wrist. They struggled.

The woman screamed. Haggard started putting her off the hack on the other side to get her away from the fight. At the same time he was shouting, "You fools, be careful with that pistol! You'll kill somebody!"

The team caught the excitement and danced nervously,

ready to run. Badly as he might have wanted to jump, the driver couldn't afford to. He had all he could handle, holding the team.

Larramore brought up his knee and struck Johnny a hard blow to the stomach. Johnny bent a little and let go. Larramore stepped clear and leveled the pistol. As he squeezed the trigger, Speck Quitman caught him from behind and spoiled his aim.

The flash blinded Johnny for an instant. The explosion set his ears to ringing. But he heard a faint cry from the woman on the other side.

The team ran. The driver jammed one foot against the brake and sawed hard at the lines to prevent them from getting completely away. As the hack pulled forward, Johnny saw horror in Larramore's eyes. Larramore pitched the gun away. Johnny spun on his heel.

Cora Haggard was going down. Milam Haggard grabbed her and cried out, "Cora!" Gently he eased her to the grass.

The three men who had been fighting stood stiff and silent now, stunned. They saw the spread of crimson across the woman's white blouse. The color had drained from her face. Her hand reached up and clutched at Haggard's shirt. She gasped, "Milam, I love you." Then the hand dropped away.

Milam Haggard cried again, "Cora!" He pulled her against him as if to try to hold her away from death. But death came despite him, and she lay lifeless in his arms.

Larramore's wits came back to him. He pointed at Johnny and shouted, "That one did it, Haggard! He's the one who fired the gun."

The lie caught Johnny by surprise, and for a moment he could not speak. He stood with mouth open and dry. He tried for words that wouldn't come. A horrified thought ran through his mind:

Haggard will believe him.

Somehow he managed to stammer, "No . . . no . . . I didn't! *He* had the gun! He was shootin' at *me!*"

But he was too late. Larramore had seized the advantage. He had said it first, and Haggard believed him. Johnny could see it in the violent hatred that welled into the tall man's eyes.

The hack driver fought the team under control and circled back. He jumped to the ground and stared wide-eyed at Milam Haggard, who still knelt, holding his wife. The driver breathed in horror, "Milam, for God's sake . . ."

Johnny cried, "Driver, he thinks it was me that killed her. It was Larramore. Tell him. You saw it."

The driver turned slowly, his face ashen. "I saw nothin'. I was too busy tryin' to hold that team. But you boys held us up, and you was robbin' a passenger. That speaks for itself."

Milam Haggard buried his face against his wife's slender neck. He held her, his shoulders trembling, while the other four men stood in helpless silence. At last the driver took a slow step forward. "Milam, we best put her aboard and take her back to Sonora."

Milam Haggard raised his head. Gently he lowered his wife to the ground. His gaze fell upon the pistol Larramore had tossed away. Johnny saw the intention in his eyes, and he stepped forward quickly. He grabbed up the gun just as Haggard was about to leap for it.

Desperate, Johnny said, "Mister Haggard, Larramore lied to you. I didn't shoot her."

Tears swam in Haggard's eyes, but a cold fury showed

through. His slow-measured words were edged with steel. "I'll remember you."

"Please, Mister Haggard, listen to me . . ."

"I'll take my wife home and bury her amongst her people. Then I'll come lookin' for you. You can stay here, or you can run, it makes me no difference. Whether it takes me a week or a year, whether I ride twenty miles or a thousand, I'll find you two. And when I find you, *I'll kill you!*"

"Mister Haggard . . ." Johnny broke off, for Haggard had turned his back. He had shut his ears and his mind.

Gently the driver and Larramore lifted the woman's body. Haggard climbed into the hack and took her into his arms. The driver turned to Johnny and Speck. "Was I you boys, I'd go back to Sonora and throw myself on the mercy of the court. Maybe the court will have some. There'll be no mercy in Milam Haggard!"

He climbed up, took the reins, turned the hack around and started back down the trail toward Sonora.

Johnny and Speck watched until the hack was gone out of sight. Speck finally broke the silence, and he was crying. "It was my fault, Johnny. I ought to've listened to you." Tears rolled down his freckled cheeks. Fear was taking a grip on him. Speck could shift from one emotion to another like he could change shirts. "We got to go some place, Johnny, and we got to go quick. Let's head for Mexico. It's only a hundred miles to the Rio Grande."

Johnny's voice was tight with shock. "And what do we do when we get there? We got no friends down there, and we got no money. We don't even speak the language enough to get by."

"But it's Mexico. The law couldn't touch us down there."

"It's not the law we got to worry about most, it's Milam Haggard. That river wouldn't even slow him down. He'd just keep a-huntin' us, and we'd just keep a-runnin'. And wherever we went, we'd be *gringos*. We'd stand out like the Twin Mountains."

Speck's eyes were swimming in tears. "But what can we do? If we stay here he'll kill us."

"Texas is a mighty big country. He can't search it all. There are places west of here where you could drop a whole army and never find it. Maybe in time he'll get tired of lookin'."

Speck said weakly, "I bet he don't ever quit. He looks like the kind that'll stay on a trail till the day he dies."

Johnny's jaw set firmly. That was the way Haggard had looked to him, too. But a man couldn't just sit and wait for somebody to come and kill him.

Speck said, "We got to get us a little money, Johnny. We could borrow somethin' from my Aunt Pru in San Angelo."

Johnny nodded soberly. "We better get ridin'."

It occurred to him then that he still held Larramore's pistol. He stared at it in loathing. He drew back his arm and hurled the pistol as hard as he could, into a liveoak motte.

He swung onto his horse and headed north toward San Angelo.

III

They rode in by night, following the stage road that crossed the South Concho at the flood-ruined settlement of Ben Ficklin. Three miles farther on, they rode by the stone buildings of old Fort Concho, abandoned a few years ago by the army when the Indian problems were over. Civilians lived there now. Most of the buildings were dark, for working people had gone to bed.

But across the North Concho, lamps still glowed along Chadbourne and Oakes and Concho Avenue. Horses stood in headsdown, hipshot patience at hitchracks in front of the Nimitz Hotel, the Legal Tender and the other saloons. Johnny and Speck rested their horses at the steep south bank of the quiet-moving river and waited in darkness, watching. Nearby stood the Oakes Street Bridge, but they had purposely shied away from it, just as they had shied away from all travelers on the road today.

Speck said, "I hear a horse comin' across. That wooden plankin' sure does make a noise at night."

Johnny nodded. "We best skip the bridge anyhow. It'd land us smack on Concho Avenue amongst all the saloons."

"There's a shallow crossin' a little ways upriver. We could use that and not run into anybody."

They moved past the deep section known as Dead Man's Hole to the shallow water. They walked the horses across quietly, trying not to splash. But their stealth was thwarted when a couple of stray dogs picked them up.

"Git!" Johnny hissed, wishing he had something to throw at the barking dogs. "Git, I say!"

Anxiously he looked around him in the darkness, afraid someone would come. A man in a picket shack stuck his head out the door and yelled angrily at the dogs to shut up. He didn't appear to see Speck and Johnny.

The huge Tom Green County courthouse, with its high stone walls and its tall cupola, loomed massively in the dim moonlight. It stood back well away from the river, with most of the town lying east and south of it. Some new development was building up in the courthouse area. Johnny had heard someone say San Angelo's population was around five thousand now, but he doubted it. It wouldn't be that big in a hundred years. San Angelo was a ranch town. With the army gone, it was dependent upon cattle and sheep, upon small farms scattered along the three Concho Rivers, and upon the freighting of supplies to ranches and settlements which lay west and south all the way to the Pecos and the Rio Grande.

Johnny had always enjoyed coming here, for San Angelo was the biggest town he had ever seen. Seemed like there was always something to watch, from a backlot badger fight up to horse races and steer roping. Holiday-seeking cowboys rode in from a hundred miles away, for this was a tolerant town that understood a man's letting off steam after months of isolation on a ranch. Long as he didn't hurt anybody and paid for what he broke, no one bothered him much.

They gave him his money's worth and showed him a time.

Since the shooting, Johnny and Speck hadn't done any talking. They had ridden in silence, each nursing his thoughts, sick with remorse and dread. Johnny didn't know how many times he had seen that woman's blood-drained face before his eyes, how many times he had heard her gasp and had seen her die in Milam Haggard's arms.

Now, in the familiar streets of San Angelo, some of the somber mood lifted. But not all of it.

Speck said sorrowfully, "It sure does hurt to come a-sneakin' in this away, like a pair of cur dogs followin' all the back alleys. I always liked to ride in on Concho Avenue screechin' like a wild Indian and lettin' the whole town know I was somebody come."

Johnny knew the ache that throbbed in Speck now, for Speck had grown up here, had played barefoot in these dirt streets when this was little more than a hide-hunter camp and a whisky village for Negro soldiers and white officers in the fort across the river.

Speck's voice was melancholy. "I sure hate havin' to leave here. It was hard, livin' with Aunt Pru, but I always did love this town. I fished up and down these rivers. I knew every horse and burro and dog by its name. I bet I could still show you the big old pecan tree where I climbed up out of the water the time of the Ben Ficklin flood." He shook his head. "A queen of a town, she is . . . a cowboy's town."

Johnny said, "Maybe things'll work out someday."

Speck's voice broke. "You saw Haggard's eyes. We can't *never* come back!"

They held up once and pulled back into an alley as a surrey passed with a man and a woman riding in it. Johnny caught the high lift of the woman's laughter and knew she would be one of the "girls" from down on West Concho, by the river. Bitterness touched him as he thought how off-center fate could be, a lady like Cora Haggard lying cold and still in death, while a woman of this kind went right on living, squealing in empty-headed merriment. Why couldn't it have been this one who had died? On reflection, he knew the thought was childish. One person could not take another's place when it came time to die. This woman had no responsibility toward Cora Haggard. That responsibility lay with Larramore and Speck and himself.

Aunt Pru lived alone in a small frame house back from Chadbourne Street. The house was dark as Johnny and Speck rode up to the rear of it. They tied their horses to the picket fence.

Speck said, "Careful now, and don't trip over a faucet. That new waterworks has piped water right to everybody's back step. Next thing you know they'll be wantin' it in the house." He moved up to the small back porch and knocked. Johnny heard no sign of life. Speck knocked again and called softly, "Aunt Pru!"

In a moment a pair of feet scuffed across the wooden floor. A glow went up as a lamp was lighted. Aunt Pru opened the door cautiously and extended the lamp in front of her to light the young men's faces while she held the door ready for a quick closing. She had pulled a cotton housecoat on over her nightgown. Her hair was rolled up. Sleepy-eyed, she squinted. She said with a start, "Speck!"

Anxiously Speck said, "Aunt Pru, would you please get the light out of our faces and let us come in the house? We got to talk to you."

The graying woman stared suspiciously as she lowered the lamp and opened the door wider. "Very well, come on in." When they were inside she said sharply, "Speck, let me smell your breath." He leaned close. She sniffed. Her eyes showed disbelief. "You don't appear to've been drinking. What on earth are you doing out at this time of night? Decent folk are all in bed."

Speck avoided his aunt's eyes. He glanced at Johnny as if seeking support. But Johnny intended to let Speck do the talking, as he usually did. Johnny had always stood in awe of this thin-faced, sharp-tongued woman.

Her gaze snapped from one to the other. "Well, there's something the matter. Speak up!"

Speck was hesitant. "Aunt Pru, there's been a little trouble."

"Trouble?" Her eyes widened. She glanced with sharp disapproval at Johnny, then back to her nephew. "I knew it; I always knew it. I knew someday you'd run too long with the wrong crowd and come dragging trouble to my door. What have you done?"

Speck's voice quavered. "Aunt Pru, we didn't go to do nothin'. It wasn't our fault, really, but we been blamed for it."

"Speck, you're evading me. What have you done?"

Speck was close to crying. "It was an accident. A woman got killed this mornin'. Man who done it, he hollered right quick that it was us, and they believed him. We're on the run, Aunt Pru. We got to run or die."

The tall, thin woman stared in horror, her hands coming up to her cheeks, her mouth open. "A killing! You've gotten mixed up in a killing!"

"It wasn't our fault. We just got the blame for it, is all."

She didn't seem to hear. She turned away from him, crying aloud, raising her face to look up at the ceiling, then dropping her chin.

"Aunt Pru, we hoped maybe you could lend us a little money. We'll send it back to you soon's we can. We wouldn't ask it of you, only we got cheated out of a whole winter's pay. That's what caused the trouble in the first place."

She turned on him with an unexpected savageness.

"Money! You bring disgrace to this house, to our name, and then you have the gall to come and beg me for money?"

Speck took a step backward, astonished at her reaction. "We wouldn't ask you, Aunt Pru, but we're desperate. We'll pay you back, I promise."

"Promise! How many times have you made me promises, Speck, and how few times have you lived up to them? Promised you'd go to school? Promised you wouldn't run around with riffraff?" Her furious eyes cut to Johnny. "You promised you'd look for respectable work, but you joined a group of common cowboys and drank whisky and caroused and made a sinner of yourself. You've drunk and gambled and debauched yourself with those painted women down on Concho and left me in shame."

Speck dropped his chin and stood in red-faced silence while she railed at him: "I knew this would happen someday. You were born with the mark of sin on you, and now it's the brand of Cain. When my sister came to me to have her baby, and no ring on her finger, I knew the mark was on you and you would come to a bad end. But I tried, God knows how I tried. I raised you and kept you because you were my sister's baby. I gave you a home and fed you and tried to teach you righteousness. But all the time I knew someday the stain of sin would show. I knew you were born to hang."

Speck's shoulders slumped. Tears rolled down his cheeks. He looked like a dog driven into a corner and whipped, a dog that had no wish to fight back.

"All these years," she drove on relentlessly, "I've known this day would come. I could have thrown her out and been spared this shame. But I was a Christian woman."

Johnny listened with anger swelling in him. He caught

Speck's arm. "Come on, Speck, let's get out of here."

Speck edged toward the door. Aunt Pru shrilled, "That's right, run! Get on your horse and run, but you can't escape your sin. It's been on you since the day you were born!"

Johnny pushed through the door, pulling hard on Speck's arm. In the doorway Speck paused. Head still down, he didn't look up into his aunt's face. But he said brokenly, "Aunt Pru, I'm sorry."

The gaunt woman cried, "Go on, get out of here! There's been enough shame on this house already." She raised her face to the ceiling. "Oh, God, what have I done? Why do you torment me so?"

"Aunt Pru . . ."

"I've done my Christian duty. Now I'm through. Go on, and may God have mercy on you!"

Speck trembled like a child lost. Johnny let go his friend's arm and took an angry step toward the woman. But he caught himself before he loosed the torrent of fury that strained within him. He said only: "My mother was a *real* Christian woman. She'd have cut out her tongue before she would've said the things you did."

He wheeled, caught Speck's arm again and hurried him out the back gate. They swung into their saddles. Johnny said tightly, "Speck, we'll go out and see my dad. Maybe he can help us."

Speck made no effort to talk. They headed north, leaving San Angelo behind them.

For a long time they rode in silence, bone-weary and sensing the weariness of the horses. Johnny watched the reflection of the moon in the river. Speck slumped in the saddle, his head down, the torment so heavy on him that Johnny could feel the weight of it himself. At length Speck asked, "What you thinkin' about, Johnny?"

Johnny hesitated. "I guess I was thinkin' about that woman, that poor Mrs. Haggard."

"I was afraid maybe you was thinkin' about Aunt Pru."

Johnny shook his head. "I'd forgot about her," he lied.

"I wish you hadn't heard all the things she said. She's probably sorry now."

Johnny's face twisted. *She's not sorry for anybody but herself.* It occurred to him she hadn't asked a single question about Mrs. Haggard—not her name, not even how the accident had come to happen. *She's never felt sorry for anybody in her life, nobody but herself.*

"Aunt Pru's really a good woman," Speck insisted. "You just got to know her, is all. I reckon I've given her a lot of grief."

And she's enjoyed it all, Johnny thought. He had known people who seemed to thrive on misery, who seemed to enjoy feeling sorry for themselves and couldn't be happy unless they were unhappy. It never had made sense to Johnny. But he could recognize the symptoms.

Aunt Pru had them all.

Speck worried, "I just wish she hadn't said what she did in front of you, that about my mother and all." He didn't look at Johnny. "I never did want you to know. I hope you don't think none the less of me, now that you know what I am."

"It doesn't make a particle of difference."

Speck brooded. "Seems like I've known about it as long as I can remember. Aunt Pru, she told me a hundred times how she took in my mother and helped her 'hide her sin.' Then I was born, and my mother died. 'God's mercy,' Aunt Pru always said. She just kept me. Sure, she rode me pretty hard, always houndin' me about this and that and the other thing, warnin' me three times a day about hellfire. But she fed me and kept me in clothes. Always said she didn't want folks sayin' she didn't do the Christian thing by her sister's boy.

"You've seen her with her bad side showin', Johnny. But she's all the folks I got. You've had a family. Me, I just got Aunt Pru. Blood kin means a right smart to you when you have so little of it. She's my aunt, and I reckon I love her."

"Never was any question about that."

"And she loves me; I know she does."

Johnny nodded. "Sure she does, Speck." But he had his doubts.

The horses had put in a long trip, all the way from Sonora. Johnny could feel his mount about to cave in beneath him. A man could drive himself to extremes when he had a reason, but he had to consider his horse.

Sometime around midnight they halted on a sloping river bottom, where ageless native pecan trees stood like silent giants, spreading a huge canopy of fresh green leaves which blacked out all the moonlight. For countless generations the Indians had come to the three Conchos each fall to gather nuts for winter food. Now the faces had changed, but the routine had not. Come fall, people from San Angelo and all around would tramp up and down these riverbanks gathering pecans to eat or to sell.

The two staked their horses. Speck voiced concern. "We oughtn't to be stoppin'. No tellin' who's behind us, or how far."

But there was no choice, not unless a man wanted to walk

off and leave a dead horse. They spread their single blankets upon the mat of fallen leaves and stretched out. Johnny was so weary he ached all over. He thought he would drop right off to sleep. But he found himself lying awake, looking up into the heavy foliage, which rustled gently in a cool early-morning breeze. The tensions of the past hours did not leave him as he had hoped they would. Lying there, it was almost as if he were still in the saddle, still plodding those endless miles, still looking back over his shoulder, fearful of what he might see back there catching up with him. His mind gave him no rest. Over and over and over again he saw the blanched face of Cora Haggard. He put his hands over his ears, and still he heard her cry.

Somehow Speck slept, but it was a nervous, threshing sleep. Johnny knew the things that went through Speck's restless dreams. Finally Speck cried out, "No, we didn't mean to!" Johnny reached over and shook him gently. Speck sat bolt upright, blinking in confusion.

"It was a nightmare, Speck. A nightmare, is all."

Speck rubbed his hand over his face and squeezed his eyes shut. "Johnny, I kept seein' her. She just stood there lookin' at me, accusin' me with her eyes, with that blood on her . . . all that blood!"

"Easy, Speck, easy. Lie down and try to sleep some more."

Speck shook his head in misery. "If I got to go through that every time, I don't think I'll ever want to sleep again."

He got up and rummaged through his warbag. Finding the pistol that had brought on the trouble, he held it a moment, feeling it with the tips of his fingers. Then he drew back and threw it into the river.

He sat on the ground with his knees drawn up and his face buried, and he began quietly crying.

IV

Tired, a separate ache for every long mile, Johnny felt a lift as the little Fristo ranch headquarters came in sight along a slow bend in the brush-studded draw. Stretched out ahead were the corrals he had helped build as a boy. There was no telling how much of his own sweat had gone into the slow, laborious digging of holes, the ditching, the tying together of cedar stakes and the tamping of heavy posts to make the fences bull-stout. He watched the big cypress fan of the windmill turning slowly in the noonday breeze, and he wondered how many times he had helped pull the suckerrods up out of that deep hole.

The first settlers had taken up the river land. Baker Fristo had arrived a shade late, with little in assets except ambition and a willing back. He had to accept rangeland away from the living water. But the day of the windmill had come just in time. He had found that his land—though there wasn't so much of it—could produce as much beef as any that lay along the river, so long as a man had windmills. It didn't matter so much where the water came from; the main thing was to have it. He had worked for wages on neighboring big outfits for cash to buy cattle and drill wells and put up the wooden towers.

Johnny and Speck rode their flagging horses into the main waterlot gate. Two high-headed cows with trailing calves eased warily around them, breaking into a run when they were in the clear. In front of the barn the riders climbed down from their saddles, stiff and groaning from the ache. Pulling off his saddle, Johnny could tell how badly drawn his horse was. They had put in an awful day yesterday. Without those few hours of rest along the river during the early morning, the horses might not have gotten here. Johnny dropped his saddle front-end down and draped the sweat-soaked blanket across it to dry. He slipped the bridle off the horse's head. The horse turned away and made for the water trough. In a moment Speck's followed suit. Johnny stood wearily with the bridle in his hand, the leather reins trailing on the ground, and watched the thirsty horses drink.

He saw his father walking out from the small frame house, trailed at a respectful distance by a short, dark-skinned Mexican cowboy. Baker Fristo was the picture of Johnny Fristo, plus twenty-five hard years. Grinding work had put a twist in his back, and he walked leaning a little forward. He favored his left leg, an unwanted souvenir from a bronc of years ago. His features were the same as Johnny's but badly abused by time and weather, the hair almost solidly gray now where it showed from beneath his old grease-stained hat. He had a three-day stubble of beard, for his wife lay buried yonder on the hill, and there was no one to tell him to shave.

The ranch was small, and it wasn't much for fancy. But what there was of it, it belonged to him. It had his sweat and blood soaked into it.

He was a plain man, and he showed his emotions. He grabbed Johnny's right hand and clamped his left hand tightly on Johnny's elbow. He squeezed so hard that it hurt. "Son, it's sure good to see you home."

"Howdy, Dad. I'm tickled to be here."

The father squeezed again, and Johnny winced. Baker Fristo stepped back for a long, critical look at his son. He extended his hand to Speck. "Howdy, Speck. I declare, you fellers look a sight. Bet you been over in Angelo celebratin' spring. Don't you-all know when to stop?"

"Mister Fristo, I'm afraid we ain't got nothin' to celebrate about."

Baker Fristo looked quizzically at his son. His grin gradually faded. "There's somethin' wrong. What is it?"

Johnny shook his head and looked at the ground. "Dad, it's a long story. I don't hardly know where to start. Reckon we could eat first? We're both hungry as a wolf."

"Sure. Me and Lalo were just fixin' us some dinner when we saw you-all ride up. We'll throw some more in the skillet." He studied his son, apprehension clouding his eyes. "You sure you ain't been drinkin'?"

"No, sir, none atall."

Baker Fristo hesitated, worry still pulling at him as he looked at the two horses rolling themselves in the dirt. It was plain that they had been ridden hard. "Well, let's mosey up to the house." He led the way. Johnny and Speck trudged along, trying vainly to keep up with him. Another day, they would have led him.

When he had finally become financially able, Baker Fristo had built the frame house to please his wife. Lord knew, she hadn't had many of the nicer things. Once it had seemed a big and beautiful thing to Johnny. Now that he was grown he could see it for the wooden box that it was. The color was faded and peeling too. The house hadn't been painted since his mother passed away. Off to one side of it stood the picket shack which Baker Fristo had first put up for his little family so many years ago. It was built of cedar posts, hewn for a fit and lashed tightly together, the butt ends set solidly in a trench. The space between the posts had been chinked with plaster. In a way, it resembled a small log cabin standing on end. The Mexican, Lalo Acosta, lived in it now.

Baker Fristo sliced steak from a quarter of tarp-wrapped beef hanging on the small back porch. Because he and the Mexican could not eat a whole beef before it spoiled, it was Baker's custom to pool beeves with several of his neighbors. Johnny stood around hungrily watching the meat frying in the pan. Impatiently he took it out of the skillet before it was completely done. Ordinarily the sight of blood running would make his stomach turn over. Like most Texans, he wanted his beef well done. But he was desperately hungry now, and so was Speck. They took the beef in big bites and ate it quickly, like a pair of starved pups.

The longer he watched them, the more Baker Fristo's eyes narrowed. "You boys are in Dutch, I can tell that."

Johnny glanced at Lalo Acosta, indicating by his expression that he didn't want to talk in front of anybody but his father. "We need a couple of fresh horses, Dad. A couple of good ones."

Baker Fristo understood. "Lalo, how about you goin' out and fetchin' up the horses?"

When the Mexican was gone, Baker Fristo leaned back with his bearded-face long and grave and waited for the story. His jaw hardened as he listened. He blinked faster, the full implication reaching him.

"Poor woman," he said quietly. "No part of it was her fault, but she suffered anyway. Wasn't really your fault either, come right down to it. But you'll be the ones who pay." He placed the palms of his rough hands together and seemed to measure his thick fingers. He glanced at Speck.

"I suppose you went by and told your Aunt Pru?"

Speck nodded.

"What did she say?"

Speck was slow to answer. He got up nervously and paced the floor. "She was awful sorry about it." He looked down. "I reckon I'll go help Lalo."

When Speck was gone, Johnny told his father bitterly about Aunt Pru. "Dad, I never did want to hit a woman in all my life. But I wanted to hit *her*."

Gravely, Baker said, "Son, she can't help bein' what she was born, any more than Speck can. What she's done for Speck she hasn't done out of love. If the truth was known, she likely hates him. But she figures he's her ticket to Heaven. She's figured to buy her way in by feedin' him and bringin' him up, even if she *did* treat him like a dog from the day he was born. Some of what's wrong with Speck today, you can blame on her."

Johnny said, "I'm glad I had you and Mother, and not somebody like *her*."

Baker Fristo looked at his hands again, his jaw quivering. "I've heard of Milam Haggard. I expect most folks have. How long do you think he'll give you?"

"They'll be buryin' her today, I guess. Likely he'll come a-ridin' when the service is over."

"How'll he know where to start lookin'?"

"He can ask the cowboys we've worked with. We didn't make any secret about where we came from, or who our folks was. Who'd have ever thought we'd need to?"

Baker Fristo frowned darkly. "So, he'll likely be stoppin' here about tomorrow. Next day at the latest."

"I expect."

Fristo took a handkerchief from his pocket and blew his nose. He tried to look at Johnny, but he couldn't. He turned and stared out the window awhile. "Johnny, I been doin' a lot of thinkin' lately. I been hopin' you'd get the roamin' out of your system and come home to stay. I need you around here."

"You got Lalo."

"Sure, he's good help but he's not like family. You're all I got left now. I been plannin' how one day soon I'd turn this place over to you. I'll be gettin' too old and stove up. This place would give you a good start. *I* started with nothin'. It's been a hard fight, but at least I've managed to build this little bit. You could build a lot more. You're young yet."

Johnny's throat was tight. "I've missed you, Dad. I've wanted to come home. But first I wanted to prove I could make a hand worth my hire to somebody else. Now I reckon it's too late."

"You could stay and try to talk it out with Haggard."

Johnny shook his head. "You don't know how he looked. If he could have, he'd have killed us and cut us up into little bitty pieces. In his place, I suppose I'd have been the same."

"Once a man starts runnin', it's awful hard to find a stoppin' place, son. He has to keep on runnin' and runnin' till finally he can't run anymore. And in the end he has to turn and face it anyhow."

Johnny's hands shook. "Dad, I just can't face him now. Call me a coward and I guess you'd be right. Maybe someday I can do it. But not now."

Baker Fristo was silent awhile. "It's my fault, in a way. I intended to talk to you but I was afraid you wouldn't listen. Now it's too late."

"Talk about what?"

"About Speck Quitman. I know you like him; *I* like him too. But he's a millstone around your neck."

Johnny stared, wanting to reply but not finding the words.

His father said, "Sure, you made a good pair when you were younger. But you've outgrown him. You're a man now and ready to take on a man's responsibility. Somewhere back yonder, Speck quit growin'. He'll never be a man if he lives to be a hundred."

"Dad . . ."

"Let me finish, son. Some folks say he's simpleminded. I don't go that far. But I *do* say he's got no imagination, no foresight. He's got no idea about the consequences of the things he does. He'd walk into a burnin' house just to get a cigarette lit. Now, that cow trader was the one to blame for what took place yesterday. But think back: if it hadn't been for Speck, it wouldn't have happened, would it?"

Johnny shook his head.

His father went on, "You ought to've said *adiós* to him a long time ago, Johnny. Stay with him and he'll get you killed!"

Johnny nodded a regretful agreement. "You're right, Dad. I've known it a long time. More than once I've started to ride off and leave him someplace, but I never could bring myself to do it. What could he ever do by himself? Now it's too late. Whatever happens to us now, we'll have to face it together."

Baker Fristo brought himself to look at his son, and his wrinkle-edged eyes were sad. Johnny had never seen his father cry but once, that when Mrs. Fristo had died. He thought he could see tears in Baker's eyes now. "Then, son, if there's no other way, you better run. You'll need some money. Whatever I've got, I'll give it to you." He paused. "Any idea where you'll go?"

Johnny shook his head. "West someplace, wherever the trail leads us. Texas is awful big."

Lalo brought in the horses. Badly as he wanted to rest, Johnny knew he and Speck needed to travel all they could. These first days would be crucial. If they could get a long-enough lead on Haggard, there was a chance he never could find them in those vast spaces west of here.

Baker Fristo took a rope out of the barn. He made a gentle underhand loop and caught a long-legged bay. "Speck, here's one that ought to fit you." When Speck bridled the bay and slipped Baker's rope off its neck, Baker reached out and snared a brown. "Johnny, you know this horse, old Traveler. I traded him off of Wilse Arbuckle. He's not much for pretty, but he'll take you all the way and bring you back."

"Thanks, Dad."

They saddled up. Lalo came out from the house with a sack of food—canned goods, cold biscuits, coffee, a little of the beef. Baker Fristo watched while Speck tied the sack on behind his saddle. He shook hands with Speck. "Good luck, boy." He turned back to Johnny. "Write me, son. Let me know you're still alive. Maybe someday I'll be able to tell you it's safe to come back."

Johnny's eyes held doubt. "Dad, we better face what's true. I don't expect I'll ever be able to come back."

Baker Fristo looked down again for a long time. "Well, Johnny, a man does what he has to. Me, I'll just have to give up some dreams. As you get older you find out most of your dreams don't really come true anyway. They keep you goin', but they don't often turn out. Still, without them a man never would amount to much."

Johnny's throat was tight and painful. He wanted to hug his father's neck, the way he had done when he was a boy. But he only gripped Baker's rough hand. "Goodbye, Dad." He swung up into the saddle.

Baker Fristo watched them ride out of sight. Finally, his shoulders slumped helplessly, he turned toward his house, oblivious of Lalo Acosta standing there, sympathy and puzzlement mixed in the Mexican's dark eyes.

"Not goodbye, son. Don't let it be goodbye!"

V

They angled northwestward from the ranch, purposely leaving a clear trail. By and by they came to a public road. They turned into it and stayed long enough to establish an appearance that they intended to remain on it.

Speck seemed numb. He followed along woodenly, doing whatever Johnny did, making no comment, contributing nothing that might help them. At length Johnny said, "We've gone far enough north. There's generally enough horse and wagon traffic on this road to blot out our tracks before long. Maybe by the time Haggard gets to here we'll have him fooled. He'll think we've headed for Colorado City and north."

Speck shrugged as if it didn't matter. "There ain't no use. There ain't nothin' goin' to fool Milam Haggard for long."

"We got to try."

Johnny saw a sandy spot beside the road, and he reined out to the left. "Time we was headin' west, Speck."

Speck only nodded and followed like a pup. Johnny dismounted a hundred feet from the road and handed his reins to Speck. He broke a limb from a mesquite and walked back to the road with it. He carefully brushed out their tracks, eliminating any trace of their having left the road. He moved slowly backward toward the horses, rubbing out all the tracks as he went. From the road there would be no visible sign that anyone had ridden away from it.

"That ought to leave us clear," he said.

Speck's eyes were bleak. "It won't fool him. Ain't nothin'
goin' to fool him."

Impatience flared in Johnny. "He's only a man. Any man
can be fooled."

"Me and you can. Other folks can. But Haggard can't."

At this point they were nearly thirty miles up the North Concho from San Angelo. They could not follow a route due west
from here, for they would not find natural water before they
reached the Pecos, not unless it had rained somewhere. And
rain in the country west of San Angelo was a thing to be trea-
sured when it came but never to be counted upon. With luck,
they might come across a windmill once in a while. Without
that luck, they might starve for water before they ever reached
the Pecos.

Still, Johnny knew there was a way. If they angled south-
westward they would strike the Middle Concho. It meant extra traveling, but it was worth that. The Middle Concho had its
beginnings west of San Angelo eighty miles or more, when
weather was wet. Chances were right now that its upper
reaches would be dry; to be safe, a man had to figure on that.
In olden times the wagon trains and trail herds venturing west
from Fort Concho had followed along the Middle Concho as
far as there was a river. From San Angelo west, the country
turned increasingly arid. With every ten miles you could tell a
difference. Early travelers had stayed with the living water as
long as they could. At best, they knew they faced long, miserable miles of dry travel between the headquarters of the
Middle Concho and far-off Horsehead Crossing on the Pecos.
It was foolhardy to start a dry trek any earlier than necessary.

Even now, with windmills increasing over the range, travel-

ers tended to stay with the old trails and the river as long as
there was any water in it. It was a conditioning bred into them,
like an old-timer watching for Indians long after the last of
them were gone.

Johnny and Speck watered the horses in the North Concho beneath the shade of tall old pecan trees whose limbs
reached well out over the river. Johnny filled their canteens
and listened to the high-pitched hum of the locusts. The afternoon was no more than half gone. If they pushed, they should
reach the Middle Concho by dark.

"Speck, you look sick. You feelin' bad?"

"I been feelin' bad ever since that woman died. I'm tired, is
all." He grimaced. "Tired. And scared."

"You're not alone, Speck. I'm scared too."

They came upon the river at dusk, and it was time, for both
of them were spitting cotton. Johnny rode Traveler over the
bank and down to the water. He slid stiffly out of the saddle and
loosened the cinch so the horse could drink comfortably. He
stepped upstream to the end of the reins, holding them because
it was too far from home to let a horse get notions about traveling alone. He dropped on his stomach to drink long and gratefully of the cool water. Finally satisfied, he pushed himself up on
one knee and wiped his sleeve across his mouth. Above him,
Speck was watering too. The horses were both still drinking.

Johnny called, "Speck, why don't you come down here
and drink? The water looks a little clearer."

"It don't matter. I figure on drinkin' it all anyway."

Johnny looked up the river. The stream here was probably
not deep enough to wet a man to his waist, and a good jumper
with a running start could almost clear it in a leap. It was a
quiet stream most of the time, in summer dropping so low that

in places it disappeared below the gravel. But once in a great while its vast dry watershed would catch a whopping big rain that brought water cascading down from the rocky hills and put the Middle Concho up on its hind legs to roar.

Johnny had noticed a bank of dark clouds forming far off in the north the last couple of hours and had made a mental note that they would do to watch. It wasn't considered realistic to predict rain in this part of the country, but it never hurt a man to be prepared.

He glanced again at Speck. "Ain't you ever goin' to get yourself watered out?"

Speck raised up, the water dripping off of his chin. "I never did know just how good water could taste."

"Leave some. We're liable to need it again."

Speck pushed to his feet. It was a considerable effort for him. Johnny could see dark circles under Speck's eyes.

"Speck, we just as well camp here. I'm gettin' hungry."

The Middle Concho lacked the heavy pecan and other timber that the North Concho had. Anyway, if those clouds moved up during the night and brought a spring electrical storm with them, Johnny didn't want to be under a bunch of trees. He'd take his chances with the rain out in the open. He'd seen lightning kill several steers beneath a tree one time. Thing like that came into a man's mind every time he saw a dark cloud.

They took the horses back up the riverbank. Johnny looked around for dry brush that would make good firewood for camp. He saw some mesquite.

"If you'll get that sack off of your saddle, Speck, I'll start a fire."

Speck turned toward his horse. His face fell in dismay. He

glanced at Johnny, unbelieving. "Johnny, that grub ain't here."

Johnny stiffened. "What do you mean, it ain't here?"

"I had it tied to my saddle. Now it's gone."

Johnny swore and looked for himself. "That knot you tied must've come loose. Got any idea where you lost it?"

Impatience had edged into his voice, and Speck reacted with a testy defense. "If I'd known when it come off, I'd have stopped and got it."

Johnny wished he hadn't been so snappish, for he knew the strain Speck had been under. Speck had ridden along so benumbed that he could almost have fallen off the horse and not realized it. Johnny took a long look down their backtrail, what little he could see of it in the growing darkness. "Might've been a mile, or it might've been before we even got out of sight of the North Concho. Cinch we can't go back and hunt for it now."

Speck stared at the saddle as if he couldn't believe it. He reached up and touched the saddlestrings. "We got nothin' to eat. What're we goin' to do?"

"We'll do without."

They staked the horses on the fresh green grass and spread their blankets. Johnny took a hitch in his belt, but it didn't stop his stomach from growling. He looked at Speck with a nagging impatience.

They lay and watched the bullbats swooping down and touching the river, then lifting and banking around for another try. By and by Speck complained, "Johnny, I sure am hungry."

"Go down there and get you another long drink of water. That'll fill you up."

"I already slosh every time I move."

Gradually, as full darkness came, Johnny grew aware of a

pinpoint of light upriver. He narrowed his eyes, wondering. Speck noticed it too.

"Campfire?"

Johnny nodded. "I expect."

Speck pondered awhile in silence. "Reckon they got anything to eat?"

"Sure, they wouldn't be out here without some chuck. But they'd remember us if Milam Haggard came along and asked."

Speck agreed reluctantly. "Still, I can almost smell supper a-cookin'."

"Forget it," Johnny snapped.

Speck was plainly hurt. He sat a long time in brooding silence. "Johnny, I'm a real trial to you."

"Go to sleep, Speck."

"I'm the one caused you all this trouble. Hadn't been for me we'd have somethin' to eat right now. Hadn't been for me, Mrs. Haggard would still be alive. We wouldn't have to be runnin' thisaway." He paused. "You know what you ought to do, Johnny? You ought to just go off and leave me!" He paused again, a long time. Then, worriedly, he said, "You ain't goin' to do it, are you, Johnny? You ain't goin' to go off and leave me?"

The fear in Speck's voice roused pity in Johnny. "No, Speck, I'm not goin' off and leave you."

Johnny turned first one way, then the other on his blanket, trying to find a position where he wouldn't feel the aches and the stiffness. He had to sleep. Hunger teased him, and he tried to force it from his mind. After a long time he drifted into sleep.

With daylight he awoke and looked up into a leaden sky. The smell of rain was fresh in the air. It would be coming down hard before long, he would bet on that.

His stomach growled its hunger. He pushed to his feet and

looked around. In the north the sky was a sodden blue. Already raining yonder.

"Speck, we just as well get started."

Speck Quitman stirred and rubbed his eyes. He blinked and looked around sleepily, trying to get his bearings. Speck was always a slow one to wake up. If there had been any nightmares last night, Johnny was not aware of them. He thought Speck probably had been so tired that Mrs. Haggard hadn't entered his mind. That was a good thing, for Speck had come close to breaking down for a while.

Speck looked at the dark sky overhead, then glanced north. "Bad enough just to be hungry. But to be soaked and cold on top of an empty belly is almost too much to stand."

"We got slickers," Johnny said curtly. "At least *those* didn't come loose from the saddles." *There I go*, he thought then, ashamed, *still laying it into him.*

"I know it was my fault," Speck conceded ruefully. "But that don't make it any easier. I'm starvin' to death."

Johnny found himself looking wishfully in the direction where he had spotted the campfire last night. He couldn't find it now in the daylight.

Speck said, "I think we ought to go over yonder and see who them folks are. Maybe it's some ranch's chuckwagon."

"You know the risk."

"And I know I'm so hungry I can't see straight."

Johnny frowned. He had tightened his belt as far as he could pull it, but it hadn't helped much. "All right, let's go."

They saddled up and rode out, following the river. It took a while. There had been no way of telling in the darkness how far away the fire had been, or on which side of the river it lay. It could have been a quarter of a mile or it could have been three times that much. Johnny didn't indulge himself in curiosity. Like Speck, the main thing which bothered him right now was that he was hungry. He looked often at the sky. The rain smell was stronger. It was a bracing smell, one welcomed by a native West Texan under almost any circumstance, for rain came too seldom.

They saw the tent first, then the old Studebaker wagon standing there with a half-wornout wagonsheet tied loosely over the bows to cover whatever goods were in the wagonbed. Two horses were staked out on grass nearby. A campfire had burned itself down low, a coffeepot sitting on shoveled out coals next to it. Johnny saw several pots and one big Dutch oven, but they looked empty. He wondered if the folks had already eaten, and thrown out what was left.

"Hello," he shouted. "Anybody home?"

It wasn't polite, those days, to ride into someone's camp and not announce yourself.

He saw a flash of skirt at the open tent flap. A girl stepped outside and looked worriedly around. Her gaze fell upon the approaching riders. She lifted her skirts a little and came running. She was young, Johnny saw, maybe seventeen-eighteen. And she was crying.

Speck's horse shied at the flare of skirts rushing straight at him. Johnny's Traveler poked ears forward but didn't otherwise flinch. The girl cried out, "Thank God you've come! Please hurry!" She tried to say more, but her voice broke, and Johnny couldn't understand her. Speck was staring at the girl in total surprise. Johnny swung down. The girl caught his arm and began to pull him toward the camp.

"Please, I've got to have help."

Johnny dragged his feet a little, watching the tent with a

considerable degree of suspicion. "Miss, I don't know what your trouble is, but we got trouble too."

With an effort she steadied her voice. "My father's in there. He's dying!"

Johnny glanced back at Speck, who still sat on his horse. "Come on, Speck. We better see what we can do."

Speck frowned. "Johnny, I don't like the smell of this."

"Come on."

Johnny wrapped his reins around a wagonwheel and followed the girl to the tent. A streak of lightning darted to the north, and thunder rolled. A drop of water struck his hand. He paused at the tent flap and looked inside. A man lay on a bedroll spread out on the ground. The hollow-cheeked face was wasted and pale. His beard was the only thing about him that wasn't a liver gray. The man coughed. Reddish foam showed on his lips.

The sight struck Johnny like a blow across the face.

Tuberculosis!

This man was a consumptive. Likely he had come to the dry West Texas region like hundreds of others from God knew where, hoping this climate would work the miracle, would bring him a cure. As a boy Johnny had come upon many of them like this, camped up and down the rivers, sleeping on the ground, taking their rest, breathing the dry air and praying for health. Some had found it. Others had found only a lonely grave, maybe a thousand miles from home.

Johnny knew the girl had judged right. This man had waited too long.

The girl dropped to her knees and touched a wet handkerchief to her father's lips. Johnny stared, a strange knot drawing up inside him. "Is he conscious?"

The girl nodded. "Off and on. Right now he knows I'm here; that's about all. He's going. I can feel it; he's going." She bit her lip and touched the handkerchief to her father's face again.

Johnny made himself move a little closer, though a cold chill ran through him. He dreaded this slow, wasting disease, and he had always avoided people who had it. "You've known, haven't you, that he didn't have much time left? You can tell it by lookin' at him."

She nodded again, dropping her hands to her knees and staring forlornly into the pale face. "But they told us this dry air might do it. We hoped so much, and we came so far. All the way from Illinois."

"You got no other folks here, nobody to help you?"

"Papa's all I've got left. When he goes . . . there'll be nobody."

The man coughed again. The girl took one of his hands and squeezed it helplessly. She looked up, desperate. "Please, he's in pain. Don't you know anything to do for him?"

Regretfully Johnny shook his head. "I never had any experience with this. I don't reckon there's much anybody can do but wait. And maybe pray a little bit."

He didn't think it would be a long wait.

Raindrops began spattering against the canvas. Speck Quitman stepped up to the flap and looked inside suspiciously. His eyes widened. Wordlessly he motioned for Johnny to come outside.

"Johnny, don't you know what the matter is with that man in there? I can tell from here, he's a lunger. Got the lung fever. You better keep out of that tent."

"The girl needs help. He's dyin'."

"He'll take you with him if you catch the lung fever. Let's get the hell out of here!"

"Speck, she needs help."

"What can you do? Can you stop him from dyin'?"

"No, but somebody ought to be here. She'll be alone."

"She's no concern of ours. She was alone before we come here. We could as easy of rode on by, and she'd be no worse off than she ever was."

Johnny didn't know what it was about the girl that had struck him so. "I can't do it, Speck. She's got too much trouble for a girl like her to handle alone."

"We got trouble too."

The girl called from the tent, "Mister! Oh, Mister!"

Johnny turned and left Speck standing there. The man was coughing again, harder than before. The girl was talking quietly, trying to hold down panic. "It's all right, Papa. We've got some help. It's all right, Papa."

Johnny knelt helplessly, knowing there wasn't a thing he could do but sympathize.

The man's eyes opened a little. He blinked, trying to focus. He looked a moment at the girl, then weakly turned his head to look at Johnny. His voice was only a whisper. "Who are you?"

"Name's Johnny Fristo, sir."

"You help . . . help my daughter. Help her."

"I'll help her."

"Please . . . don't leave her."

Johnny swallowed. He found himself making a promise he knew he couldn't keep. "No, sir, I won't leave her."

The dying man lapsed back into the shadows. There was no sound except his ragged breathing and the quiet sobbing of the girl. That, and the rain drumming down on the tent.

Rain! And Speck was out there in it! Johnny eased to the tent flap and looked outside. He saw that Speck had unsaddled their horses and shoved the saddles into the wagon. Speck squatted beneath the vehicle, his yellow slicker wrapped around him, vainly trying to keep dry. There was enough wind with the rain that the water drove in under the wagon.

"Speck, you come in here before you get yourself soaked."

Speck was resolute. "No! I'd rather take my chances with the rain. If you had any smart you'd be out here too."

Johnny shivered, for this was a cold rain, the kind that reminds you it hasn't been long since winter. It was the kind that sometimes caught fresh-sheared sheep and chilled them to death. But he could tell Speck wouldn't come into the tent.

"At least get into the wagon before you get soaked any worse."

He turned back to the girl and wished again he could do something besides just stand here and watch. When you came right down to it, there wasn't much anybody could have done now, not even a doctor. Just wait. So he waited. And at last death came quietly into the tent, touched the girl's father and peacefully took him away. It was hard to tell just when sleep lapsed over into death.

Or, Johnny wondered, was there really much difference?

VI

The girl cried softly. Johnny put his hands on her shoulders. He thought he probably should say something, but nothing came to mind, so he let it go. All he could give her was sympathy, and he couldn't put even that into words.

The rain stopped. Johnny walked out of the tent and raised his head. For a moment the sun broke through, and it struck the spot along the river where the camp stood. He looked up through the small break, and the sun struck him full in the eyes. A chill passed through him. He had always taken his Bible teachings literally, and he wondered if there was some special meaning in the way the light touched here, where a man had just died.

It came to him that this was the second death he had witnessed in three days, and he shivered again.

Back in the tent, he found the girl was no longer crying. She still knelt, solemnly looking down at her father.

Johnny said, "I expect you'll be wantin' to take him back to Angelo."

The girl was a long time in replying. "We didn't know anybody in San Angelo. We just came there on the train, and we bought this old wagon and team at a stable. We came on out because Papa thought camping on the ground would cure him."

"Seems like you came an awful long way."

"We stopped once closer in, but the man who owned the land didn't want us there. He made us move. We came here, and nobody has bothered us." She paused. "Besides, I don't have money left to bury him with. It took about all we had to get him here."

"You got to do somethin' about him."

"I know. He liked this spot. It seemed to strike his fancy the minute he saw it. I think he would have liked to be buried here."

Johnny rubbed his neck, considering. Seemed to him he'd heard that when somebody died you had to report it to the law, get death papers and such. Just to bury a man out here this way might have been all right ten or fifteen years ago, but now it was probably against the law. It was too simple to be legal anymore.

But, on the other hand, it would be a minor thing compared to the trouble he and Speck were already in.

The girl's eyes pleaded. "Will you help me?"

He couldn't have turned her down if he had seen Milam Haggard and a big posse come riding over the hill.

"We'll help you." He looked outside at the gray sky. "It might set in to rainin' again directly. I expect if we're goin' to dig, we better get at it."

He went out and looked around for a pick and shovel. He found Speck standing by the wagon, his clothes wet. "Speck, I swear you look a sight. You ought to've come inside like I told you."

Speck shook his head. "You about ready to leave here now?"

At another time Johnny might have smiled, for it struck him a little funny how Speck had lost his concern over being hungry. "Speck, her father died. We're goin' to bury him before we go."

Speck's mouth dropped open. "Johnny, we got to be a-ridin'. Haggard is liable to be most any place."

"We can't just leave this girl here with a dead body on her hands. We got to help her."

Speck looked for a moment as if he had about as soon fight as argue. But he gave in. "All right, sooner we get it done the sooner we get movin'. I'll dig, but I ain't goin' to handle him none, you understand?" He was about to say something else, but he sneezed.

Johnny said, "You oughtn't to be in those wet clothes. Maybe the girl can lend you somethin' of her dad's."

Speck shook his head violently. "No, sir, thank you, I wouldn't touch it." He took the shovel from Johnny's hand.

They let the girl pick the spot, back away from the river where no flood would disturb the grave.

That was the first time Johnny mentioned to her that they were hungry. She nodded solemnly. "I'm sorry. I should've asked you a long time ago."

"You had aplenty to worry about."

"I should've asked you anyway. I'll go fix something."

Speck started the digging. Johnny walked down to the camp with the girl. In the wagonbed he found a small supply of dry wood. She had been farsighted enough to put it under there before the rain started. In a wooden box were some canned goods, coffee, flour and sundry camp supplies. He put some of the dry wood into the firepit, poured a little kerosene over it and set it ablaze. He could see the girl through the open tent flap. She was pulling the blanket up over her father's face. Johnny turned away, respecting her privacy.

"Need any more help right now?" he asked when she came out.

"I'll be all right."

"I best go help my partner."

She said worriedly, "He's wet. I could get some of Papa's dry clothes for him."

"He wouldn't wear them. He takes some funny notions sometimes. But I'll tell him you made the offer, and thanks."

He had been looking around camp for something that would do as a headboard. All he could find was the endgate from the wagon. He took it out.

"Funny," he remarked, "I don't even know what name to put on this."

A tear started down her cheek. "His name was Edward Barnett."

"I never did hear yours, either."

"Mine is Tessie. Tessie Barnett."

With a rope Johnny and Speck lowered Edward Barnett into the grave. They stood and looked at the ground while the girl started reading the Twenty-third Psalm in a weak, strained voice. She finally broke down. Johnny took the Bible from her hands. He finished reading what she had started. Done, he added the one thing he could remember from funerals he had attended: "The Lord giveth, and the Lord taketh away. Blessed be the name of the Lord." He closed the Book and handed it to her.

She glanced up at him, and their eyes held a moment. Something stirred Johnny, something he had never felt before.

"Thank you," she said. She turned and walked back down to camp.

Speck and Johnny filled the grave and put the headboard in place, bracing it with rocks to make sure it didn't fall down.

Speck said, "Reckon anybody'll ever notice it up here? It's a ways off of the trail."

"I don't know. Maybe they won't. But it don't seem right to put a man away and not even leave a headboard to mark his passin'. Man ought to have at least that much to show that he once walked this earth. Else he'd just as well never have been here."

Speck shrugged. "Don't look like he's left much to show for him. An old wagon, a tent. Ain't much to make a man's whole life look worthwhile."

Down the slope, the girl was breaking camp. Johnny said, "Maybe it's not the money and the property a man leaves that's really important, Speck. They get scattered, and who's ever goin' to remember him by that? But he left that girl. She'll remember him as long as she lives. She'll have children someday, and she'll tell them about him. They'll remember. Come right down to it, Speck, I don't guess a marker is really so important after all."

They folded the tent and placed it in the wagon. Speck went out and got the team. Johnny looked worriedly at the girl. "Miss, what're you goin' to do now?"

She didn't look at him. "I don't know. I hadn't let myself think about it. I just know I can't stay here where he died."

"You can sell the wagon and team, I suppose, and go back where you came from."

"I've got no family there anymore. There's nothing to go back to."

"Then maybe San Angelo. It's a good-sized town. I expect a girl like you could get decent work there."

She nodded. He could still see a trace of tears in her eyes.

She had a lost look about her. She was young yet to be alone like this, to be left a stranger bewildered in a land that was alien to her, a land where she knew not a single soul.

"I have to live somewhere." She squared her shoulders, forcing herself to take courage. "How far is it to San Angelo?"

"A fair piece. Forty miles, I expect." He looked at her with worry. "Think you can make it there by yourself?"

She was plainly dubious. "I guess I could." She bit her lip. "Do you suppose . . . do you suppose I could get you fellows to go with me? I've never been by myself like this." She looked away as if ashamed. "I guess I'm scared."

Johnny saw alarm surge into Speck's face, and he moved to head Speck off. "Miss Barnett, we're goin' west. We can't go to San Angelo."

"I don't have much money left, but I'll give you what I *do* have."

"It ain't the money. I mean, if we could do it atall, we'd do it for nothin'. But you see . . . well, the truth is we *can't* go back. They're lookin' for us there."

She slowly shook her head. "I can't believe that. You've been kind to me, both of you. You couldn't have done anything bad."

Johnny couldn't hold his gaze to hers. "We did a bad thing, but not on purpose. It was an accident." He didn't want to tell her more than that. He was glad she didn't ask.

Speck's calmness even surprised Johnny. Speck spoke to the girl in a gentle voice. "We'll hitch up your horses, Miss. Too bad we can't do more." It didn't take Johnny long to figure out that Speck was simply glad to be shed of her and get moving again.

They turned the wagon around for her and headed it eastward, toward San Angelo. The girl said tightly, "Thank you again, both of you. I'll never forget this."

Johnny said, "I wish you would. I mean, if anybody asks you . . ."

"I won't say a thing."

They sat and watched her start. They watched her top out over the hill, a tiny-looking thing and all alone.

Speck wondered, "Johnny, reckon she'll ever make it there all by herself?"

"I don't know. I purely don't know."

"It's a long ways."

Johnny kept watching the girl, and that strange feeling came over him again. Suddenly he touched spurs to his horse. "Come on, Speck, we're not goin' to let her do it."

"What can we do? We can't go with her."

"We can take her west with us a ways. There's bound to be a ranch up here someplace where we can leave her with folks who'll see she gets to town all right."

"Johnny, I do believe you're losin' your head over that girl."

"I just never could sleep, wonderin' if she ever got there all right or if somethin' happened to her. Come on, Speck."

Speck grumbled, but he accepted the inevitable and followed.

VII

Milam Haggard was tired, but he had cultivated a rigid self-discipline that would not allow him to show it. Riding a black-legged dun, leading a brown horse with a small pack, he kept his back straight, his shoulders high. His flat-brimmed black hat with the round crown was pulled down low over his eyes, so that he held his chin high to be able to see out under the brim. It gave him the appearance of a man with strong pride, and the appearance was not misleading. But it was not pride which dominated him now. He burned with a grim and silent determination.

He had passed the North Concho village of Water Valley a while ago, and ahead of him lay the Baker Fristo place. He had made some inquiry around San Angelo about this Fristo. Most people had told him Fristo was a hard-working small cowman who had pulled himself up by his own bootstraps and never made trouble for anybody. But Haggard knew circumstances could forge drastic changes in a person. The mildest of men would stand up and fight for a son.

He was sure the situation here would be different from the one he had stepped into in San Angelo when he visited Speck Quitman's aunt. She had broken into uncontrollable hysterics and had cried about the shame that had been brought upon her. It had seemed to Haggard that she showed little concern for her nephew but a great deal about the disgrace that had be-fallen her good family name.

Haggard had held her in contempt, but he had stayed until

he found out that the two cowboys were likely to visit Baker Fristo. Fristo probably wouldn't tell him anything on purpose, Haggard knew. But long ago he had learned that people would usually tell more than they realized, more than they intended. A word, a glance, a set of tracks—and he might discover all he really needed to know.

Haggard rode out of the brushy draw and saw before him the big windmill, the rambling set of corrals, the barn, the fading frame house. He reined up for a long, careful look around. He studied closely the places where a man or men could hide—behind the barn, the house, a stack of unused cedar posts, a pile of barbed-wire rolls. Some of these he carefully eliminated one by one, concentrating on their shadows until he was sure nothing stood behind them that didn't belong. Still, plenty of dangerous places were left. He drew the saddlegun up out of its scabbard, laid it across his lap and gently touched spurs to the dun. He moved forward in a slow walk, watching with the tense care of a man who half expects to be shot out of the saddle.

He heard talk. His gaze caught movement out in one of the corrals. Two men were hanging a new wooden gate. Haggard lightly touched the reins and moved the dun in that direction, the pack horse following. He noted that the man facing him was a Mexican. That checked with what Haggard had been careful to find out. Fristo had one man living on the ranch with him, a hired Mexican.

The Mexican spoke quietly. The other man turned to squint at Haggard. The man made a move with his hand, and Haggard's grip tightened on the saddlegun. But he saw then that the man was only wiping sweat from his dusty face.

Now Haggard could see the face, and he knew this was

Baker Fristo. He had seen Johnny Fristo once on the street of
Sonora and again a few minutes the day of Cora Haggard's
death. That face would be burned into his memory to the last
day Haggard lived. This was the same face, except for the many
extra years to which the deep furrows testified.

"Howdy," Fristo said. He was not unfriendly. "Git down
and rest yourself."

Haggard did not do so immediately. He sat still, his gaze
sweeping the corrals, the barn.

Fristo understood. "You can quit lookin'. Ain't nobody
here but us, just me and Lalo. Nobody else."

Haggard glanced at the Mexican and saw apprehension in
the dark eyes. For a little of nothing, the man would turn and
run like a deer.

Fristo said, "I ain't lyin' to you, Mister Haggard."

Haggard let his surprise show a little. "You know me?"

"Never met you, but I know who you are. I know why
you've come. My boy's not here. Even if he was, he wouldn't
shoot you in the back. He ain't that sort."

Haggard stared at Fristo and then looked around for sign of
a gun somewhere. Fristo said, "No guns. Me and Lalo, we're
just workin' on the corrals a little. We didn't figure on shootin'
anybody."

Pointedly Haggard said, "If you know why I've come here,
you might be inclined to shoot *me*."

Fristo shook his head. "I'd rather just talk to you, Mister
Haggard."

"Talk won't change anything. You ought to know that."

"I always heard you were a reasonable man, Mister Haggard. I think the truth would change things, if you'd just listen
to it."

Haggard made no reply. Fristo gave up waiting for one. "Well, no use us standin' out here in the hot sun. It's dinnertime directly, and I'd just as well go fix us somethin' to eat. You'll stay and eat with us, won't you, Mister Haggard?"

Surprised, Haggard said, "You're askin' *me* to eat with you?"

"It's dinnertime. Nobody ever left my place hungry."

"I've come here lookin' for your boy. And you know why."

Fristo nodded slowly. "I know. I aim to try and talk you out of it."

"It won't work."

"I'll try anyway. You got to stop and eat sometime. You'd just as well do it here."

Haggard stepped to the ground frowning, studying this bent man. He couldn't remember that he had ever run into a situation like this. In a different way it bothered him as badly as his encounter with that wailing aunt. He stopped at a trough near the windmill and let the horses water. Then he followed Fristo to the frame house. He glanced for a moment at the old picket shack nearby. The thought struck him that the two young men he sought could be holed up in there. But instinctively he knew Fristo wasn't lying to him. The pair had gone.

On the front porch Fristo nodded toward a washstand on which were a bucket of water, a dipper and a washpan. "I expect you're pretty hot and dusty, Mister Haggard. Probably make you feel better to wash yourself."

As the guest, Haggard washed first, then Fristo. In the house Fristo motioned toward a rocking chair. "Set yourself a spell while I see what I can fix."

Waiting, Haggard looked around. One thing he saw was an

old wedding picture. Baker Fristo in that picture was the image of his son today. Plainly enough, a woman had lived here once. Just as plainly, she had been gone a long time. The curtains on the windows were gray now with dust and smoke. A woman had put them there, but a woman would not have allowed them to get in that condition. The dishes on the shelf bore a nice pattern and showed a woman's touch. But some were chipped at the edges, the result of a man's rougher handling. Haggard noted that far fewer cups were left than plates of the original set. Several plain white cups had been added to take the place of some broken by inveterate male coffee drinkers.

It did not escape his notice that when the leftover morning coffee was hot, Baker Fristo passed up the nicer cups and purposely took out one of the plain kind for his own use. He was evidently more comfortable with those.

I guess I would be too, Haggard thought.

He wouldn't have admitted it to anybody, but the thought of settling down and living with Cora had almost frightened him. He had lived alone a long time, Haggard had. He had lived a harsh, womanless life on the trail and in small one-room shacks in a dozen towns. He had been comfortable in austerity. Often he had wondered how he was going to reconcile himself to the change a man had to make when he married, especially when he married a lady of Cora's kind. He would not have asked Cora to compromise her ways. The adjustment would have had to be his. Sometimes he had lain awake at night wondering how and if he could actually make a success of it.

Now he would never know. He and Cora had never had much chance to find a life together.

Baker Fristo broke into Haggard's line of thought. "Afraid my cookin' ain't much for fancy, but it fills in between the ribs. It's on."

Haggard moved to the table. He had never really been hungry. He had never been one to eat much. Since his wife's death, eating had been a necessity that he forced upon himself.

The Mexican came in and sat at the table with them. Haggard noticed this. He had been at many places where it wouldn't have been done. Haggard ate slowly, forcing the food down because he knew he needed it. Fristo ate in silence, but Haggard could feel the man's eyes appraising him. Haggard found himself liking the man. It would have been easier if he hadn't.

Fristo finished eating and leaned back in his chair, his eyes steady on Haggard. "It's a hard and bitter thing for a man to lose his wife. I know, because I've been there."

Haggard was slow to answer. "Then you'll understand how I feel, and why I do what I do."

"Those boys had no thought of hurtin' your wife. If it had even occurred to them that a thing like that could happen, they wouldn't have stopped the hack. But they figured they'd been done wrong, just the way you feel you've been wronged. They made a mistake, like you're fixin' to. They'll regret it as long as they live. So will you, Mister Haggard, if you go through with this."

"They killed her. All the talk in the world won't change that."

"It was an accident. The blame isn't all theirs. It wasn't even them that fired the gun; it was that feller named Larramore."

"*They* told you that, Fristo. You can't really know."

"My boy told me, and he's never lied."

"He never killed anybody before, either."

"They're just boys, Haggard."

"They're men. They're both of age, and that makes them men in the sight of the law."

"And where *is* the law, Haggard? How come it's not with you, helpin' you hunt them?"

Haggard looked across the room, his jaw ridged in anger. "The law looked at it the way you do. The sheriff down there, he said it was an accident. He wouldn't file a murder charge. But she's dead. Nothing anybody says can bring her back."

"And killin' my son—will *that* bring her back?"

"He killed her, he and that other one. An eye for an eye is what the Bible says. It's God's vengeance!"

"God also has His mercy."

Helpless anger simmered in Haggard. He couldn't sit there and argue over this thing as if it were a cow trade or something. His wife was dead. The grief and the anger were still sharp and bitter, cutting through him like a knife. He pushed to his feet. "I'll be ridin' on. I'm sorry I stopped here."

Baker Fristo stood up too. "Please, Haggard, listen to me. Think!"

"I've *been* thinkin'. That's all I've done for days. I've hardly even slept for the thinkin' I've done. And it always comes back to the same thing: they killed my wife. I'm goin' to get them, Fristo. And the only thing I'll be sorry for is that it's *your* son."

He turned and started for the front door. He heard Baker Fristo move quickly. Instinctively Haggard stopped. Even as he turned back, his hand darted downward, coming up with the pistol from his hip.

Baker Fristo had lifted a rifle from a set of hooks on the wall and was starting to turn with it.

Haggard thumbed back the hammer of the pistol. "Stop it! Stop it right there!" Fristo hesitated a second, then kept on turning, the rifle still in his hands.

Haggard cried, "Stop it, Fristo! You haven't got a chance! For God's sake, man, I don't want to kill you!"

Fristo froze, but he still held the rifle. Eyes desperate, he looked into the bore of Haggard's pistol. The color began leaving his face. The man was scared. But Haggard could tell he was also determined, and that made him dangerous.

Fristo said, "You'll kill me, but I'll kill you too, Haggard."

"Not a chance. It's not worth the try."

"My son's life is worth *any* chance."

"You haven't *got* any chance," Haggard repeated firmly. "I'd put a bullet through your heart, and you couldn't pull that trigger. But I don't want to do it. Believe me, I don't want to do it." He waited for sign Fristo was going to relent. "Put it down now, Fristo. For God's sake, put it down!"

He could see the realization of helplessness slowly come into Fristo's eyes. And with the helplessness, a glistening of tears.

Fristo laid the rifle on the floor and stood up, his shoulders slumped, his face stamped with defeat. He looked like an old man. "I tried. I tried."

Haggard found his heart was beating rapidly. He had come within an inch of having to kill this man. It was a killing he would have regretted as long as he lived. "You've got a lot of guts, Mister Fristo. If it's any consolation to you, you can always tell yourself you did what you could. But you never had a chance, not from the first."

"It's not important that I *tried*. What matters is that I failed. And now you'll go on out and kill my son."

Haggard swallowed. He saw the Mexican come up beside Fristo, the fear somehow gone from him. He saw the intention written all across the little man's dark face.

"Don't try it, *hombre*. You just leave that gun lay there or I'll have to kill you."

Lalo slowly backed away. Haggard picked up the rifle. He unloaded it, carefully watching the two men. He started to lay the rifle across a chair, then changed his mind. "I'll take this with me out to the barn and leave it there. I'd be real glad if you-all would just stay here till I get out of sight."

He could see desperation clutching at Fristo. "You can't find them, Haggard. It's two thousand miles from here to the Canada border. They could be any place."

"You mean they went north?"

Fristo nodded, and Haggard felt somehow a little sorry for him. It was a transparent effort, born of unreasoning desperation. Had the pair *really* gone north, not even an Indian torture would have made Fristo admit it.

Haggard knew within reason they wouldn't go south again; that was where they had come from. Nobody here ever ran east, back into the settled country where it would be easy to locate them. Only one way was left: west. Anybody going west from here would almost surely strike for the Middle Concho, Centralia Draw and ultimately Horsehead Crossing on the Pecos. That narrowed it, made it easier for him.

He said, "Mister Fristo, I'm sorry for you." Then he left.

VIII

It was night now, and the storm was coming back. Johnny and Speck sat beside the wagon, watching jagged fingers of lightning shatter the black sky to the south. Short flashes illuminated the underside of ugly clouds that likely were carrying hail. Thunder rolled gradually closer, and the ground trembled.

Speck's cold was settling deeper in his chest. Johnny could hear it when Speck coughed. That was more and more often.

"Sure fixin' to rain again directly," Johnny remarked, watching the sodden clouds. "I reckon we best sleep in the wagonbed, under the sheet."

The campfire had burned down low, but in its dim glow Johnny could see the girl seated in front of her tent, staring sadly into the coals.

Speck's voice was coarsening from his cold. "Johnny, that girl is slowin' us down somethin' awful."

"We can't just ride off and leave her."

"There's some as would."

"We're bound to find a ranchhouse someplace tomorrow."

Speck didn't look at Johnny. "Kind of got you goin', ain't she?"

Johnny hadn't realized it showed. "Worried about her, is all. Things could happen to a girl out here like this."

"Get all wrapped up in a girl and you'll forget your old partner, that's what you'll do." Johnny wondered if he detected a vague resentment. Speck added, "If she was some middle-aged old maid, reckon you'd be as worried about her?"

Johnny didn't reply to that. He was afraid he knew the answer, and it didn't make him particularly proud.

Speck began coughing again. It shut him up, and Johnny was not sorry. He didn't feel like arguing. He pushed to his feet and walked down to the tent. The girl didn't seem to notice him at first. Her gaze was fixed on the glowing coals.

"Anything we can do for you, Miss Barnett?"

Startled, she glanced up. "No, thank you. I'm afraid the only thing that will help me now is time . . . lots of time."

"You'll just hurt yourself, broodin' thisaway."

"Not easy to put a thing like this out of your mind, though, especially as fresh as it is. I'm not sure I want to, not for a while yet." She looked back at the coals. "I'm sorry to be a burden to you."

"You're no burden."

"I'm keeping you here."

"We'll be all right."

"Will you? What about the man you said is after you?"

"Rain this mornin' washed out all the tracks we made up to the time we struck your camp. Rain again tonight will wash out what we've made today. I expect he'll be hard put to follow us."

That wasn't the whole truth, and he knew it. But he saw no gain in telling her Milam Haggard would follow the river, same as they were doing. It was the natural thing. Speck hadn't mentioned it, either, and Johnny hoped it hadn't occurred to him.

The girl stared into the dying campfire. The smell of burning mesquite blended well with the clean smell of oncoming rain. She said, "My father always liked the rain. Said it seemed to wash the world down and give it a fresh start. Said it needed a clean start as often as it could get one."

Johnny nodded gravely. "I wish *I* could get a clean start." He hadn't meant to say anything. But it came to him that if the girl could find concern for someone else's troubles, she might for at least a while forget her own.

Her eyes were sympathetic. "Can't you?"

He shook his head. "It'll take a lot more than rain to wash away what happened." To suit Milam Haggard, it was going to take *blood*.

"Do you have any folks, Johnny?"

"My dad, is all. And I've said goodbye to *him*. Way things are, I doubt I'll ever get to see him again."

"Then you must feel a little like I do." The cool wind came, and she shivered. "It almost makes you panic to realize all of a sudden that you're alone. Deep down, you know the pain will pass someday. But that doesn't help much right now."

Kneeling beside her, Johnny picked up a stick and idly poked at the coals. "I'll tell you somethin' my dad said when my mother died. It helped me. He said to look forward, try and put yourself into the future. He said imagine it's been a long time, that whatever has hurt you is in the past and the healin' already done. He said you know that someday it'll be like that, so try to pretend now that someday has already come."

"Does it work?"

"It helps. It's a way to borrow strength and ease the pain. Eventually you find that someday *has* come. It's over, and you've lived." He paused, solemn. "I've used it a right smart the last couple of days. Lord knows, a man needs anything he can find that'll help, even a little."

She sat awhile in a dark silence. "Your dad must be a good man."

"The best there is."

She brought her gaze up to his face. "And he raised a son just like him."

They were traveling again by shortly after daylight, the wagon wheels cutting deep into the mud of last night's rain. Turning in the saddle, Johnny worriedly studied the bold tracks they were leaving. A blind mule could follow them. Moreover, when the ruts dried they would set, a little like concrete. They would be a long time in eroding away.

Of course, Haggard probably wouldn't know the cowboys were traveling with a wagon. But their own horses were leaving tracks too. By this time Haggard no doubt had studied the tracks until he could pick these two horses out of a remuda by them. For a little while Johnny and Speck tried riding ahead of the wagon, hoping the girl's team would wipe out their tracks. It didn't work very well, and they quit trying. Johnny doubted an expert tracker like the manhunter Haggard would be fooled very long.

Nothing to do, then, but try to find a ranch where they could leave the girl, then pick up speed as they rode on west. Out there it never rained much. The constant wind would worry away at a set of tracks in soft earth until they were gone within hours.

They traveled all morning along the trace started by the Butterfield stages and followed since by thousands of wagons over the long frontier years. With the warmth of the bright morning sun, the moisture from the rain began to evaporate. The steam of it set Johnny to sweating. For Speck it was even worse. His face was flushed. He wouldn't let Johnny touch him, but Johnny knew his partner was beginning to run a fever of sorts. Speck's eyes were red, his temper short. Times like this, Johnny had found it best simply to leave him alone.

They stopped to eat a little and rest the horses. Speck was in misery, both of body and of soul. Sweat soaked his cotton shirt as he sat in the thin shade of a big mesquite. His eyes were riveted to the backtrail. It was easy to read his mind. He ate little.

"Johnny, I'm afraid I caught the lung fever."

"Where'd you get a notion like that? It takes a long time to develop the lung fever. You took yourself a cold out in the rain, that's all."

Speck nibbled at hope, though unconvinced. "You reckon that's it?"

"Sure, you'll be all right. But you need to rest awhile. Soon as we find a ranchhouse."

"We done rested too much now. Old Haggard is liable to come a-ridin' along most any minute now."

Johnny shook his head. "Not yet. He hasn't had time."

"He don't need time. He'll smell us out like a bloodhound. We need to keep on a-movin'."

"Even horses have to have rest. Here, Speck, eat a little more."

Speck waved food away. The melancholy came over him again. "You're wrong, Johnny. It *is* the lung fever. I caught it off of that girl's daddy as sure as sin."

Johnny didn't feel like going through the whole argument again, so he let it lie. Before long he was itching to go, even as he knew Speck was. Though reason told him Haggard was still well behind, the thought of the man raised something more than physical fear. The ex-Ranger's reputation was awesome. It was easy to believe somehow that Haggard stood eight feet tall, that he did, indeed, have the bloodhound's gift of scent, that with only a look he put the mark of death on a man.

A chill ran through Johnny, and he said, "Let's go, Speck."

About the middle of the afternoon they saw a trace leading off to the northwest, a faint wagon trail that had been used only enough to show it belonged to somebody. Johnny glanced back at the lagging Speck, hunched in the saddle. He pulled out into the faintly marked trail and motioned for Tessie Barnett to bring her wagon along.

Speck drew over to the side of the trail, his head down. He had nothing to say. Johnny edged his horse back beside the wagon. "Tessie . . . Miss Barnett, here's a trail. Chances are it leads to a ranch yonderway someplace. Not a big outfit, from the looks of the trail. But a ranch, anyway." He looked into her eyes, and he couldn't tell for sure whether she was glad or not. He got an odd feeling that she wasn't, really.

"Think it'll be far, Johnny?"

"No way of tellin'. We'll know when we come to it."

She glanced at Speck. "He's pretty sick. He'd be better off in the wagon."

Johnny frowned. "I expect he would." He looked toward Speck. "Why don't you sit up here with Miss Barnett? I'll tie your horse on behind."

Speck didn't argue. Johnny gave him a boost up, and he could tell Speck needed it. He couldn't have made the climb by himself. "Speck, when we find a ranchhouse, you're goin' to have to rest a spell, and no buts about it."

Speck gritted miserably, "Let's just be a-gettin' on."

They rode an hour, following the dim trail over rocky hills and through dry-looking scrub cedar timber. It hadn't rained so much here. Down yonder from the trail ran a small creek that would empty into the Middle Concho somewhere to the south. Finally, as Johnny was beginning to wonder if the trail really led anywhere, they came upon a ranch headquarters. It sat at the foot of a hill, with chinaberry trees rimming what appeared to be a small seep or spring. For a moment Johnny's spirit sagged. He had hoped for more. This was just a little box house—a one-room affair likely, or two rooms at the most. A small rock shed served as saddle house and barn. A couple of weathered brush arbors out by the shed had been intended orginally to shade the livestock. But they hadn't been kept up, and much of the brush topping had fallen to the ground, leaving big openings for the sun to shine through.

Another brush arbor stood in front of the unpainted frame house. Beneath it a lone man sat in an old rocking chair.

The thought came to Johnny that this was no time of day for a man to be lazing around the house. He ought to be out tending to work. At least, that was the way his dad had taught him. But he knew not all people looked at life that way. From the rundown appearance of the place, Johnny would bet this man spent far more time under the shady arbor than at work out in the sun.

The man stopped rocking and sat motionless, watching their approach. Nearing, Johnny saw that this was a man of forty or so, running strongly to paunch. His hair was starting to gray in spots, and he hadn't shaved in a week or two. His clothes would have stood alone if he had taken them off, which he probably hadn't done in days. He gave no sign that he was glad to see company.

"You-all lost or somethin'?" He said it to Johnny, but his gaze quickly shifted to the girl. Lazily he stood up.

Johnny eyed him closely. "You got some drinkin' water?"

The man jerked this thumb toward the house. "Back there in the cistern." He didn't move to fetch any.

Johnny said, "We been lookin' a long time for a ranch-house. This girl needs help to get back to San Angelo."

The man looked Johnny up and down. "You look to me like a healthy feller. I doubt there's anything she needs that you couldn't of give her." He stepped out from under the arbor and squinted in the sun, looking closer at the girl. "Been a long time since there was any woman at this place. If I'd of knowed you was comin', I'd of shaved and fixed up a little." His gaze fell on Speck. "You look like you'd fell off the wagon and got run over. What's the matter with *you*?"

Johnny answered for Speck. "He's sick. Got wet and took a bad cold. I was hopin' he could rest here a little."

The man frowned, still not friendly. "Sick folks take a lot of carin' for. I don't have much time."

"You won't have to do anything. We'll do it."

"I got mighty little room here, as you can see. I reckon you could roll him out a blanket under the arbor, though. Don't see how that could hurt nothin'."

Johnny felt anger rising. This was a country where most people were openhanded and ready to help, for company was scarce and friendships prized like coin of the realm. In his limited travels Johnny hadn't run into many like this before. This was an attitude alien to the time and the country. "Thanks," he said dryly. "Thanks a lot."

The man looked at Tessie again. "You said somethin' about the girl needin' somebody to help her get back to Angelo."

"I was sort of hopin' there would be somebody here who could take her."

"Ain't nobody here but me."

"Any neighbors?"

"Not for a long ways. I never did care much for neighbors anyhow. Always come a-borrowin' or wantin' help. And then they're always accusin' you of this, that and the other." He studied the girl, then turned back suspiciously to Johnny. "How come you don't take her to Angelo yourself?" When Johnny didn't answer, realization came into the man's muddy eyes. "You boys are on the dodge, that's what it is. I can tell."

Johnny swallowed. It occurred to him that this man might try to hold them in hope of a reward. He glanced around quickly for sign of a gun. He saw none.

The man looked at Speck. "Maybe he didn't catch cold atall. Maybe he's wounded."

Johnny said, "He's not wounded. I told you the truth."

"Who did you fellers rob? A bank? The Santy Fee railroad?"

"We never robbed anybody."

"Then you *killed* somebody. That's what you done, you killed somebody!"

Guilt rose hotly to Johnny's face. The girl spoke up. "They didn't kill anybody. They were there, but that was all. They weren't the ones who did it."

Johnny said, "Hush, Tessie."

The man stared at her. "How did you fit into this, girl? You look a mite green to be runnin' with the wild bunch."

Johnny protested, "We told you the truth. We found her along the trail. Her daddy was sick. He died and we buried him. Now we're just lookin' for somebody to take her to Angelo. We couldn't go off and leave her there."

The man's gaze moved to first one then the other, calculating. Mostly he looked at the girl. "I don't want to get in

Dutch with the law. I can't go harborin' no fugitives. You boys can water your horses and get a drink for yourselves. Then you got to get off of my place. The girl, if she wants to, can stay here. I'll see she gets to Angelo."

Johnny pointed to Speck. "Mister, my partner's sick."

"He'll be dead if the law finds him here. I don't want him on my place."

Angrily Johnny tried to stare him down. But the man simply ignored him and turned back to the girl. "Honey, if you want to get down from that wagon . . ."

Tessie Barnett looked at Johnny. "I don't know . . ."

Johnny stepped closer to her. "I don't like the looks of it here."

"But, Johnny, you've lost a lot of time on my account already. Maybe you'd better be trying to make some of it up."

"Speck bein' like he is, we can't move very fast anyway."

"But you wouldn't have me on your hands."

"I don't like the looks of this feller."

"Neither do I. But if he'll take me to San Angelo, that's the main thing. I'll be all right. Don't worry about me."

"I don't like it. Don't like it atall."

"What choice do you have? You'd better go, Johnny. I think if he could get his hands on a gun, he might try to hold you."

Johnny nodded. "Been thinkin' the same thing myself." He looked down, then brought his gaze back up to her face. "Tessie, I like you. I wish we could have met some other way."

"So do I, Johnny. Maybe someday . . ."

He shook his head. "There won't be any someday. We're not comin' back, me and Speck. We can't."

She leaned over. To his surprise, she kissed him on the

cheek. He felt his face warm again. "Then goodbye, Johnny. I won't forget you."

Confused, he pulled away abruptly. He reined up beside the paunchy man. "I never did get your name."

"Gerson. Gerson's my name. What's yours?"

Johnny decided to pass the question. "Gerson, you better be sure you take good care of this girl." He looked back at Speck. "Come on, Speck, we got to be movin'."

Riding away, he paused several times to look back. The first time the girl still sat in the wagon, watching them. The next time she was standing in the shade of the arbor, but she was still watching. The third time, just before they rode out of sight, Johnny saw the man standing beside her.

Johnny turned in the saddle, doubt tugging at him. He and Speck rode half an hour in silence. Speck was slumped forward, fever riding him. Johnny reined up suddenly. "Speck, we oughtn't to've left her there."

Speck made no reply.

"We don't know that Gerson. Did you notice how he looked at her?"

Speck said hoarsely, "Like a coyote lookin' at a cottontail rabbit."

"I'm goin' back for her, Speck."

Speck only shrugged.

Johnny looked about for some shade, though the day was wearing well along toward sundown, and it was no longer particularly hot. He rode to a big mesquite, took his blanket and spread it out beneath the tree. "Lie down there and rest, Speck. I'll be back directly with Tessie and the wagon."

Speck didn't argue. He almost fell out of the saddle.

Johnny hurried to help him. When he had Speck set, he swung back onto the brown horse. "Come on, Traveler, let's travel."

Moving in an easy lope much of the way, it took him somewhat less than half an hour to get back. He saw the wagon beside the brush arbor, the team standing droopheaded, not yet unhitched. The man and the girl must be in the house. Johnny wrapped the reins around a post and stepped up to the open door. He heard Gerson's voice.

"Now, girl, you got nothin' to be afraid of."

Gerson hadn't heard Johnny. The man had Tessie backed into a corner, his big left arm braced against the wall to keep her from stepping aside. His right hand was under her chin, and her eyes were wide with fear.

"Get away from her, Gerson!"

The girl cried out in relief. "Johnny!"

Startled, Gerson turned. Instantly the girl darted beyond his reach. She ran across the small room and threw herself against Johnny. "Oh, Johnny, you came back!"

Johnny's fists were clenched. "What have you done to her?"

Gerson shook his head. "Ain't done nothin'."

Tessie Barnett showed her fright. "He told me he was going to the law and tell them about you, unless I would stay here with him. He said he wanted me to be his girl."

Johnny said grimly, "You go on outside, Tessie. Wait for me."

Gently he pushed her aside. But she stayed where she was. "Johnny, he's too big for you. Don't fight him. Let's just go."

"We'll go in a few minutes." Fists tight, he started across the room toward Gerson.

He had been so angry he hadn't thought about Gerson

having a gun. But there it was, a rifle propped against a table. Gerson took one quick step and reached it. He brought it up before Johnny could move against him. A wicked smile split Gerson's bearded face. "Just keep on a-comin', cowboy. I'll blow a hole in you as big as your hat!"

Johnny stopped, his mouth dry. He looked down the bore of the rifle at the finger tightening on the trigger. His heart raced. He felt the same helpless fear that had come over him when the cow trader Larramore had brought that pistol up out of his bag.

Behind him, Tessie gave a frightened little cry.

Gerson said, "All I got to do is pull this trigger. You're on the dodge anyway. Likely they'll give me a *re*-ward."

Johnny's heart seemed to be sitting high up in his throat, pounding so hard he would have thought everybody could hear it.

Tessie pleaded, "Don't kill him! I'll do anything!"

Gerson said, "Kind of fancies you, don't she, cowboy? Maybe I ought to take her up on that. Maybe I ought to just let you ride away."

Johnny found his voice. "I wouldn't leave without her."

Gerson nodded. "I know. That's why I got to kill you. Minute I turned my back, you'd be here again, lookin' for a way to kill *me*."

"She'll do you no good, Gerson. Sooner or later she'll get away. She'll tell, and they'll come lookin' for you."

"I'll take care of that in due time."

Johnny saw murder in the man's eyes. He thought of Speck. "My partner's outside," he lied. "Shoot me and he won't let you get out of here alive."

Gerson hesitated. "The sick one? What can *he* do?"

"He can shoot."

Gerson licked his lips, worrying. He had evidently not considered Speck. "You say he's outside?"

Johnny nodded, hoping his eyes would not give away the lie. He had never felt less sure of himself.

Gerson said, "All right, we better go out and talk to him. If he sees I got you-all covered with this rifle, he'll come along easy enough." He motioned toward the girl. "You first. Ease on out that door."

White-faced, Tessie turned toward the opening. Johnny moved carefully along behind her. A dozen ideas raced through his brain, and he dismissed them all. Any sudden action might cause Gerson to kill him by reflex.

Tessie stepped through the door and down to the ground. Johnny paused in the doorway. Tensely, he said, "Tessie, move to one side."

Gerson grunted, "What's goin' on?" But Johnny stood blocking the door. The girl was instantly out of Gerson's sight.

Johnny looked off to his right and spoke loudly as if to Speck. "He's got a gun at my back. If he shoots me, kill him. He can't get out of this house without you gettin' a clear shot at him."

Johnny waited a moment, trying to work up his courage. He sensed Gerson's indecision. Even with a prisoner in his hands, the man had lost his advantage—or thought he had. Johnny got a grip on himself. "If you shoot me now, Gerson, you're as good as dead. This shack of yours will be your coffin. Now, why don't you put that gun down?"

Gerson muttered, "I don't think there's anybody out there."

"Want to stick your head out and look?"

Gerson swallowed. His hand was first tightening, then loosening on the rifle. Johnny's heart was high in his throat. He had never been a poker player because he never could carry off a bluff. He couldn't understand why Gerson didn't see through him. It came to him gradually that Gerson was as frightened as Johnny was.

Again Johnny managed, "The gun, Gerson."

Sweat popped on Gerson's face. His lips quivered. Finally, whipped, he lowered the barrel. "Tell your friend out there I'm puttin' it down."

"Hand it to me," Johnny said, and Gerson did. Johnny took it. "Tessie, come get this."

Tessie came quickly from around the corner. She took the rifle from Johnny's hand as he passed it through the door.

Johnny turned again and looked at Gerson. The fear began draining out of him, and his anger came in a rush. Before Gerson knew what was happening, Johnny was plowing into him, fists swinging.

Normally, with his extra weight, Gerson would have made short work of Johnny Fristo. But Johnny caught him by surprise. The first blow struck Gerson in the stomach. Half the breath gusted out of him, and he staggered. By the time he got his wits together, Johnny had struck him again in the stomach and once across the face.

With a roar of anger Gerson pushed forward. But surprise had cost him too much. From the first blow, Johnny had the advantage. He pressed hard, punching, slashing, driving Gerson back again to the wall. A cold fury welled up and took over for Johnny. He was only dimly aware of the pain when Gerson occasionally managed to strike him.

Gerson fought a losing battle, and he began trying to find

a way out. But each time Gerson turned, Johnny was there, striking him again, turning him back. Gerson sank to his knees, his arms raised defensively over his bleeding face.

Reason slowly returned to Johnny. He backed away, breathing hard. He looked down and found his knuckles bruised and bleeding. Each breath he drew hurt him. He paused a moment, looking.

With a sudden lunge he swung one more hard punch into Gerson's face. Gerson fell over and lay on his back.

Gasping, Johnny said, "Now, Gerson . . . don't you ever . . . point a gun at a man again . . . or take advantage of a girl." He backed to the door. "Tessie, the rifle."

Hesitantly she handed it to him. "Johnny, you're not going to kill him . . ."

He shook his head. "I ought to. I would if he made a move. Get to your wagon now, and let's be movin'."

He stayed with the rifle on Gerson till he heard the wagon move. Then he backed out the door and swung into his saddle, the rifle still in his hands. He wondered what Gerson's reaction would be when he came to the door and saw only the two of them riding away.

Johnny went by the corral and chased away a horse he found penned there. That would leave Gerson afoot. With the creek running, there would be no need for horses to come in for water, where Gerson could make an easy catch.

Johnny pulled in behind the wagon and trailed it at some distance. He rode slantways in the saddle, looking back at Gerson's house, the rifle in his hands. For all he knew Gerson might have another rifle somewhere. Johnny didn't want to be caught with his back showing. He rode like that, watching behind him, till he passed over the hill and out of sight of the house. Only then did he relax a little and look ahead of him at the wagon.

It had stopped. Tessie Barnett sat with her hands over her face. As Johnny rode up anxiously, she lowered her hands a little. They were shaking. Her face was milk-white.

"Tessie, what's the matter?"

She motioned for him to sit on the wagon seat beside her. He tied the horse on behind, eased Gerson's rifle down in the wagonbed and climbed up. To his surprise she opened her arms and pulled herself tight against him, burying her face against his chest. Hesitantly he placed his hands on her shoulders and found them trembling.

"Tessie, it's all right now. It's done."

She nodded, but she held him tightly. Her warm body pressed against him, and the effect was like strong whisky. He felt the warm rush of blood to his face.

"Johnny," she said, holding him as if she feared it would kill her to let him go, "I'm sorry to be like this. I don't know what you must think of me."

"I don't think anything bad of you, Tessie, you know that. You've had a couple of hard days."

"I wish I weren't such a baby."

"You're no baby. I don't expect any girl would have done better, and most of them not half as good."

"I won't break down this way again, Johnny. From now on I'll be strong."

"The worst has already happened. Not likely anything as bad will ever happen to you again."

Her arms were still tight around him. She raised her head a little, and he laid his cheek against her forehead. She said, "Somewhere, though, you're going to have to leave me and be on your way, Johnny Fristo. It's going to be hard for me to say goodbye."

He nodded soberly. "How come it had to be like this, Tessie? How come I didn't meet you a few days ago, when I had nothin' to run from, nothin' to be afraid of?"

"I don't know, Johnny. Maybe we just weren't meant to have any luck."

IX

For a long moment a rider sat outlined on the bald top of a rock-strewn hill to the west. Johnny Fristo felt a reflex of fear that stopped his breath and stiffened his hands on the leather lines. Then reason told him this couldn't be Haggard, and he eased. The rider wasn't tall. His shoulders were hunched a little, and his manner of riding showed he wasn't a young man.

He came down through big green clumps of *sacahuista* and reined toward the wagon, taking his time. He rode with the slack ease of a man who had done it all his life, and a long life at that. Gray hair showed beneath an old hat most people would have thrown away a long time ago. He had a salt-and-pepper moustache and tight-drawn skin that looked like saddle leather. His hand lifted in friendly greeting as he approached. Frontier times were fading into the past, but even yet it didn't hurt to let folks know you came in peace.

"Howdy." His voice was pleasant. "You-all lost?" His gaze swept them, and Johnny got the feeling that in two seconds he saw about all there was to see. But looking at the sun-squinted blue eyes, Johnny couldn't tell for the life of him what the man was thinking.

"We're lookin' for a ranchhouse."

"Mine's a little ways over the hill. Would it do?"

"I expect. We got a sick feller here."

The elderly rider eased in closer, stopping his sorrel horse beside the wagon and looking down at the feverish Speck.

"You sure do. You oughtn't to be haulin' him around."

"It isn't because we want to."

"Well, we'll take him on up to the house. Sarah'll be so glad to see company, she won't care whether they're sick or well—just so they come."

Tessie Barnett took cheer. "Sarah?"

"My wife. She's the best in the country when it comes to takin' care of the ailin'."

Tessie said thankfully, "We've found a place with a woman."

The rancher studied the girl. "You come a ways, I guess. Bet you're young married folks, headin' west to find a home."

Johnny saw the flush in Tessie's cheeks. "No, sir, we're not married. We just come across this girl a couple of days ago, down the river. She was a-needin' help."

The old rider couldn't hide his curiosity, but he didn't pry. He shoved his hand at Johnny. "My name's Dugan Whitaker."

"Fristo. Johnny Fristo. And this here is Tessie. Back yonder is Speck."

Whitaker's face furrowed. "Fristo! That's got a familiar ring to it. I used to cowboy with a feller by that name back yonder on the San Saba River. Lord, it's been twenty-five or thirty years ago. Baker, his first name was . . . Baker Fristo."

"My dad."

A grin broke across the rancher's wrinkled face. "By George, I ought to've guessed when I looked at you. But it was so long ago the Twin Mountains was just a pair of anthills. You're him all over again. Only, I'll bet you can't ride broncs the way he could."

Johnny wasn't in a smiling mood, but he smiled now. After Gerson yesterday, it was a relief to come across the kind of people Johnny was used to. "No, sir, I reckon he can still ride rings around me."

Whitaker chuckled. "I expect you do well enough. Bein' Baker Fristo's son, you've had a good raisin'. Come on, let's go to the house."

He let the wagon have the dim trail, and he rode his horse alongside. He talked all the way in. It appeared to Johnny that Whitaker was as thankful for company as his wife could ever be.

"We got a settlement now, a ways yonder over the hills on the upper reach of the Middle Concho. But Sarah, she don't take well to travelin' anymore, so we don't often go, and we don't see many folks." He watched Johnny a great deal, plainly pleased at seeing him. "Sarah knew your dad. She'll be real interested in seein' the kind of man Baker Fristo's son turned out to be."

Johnny chewed his lip. In a way it was good luck, happening into old friends of the family. In a way it wasn't. He dreaded having to explain to them the trouble he was in, he and Speck. With strangers it didn't make so much difference. Here, it would hurt.

Whitaker was talking to Tessie. "We have a daughter not much older than you. She up and married, though, and moved west. These ranches can get awful lonesome for a woman alone. Sarah'll be real tickled to see you."

Johnny brooded awhile. "Mister Whitaker, we got a favor to ask. For Tessie, that is." He explained how he and Speck had come across the girl and her dying father. The old ranchman nodded in sympathy. Johnny said, "We didn't want to just leave her there. We been lookin' for a ranchhouse, somebody to take her to San Angelo."

"And my place is the first one you found?"

Johnny frowned. "Not exactly. We came across one yesterday. Feller named Gerson."

Whitaker cut a quick glance at the girl. "You didn't leave her there with him . . ."

"Not long."

"Pity this country is gettin' so all-fired civilized. Ten years ago they'd have left the likes of Gerson danglin' off of some liveoak tree. He's been awful careless where he puts his brandin' irons."

Johnny said, "He got kind of careless yesterday."

Whitaker glanced again at the girl and read his own meaning. His mouth went grim. "There's other ways than hangin' a man. One day I'll have a talk with some of the boys."

They came in sight of a big growth of china trees, a pair of windmills and a water-filled surface tank that had been hollowed out of the ground by horse, mule and man sweat. Dugan Whitaker had a small rock house built of material hauled down a wagonload at a time from the hills. Johnny flinched, thinking about the untold hours of toil Whitaker must have put in building this place. Yet he knew the pride the old man would have in it, too, for the things a man builds with his own hands are dear to him. They are a part of him, like the hands themselves.

"Sarah," Whitaker called, "we got company."

Johnny expected to see a woman walk out onto the porch, but none did. He thought he glimpsed a face inside, back in the shadows. He couldn't be sure. He knew a moment of doubt. If he *had* seen a woman, there was something odd here.

Whitaker swung down and wrapped one of his leather

reins around a post to hold his horse. He turned toward the wagon. "Let's you and me get ahold of your friend here and carry him into the house."

They lifted Speck carefully. He had enough strength to help a little. They got their arms around him and his over their shoulders. Johnny expected to see the woman come out and hold the screen door open. She didn't. Tessie ran ahead and opened it.

Whitaker took the lead. "Right on back thisaway. We'll put him in the lean-to."

Inside, Johnny caught a glimpse of a woman seated in a chair. Only a glimpse, but it was enough to anger him a little. What kind of hospitality was this, anyway? The least she could have done was to come over and see what the trouble was. He helped Whitaker put Speck on the bed.

"Sarah," said Whitaker, "we got a sick cowboy on our hands."

The woman's voice came from right behind Johnny, and it startled him. He hadn't heard her walk up. He turned and saw her still seated, but the chair was close now. It was a chair with wheels.

"What ails him, son?" she asked Johnny. Johnny was so surprised he couldn't find his voice. The woman smiled gently. "Don't worry, this chair doesn't bother me much anymore. Not like it seems to be botherin' you."

Johnny took off his hat. "I'm sorry, ma'am. I didn't go to stare at you."

"I'll bet you're not a very good poker player. Your eyes give away what's in your head." Her smile widened, and she wheeled the chair in closer to the bed. She repeated, "What's the trouble with your friend?"

Johnny told her. She touched her hand to Speck's head. "Got fever, all right. How's his breathin' been?"

"Short, kind of. He's been in some pain."

She nodded. "I expect he's knockin' at the door of pneumonia. But he may not have crossed over the line yet. Maybe we can hold him back. First thing, you and Dugan get the clothes off of him." She wheeled the chair around and faced Tessie. "Young lady, you want to help? You can reach up into a top shelf in the kitchen and get me some whisky. I'll show you where it's at." She wheeled the chair out about as fast as Tessie could walk.

After the men had removed Speck's clothing and covered him with a blanket, Sarah Whitaker came wheeling back. Tessie brought a steaming cup.

"Now, young fellow," the ranchwoman spoke gently to Speck, "I want you to raise up and drink this. Take it slow, but drink it all." She took the cup from Tessie's hands and passed it over to Speck, keeping a hold on it so he couldn't spill it. Speck swallowed. His flushed face twisted, and for a moment he was about to spit out what she had given him. "Drink it," she said again. Slowly Speck did. The sweat was already popping out on his face.

Mrs. Whitaker said, "That's more whisky than anything else. It'll help boil the fever out of you. Now, girl, if you'll pull up the covers on him, we want to have him sweat the fever out."

Soon Speck was complaining about the heat, and perspiration was rolling from his face. When he made a weak move to push away the covers, Sarah Whitaker firmly pulled them back into place. "It's just something you'll have to go through. Later you'll feel better for it."

After a while Johnny walked out onto the front porch. Now that he had time to look around, he saw things he had missed at first. He saw a slanting ramp by which the wheelchair could roll with comparative ease off and onto the porch. Inside, he had seen how the plank kitchen cabinet had been lowered so everything would be in reach for Sarah Whitaker.

Dugan Whitaker came out onto the shaded porch after him and paused to roll a cigarette. He offered the tobacco sack to Johnny.

Johnny said, "I don't guess it's easy for Mrs. Whitaker, the way she has to get around."

Dugan shook his gray head and licked the edge of the paper. "But she does all right. It was better when our daughter was still livin' here. She was a world of help. You can't keep a girl around forever, though. When they grow up, they got a right to a life of their own. You got to let the fledglings leave the nest."

Johnny fumbled in his shirt pocket for a match. "I don't mean to ask questions that ain't none of my business, but how did it happen? Mrs. Whitaker, I mean?"

"Runaway horse and a buckboard. Had a young horse, not broke long. He boogered at a jackrabbit and commenced to run. Flipped the buckboard over on Sarah out yonder a ways." He pointed. "There where you see that whiteface bull a-grazin'. She crawled all the way to the house for help. Last step she ever took was when she walked out to that buckboard. It's the last step she'll *ever* take."

"Real bad luck."

"Don't waste time feelin' sorry for her. *She* doesn't. Everybody's got a cross of one kind or another to carry. Sarah took the one that was marked for her and made the best of what she had left. She said if it was the devil's work to cripple her, she wasn't goin' to give him the pleasure of seein' her miserable. I guess a strong spirit is worth more than strong legs." He drew thoughtfully on his cigarette. "We all got somethin' to carry, some trouble that hangs over our heads. Even as young as *you* are, I expect life hasn't been all honey and sweet-milk."

Johnny found the cigarette had lost its taste. He wondered if Whitaker was subtly fishing. Face clouding, he flipped the cigarette out into the clean-swept yard. "Mister Whitaker, before you do anything more for me and Speck, I better tell you about us. You may not want to keep us around."

Whitaker didn't look up. "You fellers are in some kind of trouble, ain't you? I sensed it from the first."

"Then why did you bring us in?"

The ranchman shrugged. "Always did consider myself a pretty good judge of men. I had a good feelin' about you, even before I found out you was Baker Fristo's son. You couldn't have done anything very bad."

Johnny told him about their trouble on the Sonora-San Angelo road, and about Milam Haggard. Listening, Whitaker turned grave.

"Boy, you know Haggard's reputation?"

"I'm afraid I do."

Dugan Whitaker's face was long and sad. He held what was left of the cigarette between his fingers and stared absently at the smoke curling upward from it. He held it so long that the tiny fire went out, and the cigarette turned cold in his fingers. "Goin' to be several days before your partner is in shape to ride. You got that much time?"

"I don't know. Might have, if the rain wiped out our tracks

down on the river. Haggard might be several days pickin' up the trail we left after we got away from the Middle Concho."

"He might, and again he might not. They say he's got a sixth sense about him." He glanced up in apology. "I didn't mean to talk like that. You know your trouble well enough without me harpin' on it."

"I know the problem all right. I just don't know the answer."

"Seems to me it was your partner that got you into this scrape. You might be able to save yourself if you'd go off and leave him here."

Johnny shook his head violently. "I wouldn't do that."

Whitaker nodded. "I didn't think you would. No son of Baker Fristo ever *could*."

If he was often harsh and demanding of others, Milam Haggard expected no less than perfection in himself. Now that he had found the trail again, he was angry, and the anger was vented in his own direction. Another man might have cursed his quarry or blamed bad luck for the five days he had wasted. Haggard had never been prone to this kind of luxury. In his view the blame was his own, and that was where he placed it.

To be sure, rain had been the main factor. It had wiped out the tracks. But Haggard did not blame the rain. He told himself he should have been more watchful. Upon finding the tracks washed away, he had pondered awhile, then gone forward on the assumption that the fugitives would continue straight upriver. But he had gone all the way west to the head of the Middle Concho and beyond that almost to the Pecos without ever finding a trace. Surely, he had thought, he would have to cut their sign somewhere.

He was certain he knew one cause for his mistake. Those months of trying to become a ranchman—of turning his back on the service of the law—had rusted him a little. But the old training and the hard-learned ability were coming back to him now. It would take something more than two cowboys to throw him again.

Backtracking, working north of the river, he had come across the trail firmly set in the dried mud. For a minute or two the wagon tracks had fooled him, for he had no reason to associate the trail of a wagon with the men he was after. But after some study he had become convinced Fristo and Quitman *were* riding along with a wagon now. Only they and God knew what for. Something else bothered him, too. Several days ago, at about the time he lost the tracks, he had ridden upon a new grave and its headmarker, the endgate out of a wagon. He had worried briefly over the possibility that the cowboys had come across someone and killed him. But considering it, he had told himself it didn't make sense for them to kill a man, then bury him and mark the grave. Hide the body, yes, but not mark the place for all to see. He had decided there was no connection.

Now, finding that the two had been traveling with a wagon, he remembered the grave and wondered again. It seemed foolish for two men under pursuit to encumber themselves with a slow-moving wagon. Unless, of course, there was something of value in the wagon that they didn't want to ride off and leave. That could even provide a motive for killing.

There was still another thing hard to fit into the equation: a woman's shoe prints. A woman was traveling with this wagon; he had no doubt of that.

He had trailed a lot of fugitives in his time. None had ever been harder to figure.

Restless now and angry at himself for the wasted days, he resolved that this would be only a setback, not a defeat. Milam Haggard knew he had time. Time, in this sort of case, was usually in the favor of the hunter, provided he faced no deadline at which he must turn back. Haggard had no deadline. He was a free agent, responsible only to himself and to God. He could follow these cowboys from now till next year, from here to Hell's front door.

And he would, if he had to.

Riding along watching the trail, he began—without intending to—wondering about himself. He had never been much given to analyzing his own motives. He had always thought in straight and simple lines. There had never been anything devious about Milam Haggard. He had always set a firm course, and everyone who knew him could predict just where he would stand. He had stood for the right and opposed the wrong, and he had not compromised, ever.

Yet now he wondered. Amid the grief for his wife—and, yes, there *was* grief—he found himself taking some sort of grim satisfaction out of this search, almost an enjoyment. He knew this shouldn't be, and it concerned him. It was as if he had somehow been out of his element awhile and on this trail had returned to it.

He told himself this was *not* his true element. He had always told himself he took no pleasure in the hunting of men. He had never killed a man except when he had to, and he had always hated it.

But now he was on a trail again, and in all honesty he

would admit to himself that he felt a satisfaction he knew shouldn't be there.

He shook his head. What *was* this, anyway? The whole notion was foolish. He had been well rid of the Ranger job. It was a job for a coyote, not for a man, riding a-horseback from daylight to dark through more long days than he could count, facing furnace heat in the summer and bitter cold in the winter, all the time trying to watch the ground for tracks while his vigilant gaze searched ahead of him. Though he would never have told anyone, there had always been a chill playing up and down his back whenever he rode into a place where someone might lie in wait for him. Every time he trailed a man, that secret fear rode with him. Haggard was cold and methodical when he stood against a man face-to-face. When he could see his enemy, fear was alien to him.

But always there had been that dread of being shot from ambush without a chance. The longer he had ridden with the badge pinned to his vest, the darker the dread had become. The luckier he was, the more certain he became that someday his luck would run out. No gambler could win forever. That was what Haggard had been—a gambler—betting his life that he was just a shade better than the other man.

He had grown sick of it, and the dread of ambush had become a cancerous thing, gnawing at him day and night. He had been glad when Cora had insisted that he turn in his badge before they were married. It gave him a reason to do what he had wanted to do a long time before.

Yes, sir, he had been well rid of that job. Cora had been the best thing that ever happened to him.

Now she was dead, and he was at it again, following a dim trail that inevitably led to the death of two men. It was a mis-

erable thing, and he knew it. Why, then, this half-ashamed satisfaction?

The saddlegun lay across his lap as he rode down toward Gerson's frame house. Warm dry winds out of the north and west
had almost obliterated the tracks now, but enough trace was
left for Haggard to follow. He saw a man sitting beneath a
brush arbor, shading himself from the morning sun. It was a
time of day when most men would be out working. Haggard
wondered whether this one was sick, lame or lazy.

The paunchy man stood up at sight of Haggard. People
had always said they could tell Haggard was a lawman almost
as far as they could see him. There was something about the
way he carried himself.

Riding up, Haggard could see a little of both awe and fear
in the man's red-veined eyes. Awe and fear were often com-
panions, and hatred usually was not far away.

The man spoke first. "Gerson's my name. Law, ain't you?"

"I'm Milam Haggard." Haggard made no move to shake
hands. He found that he disliked this man on sight. He didn't
know why; he just had an instinct that way.

"Haggard? I've heard of you. I bet you're huntin' them
two cowboys that come through here the other day. I didn't
help them none, didn't even give them nothin' to eat. I
knowed the law was after them, knowed it the minute they
come a-ridin' up here."

"How many days ago?"

The man counted on his fingers. "Five, it was. Maybe six.
They're bad ones."

Haggard frowned, his sharp eyes catching the healing rem-
nant of a cut on the man's cheekbone. Fist cut, most likely.

"They've got a wagon with them, and a woman, haven't they?"

Gerson nodded eagerly. "They do. I knowed there was somethin' the matter the minute they come in sight. . . ."

Impatiently Haggard broke in. "How about the woman?"

"They had some kind of a story about how her pa had died back down the trail, and how they brought her along to protect her. But if you ask me, they killed him. And they got that girl with them against her will. I tried to take her away from them, but they beat me up. Took both of them to do it, but they beat me up."

Haggard frowned. "How come you didn't go to the law?"

Gerson was hesitant in answering. "I figured the law would be a-comin' here soon enough."

Haggard clenched his fist. "Five . . . six days. It's a lot to make up."

"You can do it. That wagon's slow. And one of the cowboys is sick."

Sick. That made a difference. Haggard wondered how the sick one had been much help in beating up Gerson, but he didn't ask. He figured Gerson had exaggerated that part of the story to make himself look good. Chances were, if Haggard looked, he could find Gerson's description on a "wanted" flyer somewhere.

Gerson said, "One other thing, Haggard. When they left here, they took my rifle."

Rifle! Haggard's mouth went hard. No doubt about it, they meant business now. A woman with them, probably against her will. And a rifle.

It all meant one thing: when he found them, he would have to shoot fast and shoot straight!

X

They had spent almost a week at the Whitaker ranch, and now Speck seemed strong enough to try a hard ride.

In the rosy glow that came before the sunrise, Johnny Fristo tightened his cinch and looked across his horse at Speck swinging a saddle up onto the long-legged bay which Baker Fristo had given him. "Speck, you real sure you can make it now?"

Speck reached under the bay's belly for the saddle girth. "To get away from Milam Haggard, I could ride to Timbuktu."

"You still look a little peaked to me."

"Rather be sick than dead."

Johnny looked back toward the house and saw smoke curling up from the chimney. Out on the other side of the barn Dugan Whitaker was milking a Jersey cow. Johnny could hear the rhythmic strike of milk against the tin bucket as Whitaker squeezed with first one hand, then the other. Up on a shelf over Whitaker's head would be a steaming cup of coffee. Whitaker customarily carried a cup with him when he left the house. Wherever he finished the coffee, he would leave the cup. About once a week he would use up all the cups he had, and he would have to search the barns and corrals, making a roundup. Johnny had helped him with one yesterday.

Johnny said, "Time we get over to the house, they ought to have breakfast ready. Then we'll pull out."

"Let's eat and get started. I can almost smell old Haggard's breath on the back of my neck. Why he's not already here I'll never know."

A gate opened. Whitaker let his Jersey cow amble slowly out into the pasture. He shut the gate before her calf could get out with her. Whitaker came then, the bucket three-quarters full of milk and foam. He hadn't brought back his coffee cup, but Johnny didn't remind him of it. He figured a man was entitled to at least one bad habit, and this was the only one he had noticed in Whitaker.

The ranchman said, "Well, boys, this'll be your last woman-cooked meal for a while. Let's go get it." He was smiling, but Johnny thought the smile was strained. Whitaker hated seeing them leave, just as Johnny hated having to.

Except for worrying about Haggard, this had been a pleasant week for Johnny. He had spent his time working around the place, patching corrals, bracing a barn, pulling the windmill suckerrods and changing leathers. He had felt guilty sometimes about not riding out with Whitaker to work cattle. But he hadn't wanted Speck to remain here alone and helpless if Haggard came. Though, if Haggard *had* come, Johnny had no idea what he could have done. One thing sure, Johnny didn't intend to fight him.

He had enjoyed the Whitakers. Dugan Whitaker had been a man much like Johnny's own father. Sarah Whitaker had amazed him constantly with her cheerful way and her uncanny ability to get around and do what she wanted in that wheelchair. He thought Whitaker must have had trouble keeping up with her when she had the use of her legs.

Most of all, Johnny had enjoyed being with Tessie Barnett. The hardest part of leaving was going to be in saying goodbye to her. He didn't know just when he had fallen in love with her, and it didn't really matter. What counted was that he had done it without wanting to, knowing there was no future for them, hoping for her sake that she didn't feel the same way but somehow wishing for his own sake that she did.

Tessie and Sarah Whitaker had breakfast on the table and waiting for them—eggs, steak, gravy, biscuits, coffee. Sarah Whitaker smiled just as Dugan had, and it was easy to see she had to work at it. "Eat aplenty, now. There's a lot of hungry country to the west of here."

Johnny glanced at Tessie. As his gaze touched her, she turned half around, hiding her face from him.

Dugan Whitaker set his bucket of milk on the cabinet for straining. "I don't want to seem like I'm pushin' you fellers, but it's gettin' daylight outside. I think for your sakes you better eat and get a move on."

Johnny had noted at least one sign of renewed strength in Speck: appetite. All his life Speck had made a good hand at the table or around the chuck wagon. As for Johnny, he felt a wintry sadness about leaving, and he had to push to make himself eat.

Mrs. Whitaker said, "Tessie and me, we've made an agreement, Johnny. She's not goin' to San Angelo."

Johnny looked up sharply.

Tessie said, "They've asked me to stay here with them, Johnny."

"That's right," Sarah put in. "She's got no place particular to go anyway. All she could earn in San Angelo would be a livin'. She'll get that here. She's been a world of help and company to us, like our daughter used to be."

Tessie nodded, and her eyes glistened a little. "That way, Johnny, you'll know where I am."

Johnny had worried about how she would fare in San Angelo. "That's fine, Tessie." He finished eating before Speck did. He said, "Speck, I'll go bring up the horses while you finish."

He walked out to the barn, taking his time, looking around him slowly. He wanted to remember this place. In time to come it might be a refuge for him—in his mind—a place for a restful mental retreat when the world seemed to close in around him. He glanced up at one of Whitaker's coffee cups balanced on a low rafter beneath a shed, and he smiled.

He had taken several minutes before he led the horses out the gate and closed it behind him. He swung up on Traveler, leading Speck's bay. A movement at the house caught his eye. He jerked his head around and saw Tessie running toward him, skirts flaring. "Hurry, Johnny, hurry!"

She pointed, and he saw the horseman outlined atop the hill, the sun rising like a golden ball of fire behind him.

Johnny didn't need binoculars. One glance and he somehow knew with a dreadful certainty. This was Milam Haggard!

The horses, fresh and rested, spooked backward as the girl rushed toward them. "Run, Johnny! You've still got time. Run!"

For a moment Johnny sat there confused and undecided, his hands tight on the reins. What good would it do now to run? Haggard would catch them. Yet, if they stayed and waited, what could they do?

"I'll get Speck," he said, and touched spurs to Traveler's ribs. He moved into a long trot, leading the bay toward the house.

"Speck! Come a-runnin'!"

But Speck didn't come. Johnny reined up at the house and shouted again. Sarah Whitaker pushed the screen door open with her chair and wheeled out onto the porch. "Johnny, he's taken the rifle and gone out the back."

"The rifle?"

For the first time in days Johnny remembered the rifle he had wrestled from Gerson. Except for this, they would have ridden off and forgotten it.

Dropping the bay's reins, he pulled his horse about and spurred around the house. "Speck! Speck, come back here!"

He glanced again toward Haggard. The ex-Ranger was quartering across toward the ranch headquarters, his dun horse in a steady trot. A pack horse followed. Speck was hunkered down behind a cedar. Johnny saw that in a few moments Haggard would ride in front of him. It occurred to Johnny then that Haggard had not seen Speck.

Speck—if he could hold himself in check long enough— could wait where he was and shoot Haggard out of the saddle at almost point-blank range.

For just a moment Johnny knew a sense of relief. That was an out. With Haggard dead they stood a chance.

But he knew this wasn't the way. The death of Haggard's wife had not actually been their fault, but this would put blood on their hands that would never wash away. They might be forgiven for the death of Cora Haggard, but never the murder of this man.

"Speck, hold up! Don't do it!"

Shouting, Johnny spurred into a run. "Speck, for God's sake put it down!"

Haggard saw Johnny moving toward him, and Johnny saw the man's hands come up holding a saddlegun. From behind him he heard Tessie scream. Speck brought up his rifle and leveled it across a branch of the cedar.

Johnny cried again, "No!"

Speck's rifle spat flame. Haggard rocked back, dropped the saddlegun, slumped forward and spilled out of the saddle. Haggard's horse jumped clear, wild-eyed with fright.

Speck straightened and began running toward Haggard, levering another cartridge into the breech. Johnny saw Haggard try vainly to push up onto his hands and knees.

Haggard still lived, and Speck was going to shoot him again.

Johnny spurred savagely. Speck hadn't listened to him before, and he wouldn't listen now. Speck heard the horse running. He stopped to look behind him, his eyes wide and desperate. Seeing Johnny meant to stop him, he turned and began running, trying to reach Haggard and finish him before Johnny could ride him down.

Speck stopped and raised the rifle to his shoulder. As he brought it level with Haggard's bent body, Johnny reached him. Johnny leaned from the saddle and grabbed at Speck as he rode by. He succeeded only in knocking him down. The rifle roared, the bullet plowing harmlessly into the ground. In desperation Speck scrambled on hands and knees, trying to reach the rifle. Johnny quit the saddle and came running. He got to the rifle just as Speck's fingers closed on the stock of it. He kicked, and the rifle went flying.

Speck turned his face upward, and Johnny saw that his partner was frantic with fear and rage. "Let me kill him, Johnny! Let me kill him!"

Johnny grabbed his friend's arms and tried to hold him. "Speck, come out of it!"

"We got to kill him, Johnny!"

Speck began fighting like a tiger, swinging his fists, kicking wildly. For a fleeting moment Johnny had time to wonder where Speck's strength came from. Then he was too busy fighting back.

"Speck, stop it!"

Speck threw himself at Johnny, punching savagely, shouting incoherently. Murder boiled in Speck's wild eyes.

There was no time now for regrets. Johnny put them aside soberly and fought as if he had never seen Speck before, as if this weren't the best friend he had in the world. He tried to avoid Speck's face with his fists. He punched Speck in the belly and the ribs with all the power he had. Speck had to be stopped.

Speck began losing the sudden desperate strength born of his fear. The fever weakness pulled him down. He slumped to his knees, hugging his arms against his sides, tears streaming down his face.

"Kill him, Johnny! You got to kill him!"

"Speck, haven't we done enough to him already?"

"It's him or us!"

"Then it'll have to be us!" Johnny turned away and reached down for the rifle. He opened the bolt, then smashed the weapon against the trunk of a cedar. He swung it again and again until he knew for sure it was broken and bent beyond any possible use. He pitched it away and stood a moment with pounding heart as he tried to get back his breath.

He walked to Haggard, dreading to look at the man. Haggard was on his knees, hunched over in pain. He wore a pistol, but he had made no move to draw it. He seemed paralyzed. Johnny drew the pistol from its holster and pitched it off into the brush.

"Let me see, Mister Haggard. How bad did he hit you?"

If Haggard heard, he gave no sign of it. His face was flour-white, his thin lips drawn tight against his teeth in a grinding agony. His right hand was gripped against his left shoulder, and blood dribbled between his clawed fingers.

"I'm sorry, Mister Haggard. I swear to God, I'm sorry."

Dugan Whitaker came, half running, half hopping. Tessie came, too, though she halted behind Haggard as if afraid to look at him. Johnny raised his eyes. "Mister Whitaker, we got to get him to the house." He glanced back over his shoulder. "Speck, you done it. Now you come help."

They carried Haggard as far as the porch. Whitaker said, "Tessie, you run in and fetch a blanket out here. That slug's still in him, and I got to have daylight to find it."

They laid Haggard out and tore the shirt off of him. They brought whisky to give him for the pain, but he passed into unconsciousness without needing it. Dugan Whitaker tried probing for the bullet, but his old hands would not hold still.

"Johnny, it's up to you. You can save him, or you can stand back and watch him die. But remember: if you save him, you know one day he'll still come lookin' for you."

Johnny grimly studied Haggard's gray face. "Give me the probe."

He got the bullet out. They washed the wound with whisky, then Sarah Whitaker used handfuls of flour to stop the bleeding. When they could, they carried him into the lean-to. They placed him on the same bed where Speck had lain.

"Mrs. Whitaker," Johnny said apologetically, "you got another one to tend. We don't bring you nothin' but trouble."

"The Lord's wish, not yours."

Johnny watched Speck closely, wondering if he might try

again. But the spirit was gone from Speck now. He had made his try and failed. He stood with his shoulders drooped, eyes dulled by hopelessness.

Dugan Whitaker said, "Well, at least you got time now. It'll be a long while before he goes after you again."

Haggard stirred. Consciousness slowly returned to him. He blinked, trying to focus his eyes. Johnny stood beside his bed. "It's me, Mister Haggard. Me, Johnny Fristo. I just want you to know I'm sorry for what happened."

Haggard winced with pain, but he forced himself to hold his eyes a moment on Johnny. And Johnny saw the same implacability he had seen that day on the Sonora road.

Haggard's voice was thin, but it had a fierceness to it. "I won't be here long. One day soon I'll be lookin' for you again. And I vow, boy, I'll find you!"

Johnny turned away sadly, his head down. Why try to tell him again it had been Larramore who had killed his wife? Haggard hadn't believed him before. He would believe him even less now. Johnny dug into his pocket for the money Baker Fristo had given him.

"He'll be needin' a doctor, Mister Whitaker. You get him one, and pay him with this."

"You'll need that money yourself."

Johnny shook his head. "If it hadn't been for us, he wouldn't be here. Take it, please." He stopped and picked up a sack of food which Tessie and Mrs. Whitaker had prepared. "Come on, Speck. Let's go."

Outside, he tied the sack onto his own saddle, not trusting Speck to do it this time. He said goodbye first to Sarah, then to Dugan Whitaker. Last he took Tessie's hands. "Tessie, it's been awful good to know you. Take care of yourself."

"Johnny . . ." She would have said more, but the words died. She leaned forward and kissed him on the lips, then pulled her hands free and turned her back, her head bowed.

Johnny rode away, looking over his shoulder. Speck followed him like a whipped dog. Johnny kept looking back, seeing the Whitakers watching him, seeing that Tessie had turned once more and was watching him too.

Suddenly Johnny stopped his horse. "Speck, wait here. I'll be back."

He turned Traveler around and spurred into a long trot. He stepped to the ground in front of Tessie. He grabbed her into his arms with such a violence that his hat fell off and hit the ground at his feet.

"Tessie, Tessie, I don't want to leave you."

"And I don't want you to leave. But what can we do?"

"I'll send for you, that's what." He held her at arm's length and looked into her glistening eyes. "Someday, somewhere, I'll come onto a place that's so far out of the way Haggard'll never be able to find it. When I do, and when I get settled, I'll write to you, Tessie. I'll send for you."

"Promise, Johnny?"

"I promise. Now that I've known you, Tessie, I couldn't live without you anymore."

"I'll wait, Johnny, and I'll be ready. I'll follow you if you go ten thousand miles."

He held her again, once, then he turned on his heel, swung up into the saddle and rode away.

Inside the house, Milam Haggard's teeth were clenched against a searing pain. But the pain did not keep him from hearing.

XI

They quartered west by southwest, skirting the upper reaches of Centralia Draw and pointing in a general way toward ancient Horsehead Crossing. They rode dry all day through greasewood and stunted mesquite and patches of prickly pear. Not even a windmill showed on the skyline. They were west now of any living waters which would feed into the Middle Concho. This was the desolate stretch of lizard and rattlesnake and chaparral-hawk country which had brought misery and desperation to untold numbers of travelers making their way toward the unfriendly river known as the Pecos.

Before night they reached the China Pond. In front of them, and all to the south, stretched a long line of flat blue mountains. Their profile was low, but Johnny knew they were rough, impassable for wagons and difficult for horsemen. All trails led across the desert toward a scalloped opening near the northern edge. This would be Castle Gap, known for centuries as a pointer to Horsehead just beyond.

"This is a good place to stop, Speck. We got water here."

Speck only nodded. He had sulked all day, speaking perhaps half a dozen words since they had left the Whitaker ranch. This was remarkable for Speck. Instead of riding alongside Johnny, he had hung back half a length. When Johnny would slow to allow Speck to pull up even with him, Speck would draw back and keep the distance about the same. His brooding eyes avoided Johnny.

They made camp at the China Pond. Automatically Speck rode off to try to gather up some firewood. He came back without any, and Johnny used dried cowchips for fuel to cook a little supper. Later Speck sat back from the tiny fire and ate listlessly, keeping his own counsel. Johnny watched him, wondering what dark thoughts plodded through Speck's troubled mind.

"Speck, you still mad at me because of this mornin'?"

Speck didn't answer.

"I had to do it. We're not killers."

Speck's gaze touched him a moment. Resentfully he said, "You fought me. You used to call yourself my friend, and you fought me."

"I'm still your friend."

A pent-up anger began boiling over. "No, you ain't. You think you're better than I am. I've felt it comin' on ever since we stopped in Angelo. Aunt Pru told you about me, and my mother. Now I'm not good enough for you anymore. I'm trash."

"Speck, that's the silliest notion I ever heard of."

"No, it isn't. There was a time you wouldn't have fought me for nothin' in this world. Now you'd like to take that girl and ride off and leave me. But you can't because you know we're in this together. You're stuck with me and you hate it. You hate *me*."

Johnny's impatience melted away, for his pity was stronger. "You're all mixed up, Speck. I like you the same as I always did. If it's any consolation to you, what your Aunt Pru said didn't make any difference atall. I've known about your mother for years."

Speck stared incredulously. "You mean you always knew,

and you never let on?" Johnny nodded. Speck exploded. "That makes it even worse. All these years you been actin' like my friend, and all the time you was probably snickerin' at me behind my back."

He stood up and stomped off to where he had pitched his blanket to the ground. He spread it out and flopped down on his back, lying there and staring angrily up at the darkening sky.

Johnny's jaw took on a hard set. No use arguing. Speck had a haywire way of thinking, sometimes. He'd come around by and by.

At least, Johnny hoped he would.

Next morning they went on to the gap. Johnny noticed horse and cattle bones all along the way. This had always been a cruel trail. Curiosity held him in the gap awhile. Nearby he found the burned remnants of several wagons. He wondered if these were the result of some long-ago Indian attack, a bandit raid or if someone had just gotten careless with fire. If a raid, there was no question about the outcome. If an accidental fire, what had the victims done afterward? Here, so far from civilization, the loss of wagons and supplies in those earlier times could have meant the same eventual outcome: death. There was no way to know for sure now, for the charred wooden skeletons and the dark ashes had been reduced by long years of probing wind and occasional rain. Johnny sat on his horse and looked, and he let his imagination sweep him away. For a while he wished he could have been born fifty years earlier.

But eventually he heard Speck grumbling about how they ought to be going, and he grudgingly came back to reality, back to his own problems. Trouble, he knew, was something each generation shared.

No one had a monopoly on it.

Johnny pointed across the gently rolling stretch of grease-wood which lay below. "Down yonder, Speck, is Horsehead Crossing. Been a lot of history made along here."

Speck was still grumpy but a little more disposed to talk this morning. "Maybe you can see the history, but all I can see is a lizard-lick of a country that ain't worth a Mexican dollar if you got back ninety cents change."

They followed the bone-strewn trail twelve miles and came at last to the river. Here was fabled Horsehead with its sloping banks which led down to swift-moving water. This was the only place for a long journey up or down the river where the banks were such that wagons and livestock could go down into the water with a reasonable chance of coming out again on the opposite side.

A big scattering of animal bones lay along here. At this spot some thirty years before, Charles Goodnight had lost part of a Longhorn cattle herd in alkaline water and treacherous quicksands, and had pronounced the Pecos River the graveyard of a cowman's hopes.

Johnny saw a trail that angled off upriver. "This ought to lead the way up to the salt lake, Speck. That's where Dugan Whitaker told us to go."

Speck shivered, though the morning was warm. "Let's get ridin', then. This place makes my skin crawl."

They followed the wagon trail northwestward, roughly paralleling the snaking river and its line of salt-cedar trees. As they approached the Juan Cordona salt lake, the hard alkali soil began giving way gradually to more of sand. Heat waves shim-mered on the horizon as the salt basin came into view.

They met a Mexican burro train moving downriver, the

plodding little beasts carrying a heavy burden of white salt in huge twin baskets of rawhide and green willow. The ragged Mexican at the head of the train stared briefly at the cowboys, his eyes all but hidden under the wide, floppy brim of an incredibly old sombrero. He nodded, spoke a two-word greeting and walked on. Johnny watched the short-stepping burros move by him, the salt baskets bobbing from side to side with the rhythm of their walk. The Mexican *mulateros* were grayed with dust, their tattered shirts soaked with sweat and clinging to their bodies. Only one wore shoes, and these had been patched with rawhide. The rest had only simple *huaraches,* a thick sole held to the foot by leather thongs, protecting against thorns, sharp rocks and burning sand.

Johnny said solemnly, "Whenever a man gets to feelin' sorry for himself, he needs to take a look at somebody worse off than he is."

Speck grunted. "I bet they ain't got Milam Haggard lookin' for them."

The "lake" was a vast irregular stretch of shining salt, lying in an ancient basin rimmed by sandhills. The level bottom glistened in the sun, though along the edges a thin skim of dust had settled and turned it brown. There was feed here for livestock—a scattering of sand-type bunchgrasses and weeds. There was the tough green beargrass with its rapier-like stems and the tall yucca stalks. And here and there about the lake lay a dotting of camps, salt haulers of all types.

Johnny and Speck rode into two burro camps without finding anyone who spoke English. The third camp they found had half a dozen heavy wagons already full of salt and several more wagons in the process of being loaded by Mexican help. A crew sweated in the sun, their shovels slowly pitching dry salt into the wagons. A dark-skinned man saw the cowboys and came walking toward them. His beard was black beneath a crust of dust and salt. Johnny took him for a Mexican until he spoke. "Howdy. You-all lookin' for somebody in particular?"

Johnny nodded. "We're supposed to find a feller name of Massingill."

The salt freighter stared at the pair, his eyes narrowed. "You-all ain't lawmen or somethin'? Ain't got a warrant for somebody?"

Johnny shook his head. "No, sir, we just got a letter for Mister Massingill, is all. Friend of his sent it. Man name of Dugan Whitaker."

The bearded man smiled. His shoulders sagged in relief. "That's different. My name happens to be Massingill. Folks call me Gyp, on account of the Pecos River water I tote in my barrels." He reached up to shake hands. "Afraid at first you might be star-packers. I'm already shorthanded, and I sure didn't want you takin' off none of my help. You say you got a letter?"

Johnny handed him a letter which Dugan Whitaker had spent an hour in writing by lamplight the night before Johnny and Speck had left the ranch. "We're in kind of a jackpot, Mister Massingill. Dugan Whitaker, he thought you might be able to help us."

Massingill squatted in the shade of a wagon. It took him almost as long to read the letter as it had taken Whitaker to write it. His index finger followed the lines as he slowly read, his lips forming the words. At last he looked up. "A jackpot, you say? Looks to me like it's a right smart worse than that. I've seen Milam Haggard. How far behind you is he?"

Johnny explained about the shooting at the Whitaker ranch.

Massingill frowned suspiciously. "You-all must've known old Dugan a long time."

Johnny shook his head. "Never met him before."

"You sure must've convinced him you was all right. Or maybe you held a gun at his head to make him write this letter."

"No, sir, he wrote it of his own accord. He was awful good to us, him and Mrs. Whitaker both. This is the first time we ever been in trouble. They knew it."

Massingill studied them awhile, his eyes keen. They burned like the sun through a magnifying glass. Finally he nodded. "Well, if you convinced old Dugan, I guess that'll do for me. He's not an easy man fooled." He folded the letter and shoved it into his pocket. "And if Haggard has been laid up with a bullet in him, that means you got some time. We don't have to do things in a hurry. I'll make you a swap. You help me, and I'll help you."

Johnny nodded eagerly. "Anything you want."

"Well, the way I see it, Haggard will be a-lookin' for you-all to go on west. That's where any smart man on the dodge would go. So we'll fool him. Soon's I get these wagons full I'm takin' this salt south, down the Pecos River. There's ranches off down in there that a man wouldn't find in a hundred years if he didn't know where to look. It's a big country, some of it so big and dry that a hawk won't leave the nest without it carries a canteen. I'll take you down there with me, and I'll get you a job on some outfit where the whole United States army couldn't find you."

"That's mighty good of you, Mister Massingill."

"Gyp! And don't thank me till you find out how good your hands fit a shovel handle. I'll swap you a ride on my wagons in return for your muscles and your sweat. Sooner we get them wagons loaded with salt, the sooner we start down the river.

"You'll find the shovels over yonder!"

XII

Patience was part of a manhunter's stock in trade—difficult to learn, but indispensable. Milam Haggard had learned it long ago. It served him well now in this small settlement on the Centralia, for without it he could not have forced himself to remain here idle—waiting, watching, biding his time. It had been most of three months now since he had lain bleeding at the Whitaker ranch, listening to fading hoofbeats as the two cowboys rode away.

Even without hearing it, he sensed the speculation which his long stay had started among the townspeople and the ranchmen who ranged their cattle on bluestems and tobosa grass up and down the creeks and draws. He had not chosen to tell them why he had remained here, though doubtless they could guess most of it. Only one person in town, besides himself, knew the full reason.

To be sure, the whole country knew who he was and knew of his mission. They knew his wife had died as an innocent bystander in a fight along the Sonora-San Angelo road. They knew Haggard had been shot at the Whitaker ranch and that he had come riding in here as soon as he was able to mount a horse by himself, disclaiming any further help from the cowboys' friends. It was common knowledge that Dugan and Sarah Whitaker would still argue the fugitives' case to anyone who cared to listen.

It was well known also that Haggard was no longer a Ranger, that he had been unable to get official backing in his search for the two cowboys. At least two Ranger friends, to the knowledge of the townspeople, had come here to talk with him. Common belief was that they were trying to talk him out of his quest.

Why then, people asked each other, was he still here? Granted, his left shoulder was still stiff and appeared to give him some pain. But those who from afar had watched this gaunt, unsmiling man at target practice beyond the edge of town could testify that his eye was keen and his aim was ungodly straight. Haggard lived in a small shack on which he paid a token rent. Though civil enough, he made no effort to cultivate new friendships. He received no company except for a couple of ranchmen who had known him down south in the Ranger service. They stopped in occasionally to see how he was getting along, for they felt a genuine concern. He spent his time reading, exercising the shoulder and practicing at targets.

Some careful observers had noted that he always watched the mail hack when it arrived at the small general store that served as a post office. Inevitably he was among the first to be there as the storekeeper sorted the mail. It had become something of a routine, which seldom varied. Haggard would go straight to the corner where the mail was put up in small individual boxes. "Anything today, John?"

The storekeeper would always shake his head. "Maybe next time."

It had become so repetitious that the early flurry of speculation had died down, and many people largely lost interest. Most agreed he was either awaiting a renewal of his Ranger commission to make his search legal, or during his long recovery period he had sent someone ahead to track down the fugitives and now waited for word as to their whereabouts.

Whatever the storekeeper knew, he wasn't talking.

Milam Haggard had never been a drinking man. He did not believe it wise in his trade. Often he had observed how liquor had made quarry fall easy prey to a gun in the hands of a sober man.

But Haggard was a lonelier man than most people suspected, and once in a while he welcomed a visit from old friends. On such occasions, though he did not drink, he sometimes accompanied his friends to the saloon and sat there to enjoy their companionship.

Thus it was that he happened to walk into the place one afternoon and find himself face-to-face with the cattle trader Larramore.

Larramore was playing cards with two prospective cow buyers. The surprise was mutual. Larramore's eyes opened wide and frightened, his face losing color. In Sonora that day after Cora Haggard's death, Larramore had sensed how close he came to being shot when the sheriff told Milam Haggard about the swindle against the two cowboys. Though Haggard blamed the shooting directly on Johnny Fristo and Speck Quitman, he had immediately grasped the fact that Larramore's duplicity had provoked the incident. Haggard's granite fist had sent Larramore reeling. Larramore had lain terrified, not moving, knowing that if Haggard had been wearing a gun he would have killed him without ceremony and without regret.

Seeing Haggard now, Larramore arose shakily, his voice strained. "Haggard, I been tryin' to stay out of your way just like you told me. I had no idea you was here." His glance dropped anxiously to the six-shooter on Haggard's right hip.

Haggard only stared at him, his eyes hard and hating.

Larramore watched Haggard's right hand. "Haggard, I ain't got a gun on me." That was a lie, for he carried a small .38 in his boottop. But he feared if Haggard even suspected its presence, he might force Larramore to reach for it. It would have been no contest.

Haggard's narrowed eyes seemed to crackle with danger. "Larramore, those cowboys still claim you were the one who really fired the shot. I know you said you didn't, but I want to hear you say it again."

Larramore trembled. "It was *them*. They both had guns."

"That's a lie. Only one of them had a gun. And *you* had one."

"It was *them* that killed her. It was them!" The trader dropped his chin, unable to look into Haggard's face.

Haggard cut his gaze to the two men who had been playing cards at the table with Larramore. One he recognized as a rancher south of here. He took the other for a rancher, too. They sat watching in surprise, not quite comprehending. Haggard asked, "You-all have business with this man?"

One of them replied hesitantly, "He told us he knew where there was some cattle we could buy worth the money."

Haggard's voice was raw. "You'd better have nothin' to do with him. He's a thief, a liar and a cheat!"

Larramore jerked his head up. "Haggard, you got no right . . ."

Haggard's eyes cut back to him, and they were deadly. Larramore's words stuck in his throat. Haggard's voice sliced like the razor edge of a skinning knife. "Leave town, Larramore. Leave this part of the country. Next time I see you, I'll probably kill you!"

He turned sharply and started for the door. Larramore stared after him, frozen.

Haggard had just reached the door when the bartender shouted. Instinctively he jumped to one side, whirling as his right hand dropped and came up with the six-shooter.

Larramore crouched awkwardly, having reached down to his boottop for the .38. No gunman, he fired wildly. The bullet smacked into the doorframe and sent wood splinters flying. He never got a chance to fire again. Haggard's pistol roared like thunder inside the small saloon. Larramore stepped back under the driving impact. He began bending forward from the waist, the .38 slipping from his fingers. He screamed. Then the scream died off, and he pitched forward onto his face.

Haggard cautiously moved toward him, kicking the .38 out of the way. He stooped and turned Larramore over into his back, the strain bringing a stabbing pain to the old shoulder wound. "How about it, Larramore? *Was* it you who killed her?"

Larramore made a feeble effort to speak. Then he went limp. He died with his eyes and his mouth open.

Haggard pushed to his feet, the shoulder throbbing a little. He shook his head and spoke to no one in particular. "It doesn't matter, I guess. They *all* killed her."

It was a rare occasion when Dugan Whitaker came to town. Since Milam Haggard had ridden away from the Whitaker ranch on his dun, slumped over the saddle horn in pain but too proud to remain any longer under that roof, he had seen Whitaker only once. They had nodded civilly and gone their separate ways. Taking care of his place virtually alone,

Whitaker didn't have much time for coming to the settlement.

But this morning, sitting in front of the shack and watching the dark clouds which built threateningly in the north, Haggard saw the Whitakers pass by in their buckboard. Dugan and Sarah Whitaker gave him a polite nod, but nothing more. The Barnett girl only stared, and Haggard thought he saw fear leap into her face. During the time he had been at the ranch, wounded, the girl had kept her distance as if he had been a rattlesnake.

Haggard regretted that. He saw fear everywhere these days, since he had killed Larramore. He wanted respect, not fear. But that was part of the business. He had come to expect it, even if he didn't welcome it.

He hadn't been back to the saloon. He doubted he would ever go. As he heard it, the bartender hadn't even cleaned up the blood. He had purposely left it to soak a dark stain deep, into the wood. Now it had become an attraction for the idle curious. This brought a rush of resentment every time it crossed Haggard's mind. He was not an exhibitionist. Killing a man had never pleased him. He had always dreaded it, and he had regretted it when it was done.

He had thought there might be a grim pleasure in killing someone who had had a part in Cora's death. But to his surprise the sight of Larramore dead on that dirty saloon floor had brought only the same old revulsion to sicken him.

Of late he had spent much time thinking about his ranch up on the Colorado River. He had a few cowboys hired, and he felt sure they were taking care of it for him. But he wished he could go up there, find out how things looked, see if summer rains had greened the grass and fattened the cattle. He had grown to hate his vigil here. The thought of following another long trail in a lonely search for fugitives was abhorrent to him.

But again, there was his training, and his pride. He had made a vow over the fresh mound where they had laid Cora to rest. He had never broken a vow in his life. He wouldn't break this one, though sometimes he had to conjure up a vision of Cora's face to give him the strength that he could carry on this way.

Watching the Whitakers' buckboard wheel on down toward the heart of the settlement, Haggard suddenly remembered this was the day for the mail hack. And it was due about now, give or take an hour. He didn't want the Whitakers receiving their mail before he got there.

Squaring his hat, he started up the dusty road afoot. To his satisfaction he found the Whitaker buckboard sitting in front of a different store. Dugan Whitaker and Tessie Barnett were lifting Sarah Whitaker down into her wheelchair. Haggard looked east on the wagon road that led in from San Angelo. He saw dust. He wondered if that would be the mail hack.

Well, this was going to be cutting things pretty fine. He sat down on an empty bench at the front of the store to wait. His gaze drifted up and down the street, cutting back often to the Whitaker buckboard. He hoped they wouldn't come over this way before the hack got in.

The driver pulled up, the dust drifting on ahead of him. He nodded at Haggard and carried the mail bag inside. Haggard kept his seat awhile, giving the storekeeper time to put up the mail. There wasn't any hurry about it, so long as the Whitakers didn't come. Even so, it seemed it took an awfully long time. Finally the hack driver came out and nodded again, wiping his mouth. The storekeeper always had coffee ready for him. He took time to drink it before he traveled on. Haggard glanced through the window constantly to see if the mail had been sorted. The seat of his pants prickled with impatience. When he saw the storekeeper leave the mail corner, he arose and walked inside.

The storekeeper's eyes met his, and Haggard knew even before the man nodded. "It came, Mister Haggard."

"You're sure?"

The storekeeper nodded again. "It's addressed to Miss Tessie Barnett, care of Dugan Whitaker."

"Let me have it, John."

"Well, now, I can't be doin' that. It's agin the law."

"Damn the law! Give me that letter!"

"I promised I'd tell you when it came. I didn't tell you I'd give it to you. It's still the U.S. mail, Mister Haggard, till the girl puts her hands on it. There can't nobody touch it. Not you and not me."

Anger swelled in Haggard. He was sorely tempted to walk across and take the letter anyway. But judgment stopped him. Unreasoning anger was another luxury he had never allowed himself. "All right. I'll wait."

He walked to the door and started to go outside. But he saw Tessie Barnett on her way, walking rapidly several steps in front of old Dugan Whitaker. Haggard stepped back, looking quickly around him. He saw an open door leading into a storeroom. "Not a word, John." He stepped through the door and out of sight.

Tessie came in, Dugan Whitaker hurrying along in a vain effort to catch up with her. "Tessie," he laughed, "go easy. Have some pity on an old man."

Tessie might as well not have heard him. Eyes sparkling in

anticipation, she searched out the storekeeper. "Do you have any mail for me? Tessie Barnett?"

The storekeeper took his time, glancing at the open storeroom door. He knew what was about to happen. "Yes, ma'am, I believe maybe I do." He walked over to the corner and sought out a letter from among a dozen. Regretfully he placed it in her eager hands. "This what you've been waitin' for?"

Excitement leaped into Tessie's face. "Uncle Dugan, it's from *him*; I *know* it is!"

Haggard stepped out of the storeroom, unnoticed by Tessie and Whitaker. The storekeeper turned his back and walked away, wanting no part of this. Tessie ripped the envelope open, her hands trembling. "Uncle Dugan, it *is* from him, it *is*!"

Milam Haggard stepped up beside her and snatched the letter from her hands. "I'll take that!"

She whirled. Seeing him, she raised one hand up over her mouth. Her eyes were big as dollars. "You!"

Dugan Whitaker made a grab for the letter. "Haggard, you got no right!"

Haggard stepped back and turned half around, keeping the letter out of his reach. "I *have* got the right."

He skipped the opening lines, for they spoke of loneliness, and he knew all there was to know about that. His gaze dropped farther down in the letter:

This is a good ranch. A little on the plain side, maybe, but your going to like it here Tessie. Theres a good adobe house the owner says we can live in. Kind of little but big enough for two. I think we can slip down to Langtry and get Judge Bean to marry us without anybody paying us much notice.

You would never find the place by yourself. So will meet
you at Horsehead Crossing on the Pecos. Maybe Mr. Whitaker
can bring you or get somebody to. Will be there about Sept.
the 15. Bring your wagon. Will wait till you come and please
hurry.

Horsehead Crossing! Haggard crunched the letter in his
hand. September the fifteenth! Why, that was yesterday! This
letter must have traveled halfway around the world before it
reached here.

So Fristo was already there, waiting! And Quitman with
him, if Haggard was any judge.

He knew a quiet moment of triumph, then his face
turned grave. A chill passed down his back as he turned to
Tessie Barnett and saw the dismay in her eyes. It struck him
that she was a pretty girl. Silently he handed her the letter.
Sympathy touched him. Pity she had gotten mixed up in
this. Pity she had to know the heartbreak that was coming.
But she was young, and she would survive. In time she might
even learn to understand the necessity of it. Anyway, there
was no choice. The die had been cast. Haggard had long
since developed an instinct for the inevitable. The thing was
coming to an end now, as sure as the sun would rise and set
tomorrow.

The girl's eyes pleaded. "Mister Haggard, you can't do it.
Please, say you're not going to do it!"

She had as well have talked to the big wood heater that
stood cold and unused in the center of the store. Haggard
looked at Dugan Whitaker. "I'm sorry it's this way, Mister
Whitaker. I think you'd best take her home." He turned his

back and walked to the door. Tessie stared after him, the letter crushed in her hand. The dismay had turned to terror.

"No!" she screamed and went running after him.

Haggard hurried his step a little, wanting to get away from her. He went down off the porch and into the dusty street, his eyes set on the barn where his dun horse was kept stabled. Clouds were darkening overhead.

"Mister Haggard, wait!"

He tried to outwalk her. How could a man argue over a thing like this? How could he explain why he had to go on? For God's sake, didn't she already know?

She grabbed his good arm. Head high, he kept walking, his strength pulling her along. "Please, Mister Haggard, listen to me. What good will it do to kill him? Will *she* come back? Will another wrong make things right?" He walked on, trying not to listen. "I love him, Mister Haggard. If you loved *her*, you should understand that."

He swallowed, trying to shut his ears. She stepped in front of him, still holding his arm. He tried to step around her, but she was faster and blocked him. He wrested his arm free. She grabbed it again. Weary of the contest, he stopped.

"Why, Mister Haggard? Tell me why!"

"You know why. He helped to kill my wife."

"He didn't shoot her. Larramore did."

"All you know is what he told you."

"I know *him,* and I know he told the truth."

"Whoever actually fired the shot, they were all responsible. They all killed her. They'll all pay."

"He had mercy on *you.* Won't you have mercy on him?"

Haggard frowned. "*He* had mercy on *me?*"

"Speck Quitman tried to kill you. Johnny stopped him. He knew you meant to kill him, but he wouldn't let Speck kill you. He even took the bullet out of you." Haggard made no reply. She argued, "And he left every cent he had with the Whitakers to pay a doctor to take care of you."

"I didn't accept it. I paid my own way."

"But he *tried*. That's important, isn't it? He tried."

Grimly Haggard said, "Would his money buy my wife back to life? She's dead. Nothing he has done since will change that."

"Will his dying change it?"

He held silent a moment, wanting to say something but not knowing what. "Miss, I'm sorry for you, but there's nothing I can do. There's a blood debt to settle. I'm goin' to see that it's paid!"

He glanced at her face again, and he saw that her terror was gone. In its place was a stiff anger, and perhaps even hatred. "You know what you are, Haggard?" She had dropped the *mister*. "You're a killer. You're a lawman because that makes it legal for you, but if you couldn't be a lawman you'd be an outlaw. You won't listen to reason because you *have* no reason. You're like an animal; it's your nature to kill. It's a disease with you.

"You pretend you're doing this out of love for your wife, but you're lying to us, and you may even be lying to yourself. You've hunted men so long it's turned you into some kind of a wolf. Maybe it's better for her that she *is* dead. She couldn't have lived with you very long. In your own way, you'd have killed her yourself!"

Anger rushed to his face. He lifted his hand as if to strike her, but he stopped himself.

"Go ahead," she taunted him, "hit me. Shoot me, even. If you've got to kill somebody, maybe *I'll* do."

Abruptly he turned away from her. She shouted, "I swear to you, Haggard, if you kill Johnny I'll see you *dead!* Then who'll kill *me?* Where will it ever end?"

Thunder rolled in the distance. Haggard wished it were louder. He walked on, wishing he couldn't hear her, wishing he couldn't feel the stinging lash of her hatred.

Tessie stood in the middle of the street with her small fists clenched and watched Haggard walk stolidly toward the barn. Dugan Whitaker came up from behind and put his hand on her shoulder. "You can't reason with him, girl. I'm afraid the only way anybody could stop him now would be to kill him."

"Uncle Dugan, maybe *you* . . ."

"Could kill him?" He shook his head. "Tessie, I'd do almost anything for you. But that is one thing I couldn't do."

"I didn't mean that. But we've got to warn Johnny."

"It's a long ride to Horsehead. Our buckboard couldn't get there before Haggard and his horse."

"But a horseback rider might, if he was desperate enough."

"Honey, I'm old. There was a time, but I'm not that tough anymore. Haggard would outlast me and outrun me."

"*I'm* young, and I'm desperate enough."

"*You?*" His face furrowed. "It's a hard trip for a girl."

"I've been here three months. I've learned aplenty, and I've toughened a lot. I've got a good reason to make this ride. A better reason than Haggard has."

Doubt hovered in Dugan Whitaker's narrowed eyes. But there was also understanding. "You won't make it, girl. But you'll regret it all your life if you don't make the try. Come on, I know where I can get you a horse." He frowned. "But what if you *do* make it? Even if you do warn Johnny and he runs, what then? Haggard will keep on comin'. He won't stop."

"Then *we'll* keep running, Johnny and me. I should have gone with him before. I'll stay with him this time."

"That's no life, a-runnin'."

"It's better than dying. We'll live while we can."

XIII

Mean enough even in normal times, the Pecos River was on an angry rise. Sodden gray clouds loomed heavy to the north and west. A light mist enveloped this desolate greasewood barren which stretched outward in all directions from Horsehead Crossing.

Johnny Frisco stirred a glowing cowchip fire and put on a smoke-blackened can to boil a mixture of ground coffee and brackish Pecos River water. He reached under a tarp for a couple of dry chips out of a pile which he and Speck had gathered yesterday before the rain started. Chips were about the only fuel here fit to use—"prairie coal," some called them. A man could start a fire with dead greasewood, but it burned too quickly to cook with. Other campers at the crossing had long since used up any dead brush which may have stood along the river.

Speck Quitman rolled his blankets and frowned up at the low-hanging clouds. "Johnny, ain't that girl ever goin' to get here? This is the spookiest place I was ever at."

They had been here three days. Johnny was getting tired of it too. "I told you twenty times, Speck, the letter may have got held up. Not much tellin' when that Mexican got to a post office to mail it."

Speck had changed during the three months or so they had worked on that ranch way down south along the Pecos. He didn't eat much, and he didn't sleep. He smoked up all the tobacco he could get his hands on, and those hands were unsteady. Always when the work would lag a moment, Speck's gaze would lift to the horizon, and fear clouded his eyes.

He had run out of talk a long time ago.

Watching steam start rising from the can, Johnny wished they had been able to fetch along a wagon instead of depending on Tessie to bring hers. A-horseback they hadn't been able to carry much camping equipment. For one thing, he wished they had a barrel so they could fill it and let the water settle before they used it. The flooded river was carrying a lot of mud.

It hadn't tasted very good even before. Now it was about all a man's stomach could stand.

Horsehead Crossing wasn't a pleasant place to camp anyway. There was no shelter. From here back to Castle Gap, all Johnny could see was waist-high greasewood and a scattering of tall Spanish Daggers that had a worrisome way of looking like men, especially in the twilight or in a thin mist like this. He had thought at first Speck was going to come unwound here. Twenty times Speck had sworn he saw one of the daggers move, that it was Milam Haggard. Johnny hadn't wanted to bring Speck here in the first place, but Speck wouldn't have stayed on that ranch without Johnny for all the silver coin west of the Conchos.

Johnny felt an ominous presence about this place, a vague but unmistakable sense of death. For three hundred years white men had known this crossing and had used it—Spaniards first, then the Mexicans and finally the Americans. Indians had swum across here for countless centuries before that. No one knew how many men had died within a stone's throw of this spot. Johnny had found a number of graves along the trail, some of them marked, some of them not. The Pecos was deep and usually swift. Many of the men buried here had underestimated the river.

Then, too, there had been the Indians. Until twenty years or so ago, the fearsome Comanches had haunted this forsaken region. Warfare to them had been a game, though a bloody one. The Comanche War Trail to Mexico had led across here. Only God knew how many captive Mexican women and children had been dragged here in hopeless captivity. No telling how many horses and cattle the Comanches had taken here, or how many scalps. A man halfway across the river made a helpless target.

Bleached bones of horses and cattle told a silent story of hardship and death. They set the mood for this lonesome place, and a cheerless mood it was.

Even as men had used this crossing, they had cursed it.

Speck looked into the steaming can and found to his disappointment that the coffee wasn't ready. He looked eastward again, his face drawn and listless. Then he stiffened. "Johnny, I see somebody comin'."

Johnny glanced up a moment and then said crisply, "Speck, there isn't anybody comin'. Will you ever quit seein' things?"

Speck narrowed his eyes, still peering worriedly through the mist. "I'd of swore . . ." His face was grave. "He's a-comin' though, Johnny. Milam Haggard is comin'. I can feel it in my bones."

"Speck, you've felt Milam Haggard in your bones ever since that mornin' on the Sonora road. There hasn't been a day you haven't looked for him to come."

Speck shivered, and not altogether from the damp air.

"There hasn't been an *hour*!" He squatted on his heels and stared eastward, not satisfied that he had been wrong.

Watching him, Johnny felt a touch of pity. Sure, *he* had worried too, but not like Speck. Haggard had become an obsession with him. It seemed the farther they got away from Haggard, the more certain Speck became that they would be found.

Speck poured coffee into a tin cup and sucked his fingers to ease the burn he had taken from the hot can. "Johnny, what if Haggard does come? We ain't even got a gun."

"He lost us, Speck. He's got no idea where we're at. Besides, what would we do with a gun if we had it? We're not goin' to shoot him, not again."

"*I* would. If he was to die, we could live. As long as he lives he's hangin' over our heads like them clouds up there. I'd've killed him that other time if you'd left me alone."

Johnny had argued this out with Speck a hundred times. But nothing was ever final with Speck. Whatever was dwelling on his mind, he always came back to it, picking over the cold bones again and again. "And then what, Speck? He was right; we were wrong. Instead of *him* comin' after us alone, there'd have been a hundred or two of them, and we'd of been dead now instead of sittin' here at Horsehead."

"Might be better dead than to live the way we do, afraid every time we see a stranger. Seein' him all day and *her* all night."

Sadly Johnny shrugged. "Speck, I wish I knew what to tell you."

Speck kept watching the horizon. At length he pushed to his feet excitedly, dropping his cup and splashing coffee out onto the wet ground. "Johnny, it *is* somebody. Look!"

Johnny squinted. Speck was right. Yonder came a rider.

Speck blurted, "It's *him*; it's got to be. Let's saddle up and skin out of here!"

"Be sensible for once, Speck. It won't be Haggard. How could he know?"

"He just knows, that's all. He ain't human."

"He's human enough to get himself shot." But arguing with Speck was as fruitless as talking to that stack of cowchips under the tarp. Speck grabbed up his saddle, blanket and bridle and hurried out to where his horse was picketed. Johnny watched him throw the rig up onto the horse's back.

"Speck, even if it *was* Haggard, where would you go?"

"I'd head out across that river."

"It's too high. You couldn't swim it."

"With *him* after me I could swim the Mississippi."

Johnny gave up arguing. Time was when he could talk sense to Speck, now and again. Lately he couldn't reach him at all. Johnny turned to watch the oncoming rider. Something about the horseman struck him oddly.

"It's a woman, Speck. She's a-ridin' sidesaddle." The rider came nearer. Johnny exclaimed, "Speck, it's Tessie. It's Tessie!"

Speck had just finished tightening the cinch. With relief he said, "High time she was gettin' here. Only, where's her wagon?"

Johnny trotted out afoot to meet her. Recognizing him, she called his name. Johnny reached up for her and brought her down from the saddle and crushed her in his arms. "Tessie, we'd all but given you up. But why did you come by yourself?"

Her voice was urgent. "We've got no time to talk. Milam Haggard's on his way."

His stomach went cold. "Haggard?"

"He got hold of your letter, Johnny. I've ridden as hard as I could to get ahead of him. I passed him in the gap. And he knows it."

Speck had heard. His face drained. "Johnny, I told you I felt it. He's comin'." His voice cracked. "He's comin', and we're goin' to die!"

Johnny spoke impatiently, "Speck, hush up that kind of talk. We got to think."

"It's too late for that. You do what you want to. Me, I'm high-tailin' it across that river. It's still on the rise. Time he gets here maybe he won't be able to follow me."

"It's already too late, Speck. Water's too high."

"With the river we got a chance. With Haggard we got none atall."

Speck swung into the saddle and touched spurs to the bay horse.

Johnny stared after him, not quite believing. "Speck, have you gone plumb crazy? You come back here!"

Speck kept riding.

"Speck," Johnny called anxiously, "if you've got the sense God gave a jackrabbit you'll come back here!" He ran after Speck afoot. Speck saw that Johnny intended to stop him. He spurred again, putting the horse into a long trot. As Speck looked back, Johnny caught a glimpse of his friend's fear-stricken face. "Speck, for God's sake stop!"

For an instant Johnny remembered what his father had once said about Speck: *Sometimes he doesn't make good sense. He'll pull a fool stunt and kill himself someday.*

Speck spurred down the wet bank. The bay balked at going into the swirling brown water. Speck kept jabbing him with his spurs and slapping the horse's rump with his hat. Finally the bay jumped off into the river. For a moment it looked as if they were going to be all right. Speck had swum rivers before. Getting out into the fast current, he slipped out of the saddle to give the horse a better chance. He clung to the horn and the saddlestrings.

Something happened. The horse panicked and began threshing. Somehow Speck lost his hold.

Johnny watched openmouthed from the bank. "Tessie," he shouted, "bring my rope. It's on my saddle."

Tessie jerked the hornstring loose and came running with the rope. Meeting her, Johnny grabbed it and ran down the riverbank, stumbling, rolling, regaining his feet.

"Speck! Over here! I got a rope!"

Speck's arms windmilled wildly. Foamy water swirled around him, carrying him swiftly down the river. He saw Johnny and raised his hand. Johnny swung the loop and sent it sailing. But just as it touched the water, Speck went under. When the cowboy came up again, he had missed the rope.

Desperately Johnny re-coiled it and went running again, racing the current. A second time he threw the rope. This time Speck clutched it, and for a moment Johnny thought he had him. But Speck lost his hold. Once more he disappeared beneath the muddy water.

Johnny went running again. This time he knew Speck wouldn't have strength left to hold the rope. Johnny ran until he was sure he was ahead of him. He dropped down over the slippery riverbank, pulling the loop tightly around his own waist and quickly half-hitching the other end of the rope to a salt-cedar. Catching a glimpse of Speck above him, Johnny plunged into the water.

He had no idea the flood could pull so hard. It seemed a

futile fight against the swift current, but somehow he made it out into the river. The muddy, salty water burned his eyes, and it was hard for him to see. But he glimpsed Speck almost upon him. He grabbed an arm. "Speck . . ." Water filled his mouth and choked him. He pulled Speck up against him and began trying to fight the current with one arm. It was a hopeless fight. He felt himself going under. But stubbornly he held on to Speck.

He reached the end of the rope. The current pulled him so hard it felt as if the rope would cut him in two. But he kept fighting, and slowly the drag of the current against the rope drew him back toward the bank. He threshed desperately with his free arm. He choked on the bad water, but finally he felt his feet touch bottom. With all the strength that was left in him, he fought his way to the bank.

Tessie was there, wet from the rain, muddy from climbing down the steep bank. She grabbed Johnny's free arm and helped him pull up. He dragged Speck after him. Breathing hard, his heart pounding from exhaustion, Johnny pulled Speck up over the bank and out onto flat ground. Still choking, he turned Speck over onto his stomach and started trying to squeeze the water out of him.

"Here, Johnny," Tessie said, "you're done in. I'll try."

Speck's horse climbed up onto the bank and stood exhausted, hanging its head.

Tessie pumped awhile, till Johnny got over his coughing and regained his breath. Then he tried it. He was getting no response. His heartbeat quickened, and desperation began taking hold of him. "Speck," he cried, half under his breath, "you got to come out of it. Speck!"

But Speck never stirred. Tessie reached for Speck's wrist

and felt for a pulse. When she looked up her face was stricken. "Johnny, there's nothing more we can do."

Johnny had sensed it. Now tears came in a blinding rush, burning his eyes. "I tried. Speck, I tried." His throat went tight. He sat on the wet ground, his knees drawn up, his face buried in his arms. Tessie's hand was light and comforting on his shoulder.

After a long time Tessie's voice came soberly, "Johnny, I see a rider coming. It'll be Haggard."

Johnny slowly raised his head and blinked, clearing his eyes. The mist had almost stopped. He could see the tall rider pausing in camp, studying their tracks. In a moment the rider saw them. He reined the horse gently around and came on in a walk, following the river. Across his lap he held a saddlegun.

Tessie bit her lip. "Johnny, what're we goin' to do?"

Johnny clenched his fist. "Earlier, I'd have run." He glanced at Speck. "Now I don't feel like runnin' anymore. I'm tired of runnin'."

"Johnny, I've got a gun. Dugan Whitaker gave it to me."

"No gun, Tessie. Whatever happens, I don't aim to fight him. We were in the wrong."

"But now *he's* in the wrong. He told us himself: they wouldn't even give him a warrant. The law isn't looking for you. Only Haggard is."

Johnny looked sadly at Speck Quitman lying still and silent in the mud. "I wish I'd known that before."

"But don't you see, Johnny? You've got a right to defend yourself now. He's already killed Larramore. In a way, he killed Speck. Now you've got to kill *him* before he kills you."

Johnny shook his head and pushed to his feet. "No, Tessie. I won't kill him."

"Then run, Johnny! Take Speck's horse and run!"

"How far could I get? I've run too long already, and for nothin'. I'm through runnin'. I'm going to stand and face him. Whatever is goin' to happen, let it happen here. Let this be the end of it."

He turned and waited for Haggard.

Milam Haggard had camped in the gap, figuring on riding down to the Pecos crossing in the early hours of morning. He knew the two he sought were down there, for he had seen a pinpoint of firelight. He could have ridden on down and finished it in the night, but he didn't trust himself. He was tired, and the shoulder was still bothering him some. A man could make a mistake in a situation like that, when he wasn't at his best. Better to wait and rest a few hours. He would be ready in the early morning. They would not. That was the time to take them, when there was still sleep in their eyes.

This, then, was the hour he had waited for. This was the final reckoning, when all debts would be paid and the slate wiped clean, when the burden of vengeance at last would be lifted from his shoulders. It had become an oppression of late, as painful as the slow-healing wound that had bent him. He was weary of it. He would be glad when this was over and he could go home—home to the ranch. He would be glad when he no longer had to call up a mental image of Cora's face to keep driving him on.

He had been aware of someone riding far behind him yesterday, but he hadn't thought much of it. People still used this old Butterfield Trail. He hadn't even considered the girl until he saw her ride through the gap and past him this morning. Daylight had not yet come, and he would not even have seen her had she not ridden within fifty feet of his camp. She had been unaware of him until about the same time he had seen her. She had moved into a lope. He had considered saddling up and racing her to the crossing, but she had a good start on him. He would wear out his horse and maybe himself as well.

Let her go, then. He had lost the element of surprise, and he regretted that. But they couldn't go far. He had an idea the river would be up, from the looks of the heavy clouds to the north. So he would catch them soon. Sure, it was two to one, but they were only cowboys. They knew horses and cattle and ropes, but *he* was the one who knew guns. He wouldn't give them a chance to ambush him again.

"It's almost over now, Cora," he spoke aloud. "In a little while you can rest easy."

But he thought of the girl riding far ahead, and he remembered the bitter words she had flung at him in the settlement.

Who is going to rest easy? he asked himself. *Will it be Cora, or me?*

A killer, Tessie Barnett had called him.

Maybe it's better for your wife that she is dead, the girl had shouted. *She couldn't have lived with you very long. In your own way, you'd have killed her yourself.*

"It's not true, Cora," Haggard said. "We'd have had a good life. I'd have changed, for *you.*"

He had been sure he could do it. Well, almost sure. But Cora had died, and he *hadn't* changed. That much, at least, he granted the girl.

Certainly he had killed, but always for the right. He had never killed a man who didn't deserve to die, and he had never killed a man who didn't have a chance. He had killed, but he had never murdered. Of that, he was proud.

Moving toward the crossing, he reached down and drew the saddlegun from its scabbard beneath his leg. He brought it up in front of him and rode with sharp eyes watching through the thin mist. He had let these men shoot him once. He wouldn't make that mistake again. The air was wet and chill and he hunched his shoulders, wishing he had brought a coat or a jumper. But perhaps all the chill wasn't from the weather. He sensed death about this miserable place. His eyes were drawn to two unmarked mounds at the side of the hoof-worn trail. The toll of Horsehead Crossing.

Today there would be new graves.

He thought of the cowboys as he had seen them that day on the Sonora road. They were young. They hadn't meant to kill Cora. But she had died. Had it not been for them, she would still live.

Young, they were, and fated to grow no older.

Well, he had seen even younger ones die, young men who had more right to life than these, men who had done no wrong.

He saw the camp ahead, the chips aglow in the shallow firepit. He saw a horse picketed, no saddle on its back, and another horse standing with a sidesaddle. He saw tracks where a third horse had gone down to the river. There were boot tracks too.

At first he figured they were huddled down behind the riverbank, waiting to ambush him. His hand tightened on the short rifle.

Downriver he saw a movement. He made out the girl standing there, and beside her a man sitting on the ground. Watching them cautiously, he reined gently around and moved in their direction. He wondered where the second cowboy was, and the hair stiffened at the back of his neck. He considered the probability that they were trying to lure him into a trap. But presently he saw the body lying at the girl's feet. He saw a bay horse standing on the riverbank, head down, water dripping.

He thought he could guess what had happened.

Rifle ready, he rode on slowly and drew rein twenty feet from Johnny Fristo and Tessie Barnett. He looked down a moment at Speck Quitman.

Johnny Fristo said with an acid bitterness, "Yes, he's dead, Mister Haggard. You wanted to kill him, and you did."

"*I* killed him?"

"With fear. The fear of you drove him to it. So carve another notch on your gun. The credit belongs to you. Enjoy it."

Haggard's mouth tightened. For a moment he felt cheated. Then he knew relief of a kind, for in his mind this had been a just way. "Now there's only you left, Fristo."

Fristo stepped away from the frightened girl. He said flatly, "I'm here."

Haggard frowned. "I don't see your gun."

"I haven't got a gun. Never did have one."

Haggard's eyes narrowed. He hadn't considered this possibility. He nodded toward the body. "Then your friend had one. Get it. I'll give you that much time."

Johnny held still. "He doesn't have one, either."

Haggard eased down from the saddle, keeping the rifle ready, pointed toward Fristo. "He *had* one. He shot me."

"I smashed the rifle. He hasn't had one since."

Haggard stepped away from the horse, frowning. "I've never shot an unarmed man."

"If you shoot me, that's the way it's goin' to have to be."

Haggard's hands flexed nervously on the saddlegun. Somehow he found himself on the defensive here in a way that puzzled him. Few times in his life had he ever wondered what he should do; he always seemed to know. Now he faced indecision, and it was hard to cope with.

Tessie Barnett said, "Mister Haggard, you killed Larramore. You killed Speck Quitman. Aren't two men enough to pay for what happened to your wife, especially when it was an accident in the first place? How much more blood is it going to take?"

Haggard did not look at her. He kept his eyes on Johnny Fristo as he answered her, for he was not completely convinced that Fristo did not have a gun. "This one is still left. I've never hunted a man in my life that I didn't finally get him."

"Is it your wife you're really thinking of, Mister Haggard?" she demanded. "Or is it yourself?"

He did not reply.

Tessie said bitterly, "Two men dead, and you're fixing to murder another. Wouldn't your wife be proud of you now?"

Haggard tried not to listen. He reached across with his left hand and drew the pistol from the holster on his right hip. "Here, Fristo." He pitched the pistol to Johnny's feet. "Now you've got a gun."

Johnny Fristo never looked at it. "If you want me dead, you'll have to shoot me like I am. I'll not fight you."

Haggard's teeth clamped tightly. He *had* to finish this thing, had to get it behind him forever. But he couldn't just shoot down a man who wouldn't fight back. "I'll trail you. I'll hound you till one day I catch you with a gun!"

"You'll never catch me with one. I intend to never touch

one as long as I live." Johnny's voice tightened. "Mister Haggard, I've lived in hell ever since that day your wife died. I've run from you, and I've died a thousand times. Ever since it happened I've been lookin' back over my shoulder, expectin' to see you come ridin' over a hill to kill me. And when I haven't seen *you* I've seen your wife. Now all of a sudden I'm more tired of runnin' than I am scared of dyin'.

"You want to kill me? Then do it right now, right here. If you don't kill me I'm goin' home where I belong. I'm goin' to tell the world what I've done and learn to live in spite of it. I'm through runnin', and I'm through bein' scared. So shoot me if you want to. But if you're ever goin' to do it, do it now!"

He waited a moment for Haggard to move. Then he turned his back and started walking slowly toward Speck Quitman's bay horse.

Haggard brought up the rifle. "Fristo, stop!"

Tessie cried, "No, Mister Haggard. If you shoot him now it'll be murder. I'll tell them all how it was. You won't be the hunter then. They'll be huntin' *you!*"

Haggard didn't want to do it this way, but a desperation was driving him. "Fristo, for God's sake turn and face me! Don't make me shoot you in the back!" He wanted to get it over with. He felt a revulsion against himself even as he aimed the rifle at Johnny Fristo's back. But he had to end it now.

From the corner of his eye he saw Tessie Barnett reach into her jacket. He heard the click of a hammer.

What Haggard did then was pure reflex. He swung the rifle toward the girl. In horror he realized what he was doing, but he was unable to stop the motion he had started. It was lightning swift and automatic. He tried to force himself to raise the muzzle as he squeezed the trigger. The saddlegun roared. The butt of it jarred his shoulder, sending a sharp pain slashing through the old wound.

He heard himself cry out in disbelief even before he lowered the rifle. He froze, horrified at what he had done.

The pistol dropped from the girl's hand. She stared at him in wide-eyed surprise, the color suddenly wiped out of her face. Her left hand lifted toward her shoulder, and she gasped.

Johnny Fristo shouted, "Tessie!" He took two long strides and grabbed her as she started to sag. "Tessie!"

Haggard came out of his shock. He threw the saddlegun away and stepped toward the girl. "My God! Oh my God!" Blood began to spread through the shoulder of her jacket. "I didn't mean to, girl. I couldn't stop it. I tried to raise the muzzle."

Ashen-faced, Johnny Fristo was easing her to the ground.

Haggard tried to get control of himself. "I didn't mean to. It was an accident."

He realized then how futile that sounded, and where he had heard it before. He put his hand over his face.

In a moment Johnny Fristo said husky-voiced, "It isn't so bad, Mister Haggard. You *did* raise that muzzle. You just kind of grazed her."

Haggard swayed. "I thought I'd killed her." He rubbed his hand over his face again. "How could I have lived with myself?"

Johnny Fristo held the girl tightly in his arms, relief in his eyes. In a little while he said, "Maybe you'd have learned—the way *I've* had to learn."

Reaction nearly got the best of Haggard then. He trembled in realization of what he had almost done. He had almost murdered a man. Had it not been for the girl, he would have shot Johnny Fristo in the back. And then he had almost killed the girl.

Cora, I meant it for you! All that I've done has been for you!

"Fristo," he said finally, "we'd better do something about that wound of hers. She's going to be sick."

Johnny Fristo's voice was tight and grim. "I reckon I can take care of her, Mister Haggard. If you've finished your business here, maybe you'd better just go."

Haggard flinched. Then, "Yes, I guess I'm finished."

He glanced at Speck Quitman lying on the muddy ground, and he looked once more at the girl. "I'm finished." He turned toward his horse. He thought of his pistol lying on the ground where he had tossed it at Fristo's feet. He thought of the smoking saddlegun he had dropped.

But he did not pause to pick them up. He hoped he never had to look at another gun.

Swinging into the saddle, he gave one quick glance to the violent Horsehead Crossing, then reined his horse eastward toward the cleft that was Castle Gap. His shoulders were bent, and his head was down.

He never looked back.

SHOTGUN

I

The hostler at the Two Forks Livery & Grain paused in his listless pitching of hay as he saw two riders move down from the crest of the limestone hill. Harley Mills rubbed a sleeve over his sweat-streaked face and speculated as to whether he was fixing to get some customers. Hot as it was, and seeing as the stable didn't belong to him, he had as soon not have business get out of hand. It hadn't lately. With this drought on, people were playing it close to their belts. They weren't coming to town when they didn't have to, because money was tight. He went back to his halfhearted efforts until one of the horses in the corral thrust its head over the top plank and nickered. An answer came from out on the road. Mills put the hayfork aside and stepped through the gate.

The two men were strangers to him. "Mornin'," he said. "From the looks of the dust on you, you've come a ways. I expect them horses could stand a feed."

No one replied. The hostler stared a moment at a rust-bearded man hunched on a streak-faced bay, then his reddish eyes were drawn to the taller rider, a gaunt, sallow-faced man who studied him in dark distrust. The hostler felt a sudden misgiving and wished they had passed him by.

The man said, "You're Harley Mills."

The hostler swallowed, puzzled. "That's right. But I don't know you. Or do I?"

The rider said, "You didn't used to swamp stables. Time I remember you, you was cowboyin' for old man Blair Bishop."

"Used to. He fired—we come to a partin', years ago."
Harley Mills searched the seldom-explored recesses of his
whiskey-dimmed memory. Something in those deep-set black
eyes reached him. His jaw dropped.

The rider responded with a hard grin. "Know me now,
don't you?"

Mills nodded, dry-mouthed and nervous.

The tall man said evenly, "Then I reckon we'll leave these
horses with you. Me and Owen, we're goin' to go wash some
of the dust down. You take good care of them now, Harley, you
hear? Good care." Mills could only nod. The tall rider swung
to the hoof-scuffed ground and shoved the leather reins into
Mills' numb hands. He reached back to his warbag tied behind
the saddle and fetched out a cartridge belt. He took his time
putting it on while the hostler stared at the .45 in fearful fascination.

The man asked, "Things ain't changed much in ten years,
have they?" Mills shook his head, a knot in his throat. The
rider queried, "Blair Bishop still figurin' hisself the big he-
coon?" The hostler's eyes gave him the answer and he added,
"Well, things can't stay the same forever. Come on, Owen,
we're past due for that drink."

Harley Mills barely glanced at the red-bearded Owen as he
took the second set of reins. He watched the tall man stride up
the street, looking at first one side of it, then the other. Mills
led the horses into the corral, slipped the saddles and bridles
off and gave the mounts a good bait of oats. His fingers
touched a saddlegun in a scabbard as he swung the tall man's
saddle onto a rack, and he jerked his hand back as if he had
touched a hot stove.

Done, he shut the corral gate behind him and struck a stiff

trot up the street to the courthouse. He almost ran down the county clerk as he rushed through the hall and into the door of the sheriff's office. He gestured excitedly at the graying ex-cowboy who looked up startled from his paperwork.

"It's Macy Modock," he blurted, gasping for breath. "Macy Modock is back in town."

The sheriff poked his head through the door of the Two Forks Bar & Billiard Emporium. Looking around quickly, he spotted the two men seated at a small table. He stared a moment, his heavy fingers gripping the doorjamb. At length the tall man spoke to him. "Come on in, Erly. Wondered how long it would take you."

Sheriff Erly Greenwood moved solemnly, his sun-browned face pinched into a frown. He halted two paces from the table, gave the red-bearded man a quick glance, then gazed at the other. "What you doin' here, Macy?"

"Havin' a drink. Share a little sunshine with us?"

"You was in the pen, Macy. How come you out?"

"I was turned out. Got all the proper papers right here in my pocket." He tapped his shirt. "Care to look?"

The sheriff nodded. "Maybe I better." His frown deepened, and his moustache worked a little as he read. "You didn't serve out all the term they gave you."

"Good behavior, Erly. Surprise you I could behave myself?"

"Damn sure does. I figured you'd get in a fight and some other prisoner would stomp your brains out. Hoped so, as a matter of fact."

"But here I am back in Two Forks, like a bad penny."

"I want you out, Macy. Have your drink, get your horses

fed, then ride on out. I don't want to ever see you again . . . not in this town, not in this country."

Macy Modock studied his half-finished drink, a little anger flaring before he quickly forced it back. "Erly, if you'll read that paper a little closer you'll see it says I done paid up all I owe. I can come and go as I please, here or anywhere else. And after all, I'm a property owner in Two Forks. I come to see about my property."

"After ten years? That old saloon you had is half fallen in. Kids broke out all the windowlights the first week you was gone. Wind took off most of the shingles, and rain has done the rest."

"The land it sets on is mine. I come to see after my property. There can't nobody quarrel over that."

Erly Greenwood shifted his weight from one foot to the other. His jaw worked, but it was a while before any words came out. "Macy, we've had a nice quiet town here the last few years."

Modock nodded. "You're puttin' on some belly."

"Just you listen to what I tell you. If you've come to settle up any old scores, I won't have it."

A hard smile came to Macy Modock's thin, cheek-sunken face. "I got no grudge against you, Erly. You just done what you was told. The boss man snapped his fingers and you jumped. That's how it always was, them days. He still snappin' his fingers, Erly?"

Anger leaped into Erly Greenwood's face. "He's a good man, Macy. Anything he done to you, he done for good cause. If you've come back to raise hell . . ."

Macy Modock glanced at his red-whiskered companion.

"Like I told you, Owen, things ain't really changed. The years go by, people get older, but everything else stays the same."

The sheriff's voice carried an edge. "I want you out of here."

"When I get ready. Who knows? I might take a notion to rebuild."

Conviction came to Erly Greenwood. "You've come to get even with him, Macy. Don't you try."

Modock grunted. "You was just a cowboy when Blair Bishop had that badge pinned on you. You're still just a cowboy."

"That's a matter of opinion. Don't you crowd me."

Modock stared at him coldly. "If there's trouble between me and Blair Bishop, it'll be when he comes huntin' me, not me huntin' him."

Macy Modock turned away from the sheriff. He poured himself a fresh drink and held it in his hand, admiring the amber color as if he had dismissed the sheriff from his mind. Greenwood turned on his heel and left.

The smile came back slowly to Modock's line-creased mouth. "And Blair Bishop *will* come huntin' me, Owen. I'll *make* him hunt me. And when I shoot him in self-defense, not even a Two Forks jury can touch me."

II

Blair Bishop lay on his back beneath the lacy shade of a tall mesquite tree and rubbed his right hand. Why was it, he wondered ruefully, that when a man got of an age where he ought to be able to stand back and breathe good, enjoy what he had built for himself and take the pleasure of turning responsibilities over to his sons, he had to start putting up with things like rheumatism? If it wasn't in his hands, it was in his hips. If it wasn't in his hips, it was in his legs. There wasn't a part of his body that hadn't at one time or another been fallen on, rolled over or kicked by a horse.

He looked past his big gray mount, tied to a limb of the mesquite. "See anything yet, Hez?"

Hez Northcutt, sitting on a leggy dun, stood in his stirrups and squinted. "Somebody's comin'. Looks like it's probably Finn bringin' old Clarence and that sorry crew of his."

Blair Bishop pushed slowly to his feet, wincing a little as a rheumatism pain lanced through his hip. Damn it, he wasn't too far past fifty. A man ought not to have to put up with this till he was old. He took off his hat and rubbed a sleeve across his sweaty brow, then pulled the spotted old Stetson down firmly over his thick gray hair. He squinted toward a wire corral full of bawling cows and restless calves, the dust rising thick and brown and drifting away in the hot west wind. This was a corral he used twice a year in branding the Double B onto his cattle that ranged this part of his land. But the cattle in the pen didn't wear that brand. They carried a C Bar. They were thin, their ribs showing through.

This had been a hard year for all cattle, Bishop's and everybody's. Beyond the corral, stretching for miles and disappearing into the shimmering heatwaves, lay grassland brown and short, thirsting for rain. The only thing green was the mesquite trees, which had deep roots and could outlast any other living plant except the cactus.

August had come, and it hadn't rained since March. Even that had been little more than a shower, following a dry winter. The brass of the summer sky showed little sign it would yield up rain for a long time yet.

Young Hez Northcutt slipped a pistol out of its holster and spun the cylinder, checking the load. "Hez," Blair spoke gently, "you can put that thing up. You'll have no use for it today."

Hez looked at him dubiously, plainly hoping. "You sure, Mister Bishop?"

"Clarence Cass will threaten and whine, but he wouldn't fight a blind jackrabbit. And them boys with him, they're just on a payroll. They won't bloody theirselves for the likes of Clarence."

The cowboy put the pistol away.

From behind the corral, where he had been looking over the cows, another young man rode up on a stocking-legged sorrel. He turned his gaze a moment toward the dust rising on the wagon road, then looked down regretfully at the broad-shouldered rancher. "Dad, we're treatin' old Clarence awful rough."

"Clarence Cass is a user, boy. He's like a parasite tick that gets on a cow's ear and sucks blood till it busts itself. He'll use

you for all he can get out of you and then complain because
you didn't give him more. Now and again you got to treat him
rough. It's the only way you can tell him no."

Allan Bishop drummed his hand against his saddle horn.
His voice was testy. "Still looks like we could've gone and
talked to him."

Blair Bishop put his hands on his hips and leaned back,
stretching, wishing he could work the rheumatism out. Impatience touched him, but he tried not to let it take over. Hell,
the boy wasn't but twenty-two. At that age, even Blair had still
harbored notions about the inherent goodness of all men,
goodness that would just naturally come out of its own accord
if you would but reason with them. Blair Bishop had eventually had all such notions stomped out of him. His son hadn't,
yet. Blair knew some men had it in them to do the right thing,
and some didn't. The latter you had just as well not waste your
time with. Minute you turned your back to them they would
be whittling on you.

Blair thought his son made a good picture sitting there in
the saddle. Strong shoulders, straight back, an earnest young
face and square chin. In a lot of ways he looked like Blair had
looked, maybe twenty-five years ago. Except Blair had never
been that handsome the best day he had ever lived. Allan had
inherited some looks from his mother's side.

And a little contrariness, too, Blair thought. It never come
from me; I never been contrary in my life.

"Allan, one of these days this place will belong to you and
your brother, Billy. He's too young yet to take on the tough
end of it, but you're not. You know as well as I do that we've
tried talkin' reason to old Clarence. Now it's your place to
stand with me when we *show* the old beggar."

Allan's jaw was set hard.

Blair shrugged, losing patience. "All right, let's talk straight. It ain't old Clarence you're thinkin' about; it's that girl of his. Forget it, boy."

"Anything that hurts the old man hurts Jessie."

"So it'll just have to hurt her. You better forget about her, boy. She won't bring you nothin' but problems."

"You don't know her."

"I know the old man. I never knew the girl's mother, but I expect if she was much she never would've married Clarence. I been a stockman all my life. I know that if you breed a scrubby stud to a scrubby mare, you get a scrubby colt."

Anger leaped into Allan's face and he pulled his horse away, turning his back on his father.

Blair clenched his teeth. Maybe he oughtn't to've talked so rough, but he knew no way except being blunt. Though people didn't always agree with Blair Bishop, they never misunderstood him. He watched silently as his son moved the sorrel down the wagon road to meet the oncoming riders.

Hez Northcutt said: "I'm about his age, Mister Bishop. Maybe *I* can talk to him."

Blair shook his head. The cowboy had a point, but Blair rejected it. Blair had long had an easy partnership with both his sons. He still had it with Billy, who was about fifteen. But somehow the last couple or three years he had lost that open-handed relationship with Allan. At a time when two men ought to draw closer together, why was it they tended instead to pull apart? Why was it a father had to become a stranger to a son?

"He'll come around," Blair told the cowboy. "Just stubborn. Got that from his mother, God rest her."

Blair's foreman, Finn Goforth, spurred ahead of the riders so he could reach Blair Bishop first. On the way he passed Allan, and he spoke to him. If Allan replied, Blair couldn't tell it. Finn, fortyish and graying, took a curious glance back over his shoulder at Allan. "I fetched them, Mister Bishop."

"How did Clarence take it?"

"Like we'd poured coal oil in his whiskey barrel. He's bellyached all the way over here. I'll let you listen to him now; I'm sick of it."

Blair said, "I didn't figure on listenin'. I figured on doin' the talkin'." He scowled, watching his son pull up even with the Cass girl. "I wish I could talk to *him*," he complained.

"Allan's full growed," Finn commented. "You've always taught him to think for himself. You wouldn't give three cents for him if he didn't."

"Sure, I want him to think for himself," Blair said. "But I want him to think like *I* do."

Skinny Clarence Cass rode in front, hunched over in his saddle like a loose sack of bran. A short way behind him came a girl on a sidesaddle, her long dark skirt covering all but the ankles of her leather boots. Bringing up the rear were two Cass cowboys, in no hurry at all. Blair Bishop watched his son talking to the girl. At the distance he couldn't hear, but Allan's gestures made it plain he was apologizing.

Blair could tell by the pinch of Clarence's shoulders that the little man was fit to chew a horseshoe up and spit it out. A humorless smile came to Blair as he took a few steps forward. "Howdy, Clarence."

Cass reined up, his face splotched red from anger and the heat of the ride. "Bishop . . ." He had a thin neck, wattled like a turkey's.

Blair found himself smiling a little broader. He was actually enjoying this confrontation, and the realization surprised him a little. "I do believe we've got some of your cattle in that pen yonder."

Clarence Cass's anger was too much for him to hold. "Blair, you're a harsh man and a poor neighbor. An occasional beef critter of mine strays over onto your land and you abuse them and me like you was the Lord Almighty. One of these days you'll overstep yourself."

"There's more than an occasional critter in that pen; count them yourself. There's somethin' past a hundred head. And they didn't drift. Finn and Hez found where they was pushed through a cut fence. There was footprints all around where that wire was pinched. Cass footprints, I'd judge."

Cass blustered. "You got no proof of that."

"A man needs proof for court. I ain't goin' to court. I'm holdin' court of my own." Bishop's smile was suddenly gone. "Now you listen to me, Clarence, because I'm only goin' to tell you once and I don't want you to ever say you didn't hear. Your country is overstocked; I tried to tell you that last spring. Now your cows have eaten off all your grass and drunk up most of your water. You're tryin' to get them through by havin' them take mine. But I got barely enough to see my own cattle through till fall, and if it don't rain by then I'm in trouble same as you are."

For a moment he was distracted by sight of Jessie Cass. He saw her open her mouth as if to speak, then drop her chin. Well, he thought, at least she's got the decency to feel shame over the stunt her father tried to pull. Blair saw his son reach out and take Jessie's hand and squeeze it, reassuring her. "Damn it, boy," he wanted to say, "we got to stick together on this thing." But he couldn't rebuke his son in the presence of Cass and his crew; it would demean them both. He would wait.

He turned back to Cass. "Now you listen to me, Clarence. You've had all the free grass and free water you're goin' to steal from the Bishops. From this day on, we're goin' to watch our fences close. Any of your cattle we find over here, we'll run till they're ready to drop. For ever dollar's worth of grass you steal, you'll lose five dollars worth of beef. We'll run them till there's no run left in them, then we'll put them back across the fence. Now, you think you can remember that?"

Clarence Cass looked as if he was about to suffer a stroke. He tried to argue, but he couldn't. He tried to curse, but only a half-intelligible gibberish came out. His Adam's apple bobbed up and down in anger and frustration, but he sat there and took Blair's tongue-lashing without striking back.

Blair glanced at the two Cass cowboys, not expecting any trouble from them. Cass didn't pay enough to get anything but his men's contempt. Blair suspected these cowboys would gleefully blab the whole story as quickly as they could get to town. Blair looked at them and jerked his chin toward the corrals. "Them's your boss's cows in there. Go drive them back where they belong."

The two rode over to the dusty corral and swung the wire gate open. One went in and pushed the bawling cattle out while the other waited beyond the gate to get them started in the right direction. Blair Bishop swung stiffly onto his big gray horse and stood ready to see that none of the cattle cut back or ran off. They were of a common strain, mostly Longhorn, a kind progressive ranchmen were trying to breed up and get rid of. He spotted a leggy, lanky C Bar bull in the bunch. That was one reason he hated so badly to see Cass' cattle come over here, apart from the fact that he was short of grass and water himself. Bishop's place was under fence now, and he was buying better bulls to upgrade his herd. Every time a C Bar bull came over, it meant some of Blair's cows were going to fetch up a scrubby calf.

Somehow Clarence Cass got his voice back and his courage up. "You're a greedy man, Blair Bishop. You're a selfish man and no neighbor at all."

Cass' opinion of Blair was of no concern except as a matter of idle curiosity. "How do you figure that, Clarence?"

"Anybody can tell you've had all the luck. It rained more on you than it did on me. You made more grass than I did. I don't expect the Lord really intended to favor you over me; He'd of wanted you to share."

"We both had the same rain, Clarence, and that was mighty little. Difference is, you abused your land. Now you're payin' for it. Let's don't bring the Lord in on the argument."

A little distance away, Allan Bishop sat on his horse near Jessie Cass. They weren't talking; Jessie was looking shamefacedly at the ground.

Clarence Cass said harshly, "Well, if you ain't sharin', then I ain't."

"What do you mean by that?"

"That boy of yours, he ain't goin' to have nothin' from my little girl. You tell him that. You tell him if he don't leave my little Jessie alone, I'll fill his britches with buckshot."

"Don't look to me like she wants to be left alone."

"You just tell him, Blair Bishop. I wouldn't have her marryin' into no family that won't help a neighbor."

"Marry?" Blair was startled. That was the first time the

thought of marriage had occurred to him. "Hell no, I wouldn't have it either. If my boy was to pull a stunt like that, I wouldn't let him *or* her back on the place."

Cass glared. "You don't think a Cass is good enough for your boy?"

"I sure as hell don't. Now, your cows are on their way, Clarence. I'd be much obliged if you'd go with them. And take your girl."

Cass started to ride off but paused for a last word. "Someday you'll be wishin' you had a good neighbor."

"I been wishin' that for years."

III

Blair Bishop sat there awhile, watching the cattle move slowly toward Cass country, the heavy dust clouding them over and hiding them much of the time. He pitied the cattle, because he knew they would find little to eat where they were going. But if he let them stay here, they would simply starve themselves and his own as well, for if Clarence Cass got by with a hundred, he would push in a hundred more. There was no bottom to the man's shabby greed.

Hez Northcutt said, "Want me to trail along and see that they all get there, Mister Bishop?"

"Yes, Hez. And take Allan with you."

Hez looked away. "Allan's gone. Rode off toward the house."

Irritated, Blair said, "All right, go ahead. Stay behind them and don't get into no trouble. Just let them know you're back there watchin' them. That'll be enough." He turned toward the foreman, black-moustached Finn Goforth. "Finn, you and me, we'd just as well go in."

Ahead of him a long way, he could see Allan riding alone, nursing his anger.

Marry! Blair clenched his big aching fist. Sure, that Jessie was a fetching-looking girl. He had wondered sometimes if Clarence was really her father or if perhaps her mother had had a secret. Jessie was better looking than what a boy was apt to find down on Silky Row in Two Forks. But to be foolish enough to marry her! Maybe he had been giving Allan too much benefit of the doubt.

Blair Bishop had always been a summer man. Cold weather had a way of creeping into his bones, but give him hot weather and he was in his element. The sweat broke free and easy, and it seemed to take out some of the rheumatism with it. He enjoyed the touch of the hot west wind against his face, cooling him as it reached through his sweat-streaked shirt. Pride always welled up in him when he rode along letting his gaze reach from north to south, east to west, knowing that everything he could see from here was his. Droughty though it was, he had earned every foot of it, and he wouldn't ever want to give it up to anyone but the sons for whom he and Elizabeth had struggled so long. Blair had taken trail-drive money to buy the first of his holdings a long time ago, leasing state and school land to go with it. In later years, as school lands went up for claiming, he had gotten his cowboys to homestead claims. They proved them up for the required three years. Then, if they didn't want to keep the land, they sold it to Blair for a profit. A few had kept, but most had sold. Gradually the Blair Bishop ranch had grown. And with it Blair Bishop had grown too, certain he had the world by the tail on a downhill pull.

What he hadn't counted on was running out of water. The whole south end of his place was dry. In a dozen places he had dug wells in hopes of finding underground water, but it wasn't there. He found only caliche and dry sand. On the south half of the place he depended upon dug surface tanks to catch and hold runoff water when it rained. Now all these tanks were dry but one. The cattle on his entire south ranch depended upon water from one place—the Black Bull Tank.

If he could just get through this drought, Blair had sworn,

he wouldn't be caught in this kind of trap again. He was going to have a lot more good tanks to catch and hold water. He would never again have all his chips riding on the Black Bull Tank.

He jerked his thumb to the right. "Let's go by and see how that new tank is comin', Finn."

They could see the dust before they saw the tank site. Blair heard the scrape of metal against hard-packed earth. A black dog came barking to meet them. A man shouted lustily, and a pair of mules trudged out onto a mound of fresh-turned earth, pulling a long-handled fresno loaded with dirt. A man in overalls jerked up the handle, flipping the fresno forward to dump its load upon the mound, the dust swirling about him. The mules moved quicker, relieved of the heavy burden. The man shouted at them again, pulling the lines and turning them back down into a broad basin he was laboriously hollowing out of the ground. He didn't see the horsemen until they rode up on the mound. He pulled the mules to a halt and wrapped the lines around the fresno handle. He stepped forward, taking off his hat and wiping sweat onto a dirt-crusted handkerchief he had used too many times already.

"Evenin', Mister Bishop. Evenin', Finn."

Blair Bishop nodded. "You're comin' along fine with it, Joe. That tank'll catch a right smart of water if it ever decides to rain again."

Joe Little shook his head. "A right smart. But it don't look much like rain today. I may be able to build a dozen more like this before we ever see a drop."

"I hope not. I wouldn't have nothin' left to pay you with, nor no cattle to drink out of it."

A boy walked across the basin carrying a jug wrapped in a

wet towsack to keep its contents cool. "You need a drink of water, Joe? Howdy, Finn. Howdy, Dad."

Blair looked at him without surprise. "Billy, I thought I sent you to the south line camp with a wagonload of supplies."

"I already been. On my way back I thought I'd stop and help Joe awhile."

Billy looked a lot like Allan, except he was several years younger and not yet as big. One thing about it, Clarence Cass didn't have any daughters Billy's size, so maybe that was one worry Blair wouldn't have to put up with as Billy got older.

When the water jug had been passed around, Blair swung down and stiffly dropped to one knee to feel the earth in the bottom of the basin. "You reckon this one'll hold water, Joe?"

"There's caliche under it, but I ain't got it scooped down to that depth yet. I think it'll be all right."

"I sure hope so. If there's one thing this drought has taught me, it's that it's as bad to run out of water as to run out of grass. This country tends to be shy of both."

Joe Little nodded. He was a small man with a grin as bright as all sunup, his teeth shining through thick brown dust and three weeks' growth of whiskers. "Me and my mules, we can't make it rain, Mister Bishop. But if it does rain, we can sure see to it that you're fixed to catch water."

"Fine, Joe. We'll be gettin' in. You comin', Billy?"

Billy Bishop shook his head. "I'll be in for supper. I still got time to spell Joe with his mules an hour or so first."

One thing about Blair's boys, Allan and Billy both . . . they weren't afraid of work. In Billy's case it wasn't so much that he liked building tanks as it was that he liked being around Joe Little. Joe had more good stories than a man could listen to in a year. Blair always figured he made most of them up as he went along, which was harmless enough if the listener realized that and didn't take them for more than they were worth. Billy needed to learn sooner or later that not everything he was told in this world was Bible-sworn truth.

Finn Goforth glanced back over his shoulder, watching Billy take over the fresno and bring it across the basin for a fresh, deep bite of earth. "Mister Bishop, you sure Joe Little is a good influence on that boy?"

"What do you mean?"

"Him bein' a reformed bank robber and all. At least, I hope he's reformed."

"He ain't given me no reason to doubt him. He works like hell."

"He's got reason to owe you. You was the only one around here would give him a job after he come home from the pen. But that don't mean he might not take a notion someday to try it all over again. It'd be a bad experience for Billy."

Blair shrugged. "I don't think Joe would ever do that, not anymore. Anyway, a boy's got to learn for himself that it's not all rosy the way they write it in books. He's got to learn that people will lie to you, steal from you, cheat you . . . maybe even kill you. I don't think he'll learn that from Joe, except maybe the lyin' part, and Joe's lies don't mean any harm."

When they reached the barn at headquarters, Blair found Allan sitting in the shade of the building patching a stirrup leather. Blair unsaddled his big gray and watched a moment as the animal rolled in the dust, ridding itself of the saddle's itch. Blair walked into the barn and flung his saddle up onto its place on the rack, hooked the bridle over the horn and dropped the wet blanket over it all. He walked back out and stood a moment in silence, waiting for Allan to say something. Allan didn't look at him.

"Son, I'll ask Chaco to get supper fixed a little early. I'm hungry as a wolf."

Allan only glanced at him, then went back to his work. "I'll eat at the bunkhouse with the boys tonight," he said tightly.

Blair rubbed his stiff, aching right hand. "Boy, what we done today, we done out of necessity. I told you. You know that old man."

"You don't have to tell me anything about Clarence Cass."

"What goes for him goes for his kin."

Allan looked his father in the eye. "I'll agree with everything you say about Clarence. But you don't know nothin' at all about Jessie."

"Know the bull, and you know the calf." Blair turned slowly, his hip hurting a little, giving him a slight limp as he strode toward the white frame house with the tall narrow windows that he had built for Elizabeth after so many years of dugouts and picket shacks. She hadn't lived long enough to see the first coat of paint start to peel.

He saw a man sitting on the front gallery, and he paused a moment to squint. Blair couldn't recognize him at the distance, but he didn't quicken his pace. He had found long ago that good news would keep, and bad news didn't get any better for rushing it. This could be a cattle buyer, which would be good news, or it could be the tax collector.

He found it was neither. "Howdy, Erly," Blair said as he mounted the steps. "How's the high sheriff?"

Erly Greenwood had pushed up from the rawhide-bottomed straight chair and stood at the top of the steps, hand outstretched. "Evenin', Blair. How's yourself?"

"Younger than ever, except for a little rheumatism. You ain't reached that stage in life yet." He studied the sheriff with pleasure. "You're lookin' good, Erly. That Alice must be feedin' you well. Been a long time since you been out our way. This calls for a drink." He pushed open the carved front door with its oval glass and shouted, "Chaco, bring us a bottle out here."

Chaco Martinez fetched it. Blair offered it to Erly, but the sheriff motioned for Blair to take first drink. Blair did. He sighed in pleasure, wiping his sleeve across his mouth. "Some things fade as the years go by. Others just get better. Good whiskey and good friends, that's two things that always pleasure a man." He watched Erly tilt the bottle, then dropped his dirty hat on the floor and settled into the rocking chair he kept on the gallery for enjoying the evening breeze. "Chaco'll have supper ready directly. Looks like if you don't stay the night, I'm liable to have to eat by myself."

"I'll stay. I'd be half the night gettin' back to town."

Blair noticed that the warmth faded from the sheriff's face, and a worried frown replaced it. Blair considered. No, it wasn't election year; something else must be eating on him. Blair said, "We miss you out here, Erly. I've got good help, mind you, but I don't reckon there's ever been a better cowboy on this place than you was. Before you started puttin' on weight, that is."

Erly nodded. "I suppose I was a fair to middlin' hand. Times, I wish I was cowboyin' again. Seemed like then I always knew what to do."

"And now you don't?"

Erly shook his head. "Right now I'm in the water up to my neck, and it's still risin'. I got to tell an old friend some bad news, and I also got to tell him there's not a damn thing I can do."

"You talkin' about me, Erly?"

"You, Blair. I come to tell you Macy Modock is back."

Blair Bishop stopped rocking the chair. He sat in silence a minute or two, remembering, oblivious to the rising breeze riffling his thick gray hair. "You seen him, Erly?"

"Seen him and talked to him. Acts like he's back to stay." While Blair chewed his lip, the sheriff said, "I told him to keep right on movin', but I got no authority to make him do it. He's out free and legal. Long's I don't catch him breakin' the law, there's not a thing I can do about him, accordin' to the statutes." He paused. "There's a thing or two I could do *outside* of the statutes. With a man like Modock, I don't think there's many would criticize me."

"What could you do?"

"A man with his record, it'd be easy to trump up somethin' on him."

"You wouldn't want to do that, Erly."

"But I'd do it if you asked me to."

Blair Bishop passed the bottle to him again. "You know I wouldn't ask you. I wouldn't want you to."

"I didn't figure you would. So that leaves Modock sittin' there and us sittin' here, wonderin' what he's got on his mind."

"He didn't give you no idea?"

"Blair, he swore ten years ago that you'd pay for havin' him put away. He had a real good system goin' for him . . . a busy saloon, a cattle-runnin' business, even a little bit of bank robbery on the side. Hadn't been for you, I never could've nailed him. It was you that hired the special prosecutor and run all his sidekicks out of the country so the jury could get up courage to convict him."

"There's not much he could do except come right out and kill me. I doubt that he cares to hang."

"He wouldn't of come back here if he didn't have somethin' on his mind. He's still got a little money, Blair. It's been settin' in a bank drawin' interest all the time he's been gone. He could go someplace he wasn't known and set himself up decent. But he's come back here."

Blair Bishop scowled, remembering how it had been before Macy Modock was sent away. "So it leaves us out on the end of the limb."

"And Macy Modock with a saw in his hand."

Blair looked at the bottle, decided he didn't want another drink and offered it to Erly. The sheriff shook his head. Blair said, "Well, I don't intend to sit here and sweat, wonderin' about him. I'll go back to town with you in the mornin'. I'll talk to him myself."

The sheriff fretted. "I don't know if that's a good idea. It might come to a shootin'."

"Not if I don't take a gun with me." He held up his rheumatic right hand. "Look at that. Most times I can't even hold a pistol anymore, much less shoot one."

"It puts you at a bad disadvantage, Blair."

"But it puts him there too. He can't shoot a man that ain't got a gun and couldn't use one if he had it. He didn't come out after ten years in the pen rarin' to go right back."

They dismissed Macy Modock from conversation, but he remained on both their minds during the long periods of silence between the subjects they drummed up to talk about.

Billy Bishop came home finally, face and clothes covered with dust from the tank-building job. Chaco Martinez met him at the gallery and made him strip off the clothes right there and walk around back to wash before he came into the house. That, Blair thought, was what Elizabeth would have done had she lived. Chaco, cranky but competent, was no substitute for a wife and mother, though without him Blair didn't know how he would have managed the house and the care of two boys.

Blair kept looking for Allan to come up from the bunk-house, but his older son never showed. Finally he said to Billy, "Why don't you go tell your brother it's time for him to go to bed?"

Billy Bishop avoided his father's eyes. "He's not here, Dad." Pressed, he added, "He was saddlin' up a horse when I came in. Said he had an errand to run. I don't figure you sent him on any errand, Dad."

Blair shook his head, for both he and Billy knew where Allan had gone. Billy held his silence awhile, then put in, "Dad, maybe you ought to get to know Jessie better. Maybe she's not as bad as you think."

"I'm not sayin' she's bad, son. I'm just sayin' she was foaled in a poor stable."

There never was a time that Blair Bishop could walk into this house without Elizabeth crossing his mind. Times like this he missed her most of all. Maybe a mother could have talked to a son in a way a father couldn't.

IV

He was up before daylight next morning. He met his sons and Erly Greenwood in the kitchen, where Chaco Martinez was frying up steak for breakfast, humming a Mexican song about the dark ties between love and death. Blair hadn't slept much, and he guessed his face showed it. He fastened his gaze on Allan. "Son, you went someplace last night."

"Yes, sir, I did."

"You know I don't want you goin' there no more."

"Dad, I've never argued with you. I don't intend to. So that's one subject I just don't want to talk to you about."

"We *will* talk about it."

"*You* can. I'm not goin' to listen." Allan got up and started toward the door. Blair waited until Allan had his hand on the doorknob. He called, "Come on back, boy, and eat your breakfast. We'll talk about it another time."

Blair Bishop hadn't lost many battles in his life. He had an uneasy feeling he was going to lose this one. Sure, he could do one thing; he could flat forbid Allan ever to go to the Cass place again. And likely as not Allan would pack up and leave the ranch, then do what he damn well pleased. That, Blair knew, was what *he* would have done if the same situation had occurred twenty-five or thirty years ago. But of course it hadn't. Elizabeth had been one thing. A daughter of Clarence Cass was another.

The sheriff had not mentioned Macy Modock to Blair's sons or to Chaco, who would quickly blab it. Blair made a point to say nothing. Time enough for that after he had a chance to meet Modock face to face.

He sensed that people were watching him as he rode into Two Forks with Erly Greenwood. The word about Modock must have gotten around by now. Those people who had lived here ten years ago wouldn't have any trouble remembering. The rest had no doubt heard enough. He rode through town, tying up beside Erly at a hitchrack in front of the courthouse. The hostler from the Two Forks Livery & Grain came shuffling toward them as fast as he could move without breaking into a trot.

"Mornin', Mister Bishop. Reckon Erly's told you?"

Blair nodded. "He told me."

"It was me that seen Macy first, Mister Bishop. I knowed he meant trouble, and I went straight to the sheriff. I knowed that was what you'd of wanted me to do, and I done it."

Blair decided Harley Mills was casting around for some kind of reward. He also knew that anything he gave Harley would wind up being spent or traded for whiskey. Blair had given Harley a good chance once and had seen him drink it up. Blair Bishop was not much given to second chances. "Thanks, Harley. Where's Macy at?"

"A little while ago he was settin' in the Bar & Billiard Emporium. Had a redheaded feller with him. They come to town together. They both got guns on." The hostler had glanced at Blair's hip and saw no pistol there. He began to realize Blair didn't intend to give him anything, and he showed his disappointment.

"All right, Harley." Blair couldn't tell whether Harley was concerned about him or just wanting to be sure he saw the whole show. He suspected the latter. He looked a moment toward the saloon, dreading.

"Well, Erly, I guess this is what I come for."

"I'm goin' with you."

"No, you're not. I told you, you bein' there with a gun— or even that badge—might trigger somethin' off."

"What if he shoots you, Blair?"

Blair Bishop came close to making a dry smile. "Then I reckon you can come on over."

The ride into town had stiffened Blair's legs, and he walked slowly, that cursed limp plaguing him. Damn it, why couldn't a man go into his autumn years with a little dignity? His mouth went dry as he neared the building. Blair Bishop had never feared any man, and he didn't fear Macy Modock. But he disliked trouble and would ride around it when he could. Whether this meeting meant trouble or not, he knew it was a cinch to be unpleasant. He'd already had enough unpleasantness to do him for a lifetime.

The heavy bartender stepped out the front door and moved to meet him. His long moustaches drooped, and his bushy eyebrows were knitted in concern. "Mister Bishop, you know who's in there?"

Blair nodded. "I know."

"You and me been friends a long time, Mister Bishop. I don't want nothin' happenin' to you in my bar."

"Nothin's fixin' to happen. I'm goin' to talk to him, is all."

"He's been settin' there like he was waitin' for somethin'. You, maybe. I don't like the feel of it."

"If he's waitin' for me, there's no use me puttin' things off."

"You ain't packin' no gun, Mister Bishop, but he is. And so's that mean-eyed one he's got with him. They could kill you in a second."

"That's how come I left my gun at home. There won't be no trouble."

The bartender glanced at the door. "All right, Mister Bishop. But I got my shotgun behind the bar, loaded and cocked. If that Modock makes one bad move, I'll let him have both barrels."

Blair nodded his thanks. He stepped up onto the little wooden porch and through the open door. He sensed the bartender coming in behind him and moving to his place behind the bar. Blair Bishop blinked, then saw three men seated at a little table. He gave the red-bearded one a brief glance and pegged him for a gunfighter. That cinched it; Modock hadn't come here looking for sunshine and pretty songs. He turned to the tall, lanky man with the black eyes and unlighted cigar.

"Macy. Been a long time."

"Ten years, two months and twenty-one days. I counted them every one."

It relieved Blair that Macy made no move to shake hands, for Blair had no intention of doing it. He noted that the ten years had been hard on Macy Modock. The man seemed to have aged twenty since he had left here. He was thinner, his cheeks sunken in, his shoulders a little drooped. Macy's hair was shorter than he used to wear it . . . prison cut, Blair figured. And it was sprinkled with gray where once it had been coal black. But his eyes hadn't changed. They had always looked hard as steel. They were framed in darker circles now than ever before, and if anything, they were harder.

Modock motioned toward the red-bearded man. "This here is Owen Darby. We was partners, you might say, back in *school*. We worked on the same pile of rocks."

Blair nodded. That fit his first appraisal.

Modock motioned toward a thin, black-suited little man on the other side of him. "Bishop, you ain't yet said good mornin' to Judge Quincy."

Blair said, "I *never* say good mornin' to Judge Quincy."

The little man's lip turned down in an angry scowl. In Bishop's view, Quincy was a cheap, scheming lawyer who made his living defending the indefensible and hunting for loopholes in the statutes. He had never been a judge in his life, and he never would be one unless the government went plumb to hell. Someone had hung the name on him as a cheap saloon joke, and it had stuck to him ever since. Folks said "Judge" with a bit of a snicker.

Modock said, "I'll grant you the judge didn't have much luck defendin' me, but then he was up against the best legal talent that a rich man's money could buy. He's had pretty good luck in some other cases, though. I count him as a friend."

Every man to his own kind, Blair thought. "I come to town because I figured you and me might have somethin' to talk about, Macy. Do we?"

"I don't know. What do you think?" Modock seemed to sense that he held all the cards. "Bothers you, don't it, me bein' here?"

"Like knowin' there's a rattlesnake under my porch and not bein' able to get at him. It bothers me that they ever let you out. It'd bother me knowin' you was anyplace, Macy, except in jail. But you're here, and I want to know what you're plannin' to do."

Modock took the cigar from his mouth, eyeing Blair Bishop levelly, his own eyes unreadable. "Can't say that I've made up my mind. If I do, maybe I'll let you know."

"If you got any notions about gettin' even with me, Macy, you better forget them. What I done to you, you had comin' in spades. I don't want trouble with you, but I won't stand still for no foolishness."

Macy dipped the end of his cigar in his whiskey glass, soaked it a moment, then shoved it back into his mouth. "Now, what do you think I might do to you, Bishop? You was a big man before, and you're bigger now. Got you a fine ranch, lots of cattle. And me, what have I got to show for all that time? Ten years cut out of my life, cut out of me the way you'd rip the guts out of a catfish."

"You've still got a little money, Macy, from what I hear. And you still got time. You could do a right smart for yourself if you was of a mind to."

Macy grinned, his teeth clamped on the cold cigar. "And I will, Bishop; you can just bet I will."

Blair felt his hackles rise. "You'd do better someplace else. Take your money and go where they don't know you."

"But I couldn't collect what's owed me if I was to go someplace else. And I'm figurin' on collectin', Bishop. From you, most of all." He used the cigar as a pointer, jabbing it toward Blair. "I had ten years to study about you, and believe me I done a lot of thinkin'. For a long time if I'd of had the chance, I'd of just come back and shot you dead wherever I found you. But gradually it come to me that there's better ways of killin' a man than shootin' him. There's ways to kill him off an inch at a time till there's nothin' left of him but a little dab of cold sweat. I decided that's what I'd do to you, Bishop, just whittle away at you.

"I see you ain't wearin' a gun. Probably haven't in years. But before I'm done, you'll wear one. Maybe in the end you'll get so desperate you'll come gunnin' after me and I can finish the job nice and legal, in self-defense."

Color surged into Bishop's face. His arthritic right hand convulsed. There had been a time if anyone had talked to him like that he would have shot him on the spot. But that had been a long time ago, before the years mellowed him, and before an accumulation of old pains and injuries half crippled him. He said quietly, "I'm sorry it's this way, Macy. I expected it would be, but I'm sorry just the same." He turned, his big Mexican spurs jingling as he limped heavily across the pine floor and out onto the porch. A strong dread rose up in him, and a helplessness.

He walked across the street to where the sheriff waited beside the tied horses. Bishop didn't speak, so Erly Greenwood did.

"Talkin' to him didn't help, did it?"

Bishop shook his head. "The hate's as strong as it ever was."

The sheriff suggested, "What I told you yesterday still goes. Just say the word and I'll trump up somethin'."

"It'd never set right with you, Erly, or with me. No, we'll just wait, and we'll hope. Sooner or later he'll make a mistake."

"By that time," said Greenwood, "you could be dead."

Modock got up from his chair and walked to the door to watch Blair Bishop limp across the street. He saw him in conversation with the sheriff. Modock chewed the cigar savagely, his hard eyes glittering with the pent-up hatred of ten hellish years.

The red-whiskered Owen Darby spat at a brass bowl and missed. "You got your stomach churnin', Macy. I can hear it from where I sit. If I hated a man that much, I'd just shoot him and be done with it."

Modock glanced around at the heavy bartender and decided to ignore him. He didn't give a damn what a bartender thought. "Did you ever get so hungry for somethin', Owen, that when you finally got it you ate it slow and spaced it out to make it last as long as you could?" When Darby shook his head, Modock said, "No, I expect you never did, so you can't begin to understand. *You* kill a man quick, the way a wolf does. If it's a man like Bishop, I'd rather do it slow and play with him awhile, like a cat."

A young woman walked by in the street. From the scarlet hue of her crinolines, Modock surmised she might come from down on Silky Row. "Talk about hungry . . . a man don't know how long ten years can be when he never feels the touch of a woman, never hears the laugh in a woman's voice. That's somethin' else Blair Bishop owes me for . . . ten years without a woman." He glanced at the bartender. "Things still alive on Silky Row, the way they used to be?"

The bartender made no attempt to hide his dislike. "Just about. But I doubt *you're* as alive as you used to be."

Modock grunted and walked back to the table. He stared at the little lawyer. "Judge, how long you think it'll take you to go through all them deeds of Bishop's?"

Quincy sat rigid, ill at ease in the company of these two. "Some time. And it'll require some money too. A task like this is not undertaken lightly."

"You'll get your money; I promised you that. Find me the right flaws in them deeds and you'll get a lot *more* money." He leaned over the table. "Let me down and you'll eat every law book in your office, one at a time."

"Mister Modock, you have no right . . ."

Modock punched his finger into Quincy's breastbone hard enough to bring pain. "I don't give a damn about rights. You just do what I tell you!"

V

Joe Little put the can of tomatoes on the ground, opened the blade of his pocketknife and punched a hole through the tin. He punched a second at a right angle, the ends of the slits coming together in a V. He pushed the cut part down with his thumb and offered the can to Billy Bishop. Billy, trained to defer to his elders, shook his head. "You first."

Little tilted the can up and took a long swallow. He passed it over to Billy. "Boy," he said, "you got to quit bringin' me stuff like this out of your old daddy's pantry. He's furnishin' me grub enough."

"Not tomatoes or peaches or stuff like that. Anyway, he can afford a can of somethin' now and then."

"I don't know. If it don't rain pretty soon, he might not be able to buy nothin'. You got to quit it, Billy. That's stealin'."

"It's not stealin' when you take it out of your own house. That's not like stealin' cattle, or takin' from a bank, or . . ." He broke off short, realizing he was edging into deep water. "Anyway, Dad knows about it. He's seen me. And you deserve somethin' special once in a while. This is hard work, buildin' tanks."

Joe Little studied the can awhile in silence. "Did I ever tell you, boy, about the time I shared a can of tomatoes with John Wesley Hardin?"

Billy smiled. "Just happens you did. Only, the last time you said it was Billy the Kid."

Joe Little frowned. "I believe you're right. It *was* Billy the

Kid. What I shared with Wes Hardin was a pot of coffee."

Joe's black dog set in to barking and trotted across the newly dug basin. Joe stood up to look. He almost dropped the can. He said something under his breath, his eyes going wide.

Billy jumped to his feet. "What is it, Joe?" Joe didn't reply, so Billy looked for himself. A hundred yards away came two men on horseback. They were strangers to Billy.

Joe said: "If I didn't know better, I'd swear that was Macy Modock, but he's in jail."

Billy shook his head. "No, he's out. You hadn't heard?"

"I ain't heard nothin' but a hooty owl and you in a month of Sundays."

"They been talkin' a little around the ranch. They don't say much that I can hear. I remember there was hard feelin's once between him and Dad. Is he back to make trouble, Joe?"

"I don't know, boy." Joe Little shook his head. "Anywhere he's at, he's goin' to make trouble." He sagged a bit.

Billy looked at him in surprise. "You know Macy Modock?"

"I know him, boy. I've stretched the truth a mite about some of them other fellers, but I sure as hell know Macy Modock. We was . . . in *school* together. Shared a room awhile, so to speak."

"You mean you was cellmates?"

Joe Little dropped any pretense. "We was cellmates. For me, it was like bein' denned up with a rattler."

Macy Modock and Owen Darby eased their horses down into the basin and rode across to where Little and Billy stood on the fresh-made dump. Modock lifted his hand and made a dim sort of smile. "Howdy, Joe. Folks in town told me you was workin' out here."

Joe looked at first one man, then the other, worry creasing his dust-powdered face. "Folks in town talk too much. How do, Macy, Darby . . ." There was no greeting in his voice. The black dog sniffed suspiciously around the strange horses and backed off, as if deciding that if his master didn't like the company, he didn't either. He barked again from a careful distance.

Macy Modock stared at Billy. "I'd judge by the looks that this boy would be a Bishop. Howdy, boy."

Billy Bishop had been raised to be civil right up to the moment he swung his fist. "How do, Mister Modock."

Modock's attention stayed with Billy. "I swear, he sure does favor his old daddy. I bet that old man sets a heap of store in you, don't he, boy?"

Joe Little took that for an implied threat. "Macy, this boy is a friend of mine. You leave him alone."

"I'm a friend of yours too, Joe."

"That all depends, Macy. It all depends."

Modock watched the boy a minute longer, then said, "Button, I got somethin' to discuss with my old friend Joe Little. Don't you reckon you could find you somethin' to do while we talk? Go work them mules and that fresno, maybe."

Billy looked uncertainly at Joe. Joe silently motioned with his chin for him to go ahead. Reluctantly Billy walked down into the basin where the mules waited patiently, in no hurry to work again. Joe Little moved off of the dump on the side away from the wind so the dust wouldn't reach him. Modock and Owen Darby followed him a-horseback. Joe turned and said curtly, "You said you wanted to talk. I don't see we got anything to talk about, but go ahead."

"Maybe we *ain't* got anything to talk about, but I thought I'd come see for myself if it was true what I heard . . . that Joe

Little was sweatin' hisself into the ground for Blair Bishop."

"I'm bein' paid a fair wage. I got over two hundred dollars in the bank. That's more money than I ever had in my life before . . . legally."

"Two hundred dollars? Why, friend, you made that much money once in an hour."

"I said legally."

"If I remember right, Blair Bishop helped put you away, same as he done me."

"I had it comin'. I been ashamed ever since for what I done."

Modock's eyes narrowed. "Joe, I thought you had more in you. That black dog of yours yonder . . . if a man was to take a double of a rope to him, he'd tuck his tail between his legs and run. And it looks to me like that's just what you done too. You've tucked your tail."

"I'm doin' honest work and earnin' an honest dollar."

"Workin' for a man who helped send you to jail. A man who probably despises you and'd tell you so if he didn't need you to bend your back for him."

Fear began to touch Joe Little, because he knew this pair was up to something, and he sensed they had a place in it for him. Otherwise they wouldn't have come out here. Macy Modock was not a man to waste his time on people he couldn't use. "Macy, if you got any notions that include me, forget it. I'm stayin' right where I'm at."

"Followin' a plow or a fresno, lookin' a pair of mules in the rump all day? I thought you had more ambition."

"I have. Someday it'll be my own mules, my own place."

"But still mules. You're a damn fool, Joe Little. I'm sorry we wasted our time."

"I'm sorry too. I'd of been happier if I'd never laid eyes on you again the rest of my life."

Anger came into Modock's dark-circled eyes. "Next time you're kissin' Blair Bishop's boots, remember we offered you a chance to get out. Goodbye, Joe. We'll see you in hell."

"Keep a place warm for me. You'll probably get there before I do."

Macy Modock drew rein and took a long look down toward the headquarters of the Clarence Cass place. "That's a greasy-sack outfit if ever I seen one," he muttered to Owen Darby. "A man can't have no pride to live in a place like that when he could do better." The house was small and plain, evidently put up by somebody who didn't know much about carpentering and didn't learn much on the job. It showed no evidence that it had ever known paint. The corrals were of brush, mostly, some of the fences leaning. One wild bull could have torn the whole thing out by the roots.

"Fits the rest of his country," Darby put in. "Whole place looks like it'd been sheeped into the ground."

"Not sheep," Modock said. "Just too many cattle. Dry weather come, the place couldn't feed them all."

A thin, sharp-hipped Longhorn steer eyed the riders warily and clattered off into a motte of live oaks, his tail high. He looked weak enough to fall if he tried to run very hard. Modock scowled. "I remember this place the way it used to be. Cass didn't have it then. We stole some pretty good cows off of the old boy who did."

"How come he left?"

"Went broke. They split up his country and sold it off to people like this Cass."

"Maybe you helped break him."

"Maybe. It was his lookout, not mine. It's every man's place to take care of hisself. If he can't do it, he ain't got no sympathy comin'." Modock took a long sweeping look over the land. "If it'd rain some, I could make a good place out of this, Owen . . . if it was mine. And maybe before we're through, it'll *be* mine."

They rode up to the barn first, where Modock saw a man lounging in the shade, a rawhide chair tilted against the wall. It seemed to Modock that the wall might have had a little lean to it, but he wasn't sure. He wouldn't be surprised, judging by the rest of the outfit. He spotted another man asleep farther out, under a wooden water tank that stood on a platform beside a cypress-vaned windmill. "Evenin'. We're lookin' for Clarence Cass."

The cowboy jerked awake, pushing the hat back out of his face and blinking sleepily. Modock had to repeat. The cowboy pointed. "He's up at the house. Clarence, he usually takes him a little nap in the heat of the day."

That didn't surprise Modock either. From the looks of the place, he would judge that nap ran from noon till about sundown.

Owen Darby said, "If you *was* to take over this place, I don't know what you'd want with it."

"It could be fixed up. Needs some changes made. Them lazy cowboys is the first thing I'd get rid of."

Riding toward the small house, Modock caught a quick glimpse of a young woman out back, hanging clothes on a sagging wire. He glanced at Darby in surprise. Nobody had mentioned to him about a girl out here. He turned back for a second look at her, but she had disappeared quickly into the house. "Owen," he said quietly, "place already looks better."

He swung down and looped his leather reins over a fence picket. Darby took his time, following behind as Modock strode up to the house, narrowed eyes sweeping everything in sight. The door was wide open, but Modock thought it best to observe the amenities, for now. He knocked on the door frame.

From inside, he could hear the woman's voice, speaking low, and he could hear a sleepy, confused grumbling. Broke up the old man's nap, he knew. Presently Clarence Cass trudged to the door, trying to shove his shirttail into his waistband without bothering to unbutton his britches. He blinked at Modock without recognition. "You-all lookin' for somebody?"

Modock spoke with what pleasantness he was able to muster. "Yes, sir, we're lookin' for Clarence Cass, the owner of this place. You'd be him, I judge."

"Yes, sir, reckon I would."

"We'd be right favored if we could have a drink of cool water out of your cistern, sir. Then we'd like to talk some business with you."

"With me?" Cass, not completely over his nap, blinked uncertainly. "Sure, the cistern's right yonder. You-all cattle buyers?"

"No, sir."

"Then what business you got with me?"

Modock walked over to the cistern and turned the handle to lower the bucket into the well. He cranked it up again, conscious that Cass was waking rapidly now, and trailing him in his socks. He took his time about drinking the water, then passing it on to Darby, letting the old man's curiosity build. Cass repeated, "What's this business you was talkin' about?"

Modock turned to face him and motioned that they ought

to go over and sit down in the shade. It was Cass' place, but already Modock was beginning to call the turn. "Mister Cass, I understand you had some difficulty the other day with Blair Bishop."

Cass for a moment eyed him with suspicion. "I'd say that was my business. Anyway, I ain't finished with Blair Bishop yet."

Modock nodded. "That's why we came. I'm Macy Modock. This here is my friend Owen Darby."

Realization came, and Cass' mouth went open. "Modock! Didn't know you was anywheres around. I've heard about you."

"Mostly lies, I expect, sir. There was a time I had a standin' in Two Forks . . . in this whole country. It was taken away from me by schemers and liars. Oh, I'll grant you, Mister Cass, I sure ain't no preacher. I expect when I get to the Pearly Gates, it'll take some talkin' to get me through. But I'm not near what some have painted me. Some like Blair Bishop . . ." He paused. "You should know, sir. I understand he's maligned you too."

Cass nodded vigorously. "One of these days my patience'll wear thin."

Modock reached into his pocket and took out a couple of cigars, handing one to Cass, biting into the other himself. "I thought maybe it already had. I thought you might be ready to do somethin' about it."

"I will. One of these days I damn sure will."

"It could be one day *soon,* if you was of a mind. Some folks in town, they told me you'd be a real good man for me to get together with. They said you was a man who knew what he wanted and wasn't afraid."

Cass' vanity was quickly touched. "Who was it said that?"

"Some folks." Modock took out a match but didn't light the cigar. He simply chewed it while his narrowed eyes studied Clarence Cass. Feeling he had lucked upon a sympathetic ear, Cass began to unburden himself of all the injuries he had suffered at the hands of the rich and overbearing Blair Bishop. Modock listened attentively, nodding every so often and speaking softly, "That's just the way it was done to me."

Owen Darby couldn't listen to it. Scowling, he walked off to poke around the place for himself.

At length Cass ran down, and Modock said, "I can tell you've got a just grievance, my friend. And I can tell that the folks in town was right. You're the man I been lookin' for."

Cass reached down and pulled up a saggy sock. "What did you have in mind for me to do?"

"Just string along with me . . . back me up in whatever I say. We'll get even with Blair Bishop."

A sudden worry tugged in Cass' face. "But how? You ain't figurin' on killin' nobody, are you?"

"Killin'? The thought never once crossed my mind. I'd sooner scrub floors in the meanest dive in town than to kill somebody. No, what I got in mind will give us a chance to whittle Blair Bishop down, to break him piece by piece. You'll be in on it; you'll have the satisfaction. What's more, you'll have a chance to pick up some of the pieces when they fall. You'd like to have part of the Bishop ranch, wouldn't you, Mister Cass? You got a chance to get it."

"The Bishop ranch." A glow came into Cass' eyes, and he began rubbing his knuckles, enjoying the thought of it. "He's always lorded it over me, Blair Bishop has. He's got a better country, had better rain, always had all the luck when there's been others just as deservin' that the Almighty has passed by and left needful. It'd sure pleasure me . . ." He broke into a crooked grin. Modock guessed that was a sight few people had ever seen. Cass said, "I'm with you, Mister Modock. What'll I do?"

"First off, you'll let it be known around that me and Owen, we're on a deal to buy in as partners with you."

Cass' eyebrows raised. "You ain't, are you?"

"Of course not. There won't be no papers signed. Later on you can say we backed out by mutual consent. But we need a base to operate from, a reason for some of the things I figure to do. You with us, friend?"

"*With* you, Mister Modock."

They shook hands, and Owen Darby came back. Modock said, "See there, Owen, I told you this was the man."

Clarence Cass straightened his bent shoulders and stood every bit of five and a half feet tall. "I'm proud you come, Macy. I never been one to brag; I always been one to keep my silence. Still waters runs the deepest, I've always thought."

"Truer words was never spoke, partner."

Cass turned toward the house and called: "Jessie! I want you to put a pot of coffee on for these men." The girl came hesitantly to the door. Modock stared, his dark eyes widening for a moment. She was seventeen, maybe eighteen, eyes blue, face slender and nice-featured, hair the soft brown of a good Morgan colt. And her figure . . . she was coming into the full bloom of womanhood. Modock kept staring, the pulse quickening in him. He'd visited down on Silky Row a little since he had been back in Two Forks, but that was tarnished merchandise. This, he sensed, was fresh goods, untried, unspoiled.

Cass introduced the girl to the two men. "Girl," he said,

"Macy and Owen here, they're talkin' about goin' in as partners with us. I want you to fix them some coffee." He recon-
sidered. "No, by Godfrey, this calls for somethin' better than
coffee. This calls for whiskey, and I got a new bottle still un-
corked."

Modock took the bottle, but he didn't need it. The girl was
enough for now, as long as he had been without. He watched
her move about the house, and he decided. This ranch wasn't
the only thing of Clarence Cass' that Macy Modock was going
to have!

VI

In the darkness, Allan Bishop almost rode upon Joe Little's tank-building camp. He reined up sharply at the unexpected sight of Joe's mules hobbled on the short grass. The mules stirred in the pale moonlight, and in camp Joe Little called, "Who's out yonder?"

Allan's first impulse was to keep quiet and bluff it out, to make Joe think it was just a loose horse ambling by in the night. But he remembered Joe kept a shotgun in camp. He decided he'd be better off not finding out how good a shot Joe was.

"It's me, Joe. Allan Bishop."

"Allan!" Joe Little came out of the shallow basin where he had spread his bedroll. He wasn't carrying the shotgun. "Boy, you lost?"

Allan shook his head and dismounted. "I'd forgot you'd moved over here to start a new tank. If I'd thought, I'd of ridden way around and not bothered you."

"Your daddy decided he needed a second watering here close by the old Black Bull Tank. There's enough water gets down this draw sometimes to fill two tanks and leave plenty over." He eyed Allan suspiciously. "How come you out in the night thisaway?"

"Just ridin', Joe."

Little tilted his head. "Ain't but a mile or so yonder to old Clarence Cass' fence. That's where you're headin', ain't it?"

Allan nodded, uncomfortable.

"I'm not faultin' you, Allan. Ain't been many years since I

was doin' the same. I know the way your pulse beats, but the way I heard it, Clarence said you wasn't to go over there no more, and Blair Bishop said the same thing."

"I'm of age, Joe. So's Jessie, pretty near." Allan's voice tightened in resentment. "Why don't they leave us alone, Joe? We're not hurtin' nobody. We got a right to lead our own lives."

"You're too young to understand it if I told you, and Blair Bishop's too old to understand your side of it. Maybe I'm at just the right age . . . halfway between. Your daddy thinks he's doin' what's best for you. As for old Clarence, he's a miserable little whelp, and deep down I expect he knows it. Your old daddy has shamed him. Clarence hasn't got the guts to lash out at Blair, but in his eyes you're still a button. His kind can always kick a dog or a kid."

"Sorry I bothered you, Joe. If anybody asks, you didn't see me."

"You watch out for that old man."

Allan rode away thinking he knew why his brother Billy liked to visit with Joe Little. Joe had been through the grinder. Joe understood.

It went against Allan Bishop's grain to go on the *cuidado,* to sneak around like a coyote. He had grown up watching his father meet everything and everybody head on, his shoulders square and his jaw set. He doubted that Blair Bishop had ever gone to a back door or followed the moonlight shadows in his life. They would probably bury Blair Bishop with his hat on.

But Allan found himself approaching Clarence Cass' place from the back side and stepping to the ground, tying his horse in the darkness of the mesquite brush a hundred yards from the barn. Allan paused in the edge of the shadow, looking around before he set out to cross the open strip that lay between him and the brush corrals. The house lay beyond, and so did a rough-lumber shed. Allan doubted he would be seen.

He waited a long time, wanting to roll a smoke but fearing the flare of the match might betray him. He leaned on the fence and stared at the lamplighted windows of the house. Presently he saw a quick movement, something passing between him and the light. In a moment a slender figure came around the corner of the corral and paused. A girl's voice reached him gentle and quiet. "Allan!"

"Over here, Jessie." He walked to meet her and swept her into his arms. He kissed her savagely, for the wanting was stronger now that they had been forbidden to each other. They said little at first, for all the love words had been spoken so many times before. At length, Allan said, "I've got a good mind to march up to the house and tell your old daddy I'm takin' you and he can go to hell!"

"What about your *own* daddy?"

"I'd tell him the same thing, if he pushed me."

"No you wouldn't. You respect him too much; you don't really want to hurt him. As for mine, I know what he is. But still, he's my father. So we'll wait."

"This business of meetin' in the dark, it's no good, Jessie. I feel like some kind of a criminal. I expect you do too."

"We got to do it this way or not see each other at all."

"We don't have to say nothing to either one of them, you know. We could just up and leave and not speak to anybody."

"It'd be the same thing, almost. Later on we'd be ashamed. We got a whole life to live together, Allan. We don't want to start it wrong."

"I don't know how long I can wait, Jessie. Seein' you this way, it sets me afire."

"Then maybe you better not be a-comin' over here again for a while."

"Not seein' you would be even worse."

She shook her head and buried her face against his chest.

"I don't know what the answer is, Allan. We just got to wait awhile. I don't know what my daddy would do for himself if I was to leave him."

"The whole place would come apart. If you hadn't worked like a span of mules, it'd already be gone. Sooner or later you got to leave him. He won't never be no readier for it than he is tonight."

"I'm afraid to leave him right now. Things are wrong out here. They been wrong ever since Macy Modock came."

"I hear he's bought into partnership."

"That's what he and Dad say. I haven't seen any money change hands. There's somethin' wrong; I can't figure out just what. Dad hangs on him like a hound dog to a master, and yet I can tell that somehow Dad's afraid of him too. First thing Modock did was to fire our two cowhands. I could tell Dad didn't intend for him to do it, but Dad just stood there and didn't say a word. Modock's gradually takin' this place over. Dad's losin' his grip on it."

"I can't figure out what a man like Modock wants with a place like this. There's lots of better ones if he wanted to ranch."

"He's not a rancher. I don't know what he is exactly, but he's not a rancher. He scares me, Allan. He scares me to death."

"Has he done anything . . ."

She shook her head. "No. But did you ever get a sudden

feelin' you was in danger, and then see a rattlesnake? An instinct, sort of. Times I get that feelin'. I look around, and there's Macy Modock watching me."

"All the more reason I ought to take you away from here."

"No, Allan, not for a while yet, anyway. If there's somethin' wrong, I don't want to leave my dad here by himself. We'll go when it's time. Till then we just got to wait."

She kissed him again. He caught her hands as she started to leave. He held them a moment, saw she meant what she had said, then reluctantly let her go. She turned once at the corner of the corral and looked back at him. Then she was gone.

Allan Bishop went to his horse.

In the shadows, Macy Modock stood watching the girl. He had followed her when she left the house with an excuse about seeing that the chickens were shut up. He had seen her take care of that chore before dark. Modock had stood back far enough that he could not make out the words, but he could hear the soft exchange of talk between boy and girl. He had trembled as he watched the girl move into Allan Bishop's arms. Watching her now as she walked slowly toward the house, it was all he could do to keep from striding after her, overtaking her, setting claim upon her and letting the fire in him run its course. But the slow fire of his hatred burned steadier, and it prevailed. There were other things to be done first.

He looked toward the brush where the young man had gone, and where hoofbeats trailed away in the night. It would be easy to ride after Allan Bishop, to kill him and fling his body upon Blair Bishop's porch. What better way to punish the man than by robbing him of his son?

But Modock knew that would cut vengeance short. That

would put him on the run. Maybe he would have time to kill Blair Bishop, and maybe he wouldn't.

No, he would wait. All things would come to him in their own due course. He would kill Blair Bishop, but it would be in his own time, and under conditions of his own choosing.

VII

A full moon sent long shadows slanting out ahead of three riders. They moved in an easy trot across the rolling land, unshod hoofs raising dry dust to pinch the nostrils of horses and men. One man kept hanging back and looking nervously around him, twisting his skinny frame first one way, then the other.

"Macy, I oughtn't to be with you on this. If old Blair Bishop was to catch me on his country of a night, he'd turn me wrongside out. You know he's bound to miss them cattle sooner or later. You know who he'll suspicion first."

Macy Modock glanced at Owen Darby, then growled impatiently at Cass. "I wisht you'd quit your bellyachin', Clarence. I've listened to about all I'm goin' to. Hush up or I'll set you afoot, and then maybe he *will* catch you."

"Old Bishop . . . when he gets mad, he don't fool around."

"Clarence . . ." Modock's voice carried threat.

But Clarence Cass had bottled up too much anxiety to quit talking.

"You got no right to make me come along with you on a thing like this. I ain't stole none of Bishop's cows, and I didn't want to be no part of what you're fixin' to do tonight."

Modock grunted savagely. "I figure as long as we're partners we ought to share everything, the risk as well as the spoils. You been grinnin' like a possum, watchin' the boys ride out of a night to haze off Bishop stock. It tickled you, long's you wasn't a part of it. Now I figure it's time you *became* a part of it. You'll be a better partner, Clarence, once you've got your own feet muddied a little, same as ours. You won't be as apt to change your mind about things, or go around talkin' when you ought to be a-listenin'. Now catch up and stay up!"

They reached the fence. Modock dismounted, took a pair of wire pinchers from his saddle and pulled out the staples that held the wire. He had to remove them from two posts to make the wires loose enough that he could press them to the ground and let the horses walk over onto the Double B side of the fence. Clarence Cass held back, and for a moment Modock thought he would have to go fetch him. But Cass came finally, complaining all the way.

"What'll we do if Bishop catches us?"

"What'd he be doin' out this time of the night? He's gettin' on in years. He needs his rest."

"I'm as old as he is. I need mine too," Cass whimpered, watching Modock put the staples back in place so the men's entry would not so easily be noticed. They would ride out this way again, but they might not hit the same place in the fence. "Besides, I don't like leavin' that little girl of mine there all by herself with them men of yours on the place. Can't ever tell what ideas'll come into the mind of men like that."

"You know damn well what kind of ideas they have. But I told them I'd put a bullet in the man that touches her. Besides, they got an errand of their own. They'll go out and pick up some more of them Double B cattle tonight."

"Bishop won't hold still when he finds out somebody's takin' his cows."

"He's got too many anyway, dry as it is. Besides, he can't tie it to me and you, Clarence. He won't find no tracks leadin' to our place."

Cass winced. "Our place? It's still my place."

Modock nodded. "I find that awful easy to forget." He rode in silence awhile, then asked, "You sure we're headed in the right direction for that tank?"

Cass' shoulders were slumped in resignation. "I told you. The Black Bull Tank lies yonderway. It ain't fair, really. It sets on a draw leadin' out of my country. Old Bishop catches the water that runs off of my place, and he won't share none of it."

"You could build a tank of your own and stop most of the runoff."

"I will one of these days. Just never have had the time."

Modock spat, his contempt bubbling close to the surface. "You sure this tank has got a weak bottom in it?"

"I'm sure. Harley Mills cowboyed for him a few years. He told me how much trouble they had at first, makin' it hold water. It kept seepin' down through the bottom. Finally they brought all the Double B horses over here and held them in the tank bottom half a day, millin' them around so their hoofs would pack the ground. Nothin' packs like a remuda of horses."

"If we crack that tight bottom, won't take long for the water to seep right on through. Give it a few days and Bishop's Black Bull Tank will be nothin' but a black *mud* tank."

A dog barked, and Macy Modock hauled up on his reins. "What's a dog doin' way out here in the far side of a pasture?"

Cass shrugged. "Stray."

Modock listened, suspicious. "You sure you ain't led us wrong? You sure you ain't led us to a house or a line camp?"

"I'm sure. I tell you, Macy, I know where I'm at. There's not a soul lives within miles of here."

The dog barked again a time or two, but Modock couldn't spot the animal in the moonlight. He noticed that the cattle trails began converging, so he satisfied himself Cass was leading them to the tank. Presently he rode up on the dam. A few cattle which were bedded down around the water rose nervously to their feet and began to edge away. Modock whistled. No wonder Blair Bishop was so proud of this tank. Even low, it still held a considerable body of water, enough to keep his cows awhile longer if nothing unexpected happened to it.

Modock was here to see that something did happen to it. He reached into his saddlebags and pulled out three sticks of dynamite. Handing the leather reins to Owen Darby, he knelt to set the fuses, each a slightly different length. Digging a hole in the dry earth just at the edge of the mud, he laid down the stick with the shortest fuse and packed the earth around it. He walked around the tank, pausing to set a second. At the far side he placed the third, then lighted the long fuse. He came back to the second and touched it off, finished by lighting the first, then took his horse from Darby and swung into the saddle.

"We better move off a ways. These horses will throw a fit."

The first explosion made the earth tremble. Modock's horse tried to pitch. Clarence Cass' simply wanted to run. It was all Cass could do to stop him short of a full stampede. The last two explosions came close together. Modock could hear the mud splatter onto the tank dam. He heard the clatter of cattle stampeding away into the protecting brush.

It took him a minute to get his horse under control, then he forced the reluctant animal back to the tank. Where the charges had been set, Modock saw three sizable holes gradually filling with water. He was counting on the tremors having sent cracks through the tightly packed bottom. They couldn't be seen beneath the water, but Modock was confident they were there. Cass and Owen Darby rode up beside him. Cass said, "The water's still in it."

"It'll take time. Several days, more than likely. But it'll go."

"Bishop'll see them holes. He'll see the mud scattered all over."

"The mud'll dry in the hot sun tomorrow, and the cattle will tromp it back to dust. As for the holes, he can't prove they wasn't pawed by bulls lookin' for a fight."

"In his own mind, he'll know."

"Sure, he'll know." Modock grinned. "I *want* him to know that it's me and not just hard luck. But there won't be a blessed thing he can do about it, not a thing he can prove."

They started back toward the fence, Modock whistling tunelessly, letting his mind run free with all manner of good and violent dreams, the taste of triumph sweet as wild-bee honey.

The dog came charging at them unexpectedly out of the mesquite, barking its challenge. Modock's horse, still unstrung by the explosions, went straight up. Modock took a hard, dirt-eating fall but somehow held on to his reins. He jumped to his feet, holding desperately to the struggling horse. The breath half knocked out of him, Modock managed to slap the barking dog and send it retreating. He cursed, reaching for his pistol but realizing that if he fired a shot, the horse would probably get away from him. He managed finally to get a foot into the stirrup and swing back into the saddle. He spurred the horse viciously, at the same time hauling hard on the reins to keep the animal from getting its head down to buck again.

A voice came from the mesquite. "Macy Modock! I ought to've known it'd be you."

Modock's pistol was in his hand, and he bent low over the horse's neck, hoping not to present an easy target. "Who's that?" he demanded, half panicky at the thought of being caught.

Tank-builder Joe Little rode out of the brush, shotgun

pointed toward the three horsemen. He commanded the dog to heel, then approached Modock. The muzzle of that shotgun looked big as a coffeepot. Modock stared in disbelief. "What're you doin' here, Joe?"

"I got a camp over yonder, buildin' another tank for Blair Bishop, below the Black Bull." He glanced contemptuously at Clarence Cass, whose chin had dropped to his shirt collar in the agony of discovery. "First blast woke me up. Thought it was thunder, till I looked up and seen the moon and the stars. The other two blasts come, and all of a sudden I knowed. Raise your hands, Macy. You others too. You'll answer to Blair Bishop."

Modock was recovering from surprise, and he began calculating odds. He didn't like that shotgun. Even if he fired his pistol and hit Joe, he knew the shotgun blast would probably tear him in two. "It's a long ways from here to the Double B headquarters. You better ride off and forget you seen us, Joe."

"I wish I could forget I *ever* seen you, Macy, much less shared a cell with you. It takes a lowdown form of a man to dynamite another man's waterhole and starve his cattle to death. I figure you're goin' back where you come from, Macy, and takin' company with you."

"I made you an offer a while back, Joe. It still stands. Go in with us and get that land you wanted. You might even get some of the Bishop country you been workin' so hard on. Use your head, Joe, and you can wind up bigger than you ever thought of."

"Blair Bishop's a friend of mine. You, Macy, are no friend to anybody." He motioned with the shotgun. "Easy now, and slip them cartridge belts off. Drop them careful."

Modock caught a signal in Owen Darby's face. He

couldn't tell exactly what Darby had in mind, but he knew Darby was about to try something. Modock lagged, fumbling with the belt buckle. Darby undid his and slipped the belt and holster loose from his hip as if to drop it. Instead, he flipped it into the face of Joe Little's horse. The horse shied away, forcing Joe involuntarily to grab at the saddle horn and let the shotgun dip.

Modock's right hand streaked back from the buckle and came up with the pistol. He held it almost point-blank at Joe Little's chest. Horror came into Joe's face as he tried desperately to bring the shotgun back into line.

Modock fired. Joe rocked back. His horse jumped in terror. Joe Little slid out of the saddle and hit the ground with one leg crumpled.

Clarence Cass sat stupefied, watching Joe Little gasp away his life. Modock swung to the ground and kicked the shotgun away in case there was still any inclination on Joe's part to use it. But Joe was beyond thinking.

Joe's black dog growled deep in its throat and lunged in fury at Macy Modock. Instinctively Modock threw up his arm. The dog's teeth sank into it. Modock swung the pistol up under the dog's belly and fired. The dog fell away, kicking. Cursing violently, a cold rage flowing over him, Modock fired twice more into the shaggy body.

"Nothin' I hate worse than a damned dog . . ."

He rubbed his arm where the sharp teeth had dug in, bringing blood.

Cass tried to speak, but only a few terrified gasps came. Modock looked up to see Owen Darby catching Joe's runaway horse and bringing it back. Darby looked down at Joe's body. "This sure queers things, Macy. What you goin' to do now?"

Modock shook his head. "I'm tryin' to think. Just shut up and let me study it out." He cursed silently. Damn Joe Little and his stupid meddling. Modock wished Joe hadn't been here; not that he had any regret for the killing itself, but only that it made for an unexpected complication. He had felt no regard for Joe Little when they were in prison together, no more than he felt for anyone else beyond whatever use he might be. It was these unforeseen surprises that always seemed to get a man caught. It was hard to prepare for them.

Modock straightened, deciding he saw a way out. "Owen, you was sayin' the other day you wished you could break into that wooden box of a bank in Two Forks."

Darby nodded. "But you said we had bigger fish to fry, and I might ruin the whole setup."

"All of a sudden I'm changin' my mind. I think it'd be a great idea now for you to bust that bank. Our friend Joe Little was in the pen for doin' that very thing. If he was to disappear right after the bank was robbed, what do you reckon folks would think?"

Darby began to smile. "That's why I like to ride with you, Macy. You can take a disaster and make a winnin' hand out of it."

"We'll take him and his horse and make sure they're never found. Clarence, you get down here and help me with him."

Clarence Cass was almost crying, his throat quivering as he kept trying for voice. He made no move to leave his saddle. Modock railed at him without effect. Darby swung down and helped Modock lift Joe Little's body across the saddle, the frightened horse pulling its head around, its eyes spooked.

Darby asked, "What about our tracks?"

"No way we can rub them all out. We'll just have to hope

that nobody will come along till the cattle and the wind have covered them up. Unless somebody's lookin' for tracks, they ain't apt to notice them anyway."

"We can't leave that dog layin' there."

"We'll drag him off into the brush. There won't nobody find him."

Voice came at last to Clarence Cass. "You killed him! You killed him! They'll hang us now for sure!"

Modock glanced at Darby, knowing Darby had been wishing Modock would let him shut the little man up for once and for all. Sooner or later they would have to do something permanent about Cass, but not until all advantage had been taken of him. "Clarence, you quit your cryin'. Get a head back on your shoulders. Anything we done, *you* done."

"I didn't come for no killin'."

"Neither did we, but you got it, and you're in it up to your Adam's apple. Anything that happens to us happens to you too."

"Macy, I didn't know you was goin' to drag me into a thing like this. Just blowin' up a tank was all. That's what you said, just blowin' up a tank. Now I want you off of my ranch, out of this country."

Angrily Modock reached down to Joe Little's warm body and came up with blood thick on his fingers. He smeared it onto Clarence Cass' hand. Cass drew back trembling, trying desperately to wipe the blood onto his trousers. Modock said, "It won't wash off, Clarence. So from now on, your life depends on us. You'll keep your mouth shut and do everything I tell you. Everything! Else you might just wind up where Joe Little is. Come on, let's get out of here!"

VIII

The sun was starting down in the afternoon sky when Sheriff Erly Greenwood and a deputy rode into the yard of the Double B headquarters. Blair Bishop lay on a blanket on the breezy gallery of the ranchhouse, taking gratefully what little comfort he found on a hot summer day. Time had been when his conscience would have hurt him a little, napping like this when there was work to be done. But as the years went by it seemed easier to deal with his conscience on such matters. No matter how much work a man did, it was never enough anyway.

The sound of hoofs brought Blair's gray head up from the pillow. He raised up slowly, stretching, then got to his feet and invited Erly with a broad wave of his hand. "Come on up and shade awhile, Erly. It's hotter than the hinges of hell out in that sun."

Greenwood could well remember when Blair Bishop wouldn't have taken time for a noonday siesta, but that had been before the ranchman had come to terms with ambition and had learned to accept the natural rhythms of life. He climbed the steps and shook hands with the ranchman. The deputy followed his example. Blair, in his sock feet, led them into the house for a drink of cool water. Then they came back out onto the gallery, for the house caught and held much of the afternoon heat entrapped despite its tall, narrow windows.

"Blair," the sheriff said, "I come to talk to Joe Little."

Blair told him Joe was building a surface tank out close to

the Black Bull. Greenwood asked him, "Seen him today?"

"He seldom comes to headquarters, just when he needs somethin'. My boy Billy drops by and keeps him pretty well stocked on groceries and things . . . includin' the best stuff out of my own pantry. What do you want with Joe?"

"Somebody busted into the bank last night. Got off with somethin' like four to five thousand dollars."

"Joe wouldn't . . ." Blair's eyes narrowed. "He paid off what he owed the state. He wouldn't do nothing like that again, Erly. He's got a good job, got friends . . ."

"How long would it take him to make four or five thousand dollars, Blair, workin' a team of mules in this heat, sweatin' himself to death on another man's land? You can see how some of the old quick-money notions might get to preyin' on Joe's mind."

"Did anybody see him?"

"Not exactly. There was a cowboy layin' drunk in an alley. He saw the robber. Said it could have been Joe."

"Could have been? With a drunk cowboy, it *could* have been Ulysses S. Grant or Robert E. Lee."

"Just the same, I sure want to talk to Joe. He's the first one lots of folks in town thought of. If I don't talk to him, some of them are liable to come lookin'."

Blair nodded. "I'll get Billy to hitch a team to the buckboard, and we'll ride with you over there."

They found Joe's camp beside the half-finished tank, the mules hobbled to graze on the scanty grass. Blair Bishop knew the moment he saw the mules that something was wrong. He exchanged glances with Billy and found the same conviction in the boy's eyes. Joe was always working at this time of day.

Those mules didn't get the hobbles until sundown. Blair didn't have to say anything. Erly Greenwood read the signs the same way. The sheriff asked, "Does he keep a horse?"

Blair didn't answer, but Billy did. "He's always got a horse. I don't see it anyplace around."

Erly Greenwood's face went grave as he looked over the deserted camp. "You know, don't you, Blair? We'll have to send out word on Joe Little."

Billy protested. "Dad, Joe wouldn't rob nobody. He told me a dozen times he'd rather starve than to do anything like that again."

Blair sensed the desperation in Billy's voice, a silent cry for faith, for Billy had thought the sun rose and set in Joe Little. "Boy," he said unconvincingly, "maybe it's not the way it looks. Maybe old Joe just up and went somewhere."

Erly Greenwood said, "Blair, there's no use kiddin' him. Billy's old enough to take things the way they come." He turned his attention to Billy. "Think hard now, son. Do you remember anything he might've said about places he'd like to go to, things he'd like to do?"

Billy shook his head defensively. "No, sir. He said he was goin' to buy a place of his own. That's all he ever said he wanted, was a place of his own."

The sheriff commented, "Four to five thousand dollars would buy a man a right smart of a little place. He'd have to go a far piece, though. He must've said somethin', Billy."

"Nothin'. I tell you, he didn't say nothin'."

Erly Greenwood studied him apologetically but unconvinced. "All right, son, but if you think of anything later on, let us know. We want to help Joe; we got no wish to hurt him." He shook Blair's hand, gripping it lightly because of the rheumatism, but bringing pain just the same. "Sorry, Blair, I can't say I was in favor of you ever bringin' Joe Little here in the first place, but I'll say this: I liked him."

"You got your job to do, Erly. Want us to help you look for tracks?"

"Any helpful tracks will be the ones goin' *away* from the bank, not the ones he made goin' to it. We'd be wastin' our time out here."

Sitting slumped on the buckboard seat, Blair sorrowfully watched them ride off in the direction of town. The leather lines slacked from Billy's listless hands. Blair looked at his son. "Boy, sometimes life's hard that way. People we like, people we trust, they do things we can't understand, things that hurt us. It don't help to blame them. It ain't right to blame a man unless you try on his boots and walk awhile in his tracks. Whatever was drivin' Joe, it was somethin' more powerful than we know. Ain't right for us to feel hard about him."

"I'm not feelin' hard about him, Dad. I know he didn't do it."

Blair shrugged, not knowing what else to say. "Sometimes we just got to accept the things that are and not ask questions. This is one of those times." He rubbed his aching hand, wanting to busy his mind on other matters and hoping to get Billy occupied too. "Long's we're this close, let's go over and take a look at the Black Bull Tank. It does me good to see a place that's still got water."

The tank's banks were too steep for the buckboard, so Blair climbed heavily out and walked. Billy followed him. At the top of the dam, Blair stopped in surprise. He glanced at Billy, shock in his square face. "Boy, that tank ain't got half the water in it that it had the other day."

Billy's jaw dropped. "I was over here just day before yesterday. It still had lots of water in it. Somethin's happened. It's gone plumb to hell."

That wasn't language Blair had taught Billy to use, though he used it liberally enough himself. He never even noticed this time. In dismay he trudged down toward the water line. He bogged in heavy black mud almost to his boottops. "Right here's where the water line was a day or two ago. Cattle didn't drink this much, and it don't evaporate this fast."

He knelt painfully, touching the wet ground with his hand as if somehow that would give him a hint to what had gone wrong. He got up slowly, feeling as if a mule had kicked him in the stomach. Billy looked at him in alarm. For a moment Blair thought Billy's expression was a reflection of his concern over the water, but he realized that wasn't it, at least not the main part of it.

Billy said, "Dad, you better go sit in the buckboard awhile. You've turned as white as skim milk."

"I'm all right, boy, I'm all right." Blair looked at the water again, still mystified. He started around the edge of it, looking for a line that might indicate a crack in the dam. He didn't see anything.

He didn't see the hole, either, until he fell into it and went to his knees. Billy ran to help him, but Blair pushed to his feet alone, wiping the mud from his hands onto his already muddy trousers. "Damned bulls," he muttered, "pawin' holes where a man can fall in them. If they ever come up with a substitute, I'll never have a bull on the place again."

Billy observed, "They been doin' a lot of fightin', seems like. There's another bull hole over yonder."

"Bunch of bulls around here are sure in need of a shippin'," Blair growled. Pawing holes was bull nature, but at a time like this Blair had no patience with it. He glanced across the tank and became aware of a third hole which looked about like the other two. Of a sudden, suspicion hit him. The impact was almost as hard as the initial one of seeing the tank nearly dry.

"Billy, somethin' strike you funny about them bull holes?"

Billy shook his head. "Nothin' strikes me very funny right now."

"Aside from the fact that there's three of them showed up all at the same time, and the fact that they're kind of deep, don't it seem peculiar to you that they're in the edge of the mud instead of out where the sand is a little dryer? An old bull ain't goin' to stand and paw mud when there's dry ground all around him."

Billy blinked in confusion. "What you tryin' to say, Dad?"

"I'm not sure. It's just a feelin' that's come over me, or maybe somethin' I smell. There's more here than meets the eye."

"You think Joe Little went and did somethin'? He wouldn't, Dad. He wouldn't hurt us thisaway."

"Not Joe Little. I was thinkin' of Macy Modock."

"Joe would've known about it. He'd of told us . . ." Billy's eyes widened as the implication hit him. "Unless Modock done somethin' to him." He grabbed his father's arm. "Dad, we got to catch up to Erly Greenwood and tell him."

"Tell him what? We'd have to prove it first."

"But maybe Joe's in trouble and needs our help. No tellin' what that Modock might be doin' to him."

Blair knew now. Though he had nothing stronger than instinct to go by, he knew. "Whatever it is, boy, he's already done it. Macy Modock is a hard man. Whatever he felt like he had to do to Joe, it's over and done with."

"You think he killed him?"

"You'd best make up your mind to it, Billy. I'll bet everything I own. If Modock was out here and Joe caught him, then Joe is dead."

Billy's hands trembled as the enormity of the idea took hold. Tears welled into his eyes. "Then let's go after Modock. Let's kill him!"

Blair Bishop firmly took his son's arm. "No, son, that's not for us to do. Time was when it would've been the thing, but that time is gone. We'll go tell Erly Greenwood what we think. The fixin' of it is up to him."

"Joe Little was our friend."

Blair Bishop's eyes were bleak, and he knew a moment of temptation. "If I was your age and time was rolled back a few years, I'd do just what you're sayin'. But I ain't, and it ain't, and we can't. Let's get to the buckboard. If we push, maybe we can catch Erly."

They did, and Greenwood came back for a look around. What he saw did not incline him to agree. "I don't see a thing that supports you, Blair. If there was any tracks, they're gone. If them holes was blowed or dug, there's nothin' to show for it. For all I can tell, they're just what they look like . . . a sign the bulls was fightin'. The trouble with you and Billy is that you don't want to accept the truth when it stares you in the eye. Joe Little got tired of workin' and robbed that bank. You've got Macy Modock so heavy on your mind that you're ready to blame him for everything but the drought. If he's tryin' to make you sweat, he's doin' a good job of it. I bet you ain't slept a full night in peace since he came back. Now he's givin' you nightmares in the daytime."

That was strong talk coming from Erly Greenwood, who had always handled Blair Bishop with a respectful deference. But Greenwood had a looted bank in town to worry about, and the weather was hot, and he'd made a lot of extra miles that weren't taking him any closer to the man who had done the job.

Angered, Blair said, "I got a strong feelin' about this thing, Erly. You won't find Joe Little, not on this earth. If you want to find that bank money, you go to Macy Modock."

Greenwood kept his impatience in check; Blair had to give him credit for that. "Blair, I'll see you again soon's I get some time. Awful sorry about that tank."

IX

The Black Bull Tank had become only a mudhole. Blair had known that as soon as he had seen the cattle standing around the tankdam. There had been far too many for this early in the day. Usually they began gathering in the afternoon and watered, then lay around until the cool of the evening brought them back to their feet and set them to looking for grass. Blair could tell these cattle had been here since yesterday, and they were thirsty. He rode up on the dam, his two sons flanking him. What he saw confirmed his fears.

"Well, it's gone, boys. The trap's drawin' shut."

Allan nodded gravely. Billy stared, the consequences not quite so apparent to him as to his father and his older brother. "We'll just have to take them somewhere else," he said.

Blair Bishop nodded sourly, still convinced Modock had brought this trouble on him. "It means we'll have to double up cattle on another place that's already in trouble itself." He pondered a moment. "We'll haze them over onto the Harley Mills pasture. At least there we got a couple of windmill's still pumpin' all right."

Allan said, "Grass is awful short over there, Dad."

"It's short everywhere. But there's water, at least." He rode down the dam, waving his hand and hollering at the cattle. His sons fanned out on either side of him and did likewise. One cow remained. She was out twenty feet in the mud, hopelessly mired to her belly. Trembling, she shook her head angrily at the horsemen. She had obviously been here for some time, struggling vainly, fighting this mud. She was in a hostile mood toward all the world.

"Allan," Blair called, "I graduated from this kind of chore a long time ago. I'll let you do the honors. Billy, you keep gatherin' the rest of them cattle."

Allan stepped to the ground and tightened his cinch for a good pull. He rode to the edge of the mud, swung his loop and sailed it around the cow's horns. Taking up the slack, he dallied the end of the rope around his saddle horn and spurred away. The horse scrambled for footing, pulling hard. The cow's neck stretched and she bawled in rage, but the mud held her.

Blair said, "I was afraid it wouldn't be that easy. You'll have to get in there with her. Hand me your rope."

Allan took it philosophically, for this was part of a cowboy's work. Using a few choice words to describe the ancestry of a brute stupid enough to get herself into such a predicament, he took off his boots and waded into the mud.

Blair's horse was bigger and stronger than Allan's. Blair always rode a big horse, for he was an older and heavier man. He dallied Allan's rope around his saddle horn. The cow slung her head, trying vainly to reach Allan with her horns. He got behind her and grasped her tail. Blair spurred. As the horse strained against the rope, Allan lifted the cow's hindquarters. The first try didn't move her much, but on the second she somehow got her feet under her and began adding to the struggle what little strength she had left. She moved forward gradually at first. Then she broke loose from the mud's tight grip and came scrambling up out of it. On dry ground, she went to her knees. Her tongue was hanging out, and she was bawling in rage. Allan eased up to get the rope off, but she was ready to fight anything which moved. She slung her head and missed him only an inch with her sharp horns. Allan dodged back, cursing her. She got to her feet and charged him. There was nothing for Allan to do but run toward his horse, barefoot, muddy to his thighs. The horse didn't like the looks of either him or the cow, and he shied away.

Blair put his own horse between Allan and the cow and took another dally farther down on the rope. He rode away fast, jerking the cow off of her feet. While she was down, Allan slipped the rope off. He lost no time picking up his boots and getting back into his saddle. He would stay barefoot till the mud dried enough that he could rub it off.

Blair and Allan watched the cow slowly struggle to her feet. She stood shaking, tongue out and drooling saliva as she faced them in frustration and anger, tossing her head in belligerence.

"Never fails to happen," Allan said. "Do one a favor, and she turns on you."

"Female. A lot of females will do you that way. Cow, human, or whatever."

The cow decided she had made her point, and she moved weakly up over the dam to seek out her sisters. Allan looked at his father. "You tryin' to say somethin', Dad?"

Blair shrugged. "Yep, and you know what it is."

"I told you before, Dad, there's no use us talkin' about Jessie. Nothin' you say is goin' to change the way I feel about her. And I'm goin' to keep right on seein' her. I wish you wouldn't crowd me."

"If it was just seein' her, boy, that wouldn't be so bad. But it's more than that. One of these times you'll feel called upon to marry her. Sure, she looks pretty good to you now, mostly because you ain't seen a lot of other girls and got nothin' to compare by. I swear, I'd almost rather see you spendin' your time down on Silky Row in town. At least nobody there would try to tie on to you. Everybody would know just where she stood."

Allan stopped his horse. He looked his father in the eye, a quality Blair had taught him from the time he was big enough to walk. "Dad, I never lied to you, and I won't lie to you now. When the time is right, I'm goin' to marry Jessie Cass. Now, you can accept her, or you can tell us both to leave. I hope you'll accept her, because she's a good girl. But even if you don't, that won't change anything. I'll marry her. You won't stand in my way, and neither will anybody else."

Blair Bishop felt anger. He had raised his boys not to talk back to him. But he had also taught them to be straightforward and not back off from a problem. Blair struggled to put down his anger. Allan didn't seem to be in any hurry about this. Maybe something would come along to help Blair open his eyes for him before it was too late.

Blair retreated, but he didn't surrender. "Billy's probably havin' trouble tryin' to push them cattle all by himself. We better go give him a hand."

Along the way they picked up foreman Finn Goforth and cowboy Hez Northcutt, who had been riding missions of their own. The cattle drove sluggishly at first, their thirst making them contrary, and their instincts tugging them back toward the tank where they were used to watering. Every so often an animal would turn back, and only a rope would stop her. Billy was the one who most often used the rope. He was at an age when a rope had a rough appeal to him and nothing was so much fun as to stand a runaway steer on its rump. Irritably, for he was thirsty too, Blair grouched at him about rough-handling the stock. Billy would explain that he couldn't afford to let them get away.

They missed dinner, for moving these cattle to water was more important than getting back to the headquarters for a noon meal. A cowboy was conditioned to accept such things. The good of the stock was always paramount over the needs of the man.

Late in the afternoon the tall windmill showed on the short-grass prairie. It seemed to shimmer and dance in the heatwaves playing along the horizon. Riding point, Blair Bishop thought he saw a cloud of dust ahead of him, and the movement of cattle. He blinked and lost sight of it in the heat. Eyesight going bad, he decided. Looked like when the rheumatism got hold of him, it was bound to take everything else. By now he was tired and hot and thirsty and irritable. So was everybody else on the drive. He hadn't heard a man speak a word in an hour, except to use the Lord's name in vain against some recalcitrant critter.

But directly Finn Goforth trotted his horse up from the flank and pulled in beside Blair. "Do you see somethin' odd up ahead of us?"

Blair grunted. "Thought I did, but I lost it. Mirage, I figured, or just my own eyes. Times anymore I'm not worth killin'."

Finn pointed. "It ain't no mirage."

Blair sat up straight in the saddle. He stared a moment, glanced at Finn in disbelief and looked back again. "Finn, somebody's movin' cattle."

"There's nothin' up yonder but Double B range. There's not anybody supposed to be movin' cattle here but us."

Anger surged red into Blair's square face. "Rustlers! In broad open daylight!"

Finn Goforth shook his head. "That's the first thought that came to me. You know we been losin' some cattle lately, a few here, a few there. Started about the time Macy Modock come back. But they'd have to have a lot of gall to come so far onto Double B country in the daytime when there'd be so much chance of a Bishop man runnin' onto them. I can't hardly believe they'd be stealin' cattle now. Tonight, maybe, after the moon comes up, but not now."

By instinct Blair Bishop reached for his hip. He didn't have a pistol, hadn't worn one in years. He looked back at his two sons and Hez Northcutt. "Nary a gun in the whole bunch of us, Finn, except that carbine you carry under your leg. Let me have it, and I'll ride up and see what the hell is goin' on."

Goforth shook his head. "With that hand of yours, you couldn't lever it. One shot is all you'd ever get. I'll go with you, Mister Bishop, and I'll keep hold of the rifle."

Blair flexed his right hand. It was painfully stiff. Finn was right. Blair looked over his shoulder and signaled for Allan to come up on the run. He could tell that Allan had seen the other string of cattle too. "You go tell Billy and Hez to keep pushin' this bunch. The three of us are ridin' on to see what this is all about."

He swung into an easy lope that would give Allan a chance to catch up with him. The thought fleetingly crossed his mind that if it *was* cow thieves, and they were armed, one saddlegun wouldn't be much persuasion against them. But the thought was not enough to slow him. It had been said of Blair Bishop in his younger days that he would charge hell with a bucket of gypwater. Armed or not, he had seen few men who would stand against him long.

Between the three men and the windmill lay a barbed wire fence. Originally the four sections of land where the windmill stood had been homesteaded at Blair's suggestion by Harley Mills when Harley was a Double B cowboy. He had gone through the state requirements, then had sold the place to Blair and gone off to get gloriously drunk. He had never been completely sober since, and Blair had been obliged to fire him.

Next to the Mills land was a similar place Blair had bought from a homesteading cowboy named Abernathy. Unlike Mills, Abernathy had taken his money and bought a string of steers. He threw them in with a trail herd bound for the railroad and was drowned trying to swim a creek. In his honor the land was still known as the Abernathy place, though it had been in the Bishop name for years.

A double-width wire gate was marked by three tall posts. Blair moved toward them, but he saw other riders were going to get there first from the far side of the fence. Behind the riders came a large herd of slow-moving cattle, obscured by heavy gray dust. Blair recognized a tall, gaunt man whose black hat was pulled down almost over his eyes. "That's Macy Modock. Let me have that rifle, Finn."

Goforth demurred again. "I don't want to see you killed, Mister Bishop, so I better keep it. Any time you want him shot, just give me the word."

Someone dismounted and threw the two gates wide open, then climbed back onto his horse. Macy Modock pulled up into one of the gates and stopped, waiting. Beside him was the red-bearded one Blair remembered as Owen Darby. Darby had a saddlegun lying across the pommel of his saddle. Two other riders flanked them, facing toward the Bishops and Finn Goforth. None looked much like preachers.

Macy Modock held up his hand as Blair Bishop neared. It wasn't a gesture of peace; it was a sign to stop.

"Macy," Blair spoke angrily, "this here is my land, and I'll wager them yonder is my cattle. Now what the hell are you up to?"

Modock gave him that dry, flat, dangerous smile of his. "You're right, Blair Bishop, up to a point. Them is your cattle, and that where you're at is your land. But this where I'm sittin', it's not your land anymore; it's mine. I'm movin' your cattle off of it."

The surprise struck Blair Bishop like a fist. He hesitated, wondering if the thirst and the heat hadn't affected his hearing. "Your land? It's mine, and it has been for years."

Macy Modock patiently shook his head. That smile clung, ugly and threatening. "You thought it was. You thought you had defrauded the state. But after all this time you been caught up with, Bishop. You're losin' it, and I've filed claim on it."

Finn Goforth held the carbine. "Just say the word, Mister Bishop . . ."

If Blair had held the rifle at that moment, he probably would have shot Macy Modock out of the saddle, or tried to. But he didn't and perhaps that helped him take a better look at the three men who sided Modock. Finn's first shot would have to be a good one; he would never live to fire a second. "Stay easy, Finn," Blair rasped. He had no wish to lose a good foreman and longtime friend. To Modock he said, "If you think I'm goin' to stand still for you takin' four good sections of my land . . ."

Macy shook his head. "Not four . . . *eight*. Them other four sections yonder was filed on by a feller name of Abernathy. You're losin' those too. Owen here has filed on that land."

Blair flamed, "You're not bluffin' us, Macy. We got thirsty cattle comin', and you're standin' in the gate. Pull aside."

Macy's hand moved back near the pistol at his hip. "The only cattle passin' through that gate is the ones behind us, and they're goin' out, not in."

"Those eight sections have got about all the dependable water left on this ranch, Macy. They're the only place, almost, where a man can find well water just about anywhere he digs. I'm not givin' them up to nobody."

"You don't have to give them up; they're bein' *took*. You see, Bishop, you thought I was the only enemy you had. You thought when you sent me up that you didn't have any enemy left who could hurt you. But you didn't think about Judge Quincy. A little old dried-up wart like that couldn't do you no damage, you thought. But you wasn't payin' attention."

Blair Bishop listened, stewing.

Modock went on: "This land was homesteaded by Abernathy and Mills. They swore they met all the state's requirements, and they got the deeds. But did you ever look at the fine print on them papers, Bishop? No, of course you didn't. You thought anything a Bishop could get his hands on was safe forever. But there's fine print that says if there's fraud in connection with them homesteads, they can be taken back and put up for somebody else to claim."

"There wasn't no fraud."

"It was common knowledge around here that you was in collusion with them cowboys when they filed on that land.

Before they ever done it, they agreed to sell the land to you. You held them to it."

"There never was any such agreement. I told them when the time came I'd like to buy and would pay them a good price. I never told them they had to. There was a couple who didn't. They're still my friends."

Finn Goforth was one of them, but Blair saw no need mentioning the fact to the likes of Macy Modock. Finn had decided he wanted to keep his land as something to build on for his own future. He was still working for Blair, letting Blair use his land under lease and letting the lease payments stack up as savings in the Two Forks bank to buy a cow herd someday.

Modock said, "We got a signed affidavit from Harley Mills. He says him and Abernathy never actually lived on their land the way they was supposed to. They lived in the Double B bunkhouse the whole blessed time."

"They both set up shacks on their land. They lived in them the way the law specified."

"I ain't seen no shacks."

"We taken them down and reused the lumber."

Modock grunted sarcastically. "Sure. That'd sound good in court. Can you produce either man to swear he lived in the shack?"

"You know Abernathy's dead. As for Harley Mills, he'd sell his soul for a barrel of whiskey. How much did you give him?"

"Harley says you got him to swear false testimony, then forced him to sell to you or you'd expose him and get him sent to jail."

"Harley lied. He lived up to the law, same as the others. He taken his money and drank it up. That's why he's swampin' a stable."

"He claims you got what you wanted from him and then fired him."

"I had to let him go because he was drinkin' too much. You better not depend on Harley for a witness. He'll be drunk when you need him."

"I got his affidavit. What have *you* got, Bishop? I tell you what you *ain't* got; you ain't got this land no more. *We* have. And we're movin' you off it today."

Finn Goforth said deliberately, "No you ain't," and he raised the saddlegun. That was a mistake. Owen Darby's carbine fired. The horses jumped in fright. Blair saw Finn rock back in the saddle, discharging his carbine harmlessly in the air. He doubled over and slid to the ground.

"Finn!" Blair shouted. He tried to dismount, but his big gray was crow-hopping excitedly. Blair's stiff legs went out from under him as he hit the ground, and he went down on hands and knees almost under the panicked gray horse. A hoof barely missed him before Blair could crawl away and struggle painfully to his feet.

Allan was already on his knees beside the foreman and was turning Finn over. Finn's face was going gray. Blood flowed from a wound deep in his shoulder.

Blair picked up Finn's fallen carbine. He tried feverishly to lever a fresh cartridge into the breech, but his crippled hand betrayed him. He couldn't get a grip. He cursed wildly, furious at the hand, furious at Macy Modock. But the hand wouldn't function. Forcing it brought only pain.

Glancing up, he saw three men's guns leveled at him and knew that if he had been able to lever a cartridge, they would not have let him live to fire it.

Macy Modock raised his hand and motioned for his men

to lower their weapons. "Not yet, boys, not yet. Comes time to do the honors on Blair Bishop, I want to do it myself."

Blair stood openmouthed and raging, the sweat rolling down his dusty face, pain lancing through his hand from trying to force it to do something of which it no longer was capable. "Modock, I swear to God . . ."

"Just go on and swear, Bishop. Ain't another damn thing you can do."

Allan's anxious voice reached Blair. "Dad, Finn's hard hit. He won't live long if we don't get this blood stopped."

A cold chill ran through Blair Bishop as he realized how close he had come to being killed, standing there with that useless rifle in his hands. He dropped it and turned back to Finn Goforth. Allan ripped Finn's shirt open to expose the wound.

Billy Bishop and Hez Northcutt had abandoned their cattle at the sound of the shot and came loping up excitedly. Hez jumped off to see about Finn. Billy glanced at Finn, saw the blood, then spotted the saddlegun lying on the ground. He reached for it, but Blair managed to grab him.

"Boy, don't touch that rifle! Can't you see they're fixin' to kill you?"

Billy cried in fury: "He's the one that killed Joe Little. Now he's shot Finn."

Macy Modock said coldly, "Go on, Blair Bishop, let him pick it up."

Blair sensed they wouldn't withhold fire against Billy. They would cut him to pieces. Blair pushed Billy back, putting himself between the gunmen and his son. "No, Modock, you're not goin' to get at me by killin' these boys of mine."

Allan methodically wadded a handkerchief against Finn's wound, trying to stop the blood. When that handkerchief was soaked, Blair handed him one from his own pocket. If the wound didn't kill Finn, those dirty handkerchiefs probably would, Blair thought darkly.

"Billy, you and Hez ride up to the ranch. Billy, you go to town and fetch a doctor to the house. Get word to the sheriff too. Hez, you load up the buckboard with blankets and bring it here in a run. Allan and I'll take care of him the best we can till you get back."

Billy said, "How about them cows?"

"The hell with the cows. We got to save Finn."

The young cowboys rode off together in a lope that Blair knew was likely to kill both horses if they didn't slow down. They would, when excitement gave way to judgment. Allan and Blair carried the foreman gently to the shade of a thin mesquite tree and laid him on the ground. The blood gradually stopped.

On the other side of the gate, the riders arrived with the cattle they were pushing for Macy Modock. Blair watched in helpless anger as they drove them through the double gate and then chased them into a run that would carry them a considerable distance out across a waterless pasture.

Modock rode over and looked down from the saddle, the hard smile still making a slash across his thin face. "Too bad about your man. Owen Darby's slippin' in his old age. Time was when he'd have got this feller in the heart and you wouldn't have to be fussin' over him thisaway. You'd just dig a hole for him, is all."

"Did you dig a hole for Joe Little?"

Modock never changed expression. "You ain't found it, have you?"

Blair said, "Soon's I get Finn took care of, I'll be back. I'll bring plenty with me."

Modock was unmoved. "It ain't your land no more. It's mine, or fixin' to be. Judge Quincy's been over at the State-house the last four days. I got a wire from him that he had everything fixed. That land is mine and Owen Darby's. We're goin' to put the Cass cattle on it."

"They don't just take a man's land away without goin' to court."

"If you want to press it, I reckon you can have your day in court. But you'll lose. Judge tells me that's a cinch. And mean-time, as they say, possession is nine points of the law. I sure as hell got possession. And I got some boys yonder tough enough to see that I keep it."

"Without that land, I got a bunch of cows that don't have water to drink. You won't keep me off."

"Seems to me I heard about my partner Clarence Cass tryin' to tell you he had the same problem. And I remember what you told him. So I'm tellin' you the same thing, Blair Bishop, with one extra addition: any of your men tries to come onto my land, I'm givin' my boys orders to shoot him."

Blair Bishop stared at Finn's saddlegun, still lying where it had been dropped. From here, if Allan would lever a cartridge into it for him, Blair was almost sure he could shoot Macy Modock as the man rode away. Blair made a move toward the rifle then stopped, knowing he couldn't do it that way.

He might curse himself the rest of his life for missing the chance, but he couldn't shoot a man in the back. Not even Macy Modock.

X

For the better part of an hour the doctor labored in flickering light while first one man then another held a lamp close. But finally he straightened in resignation, wiping a handkerchief over his bald head and his sweat-glistening face. "I'm sorry, Blair. Did all I could, but Finn Goforth is gone."

Cold lay in the pit of Blair's stomach. Even as he had paced the parlor floor, pausing periodically to stare blackly out into the darkness, he had known it would end this way.

The doctor said, "If I'd been close by when it happened, maybe I could've saved him. Even then it would've been close." He began putting his instruments into his bag.

"Doc," Blair rasped, wanting comfort and not knowing where to find it, "it's midnight. No use you ridin' to town now. We got a bed for you and a couple of stiff drinks to help settle you if you need them." The doctor nodded his acceptance. "God knows I need them."

Blair added, "Could be we'll need you again anyway. When we've done right by Finn, we'll be goin' back over there."

"With the few men you've got?"

"I'll have more. I'm fixin' to send the boys out to round up all the friends we can muster."

The doctor poured a liberal drink out of a bottle Blair fetched from a cabinet. He sat down wearily, taking one stiff drink that twisted his face, then sipping easier on the rest of it while he pondered. "You have two sons, Blair. Tomorrow one of them—maybe both—could be lyin' here where Finn is."

"It's our land. It'll be the boys' land one of these days . . ." Blair rubbed his cramped, aching hand. "Maybe not so long off."

"Your land. And you'd expect your friends to come and die for it with you? That's a lot to ask of friendship, Blair."

"No more than I've done for some of them." He didn't have to tell the doctor how it had been in earlier days, about the Comanche raids and the like. Doc knew. "This fight ain't just for me or my boys; it's for all these people. You remember how bad it used to be when Macy Modock was here before. If we let him get a foothold, it'll be the same way again."

"You're still not the law, Blair. We've got a duly elected sheriff in this county. It's up to him to handle it."

Blair's left fist doubled. His right one couldn't. "Erly can't do it all by himself." He turned to his sons, to Hez Northcutt and to chunky Chaco Martinez. "Saddle up. You got some ridin' to do."

He stepped out onto the gallery with them. From the darkness came the sound of a running horse. Blair motioned for the others to wait. "Could be the sheriff," he said. Nobody had been able to find him earlier. The lawman was still scouring the country for Joe Little.

The horse loped into the open yard, and Blair saw the flare of long skirts. He frowned as Jessie Cass reined to a stop and jumped down in front of the house. Her eyes went straight to Allan. "Allan," she cried, "are you all right?"

Allan hurried down the steps and grabbed her into his arms. "Jessie, what're you doin' here?"

"I heard them say they'd shot somebody. They didn't say who. I was scared to death it was you. I'd of died if it was you."

Blair Bishop watched hard-eyed as Allan held the girl tightly. "It was Finn. He's dead, Jessie."

"Dead?" She sobbed quietly. "I've been afraid it would come to somethin' like this. I've been tryin' to tell Dad . . ."

Blair moved stiffly down the steps. His voice was cold.

"You go on home, girl, and you tell your daddy somethin' else. You tell him he picked himself the wrong partners if he has any notion of gettin' his greedy hands on some of the Double B for them scrubby cattle. You tell him a good man died here tonight, and I'm holdin' him responsible right along with the others."

Jessie turned from Allan, but she still held his hand. "He can't do anything," she said brokenly. "All those men . . . bad men . . . they've got him scared to open his mouth. They're breakin' him down, Mister Bishop. They've taken over."

"He asked for it. He let it start. I got no sympathy for Clarence Cass, but one thing I'll sure as hell promise him: I'm goin' to protect what's mine. He ain't goin' to get any of this land, either by stealin' it or by marryin' off his daughter to it. If I got to bury your old daddy along with the rest of them, then that's just what I'll do. You go tell him that, girl."

"Please, Mister Bishop, you've got to understand how it is . . ."

"I *know* how it is. I lost one good man findin' out. I got a strong hunch I lost another and just can't prove it. So you go tell him what I said. Tell him if he's got half the brains God gave a jackrabbit, he'll pack up and leave this country on the fastest horse he's got. And you better go with him."

Allan tightened his hold on the girl's hand. "Jessie's not goin'."

Blair's eyes narrowed. He gave the girl a long, hard look, then turned to Allan. He thrust his jaw forward. "Boy, we got a good man dead in yonder. I don't want to ever see Clarence

Cass' miserable whinin' face again, and I won't have this girl around to remind me of him." To the stricken girl he said evenly, "Now get on that horse and go home, girl. Don't you ever come here again!"

Crying, she tried to leave. Allan held her. Stubbornly he faced his father. "I've told you how it is with us. Anywhere Jessie goes, I go with her!"

That shook Blair Bishop. He said, "You know what we got to do tomorrow. If we don't do it, Finn died for nothin'. Would you turn your back on us at a time like this?"

"Not unless I was forced to it. Don't you force me."

"The choice is yours. I don't want that girl here. Not now and not ever."

Allan eyed his father an awful moment, then the girl. He gripped Jessie's hand so hard she flinched. "Jessie, I got a duty here. I'll see it through. When it's done, I'll come for you and we'll *both* leave this country. You go on home and get your things ready. Chances are I'll be there sometime tomorrow."

Blair Bishop swallowed, but he tried not to let the bitter disappointment show. He turned away from the couple and walked out into the yard, struggling for control over the grief and anger which shook him. He could hear Allan talking softly to the girl. "He's speakin' for himself," Allan was saying, "but not for me. Soon as I go to fetch you, you can say goodbye to that place. You won't ever have to go back there."

Blair didn't look, but he could tell Allan was helping the girl onto her horse. "Allan," she said, "be careful. Those men had as soon kill you as look at you. Maybe a little rather."

"I'll be careful. You do the same."

The horse moved away. Presently Blair heard his oldest son walk up beside him. "She's gone, Dad, and you won't have to look at her again. Soon's we get this quarrel with Modock over with, I'll be leavin'."

"It's your choice to make, son," Blair said stiffly.

"Always remember, I didn't want to make it."

By daylight the first people came. A neighbor brought a pine coffin that he had stayed up through the post-midnight hours to build. His wife had padded the interior of it with dark velvet cloth. The men filed through the Bishop parlor to view Finn Goforth in the simple coffin. Then they gathered on the gallery in angry silence, for Finn had been a man without an enemy, except those he inherited through Blair Bishop.

Blair sat in the parlor quietly receiving the people. Few women came, because what lay ahead this day was for the men to do. Nobody talked about it, but Blair sensed it was strong on everyone's mind. Mentally he tallied the men as they arrived. About ten o'clock he pushed painfully to his feet. He looked a minute into the faces of men he counted as friends—ranchers, cowboys, people from town. They had come to side him in his hour of need, for they realized it was their hour too.

Allan Bishop waited with the rest. Blair wished that he could undo what had been said in the dark of night, but it lay between them like a strong adobe wall. He nodded at Allan. "Let's go, son."

Billy Bishop came out of his bedroom, shotgun in hand.

Blair caught his arm. "Billy, you're not of age for this. When we've finished buryin' Finn, you're comin' back to the house."

"I'm old enough. There's not nobody can shoot this thing any better."

Blair's voice carried in it a firmness that plainly brooked no argument. "You're stayin' home, son."

The burial was soon over. Without saying anything, Blair Bishop limped out and swung heavily upon his big gray horse. The other men followed suit. The only sound was of stamping hoofs and creaking leather. For a moment Blair caught the reluctant look in Billy's eyes. Blair wanted to know *one* son would be home when he came back . . . if he came back.

He set out with a dozen riders behind him. Before he had gone a mile, he picked up three more. They moved in a stiff trot, saving the horses but steadily putting the miles behind them. Blair led them in an arc that would allow them to pick up most of the cattle. The ones Modock had herded out of the pasture probably would be scattered in the general vicinity of the gate, wanting back in for the water they were accustomed to. The others which Blair and the men had driven yesterday probably would be strung out halfway to the Black Bull Tank by now, instinct taking them back.

The horsemen picked up the scattered cattle as they found them and bunched them gradually, pushing toward the double gates. The animals were dry now, slobbering for want of water. They moved sluggishly, instinct telling them they were being pushed away from water rather than toward it. The dry ground went to powder beneath the scraping of their sharp hoofs, and dust rose in a choking veil of gray.

Finally Blair could see the tall gateposts which marked the location of the fence. And he could see the dark figures he knew were horsemen, waiting to stop them. "This time, Macy Modock," he muttered, "you'll move aside or get trampled."

The day was hot, but the sweat which broke over him was cold. He counted the men at the gate. Six. He had them outnumbered by more than two to one. He said nothing. He simply touched spurs to the big gray and moved into an easy swinging lope, leaving the cattle. Without looking back, he knew the men behind him would follow his lead. The thought gave him satisfaction, knowing he had friends strong enough in their faith to follow him into the muzzles of professional guns. But the responsibility was heavy too. For half a moment he felt the hard tug of strong doubt. But this left him in a rise of bitterness as he recognized the thin form of Macy Modock slacked on his horse just beyond the wire gate.

Blair pulled a shotgun out of his saddle scabbard. He had left his rifle at home because he feared his right hand would allow him poor use of it, at best. But he could handle this shotgun. For one shot, at least. He would make that shot a good one, or he would never get a second.

His horsemen pulled up on either side of him, presenting a broad, massive line bristling with weapons. Blair studied the men across the fence. Each had a rifle or a pistol in his hands. Mostly rifles.

We can't help but win, he thought, *but there's liable to be some good men fall*.

The alternative was to be able to convince Modock of the hopelessness of his situation, and failing this, to get Modock with a first shot that might—given luck—be the only one fired. One more man dead among Blair's good friends was one more man too many.

Maybe Modock would see reason when he looked into all those guns.

One of the wire gates lay on the ground, thrown back out of the way. A horseman rode through it, his hand raised. Blair felt surprise. This was sheriff Erly Greenwood.

"Erly," Blair said, "my boy told me he couldn't find you last night."

"I got in awful late. What I found didn't cheer me none. Blair, you got to call this off."

"*Me?* You get Macy Modock to call it off. He's the one makin' the grab, startin' the trouble."

Erly Greenwood appeared considerably agitated. Blair surmised he had been arguing with Macy Modock before the ranchers arrived. He probably hadn't gotten anywhere with Modock. *The only thing Modock understands is a .30-.30 slug, or a dose of buckshot,* Blair thought.

The sheriff appeared almost in despair. Blair hadn't slept any last night, and he guessed the sheriff hadn't either. Greenwood said, "Blair, you got to back off. Somebody'll get killed here sure as hell."

Blair shook his head. "I come to put my cows back where they belong. They're goin' through that gate, Erly, before the sun's an hour higher."

"You got good men with you. Friends of yours, friends of mine. You don't want their blood on your conscience."

"They know what's at stake here. They know what it might cost. They figure this is for them as well as for me. Them thirsty cows back yonder are mine. But next week or next month they could be somebody else's. We've decided we're goin' to stop the thing before it ever really starts. We'll stop it here."

"I'm askin' you to back away, Blair."

Blair frowned, beginning to be puzzled. "You askin' me as a friend, Erly, or as the sheriff?"

"As a friend first. If you won't do it as a friend, then I'll ask you as the sheriff."

"Them cows yonder, they can't wait much longer. They're dry. I'm takin' them to water. That's my land."

"Maybe it's not, Blair."

Blair stared, incredulous. "You better explain that."

"Judge Quincy got in from the Statehouse. Brought a court order with him. It's an injunction to keep you off till there can be a hearin' on whether you got legal title or not."

"Legal title? I've had title for years."

"Seems like Quincy dug up somethin' that casts a shadow over your deeds, Blair. The court orders everything held still till there can be a hearin'. Now, I'm askin' you again to turn back."

"Erly, you wouldn't side with Modock."

"You know me better than that. But I got to uphold the law, and a court order's the law. So back off, Blair, please."

"And if I don't?"

"Then I got to try and stop you."

"You wouldn't shoot me, Erly."

"But I might block that gate till you shoot *me*."

Dry-mouthed, Blair looked awhile at Erly Greenwood, then at the barbed wire fence and at the windmill far beyond it. He looked at the riders who faced him across that fence, and most of all he stared at Macy Modock, the hatred aboil in him.

"This is twice now you've let me down, Erly."

"Not through any choice of mine, Blair. I'd resign this badge before I'd hurt you. Right now I'm just tryin' to keep you from hurtin' yourself."

"What about my cows?"

"You push them up to the gate and I'll make Modock drive them to the mill for water, then bring them back to you. But you keep your men on this side."

"One waterin' saves them for one day. What about tomorrow?"

"I don't know, Blair. Honest to God, I don't know what you're goin' to do about this problem."

"Modock may not want to water them even this once."

"Right now he needs the law. He's usin' me and knows it. I'll tell him he'll do it or I'll shoot him."

Blair pondered, all his instincts telling him to fight, to make this a showdown and get it over with while the odds heavily favored him. Another time, they might be heavily against him. He studied the guns across the fence and felt his hands cold-sweaty against his own shotgun.

We could do it, he thought, wanting to go ahead. *We could do it so easy . . .*

He watched Macy Modock running his ready hand up and down the rifle he held lying across the pommel of his saddle, its muzzle vaguely pointed in Blair's direction. Blair gauged the distance and knew he would have to move closer for this shotgun to take good effect.

To move closer, he would have to ride over Erly Greenwood.

Blair looked to one side of him, then to the other, at the men who had come to cast their lot with him. Guilt touched him, for if he backed away now, he was letting them down.

But he couldn't go against Erly. His shoulders slumped. "All right, Erly. But don't you let me down a third time."

He saw triumph in the way Macy Modock relaxed, letting the rifle droop, and resentment roiled in Blair Bishop. To Greenwood he said, "You make it clear to him that I ain't givin' up, not by a damn sight. I'm just backin' off this time because you asked me to. We'll give the court a chance." His eyes narrowed. "But the court better come through right, because that's my land, and I won't stay off of it long."

He turned his horse and started back toward the herd, to bring it up to the gate as Erly had said. One of his neighbors spurred up beside him. "You don't have to call it off on our account, Blair."

"It's over with, John. At least, for today it's over with."

The neighbor frowned, looking over his shoulder toward the fence. "Then it's over for good and all. Ever give Modock a toehold, the only way you'll be shed of him is to kill him."

They brought the cattle and turned them through the gate. Blair could tell Modock had no inclination to receive them and drive them up to water, but Erly Greenwood brooked no argument, and at the moment Modock was heavily dependent upon Greenwood's reluctant backing.

Gradually the neighbors dropped out and began riding away, saying little or nothing to Blair Bishop, talking little even among themselves. Blair watched them silently, sensing the disapproval of many who had come here angry enough to fight. To them, Blair had backed down. Blair Bishop, the old warhorse, was showing his age.

It shook his self-confidence, for in his own mind he still didn't know whether he had been wrong or right. Maybe he should have gone ahead and carried through his threat. Now it was too late. The moment had come, the iron had been hot, and he had not struck. The moment might not come again.

Maybe they *were* right. Maybe Blair Bishop *was* showing his age. Maybe he should turn it over to his sons.

But he couldn't do that. Billy was not of age. And Allan was standing firm on his promise. The confrontation over and the danger past, Allan had ridden away to get Jessie Cass.

Blair hung his head, beaten.

XI

The confrontation at the fence hadn't turned out the way Allan Bishop had expected. He had thought Blair Bishop's show of strength would have put a quick end to it, either in a volley of gunfire or by Macy Modock's capitulation in the face of heavy odds. He had really anticipated the latter, for Modock might have been vindictive and he might have been greedy, but he was not a fool. What Allan hadn't expected—and knew his father hadn't either—was Erly Greenwood's being forced to take a position that gave the decision to Modock.

Now the question remained unresolved; the problem bore on Blair Bishop heavier than ever. Allan felt a keen sense of guilt, leaving this way when it was plain his father faced deeper trouble. He knew how it would look; many would call him a quitter, deserting Blair Bishop in his hour of greatest need. Allan hadn't wanted it this way; Blair had made the ultimatum. Given any way out, Allan would have stayed and seen it through. But not at the risk of losing Jessie Cass. No telling what things were like at the Cass place anymore. Allan had made up his mind he wouldn't leave her there another day, another night.

He wished he had taken time to go to the ranch for a wagon. He figured the ranch owed him that much, for as a Bishop son he had never drawn any regular wage. But maybe now would be a good time to fetch Jessie, when Modock and his crew and Clarence Cass were occupied watering the

Bishop cattle and driving them back out of the contested pasture.

Allan had no particular fear of Modock. He realized the man was reputed to be fast with a gun, and word had drifted down that Owen Darby was fast too. But Blair Bishop had always maintained and taught his sons that speed wasn't the only thing which mattered. Coolness and deliberation counted for a lot. Allan figured he had both, but he had never had occasion to test them under fire. The deliberation part told him if he could avoid a fight, he was that much better off. And getting Jessie out while everybody was gone might be a good way to sidestep trouble.

Don't run from a fight, Blair had taught his sons, but walk away right gingerly if you can.

He rode boldly up to the small, slipshod frame house that seemed to show a slight lean toward the east. West wind was pushing on it all the time, Allan thought. Somehow the whole character of Clarence Cass seemed reflected in his poor drab house.

"Jessie," he called, "you in there?"

Jessie Cass had already seen him. She ran out, almost stumbling on the wooden doorstep. He took her into his arms a moment, then released her. "You got a horse here you can ride, or have we got to ride this one double?"

Surprised, she said, "You're really takin' me away from here?"

"Told you I was."

She had been crying; he could tell by the redness of her eyes. "The fight," she asked quickly, "is it over?"

"It never started. It's a standoff of sorts, but I reckon Modock has got a little the better of it."

Her voice was bitter. "I wish somebody would kill him. If somebody doesn't, there'll be other men die."

"That's no way for a girl to be a-talkin'."

"You haven't been here. You haven't seen him and listened to him. He's a little bit crazy, Allan."

He could tell by the way she spoke of Modock that she was afraid of him. "You won't be troubled by him no more. You got anything you need to pack, anything we can carry horseback?" He knew she didn't have much. Everything she owned could have been stuffed into a cowboy's warbag without crowding the puckerstring. Cass had never been one to spoil his daughter by teaching her vanity and a taste for worldly goods.

"I'll pack it," she said, "while you go saddle my horse for me. You'll find him grazin' down yonder in the draw, most likely."

Riding out, Allan saw a man standing in the open door of the shed, swaying. He recognized Harley Mills, once a Double B cowboy, mostly now a stable-sweeping drunk. Resentment touched Allan as he thought of Mills' falsely swearing that his homestead claim had been fraudulent.

"What're you doin' out here, Harley?" he demanded, but Mills didn't answer him and didn't have to. Allan could guess. He decided the man represented no threat to him and Jessie, so he rode on down to the draw. He found the horse, tossed a loop over its neck and led it back to the shed. Mills watched indifferently while Allan flung the sidesaddle onto the dun and led it to the house. Jessie came out carrying a faded carpetbag. "My mother's," she said. "It's about all she left me except a cheap ring and a locket."

"And the prettiest face in the country," Allan told her. He

gave her a lift into the saddle. She looked around a moment, tears welling into her eyes. He asked her, "Any regrets?"

"I hate leavin' Dad. He's in trouble."

"Nothin' your stayin' could do to help him out of it." But Allan could respect her feelings, for he had the same kind himself regarding Blair Bishop.

"Where we goin'?" she asked.

"To town. I figure we'll get married there. Wouldn't be proper for us to go ridin' around all over the country together without we do the right thing first. And I got some money of my own in the bank. I thought I'd get Mister Karnes there to give me a letter of some kind so we can draw against it wherever we go. Then we'll just strike out a-lookin'. I'll find me a job on a ranch somewheres."

She said gravely, "You don't want to leave your old daddy any more than I want to leave mine."

"We got any choice?"

"I reckon not."

"Then we better be movin'. Longer we wait, the more likely we'll run into your daddy's friends."

They had already waited too long, but they didn't find out for a while. They rode side by side several miles, saying little, exchanging occasional glances but mostly keeping their own individual counsel, mulling over the intolerable conditions that had brought them to this necessity of riding away when neither really wanted to.

"Things'll work out," she said after a time. "You'll see."

He found no conviction in her voice, and there was none in his. "Sure they will."

It was on his mind that either probably would turn and go back if the other would but suggest it. Increasingly he knew he didn't want to go like this, and neither did she, leaving so much uncompleted, so much trouble still in the air. He was on the point of saying so when he saw riders coming toward them on the Cass wagon road.

Jessie gasped, "Modock!"

Allan stopped. He looked around quickly, but he saw no way to avoid the riders without running. It was contrary to all his upbringing to run. He hoped Modock still had the sheriff with him, for Erly Greenwood would see to it that there was no trouble. As the riders neared, he sagged. The sheriff must have gone back to town. Allan told Jessie, "Stay back a little. If there's a fight, I'll need room."

Clarence Cass was the first of the riders to speak after they closed the distance and stopped their horses in a crescent around Allan. He looked at his daughter in sharp surprise. "Jessie, what you doin' out here thisaway? I've told you I don't want you havin' no truck with this Bishop."

She didn't answer him. Modock spoke. "Ought to be plain enough to you, Clarence. It's plain to me. That boy yonder's a true son of his old daddy. He was fixin' to steal that little girl from you."

Allan said defiantly, "Jessie and me, we're goin' to town. We're fixin' to be married, and then we're leavin' this country."

That brought surprise even to Modock, who had never thought of the Bishops except as a cohesive unit. It hadn't occurred to him they might split away from each other in disagreement. "You meanin' to tell us you'd leave your daddy in the midst of a fight? I'm disappointed in you. You ain't a true Bishop after all. Givin' the devil his due, I'd say that Blair Bishop wouldn't never run out on *nobody*."

"I'm not runnin' out; I been *put* out. If it was up to me, I'd stay and fight you, Modock."

The tall gunman frowned, chewing quietly on something as his eyes dwelt on Allan. "Well, I'd say you got a good chance to do that right here, because I done made up my mind you ain't takin' that gal noplace."

"You got no hold on her."

Modock said, "Then I reckon I'll *put* one on her."

It came to Allan with sudden impact, a thought that had never quite reached him before. Modock had a hunger for this girl, just as Allan did. And he became certain this was as far up this road as he would get unless he could somehow beat Modock. He could see death in Modock's hard eyes.

Allan felt trapped like a fly in a spiderweb. His heart quickened. He tried to look around him without giving away his anxiety. They were moving to box him in, the red-bearded Owen Darby passing around to get behind him. But Jessie was still back a few feet, out of it. She could, if she would, spur clear. Then it would be a matter of a horserace whether they could catch her or not. Allan said to her, "Jessie, light out of here. Don't you stop till you get to Dad. You tell him—"

Modock broke in. "She ain't fixin' to tell him nothin'. And neither are you."

Allan sensed that Jessie wouldn't do what he told her; she wouldn't run off and leave him here. He could see the intention in Modock's eyes and knew at any second Modock would reach for the pistol at his hip. He tried to remember all his father had told him about keeping his head, but none of the admonitions seemed to hold for him now. He found himself drawing inexorably toward a contest. Even as he realized he couldn't win, he found himself easing his hand down toward the butt of his pistol. *Don't be a fool,* he told himself, *they'll kill you.* But then he told himself, *They'll kill you anyhow. At least, take Modock.* He ducked low in the saddle, his hand darting for the gun.

Modock moved so swiftly Allan barely saw. He caught the swift streak of the man's pistol coming up, saw the flash and heard the explosion before his own hand had more than grasped the butt of his weapon. The bullet smashed into him like the strike of a sledge, driving him backward out of his saddle. He felt the frightened jump of his horse and felt himself suspended a moment in midair before he knew the sensation of falling. He struck the ground almost beneath his horse's hoofs.

Modock grunted. "He ducked just as I fired. I didn't get me no clean shot. But I don't reckon he'll duck again." The excited horse was in his way as he leveled the gun toward the sprawled body on the ground. Modock shouted impatiently, "Hyahhhh! Get out of here!"

Jessie Cass was on the ground, screaming at him. Before the horse galloped off in panic, clearing the way, Jessie had thrown herself over the downed boy and was looking up at Modock with eyes ablaze. "No! Don't you shoot him again."

Impatient, Modock gestured with the gun barrel. "Git aside, girl."

"I won't move. To shoot him, you'll have to shoot me first."

Owen Darby coldly rode up on the other side. "I can get him from here, Macy. She can't cover him from both of us."

Jessie Cass glanced back in desperation, knowing Darby could and would.

Clarence Cass brought himself up to mild protest. "Macy, you don't really need to do it. He's old man Blair's boy. Folks'll raise hell. You can leave when you've finished what you come to do, but me, I got to live here."

Modock flashed him a look of disgust. "Old man, you ain't ever really seen *nothin'* clear, have you? I don't figure on leavin' here at all. And I won't be finished with what I come to do till all these Bishops are put away in a pine box. This one is just the first." He turned his back on the frightened old rancher and tried to see a way to aim past Jessie without hitting her.

Jessie saw he intended to do it. She straightened, got what control she could muster and told him: "Go ahead, then, if you have to do it, but you'd better shoot me too. If you don't, I'll get you, Modock. Somewhere, somehow, I'll get hold of a gun, and I'll kill you. If I can't get a gun, I'll get a knife, and some-day you'll doze off and forget to watch me, or you'll look away a minute and I'll drive that knife into you to the hilt. I'll kill you, Macy Modock. I promise, I'll kill you!"

Modock blinked, unprepared for her savage response. A chill touched him; he hadn't guessed it was in her. Yet, he could tell she meant every word, and she would carry through if it cost her life. He lowered the pistol. "Hell, maybe he'd be worth more to us alive than dead anyway. Long's we got him laid up with a bullethole bigger than a bushel basket, he won't be goin' noplace, and neither will she. Could be he'll make us a hole card if we need it to use against old Blair Bishop. Catch that horse, somebody, and we'll throw him across the saddle."

Jessie pleaded, "He'll bleed to death."

"Let him bleed. Weaker he is, the less we got to worry."

They threw him roughly up onto his horse. Jessie had used a handkerchief to help stanch the blood, and now she rode close beside him to help hold him onto the saddle. Modock glared at her.

"All right, girl, you got him. Now you better remember this. *We* got him too. First bad move you make, we'll blow him out like a lamp. You listen to every word I tell you and you do what I say. Long's you pay attention, that's how long he stays alive. Now, let's git movin'."

XII

Blair Bishop drew rein in front of the Two Forks Livery & Grain, stepped down and limped heavily into the big open door. "Harley Mills, where you at? Harley, you git yourself out here! I come to talk to you!"

He caught a shadowy movement toward the end of the horse stalls and walked angrily in that direction, cursing a little in pent-up bitterness. He slowed as an old man stepped out into view. Blair broke off the profanity. "I took you for Harley. Where the hell is he at?"

The old man shrugged. "He ain't been here in two-three days. He just up and quit his job; said he had enough money he didn't have to shovel horse manure no more. Ain't seen him since."

Blair Bishop seethed in frustration but decided this was only a momentary setback. Depending upon how much money Harley had been given, he would be either in one of the saloons drinking his fill or out someplace sleeping like a man pistol-whipped. Harley was one of those bachelor cowboys who had never had a wife and didn't need one; whiskey was both his comfort and his personal hell.

"I'll find him quick enough," Bishop gritted, turning.

"I heard what he done," the old man said. "He was lyin', wasn't he?"

"He was lyin'."

"Don't think too harsh of him, Mister Blair. He can't control himself when it comes to whiskey. He'd do anything to get it."

"I don't plan to hurt him much; just bust his head if he don't tell the truth."

Followed by his son Billy, Blair tromped from one saloon to another, impatiently inquiring after Harley Mills. To his surprise, he found no one who had seen Harley in a couple of days. Harley had bought several bottles and dropped out of sight. A thought struck Blair, and he started back down the saloons, inquiring if anyone had bought any unusually large amounts of whiskey lately. At the third place, he found out Judge Quincy had bought a full case. That was strange, for Quincy was, at most, a light drinker. Whatever his shortcomings might have been, an affinity for alcohol was not one of them. His legal mind, if devious, stayed nevertheless sharp.

Blair stood outside the saloon door with young Billy, grinding his teeth. "He took Harley's deposition and then hid him out, that's what he done. He's hidin' him someplace to keep us from gettin' any chance to shake the truth out of him."

"Ain't many ranches around here would do that to you, Dad. By now they all know what Harley done. No friend of yours would help Macy Modock."

"No reason a friend of mine would have to. Ten to one they got Harley at the Cass place where Modock can keep an eye on him till he needs him in court."

"Well, then, let's go out there and git him."

Blair shook his head. "This mornin' the odds were on our side. If we was to ride out there, they'd be on Modock's side, and don't you think for a minute he wouldn't use them. He'd cut us both to pieces. And he'd have a legal leg, because we'd be the trespassers, not him."

"Then we can't touch Harley Mills?"

"Not unless he runs out of whiskey and comes to town. I'm goin' to leave word around with some friends to keep an eye out for him."

"Modock'll figure that. He won't let Harley run out of whiskey till he's through with him."

"Which only leaves Judge Quincy."

Billy grinned humorlessly and rubbed his knuckles. "Come right down to it, he's the cause of all this trouble. Without him, Modock couldn't of done a thing, hardly. Let's go work on him."

"We'll go *talk* to him," Blair corrected his eager son. "And I'll do all the talkin'."

The moment Blair Bishop's shadow fell across his door Quincy was on his feet. He hurried behind a long table spread with papers and law books and turned defensively. "Blair Bishop, I been promised the sheriff's protection. You lay one hand on me and I'll sue you for every acre you got, every cow . . ."

"Settle down, Judge." Blair's voice was dry. "I come friendly. No, I take that back . . . not friendly. But I come peaceful. All I want to do is talk."

"We've done our talking. Anything else you have to say to me you can say it in court."

Blair eyed him thoughtfully. "I ain't no lawyer, Judge, but through the years I've picked up a legal word here and there. One of them is *perjury*. Another is *disbarment*."

"You'll not get away with threatening me. Intimidation is against the law . . ."

"I ain't threatenin', and I ain't intimidatin'. Let's say I'm askin' for a little bit of legal information, and I'm willin' to pay the goin' fee for it. My question is this: how does a man go about filin' for disbarment of a lawyer who knowingly builds up a case based on perjury . . . who maybe even personally bribes a witness to give false testimony?"

"You're still trying to intimidate a legally licensed attorney into defaulting on a client, Blair Bishop. The bar will not hold still for it."

"I never mentioned your name; never mentioned nobody's name. I just asked for a piece of legal information. If you don't care to answer it, I can go to somebody else who knows law. Maybe the district judge . . ."

Blair's leg hurt; he'd slept little, and he had done a lot of riding. He shifted his weight. Quincy took that for a move forward, and he cringed. "Bishop, don't you come any closer. I have a gun in here. I'll use it."

Blair heard footsteps scrape across the threshold, and he saw relief flush over Quincy's face. Quincy said, "Sheriff, you sure took your time getting here."

Blair glanced back at Erly Greenwood. "Howdy, Erly. Seems like a man runs into you almost everyplace these days, except when he needs you."

"Maybe you do need me right now, Blair. Maybe you was about to do somethin' that could cost you more than you could afford to pay."

"I wasn't goin' to do anything to him. I'm as close right now as I ever care to be. The smell of him would kill cotton at forty paces."

Erly studied Blair Bishop gravely. "Blair, you got trouble enough without makin' it worse. Why don't you go on home and get some sleep? Then maybe you'll be in a better position to think things through. Better yet, you come on over to my house and bunk down awhile. You'll see things clearer."

"I'm tired, but I ain't blind. I see things clear enough. Quincy bribed Harley Mills into makin' a deposition that he homesteaded his place through fraud and that I was the one put him up to it, so I could buy the land from him. You know it's a lie; Quincy knows it's a lie. But some visitin' judge from another part of the state won't know it's a lie unless Harley or Quincy owns up to it. I come to talk sense to Quincy."

"And I come to talk sense to you, Blair. A mistake right now could cost you your case."

"I ain't fixin' to lose my land, Erly, not to a set of lies told by a crooked lawyer and a whiskey-soaked stable sweeper."

"You *could* lose it. You got to walk easy till this thing has come to a head. You got to keep your distance from Judge Quincy. It's my job to give him protection."

"Seems to me like you been takin' your job awful seriously here of late."

"I always did, Blair." Erly shook his head, taking a hard, long look at Quincy. "And there's never been a time I ever hated it till now."

Quincy watched the sheriff until he found confidence in himself. "You're letting your personal feelings influence you, Greenwood. A peace officer cannot afford to do that."

"A peace officer cannot afford to let his personal feelings be an influence in what he does," Erly corrected him. "There's no law can keep an officer from havin' them. You know mine. Somethin' for you to keep in mind if ever I catch you steppin' over the line."

The sheriff followed Blair and Billy out into the street. Blair stood slumped, exhausted in body and spirit. "Seems like every way I turn, they got me boxed, Erly."

"I'm sorry they've made me a party to it. Only way I could change it would be to resign, and that wouldn't help anything. The next man couldn't do no different, not and live up to his oath."

"Don't resign, Erly. Maybe they'll make a mistake. Then we'll need you behind that badge."

"And if they don't make any mistakes?"

Blair thought awhile. "Then I'll need you to keep me from makin' one and killin' them all."

Erly walked along with him. He didn't have to move very fast, for Blair was dragging some. He said, "Blair, I still wish you'd come out to the house and rest awhile. You need it."

"I got a lot of thinkin' to do. I think better at home." It occurred to him to ask, "You never have found any sign of Joe Little?"

Erly shook his head. "None at all. He's plumb left the country."

"I don't agree with you. I still believe he was the first mistake Macy Modock made."

"You keep thinkin' that, Blair, if it'll make you feel any better."

"It don't help my feelin'. But it helps keep me convinced that one way or another, I got to stop Macy Modock. Only thing bothers me is, how many more men will he kill before I get *him?*"

Harley Mills was well into his second bottle for the day, but his vision wasn't so foggy he couldn't see that one of the horses was bringing somebody wounded. The thought filtered through his brain that he could've told them old Blair Bishop would fight like a mountain lion with its tail in a steel trap, that they wouldn't come home in one piece. But they hadn't asked him. They hadn't asked him much of anything, come to think of it.

Well, it wasn't going to be any bother to him one way or the other. The hell with them. Soon as they got that court hearing over with and paid him off, Harley Mills was going to be long gone out of this country. He didn't give a damn then if Modock and all of his bunch got shot into pieces too little for chili. In fact, he almost hoped they would. He found it impossible ever to feel easy in the presence of Modock or Owen Darby. He never got over the feeling that Darby would shoot a man just for the fun of seeing him jump and fall, and that Modock had some devil chewing on him all the time. Mills would be glad to get the money in his hands and run. It had occurred to him more than once that for the amount promised him, Modock probably wouldn't hesitate to kill a man.

I'll be sober that day, Mills pledged himself, *and I'll have eyes in the back of my head. Once I get paid off, all they'll see of Harley Mills is a blue streak and a little cloud of dust.*

He didn't care enough to get up and go see who was wounded; he didn't know any of these Modock men anyway, and if it was old man Clarence the world would be that much better off, in Mills' view. But his interest was aroused a little when he saw Cass' girl, Jessie, jump down from her sidesaddle. The way he had seen her ride away from here earlier with that young Bishop, he had figured she was gone for good. Mills blinked as they led the wounded man's horse up to the shed where he lay with the bottle. To his surprise he recognized Allan Bishop. Mills staggered to his feet, stumbled over a pitchfork and got up again. His first thought was, *He'll tell old Blair where I'm at and he'll come after me with a bullwhip or a gun.* Then he realized that the shape Allan appeared to be in, he wouldn't be going anywhere. Mills tried to figure out how come they had brought young Bishop here, but liquor had left him no chance with logic. Nothing came very clear to him except that an uncomfortable situation was becoming increasingly bad.

"Move over, Mills," Macy Modock said curtly. "We got to have that cot you been lyin' on."

Mills stared in confusion at the unconscious Allan Bishop. "How come him to be here?" He was too puzzled even to feel resentment over being done out of his cot. He would have to sleep on the hay now.

"We shot him," Modock said.

"Old man Blair'll come huntin' him, and there'll be hell to pay."

"Bishop figures he run off with the Cass girl," Modock said. "He won't be lookin' for him."

Mills stared down at the blood-streaked face. "He goin' to die?" He had punched cows with Allan, back when Allan was just a kid. He had been a good-enough kind of a button, Mills had always thought, considering that he was the son of a big cowman like Blair Bishop. A little humility wouldn't have hurt him none, but Mills wouldn't have wished him a bullet. "Somebody better fetch him a doctor."

"No doctor," said Modock. "The less Blair Bishop knows, the better. I'll tell him myself if I think the time is right."

"What if that boy was to die?"

"Then I'd give you a shovel and tell you to go bury him, since you're a friend of his. And if you said a word to anybody about it, I'd see that you was buried right next to him. Do you get that through your head, Mills?"

Harley nodded, fearing the man. But he had another fear

too. "If Blair finds out about this, I sure don't want him thinkin' I had anything to do with it."

Modock snarled. "You and old Clarence . . . neither one of you has got sense enough to see daylight. Time I get through, Blair Bishop won't trouble *nobody*."

Harley Mills sat on the ground and silently pulled at the bottle as he watched tearful Jessie Cass and her father dig the bullet out of Allan and wrap clean cloth around the wound. He listened to Clarence Cass complaining. "I didn't noways figure on nothin' like this. I ain't a-goin' to stand for it. One of these days I'm goin' to walk up to Macy Modock and I'm goin' to tell him . . ."

Mills snorted to himself, feeling better in the knowledge that he wasn't the only coward on the place. *You ain't goin' to tell him nothin', Clarence, same as I ain't goin' to tell him nothin'. You're goin' to listen and say yes, sir. Difference is, I'm goin' to get my money and ride out of here. What're you goin' to get, Clarence?*

XIII

Blair Bishop lay down for a fitful nap when he got home, but he arose for a supper quickly cooked by Chaco Martinez. Mostly he drank coffee. It didn't make him feel any easier, but it woke him up. He stayed awake long past his accustomed bedtime, bolstered by a notion that Allan would get over his anger and come on home. He didn't really believe his son would leave here at a time like this, angry or not. And Blair had cooled too, in the face of so many other problems. He could remember how strongly the tides of young manhood had surged in him when he was Allan's age and could, now that he was calmer, understand why the boy would turn his back on father and home in favor of a girl. Blair sat on the porch a long time, sometimes rocking, sometimes still, listening vainly for hoofbeats. He fell asleep finally and woke up with a crick in his neck. Sadly he made his way to bed, knowing Allan wasn't coming.

Next morning he was up early, problems still unresolved. He knew what he had to do about one of them, and he had to do it quick. He had to get a lot of cattle off of his land in a hurry or he wouldn't have anything left except their sunwhitened bones.

He ate his breakfast at the bunkhouse with the men. "Bad as I hate to," he told them, "we got to take a deep cut into the cow herd. We can't sell them at home. It's so dry that most people here are more of a mind to sell than to buy. We'll make a drag on our oldest cows and drive them over to the railroad.

Maybe we can get a decent price for them in Kansas City."

Billy Blair put in, "Seems like an awful pity to have to sell off them good Double B cows."

"Be a worse pity to watch them die for water. If we can save the young cows, we'll at least have seed."

"There was a time," Billy said, "when you wouldn't have done it this way. You'd have took care of Macy Modock and everything would've been all right."

Blair frowned. It surprised him, the quick-fighting spirit Billy was showing these days. Blair wondered where his son had gotten this sudden contrariness from; certainly not from his father. "Times change, boy. There was a time years ago when I could've killed Modock and nobody would've said a word."

"You sorry now you didn't?"

Blair thought about it a minute. "Maybe. For some things in this world, there's no cure as dependable as a good old-fashioned funeral."

He took the small crew to the Black Bull pasture where yesterday's trouble had been. There the water problem was most immediate, and most acute. The cattle had been watered yesterday. Today there wouldn't be enough. The cowboys made a broad sweep of the pasture, pushing all the cattle before them. As they moved, Blair Bishop rode back and forth among them, cutting out the younger cows carefully as he could without disrupting the herd. No use walking them extra miles for nothing. He kept the big steers in the herd, and the older cows, and the steer calves and yearlings. These were expendable. These would walk the better part of two days to the railroad.

When he had finished cutting the herd, Blair looked back

for sign of Chaco Martinez. He had told Chaco to load the chuck wagon and bring it, for cowboys had to eat along the trail. They had to have changes of horses, too. He sent Hez Northcutt to round up the remuda. Then Blair took the point and let Billy and the rest of the riders string the herd out behind him. Some of the cattle were bawling, for they already had walked miles in the roundup and were showing thirst. They would have to skirt around Clarence Cass' land, for they would find no welcome there, Blair knew. But beyond Clarence lay the Finley ranch, and John Finley would spare water for a neighbor's passing herd as long as a drop was left.

They walked the cattle through the heat of the afternoon, thirst cracking Blair's dry lips as he rode along watching the dancing dust devils and peering toward the shimmering horizon line that changed but slowly in the deliberate pace of the herd. Chaco rode ahead and off to the right, keeping the wagon out of the herd's dust, for cowboys who ate dust all day didn't want to find it in their supper at night. Along late in the afternoon Blair called Billy up to take his place on the point and loped ahead to find John Finley and get permission to water the herd.

Blair's conscience hurt him as he watched his cattle watering by twilight, the stronger cows hooking impatiently at the weaker ones, fighting their way down to the deeper water. John had only a surface tank, much like Blair's own Black Bull Tank had been. When it emptied, that would be all of it until rain came again. But John hadn't had the heart to turn down Blair Bishop in his time of trouble. Blair shouted at the men, "Let's keep them movin'. Let them get enough water, but don't let them stay too long." Normally he would have bedded the cattle for the night near water, but this was not a normal situation. Soon as they had slaked their thirst, Blair moved out on point and had the cowboys push them a couple more miles to get them away from John's dwindling tank. Maybe they hadn't had all the water they wanted, but they had had enough to see them through another day's drive. There would be water again at the railroad.

The cowboys strung the cattle out in the cool of the morning and walked them steadily, pushing for all the miles they could get without hurting the stock. As the day wore on and the heat came up, the cattle slowed, bawling in distress. Blair plodded along, matching his pace to that of the cattle. He had water in a canteen, but he used it sparingly. Somehow it didn't seem right for a man to drink when his stock was suffering. Blair rode steadily and suffered with them.

Sometime after noon he began noticing the clouds change. Up to then, they had been the same puffy white clouds he had watched drift aimlessly across the sky all the dry spring and summer, leaving no benefit other than a brief respite from the sun's burning heat as they passed over the land. Now, however, the clouds seemed to thicken and turn darker.

Could it be that a summertime rain was coming up? Blair felt his pulse quicken a little at the thought. It wasn't often that a drought broke in this country in August, but sometimes a man got lucky and caught enough hard, pounding rain to run the draws and fill his tanks, to revive the grass and keep its roots alive until the more generous fall rains gave it one last chance before winter.

As the clouds became a leaden gray in the north, excitement built in Blair Bishop. He was tempted to stop the herd. If it would just come one of those old-timey chip floaters and fill his tanks, his cattle would have water enough. He wouldn't have to sell them.

But he knew that since he had gone this far, he had as well go the whole way to the railroad. The grass would revive better and the land would hair over sooner if he got some of the excess cattle off of it.

Riding point, he came to the creekbed where a flash flood had swept the cowboy named Abernathy to his death years ago. The creek was bone dry, as Blair had known it would be. Watching the clouds, he had a feeling it was a good thing the crew would have time enough to get the herd across before the rain started.

He was tired, and he was still desperately thirsty, but it didn't bother him now. He didn't seem to feel it. All he could feel was a faintly cooler wind coming out of the north, out from under those beautiful clouds. *Any minute now, she's going to start,* he thought. *Any minute now, we're goin' to get ourselves soaked.*

A drop of water struck his hat brim, and he turned his face up to the sky. A couple more drops splattered across his nose and his mouth. He turned in the saddle and gave a loud holler that would carry all the way to the drag end of the herd.

But something happened. Even as he watched, the cloud began to split almost directly overhead. He could see blue sky through a rift. As quickly as they had made up, the clouds broke apart and began drifting away. Blair watched dry-mouthed and stunned.

He had seen clouds break up like this more times than he could ever count. But he had never seen a time he had so desperately wanted it to rain.

The sun broke through, as hot as it had ever been. Blair pulled his hat down low to protect his eyes from it. His eyes were burning a little, somehow; must have gotten dust in them. His throat was tight. All of a sudden he realized anew how thirsty he was, and how far it still was to the railroad. He slumped in the saddle and rode along in silent misery.

Late in the afternoon he summoned Billy. "Looks to me like we ought to make it to the shippin' pens about dark. I was thinkin' me and you would ride in and make arrangements with the agent for water and hay. Ain't likely they can spot cars for us till tomorrow sometime."

Billy nodded and went back with orders for someone else to take the point. Then he reined in beside his father, his dusty face proud. This was a sign he was coming of age; this was the sharing of a man's job. Any kid could drive cattle; it took somebody responsible to handle the business end of a ranch.

Blair studied his youngest son as they rode and he liked what he saw. Give the boy a couple-three more years and he would be the man Allan was. Maybe if Blair was lucky, Billy wouldn't fall in love with the wrong woman, either. Time had come, Blair guessed, to talk to him straight-out about things like responsibility, and women and such as that. Maybe that had been the trouble with Allan; maybe Blair hadn't talked to him enough.

I won't make that mistake with Billy, Blair thought. *I'll sure talk to him. But not today; I'm too dry. I'll get around to it one of these days, when the right time comes.*

Blair saw dust rising from the railroad shipping pens and knew another herd was there ahead of him. Late as it was already, he figured it unlikely that herd would load out tonight.

"That's too bad," he said. "I'd figured we could turn them

cattle into the pens on hay and water. Then we wouldn't have to fool with them."

Curiosity would normally have carried him by the pens to look at the cattle, but he had too much on his mind now to spend time on idle things. He rode straight to the depot. Every bone in him ached as he handed his reins to Billy and limped up the plank steps. Billy tied the horses and followed him. First thing Blair did was to find the water bucket and empty the dipper three times . . . twice down his throat and once over his head. Handing it to Billy, he turned and sought the railroad agent. The agent was a fairly new man, for Blair didn't recognize him. He said, "I got a herd of cattle comin' in directly. Blair Bishop, from over at Two Forks. Need cars to take them to Kansas City. Tonight we'll need hay and water."

The agent explained what Blair had already seen, that another herd had preceded him and had occupied the corrals. "However, we have a large water lot with troughs in it. You can bring the cattle, water them good, then take them back out and herd them on the prairie till the train comes tomorrow."

"That'll have to do," Blair said. The agent sat down and began filling out the papers. "Bishop," he murmured. "Blair Bishop. I believe I've shipped cattle for you before, Mister Bishop. What's that brand again?"

"A Double B."

The agent looked up in surprise. "Perhaps I misunderstood you, Mister Blair. You talked as if your cattle were still to come in."

"They are. They'll be here in an hour, give or take a little."

"But most of those cattle down there waiting for shipment

are Double B too. Let me see." He riffled through a sheaf of papers and came up with one. "Yes, it says right here: Double B. Bishop ranch. They were signed for by one of your cowboys."

Blair looked incredulously at Billy, then back at the agent. He reached for the paper. "Let me have a look at that." His gaze went quickly down the paper till he reached the signature at the bottom. "That's no cowboy of mine. I never heard of this man."

The agent blinked. "But those cattle carry your brand, and your name . . ." He stood up solemnly. "We've got a deputy sheriff here. I think I'd better get him."

Blair nodded, suddenly grim. "I think you'd better. We'll go with you."

They found the deputy relaxed in the shade at a livery barn. This was a different county than Erly Greenwood's, and Blair didn't know the lawman. But he thought by the look in the man's eyes that he probably savvied his line of work, for he had a riot-stopping stare. The deputy had heard of Blair Bishop. He shook hands. "My name's Hawk. Family name. Folks around here nicknamed me Bird. I'd still rather it was Hawk."

"Hawk," Blair said, "the agent tells me there's cattle in them shippin' pens carryin' my brand. There oughtn't to be. I'd like you to go with me to investigate."

The deputy was immediately all business. "I'll saddle my old pony and be right with you."

It didn't take him a minute. Blair turned to his son. "Billy, if I'd had any thought of trouble, I wouldn't of brought you. I want you to stay here."

Billy's reply wasn't argumentative; it was a plain statement of fact. "Like hell I will. I stayed home the last time."

Momentarily inclined to raise Cain with him, Blair decided against it. At Billy's age he had taken on all of a man's responsibilities and was the veteran of two Indian fights. "All right, boy, but you watch yourself."

They rode to the shipping pens in an easy trot. Blair took the shotgun out of his scabbard, painfully loaded it with an aching hand and laid it across his lap to be ready. Hawk eyed him warily. "Mister Bishop, we'll talk first."

"That," Blair said, "depends on them."

Two cowboys were in a corral spreading hay. Blair needed only a glance to know that the cattle in the pen were his. They carried the Double B and his earmark. He told the deputy so.

The deputy said, "I know them two hands, Mister Bishop. They been around town here lookin' for work. I didn't figure them for thieves."

"Can't always tell by looks. Damn few cow rustlers go around carryin' a sign."

Without dismounting, the deputy hailed the two cowboys over to the fence. They came without apparent suspicion, until they spotted Blair's shotgun casually aimed in their direction. That stopped them in consternation. "Boys," the deputy spoke, "we come to talk to you. We want to know whose cows them are yonder."

One of the cowboys moved up cautiously, his eyes never leaving the shotgun. "They belong to a feller name of Bishop. Lives over at Two Forks."

The deputy asked, "Do you know Bishop?"

"No, sir, never met him."

Blair demanded, "Then what're you doin' with them cows?"

"We was hired to help drive them up here and see they got shipped all right."

Blair eased off with the shotgun, for he began to suspect these men were the inevitable innocent bystanders who get hurt in every fight. "Who hired you?"

"His foreman. Leastways, he said he was." The two cowboys were beginning to sense the way the wind blew. "Said he'd pay us ten dollars apiece to help make the drive and stay till the shippin' was done."

"He paid you yet?" Blair asked.

"Not yet."

"Then you've likely lost ten dollars apiece. I'm Blair Bishop."

The cowboys gave each other a sick look. One of them tried a weak smile that didn't work. "Somehow, I was startin' to suspect that. Last we seen of that foreman, him and a pal of his was over in the Legal Tender havin' a snort and waitin' for the train."

The deputy motioned. "You-all come with us. You'll have to point them out."

The cowboys were eager, for by now nobody had to explain the situation any further to them. They might come out of this broke, but they wanted to be sure they came out of it clean. There had been a time not too long before when a man caught with somebody else's cattle stood a good chance of looking up a rope at a nice, sturdy tree limb. Climbing into his saddle, one of the cowboys studied Blair the way a jackrabbit might study a wolf. "Mister Bishop, I bet you ain't even *got* a foreman." Blair said, "I did have. He was killed."

The cowboy pleaded, "We didn't know. We needed work, and we took him for what he said he was. We sure don't want no trouble."

Blair said, "You just point him out, and you won't be in no trouble."

They reined up a few doors from the Legal Tender and went on afoot. All but Billy. Blair told him to ride around to the back door. If anybody came running out, Billy was to detain him. Blair figured it would be much safer out there than in the saloon.

The front doors stood wide open, and all the windows were up, for the heat still lingered here into the dusk. The cowboys walked in front of Blair and the deputy. They paused at the door. One pointed. "That's him, the one yonder with the ventilation holes punched in his hat." Blair squinted. Two men sat at a small table, a bottle half emptied in front of them. They had both been with Macy Modock at the Harley Mills fence.

He realized he had never thought to count the cattle Modock had pushed out of that pasture. Other things had seemed far more important at the time. Now he knew Modock had probably shorted him, depending upon there being no count. And he realized where some of the other cattle he had been missing must have gone.

The cowboys stepped back out of the way. Blair moved into the saloon, flanked by the deputy. The two men looked up. Recognition was instantaneous. Both jumped to their feet.

Other men in the saloon dived for cover as the one who had posed as foreman whipped a pistol out of his waistband, his eyes on Blair. *He'll take me first,* Blair thought, bringing the shotgun up into line and stiff-handedly pulling the trigger. Even as the weapon boomed, he knew he had jerked too hard and had missed. But the reaction to the blast threw off the cow thief's aim. His shot went astray. He never got a chance for a second one. The deputy's pistol roared, and the man staggered back.

The second man never made a move toward his pistol. He ran for the open back door. Blair leveled the shotgun at him, but he had no time to reload. The deputy was too engrossed in seeing that the first man didn't fire again to do more than glance at the second. The man hit the door in a dead run.

Blair heard Billy cry out for him to stop. Shots were fired, and Blair could hear horses' hoofs as he limped toward the door, feverishly trying to reload the shotgun and fumbling it. He hit the back step and saw Billy Blair running toward a fallen man. A horse galloped away in panic, stirrups flopping.

Billy stood over the man, smoking pistol in his hand. Blair rushed to him, followed by the deputy and the two cowboys. Other men from the saloon trailed in curiosity.

The deputy looked at the man, who lay sprawled on his stomach. He turned him over, puzzled. "Where'd you hit him, son?"

"I didn't," Billy said, barely above a whisper. "I missed him." He trembled from shock. "He grabbed a horse and tried to run off. He was lookin' back at me. He didn't see that clothesline."

The deputy felt for a pulse, then laid his ear to the man's chest. "You can tell by the way his head lays that he broke his neck. See that rope burn? Done the same as if he'd dropped through a trapdoor with a hemp necktie on."

Blair Bishop placed his hand on Billy's shoulder. "Good thing it turned out this way, boy. You're a shade too young to have a man on your conscience."

"In a way," Billy said regretfully, "I did do it."

"He wasn't runnin' from you, really. He was runnin' from a hangrope. He missed one and found another." Blair turned back to the deputy. "The other one . . . he dead too?"

The deputy nodded. "Been a poor day for cow thieves."

Bishop scowled. "And for me too. I wish we could've got them alive . . . one of them, anyway. Now we got no way to prove Macy Modock was behind them. Far as any court can tell, they was workin' for themselves."

He had explained a little about Modock to the deputy as they had ridden in from the shipping pens. The deputy shook his head sympathetically. "Sorry, Mister Bishop."

"Can't be helped. At least we all still got our health." He rubbed his hurting hand. "Most of it, anyway."

The deputy said, "I reckon now you'll want to claim your cattle."

Blair nodded. "Long as they're already here, I'd just as well ship them with the others I got comin' in. No point in drivin' them back to a dried-out range." He turned to the two cowboys. "You said they promised you ten dollars apiece. I got a herd out yonder. I'll pay you ten dollars if you'll meet them and help bring them on in."

"Fair enough, Mister Bishop." The cowboys rode off in the direction Blair pointed, glad they hadn't found themselves neck deep in trouble.

Blair and Billy rode to the pens again. Blair sat outside the fence on his horse, looking across at some young heifers he wished he could save. Billy rode on around to look at the rest of the cattle. Presently he came back. "Dad," he said urgently, "these ain't all yours."

Blair was a little surprised, though he realized he shouldn't be. A cow thief was not likely to be particular. "Whose are the rest of them?"

"There's a bunch of C Bars in there, too. Clarence Cass."

That *did* surprise Blair, till he had time to think about it a little. Gradually, though, it all began to fit. He laughed dryly when the full irony of the situation came to him. Cass was offering sanctuary to Macy Modock, hoping to see Modock break Blair Bishop, and all the time Modock was stealing from the old man too.

"Cast thy bread upon the waters . . ." Blair Bishop mused. "I reckon old Clarence's bread must've been a little moldy."

XIV

Macy Modock was napping out the afternoon heat when Owen Darby gripped his shoulder and shook him. "Somebody's comin' yonder," Darby said. "Can't tell yet who it is, but I'm pretty sure it ain't Jim and Charlie back from the railroad."

Macy Modock got to his feet and wiped the sweat from his face. He strode out into the yard, softly cursing the interruption and looking down the wagon road. Recognition was slow in coming, but when it came he was suddenly wide awake. "It's Blair Bishop. And he's got the sheriff with him." Modock turned quickly, barking orders. "Owen, you put one of the boys out in the shed to watch that girl and the Bishop boy. No . . . come to think of it . . . you better do it yourself. Tell that girl if she makes as much as a howdydo you'll blow that boy's brains out. And keep Harley Mills out of sight too. Old Bishop'd just love to see him here."

Darby strode to the nearby shed. The rest of Modock's tough crew strayed up from one place and another. Clarence Cass shuffled out of the house sleepy-eyed. "What's goin' on?"

Modock spat, "You just stand back and keep your mouth shut, Clarence. One wrong word and I'll bust out what few teeth you still got left."

Cass stood blinking, trying to figure what he had said wrong.

Modock didn't trust even Darby to do a job without supervision. He looked into the shed. He found Harley Mills seated on the hay-strewn floor, his back to the wall, a near-empty bottle in his hands and an empty look in his eyes. Allan Bishop lay in a fever, half out of his head. The girl sat in a rawhide chair beside the cot, placing wet cloths over Allan's face every now and then. Her eyes hated Modock as she looked up. Owen Darby stood with his back to the wall, pistol pointed at Allan.

"I told her like you said, Macy. If they see her, or hear a sound out of this shed, the boy's dead." Argument showed in his eyes. "But hell, Macy, there ain't but the two of them. You been wantin' to kill Blair Bishop all this time. It'd be easy now."

"Too quick. I ain't got him to his knees yet. Anyway, we'd have to kill the sheriff too. I don't want to run no more. I want to do this in a way that when it's over, I can stay here and en-joy what I've got." He looked at Jessie.

Darby shrugged. "However you want it, Macy. Just seems to me sometimes like you sure go about things the hard way."

"But it's my way. Don't you mess it up."

Modock checked his pistol to be sure it was fully loaded, then walked out into the yard. He didn't plan to use it, but a man never could tell. He stood waiting beside a nervous Clarence Cass while the sheriff and Blair Bishop took their own sweet time about riding in.

The sheriff spoke first. "Howdy, Clarence. Modock."

Blair Bishop looked at Modock, but he spoke to Cass. "Clarence."

Ranch country custom called for a man to invite any visi-tor to light and hitch, whether he be friend or enemy. But Modock had never been one to concern himself over any cus-tom but his own. "Sheriff, you're welcome here any time." He pointedly left out Bishop.

Blair Bishop observed with a touch of sarcasm, "I'd always thought this was Clarence Cass' place." He glanced at Cass in a way that was like rubbing salt into an open sore.

"Me and Clarence is partners," Modock said.

Bishop grunted. "I'm glad to hear that. I thought you'd taken plumb over." He was still looking at Cass, making sure the point wasn't lost. It wasn't.

Modock growled, "You didn't come over here to say howdy."

The sheriff shook his head. "No, we didn't." He looked at the men gathered loosely around Modock. "Seems to me like you had a couple or three more men when you throwed Blair's cattle out of that pasture."

Suspiciously Modock said, "A couple. Does that make any difference?"

Blair Bishop braced his hands against the saddle horn and leaned forward, shifting his weight to one side to ease an aching leg. "We was over at the railroad yesterday. Drove a bunch of cattle there to ship. We found another herd had got there ahead of us. Funny thing about them cattle. Big part of them was wearin' the Double B brand."

Modock frowned. "I wouldn't know nothin' about that."

"There was a couple of your friends over there with them. One was shippin' the cattle and signin' himself as a sales agent for me. The money was supposed to come back to him."

The sheriff said, "To've got them cattle to the railroad yesterday, they had to be gone from here two or three days. Don't a thing like that make you suspicious, Modock?"

"A couple of my boys quit me after that set-to over at the fence. They was nervous about all them guns. Maybe they decided to take a little somethin' with them as they went."

"Maybe so," said Bishop. "Now, Macy, you'll be glad to know that the money for them cattle will all come to me."

"Always tickled to see the right thing done." Modock's dark eyes were a-glitter with anger. "What did you do with them two boys?"

The sheriff said, "They're buryin' them today."

Modock's eyes momentarily flashed a fury he was helpless to hide. He had figured on that money . . . had counted on getting it. Losing it threw a monkey wrench into a bunch of things, but he said, "I reckon they had it comin'. If there's anything I got no use for, it's a thief."

Bishop glanced at the sheriff. "Well, Erly, since Macy wasn't noway involved, I reckon we got no more business here." He started to pull away, then looked at Clarence Cass. "Clarence, I was wonderin' about that daughter of yours. I don't see her noplace around."

Cass shook his head, trembling. "No, you don't."

Bishop nodded solemnly. "Then I take it she's gone. My boy Allan, he said he was goin' to come get her. I hoped maybe he'd come to his senses." Bishop showed disappointment, and he looked a moment at the ground. Then he brought his gaze back to Cass. "One other thing, Clarence. You took any count on your cattle lately?"

Cass' mouth came open in puzzlement. "No, why?"

"Because all them cattle over at the railroad wasn't mine. A big bunch of them was yours." Bishop paused, watching an explosive reaction in Cass' whiskered face. "Since they was already in the shippin' pens and since you're overstocked anyway, I told the station agent to go ahead and load them out for Kansas City along with mine. The payment will come to you."

Clarence Cass' face was flushed. He looked sharply at Modock, then away. Bishop added with an evident touch of malice, "The station agent told me them wasn't the first of your cattle *or* mine that've been shipped lately. Been several other loads gone out. Naturally my first thought was that Macy Modock done it. But from what he tells us, I guess he didn't . . . seein' as you're such good partners." His voice went bitter. "Surely Macy wouldn't have no call to be stealin' from himself." Bishop pulled his horse away. "*Adiós,* Clarence."

Clarence Cass seethed, and Modock knew it, but he didn't give a damn. He stood simmering in his own frustration over loss of that herd, and over the fact that Bishop and the sheriff were wise to him, even if they lacked evidence to make a legal move. He would have the devil's own time getting any more Bishop cattle out from under old Blair's nose. And Modock wanted that money.

Owen Darby walked over from the shed, squinting after the departing riders and making it plain he had rather have seen them lying here on the ground. "How come Bishop to bring the sheriff, since he didn't make no move against us?"

"Protection. Knew we wouldn't do nothin' long as the sheriff was here."

"But I don't see what he come for in the first place."

"Sniffin'. He's an old bloodhound, that Bishop. Lookin' for that boy of his, for one thing. Lookin' for anything he might be able to use against us. And lookin' for a chance to stir up trouble between us and Clarence."

Cass could contain himself no longer. "You been stealin' from me, Macy. We made a deal, and then you turned around and went to takin' my cattle."

"Shut up, Clarence."

"Damn you, Macy . . ." Cass' fury had momentarily over-come his fear. "Damn you for a double-crossin' thief!"

Modock's short fuse went up in smoke. He brought his fist around and struck the old man square in the face, hitting him so hard that Clarence went down on his back. Nose bloodied, the rancher raised up onto one elbow. "Damn you all to hell, Macy! I'm goin' to ride after the sheriff and tell him . . ."

Modock reached down and grabbed Cass' shirtfront, sav-agely hauling the old man to his feet and striking him down again. His voice dropped to almost a whisper—a deadly one. "If I thought you would— If I thought there was even a chance you would do that, Clarence, I'd wring your scrawny neck the way I'd kill a rooster."

Cass tried to crawl away, and Modock kicked him hard enough to have caved in his ribs if he had hit him right. "But you ain't goin' to do it, old man. You got too much blood on your own hands. You ain't goin' to say a word . . . not one little bitty word. You was there when we killed Joe Little. You was with us when we broke into the bank to make it look like he done it and ran off."

"You forced me to go with you to the bank. And I didn't have nothin' to do with that killin'. You-all done it."

"You was there. You was an accessory. The court that hangs us hangs *you*. So you'll keep your mouth shut, Clarence, or I'll shut it for sou. And when I shut it, it'll stay shut for good." He grabbed the old man again and pulled him up, tak-ing such a grip on the shirtfront that Clarence nearly choked. "Anything you don't understand, Clarence?"

The old man sobbed in fear. "No, Macy, no."

Macy dropped him. Clarence lay on the ground at Modock's feet. Modock's anger led him to say the rest of it.

"Sure, we was stealin' your cattle. You was too lazy to get out and look, and too stupid to've seen if you'd been out. I was goin' to steal you blind and buy you out with the money from your own cattle. I already had Judge Quincy draw up the papers for you to sign when the time come. You'd of took your money and left this country, and this ranch would be mine. This ranch first, then Blair Bishop's. And all the people that stood around and rubbed their hands when Macy Modock went to prison, I'd have them sweatin' blood."

Cass murmured, "Blair Bishop'll stop you now."

"There ain't nobody stoppin' me. I was goin' to pay you for this ranch, but now I'll have it without payin' you, Clarence. You'll sign them papers for nothin'. You'll sign them because you know I'll kill you if you don't."

"This ranch is all I got."

"Not anymore it ain't. I'm takin' it."

"But what'll me and Jessie do? Take this away and we got nothin'."

"I'm takin' Jessie away from you too, old man. I been wantin' her since the first day I ever seen her. I've held off with her till I could have it all. Now I'm *takin'* it all." He leaned down. "Get up, Clarence. You got papers to sign."

The old man wept. "You'll kill me when I do."

"I'll kill you if you don't."

"I won't sign them, Macy. I won't sign them."

Modock hauled him to his feet. "You will. I'll put you out in that shed and let you look at that Bishop boy awhile. You figure how you'd like to be in the shape he is. You'll sign." Modock shoved him toward the shed. The old man stumbled and went to his knees. Roughly Modock picked him up and shoved him again. "Git in there, Clarence. You'll git in there till you've made up your mind. I ain't foolin' with you no more; I ain't goin' to soft-talk with you. I'll come in ever' so often and stomp on you a little bit to help make up your mind."

In the shed, Modock looked a moment at the girl, and he felt a strong urge to grab her by the hand and drag her over to the house. But he would wait; she wouldn't try to go anywhere as long as that Bishop boy was there and helpless. Taking her now might cause old Clarence to do something foolish and not ever get around to signing those papers. Moreover, he still had Harley Mills here, and he depended upon Mills' testimony to help him wrest that land away from Blair Bishop. Mills was a man of no particular character, but even a bottle bum might climb out over the fence if he saw Modock use force on the girl.

"Keep an eye on them, Owen," Modock said to Darby. "Old Clarence has got some thinkin' to do."

Darby nodded. "Want me to help him?"

"I'll take care of that, Owen. You might overdo things, and a dead man don't write very good."

Clarence Cass withered up into a huddle of misery. He sat hunched on the floor, tears running down his cheeks and into his beard, his thin shoulders shaking as he wept in helplessness.

Jessie looked at him in a mixture of disappointment and pity. "You're dead if you sign them papers."

"I'm dead if I don't."

"I heard what you was sayin'. What's this about you bein' there when they killed somebody, and about the bank?"

Cass told her, his voice broken in despair. "I didn't go to do it. I been an honest man all my life; you know that. It was Modock; he forced me into it."

"You don't think for a minute that he can let you leave here alive, knowin' what you do? He knows sooner or later you'd break down and tell somebody, then they'd come after him. Once he gets your name on them papers he wants, you're dead. We're all dead."

"Not you. He wants you."

"I'd as soon be dead. Anyway, he'd get tired of me, and then he'd have to kill me too because I know the whole story now."

The old man buried his face in his hands. "I never knowed it would end thisaway. I was so filled with hate for Blair Bishop, I'd of done anything Modock wanted me to." In a minute he looked up, a little hope in his eyes. "Maybe if we promised him we wouldn't ever say nothin' . . . maybe if we promised we'd leave this country and not ever come back within three hundred miles . . ."

"He won't let you leave here, or me," she said gravely. "He'll kill Allan first, and then you . . . and eventually me. The minute you sign them papers, it's over for all of us." She looked at Harley Mills, who slacked against the wall on the far side of the shed. Mills was drunk, but he had heard enough that alarm was beginning to reach him. He kept trying to focus his eyes on Owen Darby, who sat with pistol in his hand, listening and smiling to himself. Sunlight kept striking Mills in the face through one of the several big holes in the west wall. He would blink and move a little, but in a minute he would sag a little and the sun would hit him again.

The expression in Darby's face showed plainly that every word the girl said was true. Jessie spoke to Mills. "If you're not stupid drunk, Harley Mills, you better think a little bit about your own situation. Sooner or later Modock's goin' to decide maybe you've heard too much and seen too much too. Once he's got what he needs from you, you'll be in the same fix as the rest of us."

Darby snarled at her. "Shut up."

Jessie took a cloth from Allan's head and soaked it in a pan of water while she put a fresh wet cloth in its place. "And if I don't?"

"You may've got into Macy's blood, but you ain't got into mine."

Old Clarence looked fearfully at Darby. "You'd kill a woman?"

Darby raised the pistol a little, then lowered it. "Takes one bullet for a woman, same as for a man. I can buy all the woman I need in town for five dollars. This one wouldn't be no loss to me."

Clarence buried his face again. "Oh, God, little girl, what did I get you into?"

Macy Modock waited a long while before he came back into the shed. He had calculated on the wait to shatter Clarence Cass' nerves. He stood in the door, the afternoon sun ominously casting the shadow of his tall frame across the shed floor. "I got the papers laid out on the kitchen table. You ready, Clarence?"

From somewhere, Cass summoned strength to say, "Go to hell, Macy."

Macy Modock gave him a kick that sent him backward, arms flailing. Modock took a long stride and stood over him. "Sometimes I get awful short of patience, Clarence."

Clarence Cass drew up in pain, shaking his head. "I ain't signin'. I ain't signin'."

Darby stood up. "Why don't you go take yourself a drink, Macy? Let me argue with him a little."

Angrily Modock said, "Just don't kill him . . . quite." He turned on his heel.

Darby enjoyed his work. He kept it up until Jessie jumped from the unconscious boy's side and threw herself against Darby, striking at him with her fists and cursing him in language a girl wasn't supposed to know. Darby grabbed her shoulders and flung her roughly into the hay.

Harley Mills had sat bleary-eyed and fearful during the beating of the old ranchman. At the manhandling of the girl, he pushed to a wobbly stand and took a halting step forward. "Now you just looky here . . ."

Darby turned on him. "Sit down and shut up, drunk. Take another slug of whiskey and don't pay no attention to what don't concern you."

Modock came back presently. He saw the girl first, disheveled, the hay clinging. His angry eyes cut dangerously toward Darby.

Darby said, "She come at me a-fightin'. I just shook a little sense into her, is all."

"She's mine, Owen, and you damn well better remember it." Modock leaned over and grasped the old ranchman's shirt-front. "Clarence . . ." He shook Cass, but he got little response. He let go, and the ranchman fell back. Modock straightened, speaking sharply to Darby. "I told you not to kill him. He ain't no good to me if he ain't in shape to sign his name."

"He ain't hurt. He's just a cowardly old man playin' possum on you."

Modock towered over Cass, hands on his hips. "Listen to me, Clarence. Don't pretend you can't hear me. I'll be back in a little while, and you better be ready to sign. Else I'll take a horse and a rope and I'll drag you up and down that brushy flat yonder."

Three of Modock's hands confronted him as he stepped out of the shed. Modock could see trouble in the way they looked at him. One had elected himself spokesman. "Macy, we don't like the way things is shapin' up."

Modock stiffened. "What's the matter with them?"

"First thing, you oughtn't to've sent Jim and Charlie out by theirselves with that herd the way you done. Maybe they wouldn't of gotten killed. And besides that, takin' land and cattle away from a big man like Blair Bishop is one thing. Beatin' the life out of a weak-backed old man like Clarence is somethin' else; we don't like the smell of it. And we don't like what you got in mind for that girl either. When you can buy more women than you'd know what to do with, we don't like you misusin' one."

Modock's hand was near the butt of his pistol. "Any one of you feel like he's man enough to stop me?"

The men looked at each other, then at Modock. "Maybe we can't stop you, but we sure don't aim to stay around and help you. We're goin' on, Macy."

Macy Modock boiled in frustration. He wanted to draw and shoot them like the slinking dogs that they were. But he knew it was unlikely he could beat all three. "Then go on, damn you. Run like a pack of rabbits. Ain't nobody needs you around here."

But as he watched them saddling their horses to leave, he felt the whole thing beginning to trickle away between his fingers. He *did* need them. He needed the force they represented. He couldn't do this thing alone, just him and Darby. Damn

them for cowards! Damn them for quitters! He watched them
leave and trembled in helpless fury. He drew his pistol and
nearly gave way to an urge to kill them all. But as the men
rode, they were all turned in their saddles, watching him until
they were well out of range.

Modock stared after them, the fierce anger burning
unchecked. When they were beyond recall, he turned sharply
and strode back into the shed. Roughly he yanked Cass to his
feet. "I've pussyfooted all I'm goin' to. We're goin' into that
house, Clarence, and you're signin' them papers if you do it
with your last dyin' breath!" He flung Cass through the door.
The old man went down on his knees, but Modock didn't let
him stay there. Modock half carried, half dragged him to the
house while Jessie Cass stood in the shed door and watched,
her hands to her mouth. Harley Mills swayed with one hand
braced back against the wall, sobering under the impact of violence. Owen Darby walked to the door and shoved the girl
back. "Sit down!" he said roughly, and then stood in the doorway, a hard smile across his face as he watched the house and
imagined what Modock was doing in there.

Modock pushed Clarence Cass toward the kitchen table
where he had the deeds spread out. A pen lay atop the papers,
and an ink bottle beside them. "Sign, Clarence. Sign them papers or I'll kill you where you stand!"

Clarence Cass sobbed aloud, because he could see death in
Modock's fury . . . death whether he signed or whether he
didn't. Modock struck him. "Sign!"

Cass sank into a chair. He reached for the pen, jabbing the
point at the ink bottle without realizing he had to unscrew the
top.

"Open it first, you stupid . . ."

Cass fumbled with the bottle, got the top off, then let the whole thing slip through his fingers. The bottle hit the floor rolling, the ink spilling. Before Modock could outrun it and pick it up, it was empty. It didn't have ink enough left to wet the pen. Modock hurled it against a wall, then turned and struck Cass again. "You'll sign if you have to do it in your own damned blood!"

Cass huddled in the chair, trembling like a cottonwood leaf. He said, "I think I know where there's another bottle."

"Get it!"

Cass pushed shakily to his feet. He walked into the room where he customarily slept and swayed forward, catching himself on a battered old chest of drawers. He paused a moment, summoning strength, then pulled out the drawer. He reached into it, his hand hidden momentarily from Modock. When he turned, he held an old pistol in his hands. His eyes were desperate. He shrilled, "Die, Modock!" and pulled the trigger.

It clicked.

Modock couldn't risk the next one doing the same. His own pistol came up and leveled swiftly. Even as he squeezed the trigger, he knew he had lost this ranch.

The gun thundered. Clarence Cass was driven backward against the window. He fell through it and out in a shower of glass. He lay hanging, his knees bent across the windowsill, his arms slacked, his limp hands touching the ground outside.

Modock picked up the fallen pistol. He flipped open the cylinder and shouted aloud. "Empty!" He hurled it through the broken window, knowing Cass was dead, knowing that by grabbing up an empty gun he had wiped away all Modock's hopes of taking this land. Modock leaned out the window and cursed him and emptied his gun into the frail body.

At the shed, Owen Darby stood transfixed. He had heard the commotion in the house, heard the shot and saw Cass fall backward through the window. He watched hypnotized as Modock fired again and again in fury and frustration.

Jessie Cass had known when her father went into that house he had little chance of leaving it alive. To her he was dead before she ever heard the first shot. She flinched, and she cried out, but she had already given up.

"It's Allan next," she rasped to Harley Mills, "and then you, and then me."

She pushed to her feet as the other shots began. Outside the shed, she could see Darby standing frozen, forgetting about the people in the shed because of his fascination in the scene at the house. He held the pistol loosely in his hand, forgotten in the excitement.

Her blood like ice, she stared at the pistol. Her hands flexed, and she considered her chances of running out and grabbing it. They were nil, for Darby's strength would be too much.

Harley Mills was sobering fast. From the pile of hay he took the pitchfork and staggered forward. Jessie saw what he was trying and knew he was in no condition to carry through. She wrested the fork from his hands, took a firm grip and rushed.

Darby heard. He turned, bringing up the pistol. She speared his hand with one of the sharp tines, and he let the weapon drop. She kicked it aside. Holding the bleeding hand, he stared at her a moment in rage, then rushed her. She dropped the butt end of the fork to the ground to brace it. The force of his rush carried him headlong into the tines.

Darby screamed and fought against the embedded fork. He

managed somehow to pull it free. He staggered, holding his
arms tight against his belly as he cried to Macy Modock for
help. Jessie grabbed up the fallen pistol and rushed back into
the shed.

Modock ran out of the house, eyes wide in confusion. He
saw the staggering Darby and started toward him. In panic,
holding the pistol in both hands, Jessie fired. She missed him
by a long way, but she stopped him. He ran back around the
house.

Darby kept crying out, staggering until loss of blood
brought him to his knees. He called to Modock for help, but
Modock was in no position to assist him.

Mills was cold sober now. Darby's cries chilled him.

"For God's sake, girl, shoot him. Put him out of his misery."

Milk-pale, Jessie shook her head. "I've used up one bullet.
We may need all that's left."

In blind agony, Darby crawled up the tank dam and over
toward the water that lay beyond the deep mud. Presently he
went quiet. Jessie shuddered. "You watch that side of the shed
and I'll watch this one," she told Mills. "We can't let Modock
slip up on us."

Modock waited awhile before he showed himself, calling
from the corner of the house. "Girl, you can't hold out in
there by yourself. That boy's no help to you, or that drunk.
You throw the pistol out here where I can see it. There won't
no harm come to you. Wouldn't be no reason for it anymore."

Her throat was dry and tight, and her heart throbbed in
fear. She didn't answer. She held the pistol in both hands and
braced it against the doorframe, sighting down the barrel.

Emboldened, Modock stepped out a little farther. "Girl,

you better listen to me. I got more time and patience than you have."

She squeezed the trigger. Through the smoke she saw splinters fly from the corner of the house. Modock rushed back out of sight.

"Would've been better," Mills said, "if Darby had died here in the door. We could've got the cartridges out of his belt."

Jessie nodded, her hands trembling as she lowered the smoking pistol. This was a six-shooter. She had fired two shots. Provided that Darby had kept it fully loaded—which she was sure he would—she had four shots left.

Modock leaned out from the corner of the house and fired deliberately at the shed. Jessie dropped to the floor as the bullets smacked into the wall over her head. When she had time to think, she realized Modock must have purposely aimed high.

He still wanted her alive, she knew. He was trying to scare her, and he was doing a good job of it.

She raised up, her instinct to fire back at him, but she knew the shot would be wasted. He was probably trying to lure her into doing just that. She sank to her knees, the pistol across her lap. Warm tears ran down her face.

"Girl," Harley Mills said, "you better let me have that gun."

She looked up at him and saw he was shaking. "No," she said, "you got way too much whiskey in you. You'd wind up killin' us instead of Modock."

Presently Modock fired again, still aiming high. Jessie ducked involuntarily and cried out as splinters showered down. She heard a horse running excitedly in a corral behind the shed. Through a crack in the wall she looked at the house, and a fresh hope began to rise.

"Mister Mills, he's still behind the house, or in it. He can't get away from it very well without me seein' him. That's his horse behind the shed makin' all the commotion. You could catch that horse and saddle it without exposin' yourself to Modock none. There's a wagon behind the shed too. You could go down into the draw, fetch up the team, and we could hitch it to the wagon. We could load Allan into the wagon and light out of here in a dead run. Modock bein' afoot, there wouldn't be no way he could stop us once we started."

Mills shook his head fearfully. "I don't know. If he was to ever get a clear shot at me . . ."

"He won't, if you watch how you handle yourself. Anyway, I'll keep the house covered."

"Girl, you can't even hit that house, much less hit Modock."

She flung all her anger at him. "Have you got a drop of red blood left in your veins, or has it all gone to whiskey?"

He dropped his chin. The violence had largely cleared his mind, though his reflexes were still not coordinated. "I didn't come out here to get killed."

"You came out here to lie your way into some whiskey money. Maybe you've learned now you don't get nothin' you don't pay for. Are you goin' out there and catch that horse?"

Slump-shouldered, Mills took a bridle from a hook and a rope from a saddle that had belonged to Darby. Jessie went back to watching the house. She could hear the horse running around and around the pen and could hear the swish of the loop as Mills tried several times to catch him and missed. But finally from the sounds she knew he had caught the horse and was saddling him. She stepped to the shed's corral door long enough to see Mills swing into the saddle. She called, "You bring back that team, do you hear?"

Mills bare-heeled the horse into a lope and bent low over the saddle as he left the pen. He angled in such a way that he kept the shed between him and the house until he was out of range. Jessie went back to her vigil by the front door and waited for Mills to return. She felt of Allan's forehead and found it hot. Allan mumbled feverishly, unaware of what was going on.

"We'll be out of here directly," she murmured. "Just as soon as Mills gets back with that team."

Time moved rapidly enough at first as in her mind she followed Mills down into the draw. She knew where the wagon team usually grazed, and how long it would take Mills to get down there. She visualized his picking them up and starting back toward the barn. She followed his progress all the way.

"He ought to be comin' just about now," she said to the unconscious boy. "We'll hear him any minute."

The minutes ticked by slowly then, no sound coming. Maybe the team had grazed farther than usual, she tried to tell herself. Even a horse doesn't do the same thing every day; even a horse likes variety. She allowed the extra time, mentally beginning over, giving Mills a fresh start back from the draw. Still he didn't come.

For a long time she resisted the obvious: he wasn't coming back. But finally the realization forced itself upon her against her will. For the first time she broke down and openly cried.

XV

It was dusk now. Jessie knew that only so long as there was still light could she keep Modock pinned behind that house. Even then, there was no way to be absolutely sure. He could walk away, carefully keeping the house between him and the shed, and she would not see him. If he walked far enough to lose himself in the brush, he could get completely away, or he could circle back and come up on her from behind.

But Modock was still at the house. She heard him call. "Mills is gone now, girl. That boy can't help you, so it's just me and you."

She didn't answer him. He waited a little, then said, "You can't hold out. Sooner or later you got to give up. Do it now and I promise I won't do that boy no more harm. You and me, we'll ride out of here together."

She knew he was lying. For a while there had been some possible advantage to him in keeping Allan alive. Now there was none. She knew his hatred for Blair Bishop was so intense that he would kill Allan simply for revenge on Allan's father. And when he was done, he would still carry Jessie away with him. There was no bargaining with a man who knew no honor.

"You stay away, Modock," she cried. "You stay away from us."

He showed himself, and in a moment of desperation she fired again. Instantly she realized she had made a mistake.

That was it: he was trying to lure her into using up her cartridges. Once she had done that, all he had to do was walk in and take her.

He waited a time, then called to her again. "It's up to you, girl. I ain't goin' to put up with this all night. If I have to, I'll kill that boy."

To make his point, he fired at the shed. She saw the thin wood wall crack where the bullet struck, very little above Allan's cot. Modock knew the position where Allan lay. If he made up his mind to it, he could fire through the wall and kill him. And if a pistol wouldn't do it, there were a couple of rifles in the house at Modock's disposal.

Jessie took Allan's feverish hand and stared at him. She ran her fingers through his tousled hair. "If I move you," she said, "that wound is liable to break open and bleed some more. If I don't move you, he'll kill you sure. I got to do it, Allan. Try to help me if you can. I got to do it."

She didn't think her words ever got through to him. She reached under his shoulders and tried to lift him. He was too heavy. She could drag him off the cot, but then she wouldn't be able to keep him from falling, and that would hurt him for certain. The big problem was to ease him somehow to the floor. She mulled over it a moment, then reached across him with both hands, lifting the far edge of the cot, tipping it gradually toward her, pressing her body against his to keep him from falling. The lifting was heavy till she had the cot tipped halfway up; then the problem was to prevent the cot from falling too fast and Allan from tumbling. She held the cot most of the way. By the time it became too heavy for her, Allan was almost in her lap. He slid gently, and she had him. She cradled him in her arms a moment, pressing her cheek against him. He mumbled fevered words that had no meaning.

Modock fired again, and she saw a ragged hole appear in the wall where Allan had been. Modock had a rifle now. He had given up fooling around. Jessie lay on the ground, her arms around Allan, and began laboriously dragging him away. She crawled a few inches at a time toward the back of the shed, while Macy Modock methodically sent slug after slug tearing through the wall.

If she hadn't moved Allan, he would be dead by now.

She didn't stop dragging until she had him almost to the back wall. She looked around for anything she could pile up between him and the wall that faced the house. She flung down Darby's saddle and one of her father's and also her own, knowing all of them together might not be enough to stop a rifle bullet. She piled up the horse collars and the harness and several sacks of grain that had been bought for the chickens.

"He's dead now, girl," Modock shouted. "No point in you tryin' to protect him anymore. You come on out here and throw that gun away."

The clapboard walls were shoddily constructed, like everything else on the Cass place. Jessie could watch the house through spaces between the boards. She saw Modock step out experimentally in the dusk, inviting her to fire at him. She wanted to, but she resisted. She held her breath, taking in a gasp of air once in a while, then holding while she watched Modock. He waited a while for her to fire then moved a few feet forward and stopped again.

"Girl," he called, "do you hear me?"

She made no reply. He took a few more steps, and she could see his face clearly. In his changing expressions she could almost read his mind. He was suddenly becoming fearful he had hit her with some of those shots intended for Allan

Bishop. He came forward again, halting occasionally, still not sure.

"Girl, are you all right? I want you to answer me."

The closer he came, the surer he seemed to be that she had been hit, and the less caution he showed. Jessie sat up, holding the pistol firmly in both hands, arms extended stiffly. She aimed at the doorframe, waiting for the moment he would step through into full sight.

She couldn't see him now, but she could hear the slow tread of his boots. She caught a deep breath and held it.

He came through the door, pistol ready. "Girl?"

He couldn't see her immediately, not in the darkness at the back of the shed. His gaze went to the overturned cot and the blankets.

Jessie saw him over the sights, took a firm grip on the pistol and pulled the trigger. Modock jerked, and she fired again. Black smoke billowed, hiding him from her view.

She heard him cry out in surprise and pain, and she heard his footsteps running again across the yard. She dropped onto her stomach and peered out through the spaces. She saw him half running, half hopping as he disappeared behind the house.

She hadn't killed him, but she had drawn blood. He would think a long time before he came again.

And Jessie knew she would have to think a long time before she fired at him, for the next shot would be her last. She had but one bullet left.

Allan whispered, "Jessie." She turned quickly to him and saw his eyelids flicker a little. The gunfire had stirred him at last. She put her arms around him and lay against him and put her cheek to his burning forehead. "Lie easy," she said, "just lie easy. Everything will be all right."

Then it was dark and she could see no more. All she could do now was lie here by Allan and listen fearfully. With the darkness came all the night sounds of the crickets and the night birds and the far-off bawling of a cow in search of its calf. But no noise came from the house. Jessie listened intently, trying to separate each sound and analyze it, looking for menace in the light summer wind that rustled the leaves, chilling at the sudden yip of a roaming coyote far out on the prairie.

The dark hours dragged by. She had cried some at first, but now the tears were dried. Hands that had been cold-sweaty against the gunbutt held it now as firmly as ever, but they too were dry. She no longer stirred at every sound; she had listened to them so long that she knew now which ones were natural.

When Modock came—and she was still sure he would— he wouldn't find her in panic again. He would find her ready. With the one bullet she had left, she would kill him if she could. And if she didn't kill him, she would force him to kill her. He wasn't going to have her . . . not alive.

She had no way of keeping up with time. She didn't particularly want to, for she felt sure Modock would make his move before daylight came again, and she was not eager to see the night end. But she knew midnight must have come and gone when she heard the sounds. She pushed to her elbows, listening, trying to pin down their source.

She doubted Modock would try the front door again. Perhaps not the back one, either, for he would not want to be as plain a target as he had been before. She expected him to slip up to the wall, for it had plenty of holes and cracks that he could see through without unnecessarily exposing himself to fire. Probably he would try to wound her just enough to put her out of the fight. A wounded girl was better than a dead one, he would probably figure. She lay holding her breath, listening.

The sounds were louder. He must be easing closer. She took a deep breath and then held it again.

Where was he? For God's sake, where was he?

Then she recognized the sounds: horses, running. It wasn't Modock! It was somebody else, somebody coming.

"Allan," she cried, "do you hear it? They're comin' to help us."

She judged that the horses were in the draw now. They would be here in minutes.

She heard something else, too—a man afoot, hurrying across the yard. Modock was coming. This was his last chance, and he was going to use it. He wasn't making any effort to slip up on her. He didn't have time. She knew he was coming straight for the door. She sat up, bringing the pistol into line, both hands gripping it steady. When he came through that door she would get him. This time she wouldn't miss.

The dark shape suddenly hurled itself at her. Crying out involuntarily, she squeezed the trigger. The flash seemed to light up the whole shed, and she saw the shape fall.

But it didn't fall like a man. It fell limp and lay flat.

In anguish, Jessie realized Modock had tricked her out of her last shot. He had flung a blanket through that door, and in the darkness she had thrown away her last chance. He stood now where the blanket had appeared.

"That's all of it, girl."

Not quite all. She threw the empty pistol at him in desperation and pushed to her feet. She didn't wait for him to come to her; she rushed at him, pummeling him with her fists, crying out in her hatred of him. He put his pistol away, grabbed her hands and pushed her back. When she came at him again, he lashed out with his fist and caught her chin. She fell to her knees, stunned.

"You're a fighter," he rasped, "I'll admit that. I just wish I'd of thought about that blanket trick hours ago. Then I'd of had some time with you. Now I got no time left, and no patience. You've caused me all the grief I'm goin' to take." He drew the pistol and shoved it at her. "Give me one more bit of trouble and I'll kill that boy yonder. Then, if I decide to—and I may—I'll kill you too."

The horses loped into the yard. A deep voice called out.

"Allan! Allan, boy, where you at?"

Helpless to resist anymore, Jessie crawled to Allan and put her arms around him. His eyes were open, and he was trying to clear them. "Jessie?" he said, his voice only a whisper.

"Yes, Allan, it's me."

"Jessie, what's goin' on?"

"Your dad is here. He's outside. But Modock is in here with us, and he's got a gun."

From the sounds, Jessie could tell the men were dismounting in the yard and spreading out. She recognized Blair Bishop's voice calling again. "Allan! Jessie! Are you-all here?"

Jessie cried, "Stay away, Mister Bishop! It's Modock!"

Modock pulled back into the shadows, nearer Jessie and Allan. "Like she says, Bishop, we're all in here together. Why don't you come on in . . . if you want this boy killed?"

There was silence for a moment, then Bishop said, "Modock, whatever quarrel you got, it's with me, not with my boy or that girl."

"That's right, Bishop, it's you and me. It's always been you and me."

"Well, then," Bishop called, "what do you want?"

"Just you, Bishop, just you."

"You got me, if you'll let them kids go. What do you want me to do?"

"Make them men of yours git away . . . plumb away. Just you is all I want to see out there. Just you and two horses . . . one for you and one for me."

Jessie could hear Blair Bishop quietly giving orders and the men pulling back.

Modock said: "You give them orders that I get to ride out of here clean. And you're goin' with me."

"They heard you," Bishop said. "It's the same as an order from me."

Modock moved closer to the door, satisfying himself that the other riders had remounted and moved back. "All right, Bishop, you come closer where I can look at you."

Jessie could hear Bishop's footsteps and made out the heavy shape of him, dark against the open door. Modock gloated. "Well, it didn't turn out the way I figured on, but I got this one thing I was after. You did come to *me*. Drop your pistol."

Bishop raised his hands a little. "Ain't got one, Macy. These old hands, I couldn't use one if I carried it, so I don't bother myself packin' the weight."

Jessie became aware of a slight scurrying noise at the back wall. She looked around, mouth open in wonder. She saw the barrel of a shotgun poke through a knothole a little above her head. She saw it move up and down, its holder outside trying vainly to draw a bead on Modock.

At the bottom of the wall was a hole big enough for a cat

to move through. Quietly she leaned forward and eased her
hand out. The shotgun muzzle quickly disappeared. She felt
the touch of cold steel, and then the touch of fingers, gently
pressing the shotgun into her hand. Carefully, her eyes on
Modock, she began pulling the shotgun into the barn.

Modock was busy glorying over getting Blair Bishop into
a trap. He had his back turned to her. She kept pulling the
shotgun until it was clearly inside, then cautiously brought it
up. She almost had a bead on Modock when Blair Bishop
stepped fully into the barn.

Her heart sank. She couldn't fire without Bishop sharing
the blast.

Bishop was saying: "I'll go with you, Macy. But first I got
to see about my boy. I got to be sure he's alive."

Modock backed away, giving Bishop room to pass by. But
it wasn't enough room that Jessie could get a clear shot. And
she knew that when he turned to let his gaze follow Bishop, he
would see the shotgun in her hands. She lowered it, laying it
lengthwise beside Allan Bishop, hoping Modock wouldn't spot
it in the darkness.

"He's alive," Modock said. "That girl has kept him alive in
spite of all I could do. But go see for yourself. Then you and
me are ridin' out of here, Bishop. You're my ticket for a free
passage."

Blair Bishop limped over and dropped to one knee. "Allan?"

Allan whispered, "Dad." Bishop rasped, "Thank God." He
raised his eyes to Jessie and looked at her a minute. "And thank
you, girl."

He reached out for her hand. She caught his fingers and

gently guided them down to the shotgun. She saw the surprise show for a second in his face before he covered it. Bishop bent over as if to hug his son.

"You've seen him," Modock said. "Now come on."

"I'm comin'," Blair replied, his back turned to Modock as he slowly arose, holding the shotgun against his body.

Jessie flattened herself beside Allan. Blair turned, getting as good a grip on the shotgun as his stiff hands would let him.

Confident of Blair's helplessness, Modock had let his pistol sag. He saw the shotgun too late. Giving a startled cry, he tried to bring up the pistol. Bishop didn't give him time. The blast knocked Modock to the floor. He rolled halfway through the door, gathered one knee up as if to push again to his feet, then slumped forward and died there.

Blair Bishop said, "Harley Mills didn't have it in him to go back with the team, once he got clear of the place. But he did work up enough courage to come and tell me. I reckon that took some guts just in itself."

He stood at the foot of Allan's bed in the Bishop house, looking at a weary Jessie Cass, who ought to have been off somewhere asleep but wouldn't leave Allan's side. She sat in a chair by the bed and watched Allan.

"I don't know what these boys are comin' to, this day and time," Blair went on. "There wouldn't none of this of wound up the way it did if my two boys had listened to what I told them. I tried to raise them different, but they're just plain contrary. Got it from their mother, God bless her. Allan first. I told him to stay home and not be runnin' off to you, but he went anyway, and you see what become of him for it. Then Billy . . . when Harley Mills come by, I told Billy to stay home. He was too young to get into a fight like this, and I didn't want to lose *two* boys. He come anyhow. And when I told him to move out of the way with the others, he took the shotgun and run for the back of the shed instead.

"No, seems like I can't tell them boys nothin' anymore. And it's probably a good thing."

Jessie nodded wearily, agreeing with him, though she was plainly too tired to know half of what he said. It looked to Blair as if she would drop off to sleep in that chair, and maybe he ought to go away and let her. But he had one more thing he wanted to say. "I never been wrong but very few times in my life, and I hope I ain't never wrong again. But I was wrong about you, girl. I'll make it up to you, any way an old man can find to do it."

"You just give me Allan, Mister Bishop, and that's all the makin' up you'll ever have to do."

"He's yours. He ought to be up and goin' again pretty soon. September's just around the corner. I feel like we'll get a good rain then, and everything'll look better. How would you like a nice big September weddin', girl?"

She smiled. "I'd *like* a September weddin'. In the rain."